This book is published by
Grosvenor House Publishing Ltd
Link House
140 The Broadway, Tolworth, Surrey, KT6 7HT.
www.grosvenorhousepublishing.co.uk

This book is a work of fiction. Any resemblance to
people or events, past or present, is purely coincidental.

A CIP record for this book
is available from the British Library

ISBN 978-1-78623-701-9

ABBOTS FORD

The Abbots Ford Trilogy covers the
Twentieth Century, tracing four
generations of a family in a Somerset
village, focussing mainly on the women.
Through two World Wars, and
unprecedented social change, these
women strive to keep their families on
course and their working lives viable.

THE AUTHOR

Elizabeth Davison was born and lived in
London, but spent much time in Somerset
staying with her mother's best friend.
Her visits continued for many years and she
always enjoyed her time spent there.
This book is a reflection of her impressions
and feeling of her love of life in the
West Country.

Elizabeth Davison

Beneath the Hill

ELIZABETH DAVISON

Book One of
The Abbots Ford Trilogy

Grosvenor House
Publishing Limited

BENEATH THE HILL

In Beneath the Hill, Flora and her siblings, Charles,
Louise and Bill, are growing up as the Twentieth Century begins.
Flora marries handsome Seth and sets up home.
By chance, she discovers that she has the ability to join
Ellie Bates, the village midwife, in her work.
Flora combines work with bringing up a family,
and does not escape the stresses which assail her situation.
The lives and loves of her family and friends are no
less involved. The First World War demoralises and diminishes
the village, but life has to be rebuilt, even after
the tragedy of irreplaceable loss.

Chapter One

SEPTEMBER 1906 – EASTER 1907

The last long pink-red rays of the sun slid behind the hill that dominated the village of Abbots Ford, taking with it the remains of a lingering autumn day. The sky was tinged turquoise as Flora made her way towards her parents' cottage. She smiled softly to herself. She was carrying a muslin-covered bucket of fresh milk. Tonight was the Harvest Supper. Everyone went to Harvest Suppers, even the little children. This one was going to be different, especially now that she was seventeen. Almost reluctantly, she reached the cottage. "Hello," she called, opening the inner door to the welcome warmth of the living room.

"Hello love. Let's have that milk," said her mother, turning from the pots on the range to welcome her elder daughter.

"Bit chilly now the sun's gone," commented Flora, kneeling in front of the fire.

"Get out of the way!" moaned her younger sister, Louise, crossly. "I was here first!"

"Take no notice of her," their mother told her. "She's been a cross-patch all day."

"I wonder why!" Their brother Bill came in from the scullery drying his face with a towel.

"Why's that then?" asked Flora laughingly, joining in the teasing.

"No reason," Louise stated abruptly.

"Someone wants to get all done up like a young lady," sang her brother.

"I am a young lady and you know nothing about them," snarled Louise threateningly.

"Now then, that's enough. Get yourselves organised and lay that table. Your father and Charles'll be here before you know it," said their mother.

The girls busied themselves preparing the table for the family's meal, while their mother prodded and stirred the contents of the simmering saucepans. She wiped her forehead with the back of her hand.

"Get your great feet out of my way and give me the towel a moment," she demanded.

Bill moved himself and ducked when his mother threw the towel back at him. She glanced anxiously at the clock, judging when her menfolk would arrive from clearing up after milking.

They heard the voices long before they arrived. William Henty came in first, followed by his eldest son. The muscular older man laughed as he appeared.

"Well, whatever you do say, lad, whatever you do say. Can't be doing with new-fangled contraptions on my farm!"

"Hello, my love," his wife greeted him and took his coat and hat to avoid their being thrown on to the leather sofa.

It was a worn leather sofa; black and curved up at one end like a chaise-longue, though this one could not be regarded as anything with a French name. The horse hair filling thrust out along the side, however much Louise attempted to mend it.

"That's better." William took his seat at the head of the table. His open face glowed from the cold water wash. Charles joined them and the girls helped their mother to serve the food. Supper, or high tea as some called it, was a smaller version of dinner in the middle of the day. Tonight it was thick slices of home-cured ham, over which they poured vinegar, served with bread, but no butter.

"Get everything done all right?" asked Louise.

"Yes. Good day for it, weren't it, boy?" replied William.

"Almost done, Ma," agreed Charles, enjoying the warmth and food.

"Our Flora's becoming a big strong girl," her father told them. "See her coming up from the back field with the cows? Could've been a lad!"

"Oh thank you, Dad." She laughed, taking it in the spirit in which it was meant.

They washed down the supper with large cups of hot, sweet tea while Bill tried to kick his younger sister's shins beneath the table.

"You are such a cry baby." She tried to be condescending and then spoilt the effect by retaliating.

"How many times do I have to tell you two?" demanded their mother.

"That's two less for the Harvest Supper, I reckon," said William good-naturedly.

"Come and help in the scullery, Louise," suggested Flora, shepherding her sister away from Bill.

"Reckon you'll be looking forward to this evening," said her mother as all three cleared away the debris of the meal.

"I reckon I am," Flora agreed shyly.

"I wish I didn't have to wear that stupid frock," complained Louise. "I don't want to go."

"You'll be all right once you're there," comforted her mother. "Won't she, Flora?" The older woman looked pleadingly at her eldest daughter.

"Yes, 'course you will. Come up in a minute and I'll help you get ready."

Flora carried the water jug carefully up the oak stairs and set it down on the marble top of the washstand. She busied herself, moving the bowl to the centre, taking the lid off the soap dish and unravelling the towel from where it was neatly folded on the bar at the side. She climbed out of her working clothes, which included an old frock and apron, and laid them on the chair. Brushing back her hair, she tied it up neatly away from her face and neck, humming tunelessly to herself all the while. Then she poured half of the water from the jug into the bowl and started to wash.

The room was large with a sloping ceiling and small dormer window. The floor sloped too, towards the tiny room next door where her brothers slept. Pretty floral curtains screened the window and hung over dormer spaces where both girls stored their clothes and trinkets. The washstand stood at the far side of the room, away from the window, where it was almost always gloomy and dark. The girls shared a huge brass bed with a feather mattress, which needed vigorous shaking every day.

A beautiful patchwork quilt and pretty rag-rugs lent colour to the room. Opposite the bed, against the only full-height wall, stood an enormous oak wardrobe with a mirrored door.

Flora soaped her face and thought about her pink-striped frock. Would it look too young? She ran the flannel over her white limbs and supple body and smiled into the mirror at her brown face. She was a striking girl with long, straight, dark hair, deep brown eyes, a strong chin and a warm smile. She was excited about the Harvest Supper Dance at the village hall, because she knew that Seth Hawkes would be there. They had known one another all their lives, but had only begun to smile and nod in church in recent months. Their parents knew each other well, but there was never much time for socialising in the farming community of Abbots Ford. The young people had been formally introduced the previous Sunday when their fathers had stopped to talk about the harvest.

Louise burst into the room and went to the frock hanging on the outside of the wardrobe. Fingering the frill around the high neck, she admired their mother's dressmaking skills, saying, "I don't want to be a farmer's wife – I'd like to make clothes, be a seamstress."

She pulled at the hem, straightening it and then puffing it out.

"Mother showed me all I need to know, and I made most of this one," she stated, with all the arrogance of a fifteen-year-old.

Louise, like Flora, had helped at home since leaving the village school and she knew that the only alternative to marrying a farmer would be to be sent away to one of the grand houses in Bristol or Bath to work in service. This had been discussed the previous year when she left school, but their parents, Louise and William, had decided to keep her with them a while longer. Flora had been a good teacher to the younger children and had enjoyed helping 'old Miss Taylor' with some of the rascals. Once she had left school, she had blended in, helping her mother to run the house, caring for her grandparents, and helping with the animals and poultry that her mother kept. She was sensible and dependable, but occasionally her temper would surface and that was when her family kept out of her way.

Flora towelled herself dry and climbed into her voluminous cotton underwear and chemise. While she brushed her shining hair, Louise fiddled with her buttons and laces and bemoaned the fact that she was considered too young to wear a grown-up frock.

"You'll be allowed to go next year," comforted Flora.

"Next year is forever," whined Louise.

She could not wait to grow up and chafed at the conventions that bound her to childhood in Somerset at the beginning of the century.

"Come and use the rest of this water. It's still quite hot," encouraged Flora.

Louise grudgingly did as she was bid and each girl helped the other with buttons and bows to be done up or tied.

"How shall we do our hair?" asked Flora.

Louise was more fair haired than her sister and had slight glints of red sprinkled through her long, thick, curly hair.

"Up and down." Louise grinned, joining in the excitement of the occasion.

Flora brushed Louise's hair and, pulling the front and sides upwards, tied it in a blue ribbon, leaving the mass of hair to flow down her back.

"There, you look really grown-up!" Flora said enthusiastically. "Look in the mirror."

"Yes, I do, don't I?" Louise regarded her image with some surprise.

"Pinch your cheeks before you go in and they'll go pink," instructed Flora. "And bite your lips, but not too hard!"

Louise suddenly threw her arms around her sister. "Thanks," she whispered.

"Daft thing," responded Flora fondly.

"See you there," Louise told her more confidently.

At sixteen, she would be considered a young lady. Flora went downstairs and presented herself to her mother for her approval.

"You look lovely," she said proudly. "Remember, Aunt Elsie and Uncle Ed will be there to look after you."

Flora knew that her mother was fussing because she was aware that Seth's dark good looks were the cause of the shining eyes and slightly flushed face before her.

"You'll need your shawl tonight!" her mother called, too late, as Flora ran off up the lane towards her aunt and uncle's cottage.

When they arrived at the village hall, the dance was already in full swing. The hall was decorated for the celebration with bunting and coloured oil lamps, looking festive. People were whirling around with shouts of laughter and shiny red faces. Flora danced the next dance with her Uncle Ed, scouring the knots of people for a glimpse of Seth. At first, she thought he had not come, but then a noisy group, including her brother, Charles, was pushing through, some holding tankards high above the dancing crowd.

"Mind yourselves, lads!" called Charles.

"All right," came the reply.

"These young ones!" muttered a middle-aged matron.

"Lock up your daughters!" said another laughingly.

Seth took Flora's hands and swung her away from her uncle.

They danced, ate and drank, hardly taking their eyes from each other. Seth exchanged banter with some of the other lads and was polite to older folk, but his eyes always returned and rested on Flora. Sometimes she would meet his, but then she lowered her lashes, embarrassed by the attention.

They had organised a 'Farmer's Girl' competition. The contestants walked through the middle of a cleared circle amidst much noise and laughter. Flora had been too shy to join in, even though Seth and his friends had tried to persuade her. The girls looked attractive in their best frocks; they were fresh-faced and healthy. One or two were bold and spun slowly around in the middle of the circle as if to show their charms to better effect. One was a girl of Flora's age named Mary Hessop and Flora had to admit that she was pretty. They elected Emily Hastings as the 'Farmer's Girl of the Year', a tall, lively girl with long blonde hair.

At last it was time for the final dance and Seth's tall frame towered over Flora as they swung around in a waltz. He had a tanned, broad face with deep-set, startling blue eyes, and eyelashes any girl would be glad to have. His dark hair was combed straight back, but, with all the exertion, tendrils had escaped, making him look like a gypsy. Aunt Elsie, enjoying the occasion, waltzed over by herself to ask if they were ready to walk home, and Seth agreed that they were. Although there was a chill in the air, Flora did not notice it. Seth walked beside her, her aunt and uncle just ahead.

"So you've been helping your dad?" he enquired.

Flora agreed and explained that, mostly, she helped her mother at home. On the way back, they called in briefly to see that all was well with her grandparents, then, calling farewells to her aunt and uncle, carried on to Flora's house a few minutes' walk further on. Seth took her hand as they walked in the moonlight. At first, she thought she would snatch it back, but it seemed right. When they reached Orchard Cottage, she turned and thanked him for seeing her home and made to go inside. He caught her hand and asked if she would like to go for a walk after church the next day.

"I can't go straight after church..." she said tentatively.

"Then you can come in the afternoon?"

Flora said she would have to ask her parents and she would let him know after church the next morning. She turned and darted inside, leaving Seth to walk home pondering his feelings, which had been greatly stirred by this vivacious girl.

+ + +

The autumn sun shone on the ancient stone of the village church. The church itself was ablaze with offerings to celebrate the harvest; it had been a good year. The last notes of *All is safely gathered in* faded and the vicar gave the blessing. As the congregation said their own silent prayers, little children peered through their fingers at the stunning display of fruit, vegetables, bread and a generous sheaf of corn. As they filed out, Rev. Orrins stood at the door while everyone said their farewells. Mrs Wilton, one of the pillars of the village, stopped Flora's mother to discuss the distribution of harvest gifts to the elderly and needy in the parish.

Seth bounded over and stood twisting his hat in his hands, coughing slightly and clearing his throat.

"Father, you know Seth Hawkes, don't you? He walked home with me last night."

"Ah, James' lad, eh?" Her father grinned.

Flora asked him if she could walk out with Seth for a while later that afternoon.

"Don't see why not – but I have to drive your mother to Stoke Magna – why not come in the trap with us for the run?"

Flora turned enquiringly to Seth, who merely nodded, red-faced.

"See you later, lad. Two o'clock sharp," ordered her father as he gently steered Flora towards her mother.

The journey was pleasant; it was mostly a long, straight road to Stoke Magna and Samson, William's big bay horse, was a steady puller. When they reached the small town, Flora, Seth and her younger brother, Bill, went walking while her mother and father conducted their business. They strolled past the pretty church and saw tidy children filing neatly in for Sunday school carrying their small stamp albums, ready to put in that Sunday's stamp to show that they had attended. Bill strutted, aware that he was now considered too old for Sunday school, and feeling very grown-up. The road to the far side of Stoke Magna was little more than a track, where even a horse and trap had trouble passing through the parts where cottages edged the lane. When they found themselves leaving the village, they decided to turn and walk back to the farm where they had left Flora's parents. The autumn sun shone softly, giving a warm glow to the grey stone cottages and highlighting leaves where they had turned red and gold as they perished. Flora felt content as she walked side by side with Seth, glancing up at him occasionally as she felt his eyes on her.

"Do you like our Flora?" asked Bill guilelessly.

"Yes, Bill," Seth replied casually. "She's the girl for me."

Flora blushed prettily, and both Seth and Bill laughed; Bill because he had embarrassed his sister and Seth because he knew that Flora felt the same about him. They passed a magnificent horse chestnut tree and Bill exclaimed at the size of the conkers.

"Look at those! Can I have some?" He looked eagerly at Seth, who found a piece of wood with which to aim at the bunches of succulent pods.

Seth stretched and jumped, showing off, and succeeded in felling a number of conkers. Both he and Bill enjoyed opening their green cases to reveal the shiny, moist seeds.

"Look, sis, look at the size of this one!"

Bill held the prize in his hands and looked at them as they continued their walk.

"Thanks, Seth," he said.

"That's all right, Bill. I used to go conkering in Abbots Woods a few years ago. You should try down there."

Flora looked at Seth as he and Bill discussed the finer points of playing 'conkers'.

"Put 'em in your mother's oven before you play," advised Seth.

She smiled inwardly. This tall, handsome twenty-year-old was Bill's age in some ways, but somehow, it made her even more sure how much she liked him.

NOVEMBER 1906

The main road from Bristol ran straight through the village, while tiny lanes meandered into the countryside on either side of it. Weathered stone walls edged the lanes, tracing their progress over the hilly meadows or through tree-lined byways and wooded estates. Church spires and towers glimpsed through trees signalled small communities tucked into the Somerset countryside.

Salisbury House stood on a corner surrounded by its beautiful gardens, marking the beginning of Abbots Ford. Further on, the chapel sat forward, its doors opening straight onto the narrow path as if to encourage worshippers inside. Redford's, the abattoir and butcher, was situated at the main crossroads. They had built a shop on the front and had become the General Stores as well. Once on the wooded steps and inside, there was an upholstered wood floor and evocative smells of tea, coffee, candle wax, oats and spices. A minor maze of passageways led from the shop to the back, where Angus Redford and his son, Graham, served with cheerful bonhomie. Almost opposite, Wilton's the Drapers stood sideways on, facing the traveller entering the village with pastel displays. The Partridge Inn faced a minute village square, served by a horse trough, so that patrons could leave their horses to take refreshment while they enjoyed the hospitality of Mr Smythe and his sons.

The village was a cohesive community in the West Country unsullied by its proximity to the relative decadence of urban Bristol. Generations of families had farmed the area and all the families knew each other and knew their place in the virtually self-contained hierarchy of Abbots Ford.

Near the top of the hierarchy was Silas Bartrup, who baked delicious bread and cakes for villagers, helped by his son. His wife, Margaret, was one of the stalwarts of the church; it was she who organised the rotas for cleaning the church and arranging the flowers when required. Almost opposite Bartrup's Bakehouse was the village church; made of grey stone, it had a square tower. The windows were not large and, in the main body of the church, were plain glass. Sometimes in the winter it was as cold and grey as a prescience of the grave. The mood in spring or when the sun shone was different; shafts of sunlight lifted the colour of the old oak pews and picked out the gold leaf in the decoration around the pulpit. The churchyard harboured generations of farmers and their families, and spread out on either side; in one direction towards the plum trees of Orchard Cottage, and in the other, the land around the village school.

Mr John Williams was the crusty, balding headmaster whose wife had died some five years before. He ruled the school with a rod of iron and mobile eyebrows, and was ably assisted by old Miss Taylor, who wore wire-rimmed spectacles and managed to be both stern and whimsical at the same time.

At the far end of the village was the old iron church hall, where most of the village gatherings were held. Rough grass surrounded it, bisected by an earth path, and it was often mistaken for part of the Smithy, which was next door.

Thomas Bates, the village blacksmith, was a taciturn man whose wife, Ellie, was the lying-in woman. They had four children of their own, two little girls and two boys, who at ten and twelve years old were already helping their father.

Seth Hawkes loved horses and was often to be found at the forge giving Tom a helping hand or just standing talking while he fashioned a horseshoe. The horses would wait patiently as if they knew he was helping them; they stood, changing the weight-bearing leg occasionally and swishing their tails. The Smithy was an immense old barn reached by a grassy paddock through a five-bar gate. The earth floor was sprinkled with straw and the forge itself was built with brick and set like a fireplace with a chimney at the far end of the barn. Around the walls, there were all manner of tools, instruments and pieces of wood and metal. The anvil stood near the fire so that the worked metal was always red-hot. Close by was a huge tub of water to cool the shoes, ready to fit on the horses.

Thomas was a muscular man with enormous hands. He was always quiet and gentle, both with the animals he tended and with people. His dark curly hair and beard made him look like a giant, or an ogre from a fairy tale, yet he was known to have a quiet, dry sense of humour.

"He's a beauty, Tom," observed Seth of the horse Tom was shoeing.

"He's Sir Matthew's hunter, lad. Bit high-strung."

"How many hands would he be, about thirteen?" asked Seth.

"Yes. Whoa, boy, whoa," murmured Tom as the elegant hunter became restive.

"Good day to you, young Seth," called Tom's wife, Ellie, as she came through the barred gate, taking a shortcut to the house through the forge.

"Nearly dinner time, Tom. You as well, Seth, if you've a mind to."

"That's all right, Mrs Bates; I'll be getting back now," replied Seth.

The gate moaned again as Flora appeared and opened it for her father to drive in.

"Hello, Flora," said Seth, surprised. He stood away from the door jamb on which he had been leaning.

"Morning Tom. Morning Seth." Flora's father got down from the trap.

"You doing Samson's shoes this afternoon, Tom?"

"Yes, lad. Nearly finished this one. I'll have my dinner and be doing him in about a half hour. That all right?"

"Yes. I'll go around home and be back. About three o'clock all right?"

"Right," mumbled Tom.

"I'll walk along with Flora and her father, Tom. Farewell for now," said Seth.

He held open the gate for them and they walked briskly along through the village towards Church Lane. It had been pleasantly warm at the forge, but the late autumn day was cold. When they reached Orchard Cottage, Flora's father went straight inside. The cottage sat sideways-on to the lane, so that the gable end, covered in ivy, faced the road. It was constructed with uneven blocks of grey stone and had a slate roof. Tiny square-paned windows nestled under the eaves of the roof upstairs and peered out like friendly eyes downstairs. A porch roof sheltered the low front door, which was made from oak. The long front garden ran parallel to the lane. A wooden fence separated the garden from the orchard, which ran along beside both cottage and garden, and around towards the main road. Chicken coups took up the rear of the orchard, but the chickens always escaped and had the run of the place, even strutting around the garden and inside the cottage if nobody stopped them. Flora and Seth smiled at each other.

"Will you come walking with me again this Sunday?"

Seth rubbed his hands together and looked down at Flora's pink face.

"Yes, I'd like that," she said.

"In the afternoon, after dinner?" he asked.

"Yes, see you then." Flora watched as he turned and strode back to the main road.

His broad shoulders moved as he swung his arms strongly, and she could tell he was exuberant. He turned, flashed a smile and waved.

He's a nice-looking boy, thought Flora as she went down the steps and into the cottage to help her mother prepare their meal.

+ + +

"Hello!" Seth called out as he bobbed his head to enter the tiny doorway of Orchard Cottage. He stood waiting for a reply in the small square space that served as a hall.

The door to the cottage living room was open and Mrs Henty came forward to greet him, still wiping her hands on a cloth.

"Come in, Seth, she's almost ready," she informed him.

Seth twisted his hat between his hands.

"Sit down. You've grown even taller than your pa, haven't you?" she observed.

Young Louise opened the door at the bottom of the stairs and came down, holding it wide open for her sister. Seth stood up, just missing the room's central beam.

"Hello, Flora."

"Hello again, Seth," she replied.

They had already met, briefly, after church earlier.

"We'll see you later, Mother." Flora turned to smile at her mother and sister, and bowed her head to go through the door and out to the front path with Seth.

He gave her his hand to go up the two steep steps to the lane, as though she had never managed them on her own before. Embarrassed, she pulled her hand away and they set off side by side up Church Lane towards Upper Abbots. They waved to Mrs Percival, who was a widow, as they passed her cottage. Flora blushed, as this was the first time she had walked out with Seth on her own.

"Seems you're embarrassed to be seen with me," he observed.

"No, I enjoy being seen with you, Seth Hawkes," replied Flora.

They walked slowly and companionably past her aunt and uncle's cottage.

"Your Charlie enjoyed himself at the dance, didn't he?" commented Seth.

"Yes. He's a good lad. He's beginning to be a real help to our dad, too, with the farm and all."

"Keen on Emily Hastings, is he?" enquired Seth.

"Charlie's keen on every pretty face." Flora laughed.

They arrived at a pair of cottages and Flora stopped.

"Mother wants me to take these cakes in to Gran and Grandad. Shall you wait here or come in?" she asked.

Seth followed her down the narrow path and Flora tapped on the door as she went straight in, calling out to her grandmother. Victoria Bartrup came out from behind a curtain drawn across the door to ward off draughts.

"Hello, Flora, what a nice surprise. Who is this then?"

"You know Seth Hawkes, Gran," said Flora.

"Oh, yes. Grandad knows your family well. How do you do, Seth?"

"Pleased to meet you, Mrs Bartrup," said Seth politely.

"Thank your mum for the cakes. I'll see her tomorrow, Flora," said the elderly lady, watching fondly as they left to continue their walk.

They waved before they turned the corner by the wall. There were leaves everywhere and Flora kicked them with her leather-booted foot. She watched while they scattered and ran, crunching along the edge of the lane, which narrowed so that they had to walk close to the fence of two cottages.

"Hello, Mr Saunders." Flora smiled.

An elderly man was working on a vegetable patch at the side of the cottages, turning the soil.

"Hello, Flora. How are you?"

"Fine thanks. You keeping well?"

"Getting old! Tell your dad I'll be along tomorrow."

Mr Saunders had handed his farm over to his two sons, Michael and Jacob, but he lent a hand whenever he could around the village.

They walked on past other cottages, and Peartree Farm, where the lane became a track with grass growing in the middle. Flora pulled her shawl more closely around her neck and their bodies lent forward as the hill grew steeper. They spoke of their families and

Flora told of her brother, Jacob, who had died aged three. Flora had been six at the time and she continued to miss him.

"Mother never ever talks about him," she explained. "He was a dear little chap."

They walked the mile to the top of the hill in thoughtful silence.

"We lost Grandma Bryant in January and I still miss her," Seth told Flora sadly. "Grandfather Hawkes died a few years ago now. I remember his funeral. First one I ever went to." Seth squeezed Flora's hand as he spoke.

They carried on until they reached the crest of the hill, looking down over Abbots Ford. Each had made the journey many times, for the hill was a favourite place with villagers. The walk was picturesque, with trees overhead enclosing the path in parts. Primroses grew in abundance on the banks in spring, and poppies, cowslips and buttercups brightened the way through the year. At this time of year, the colours delighted the eye as leaves were shed, hedgerows turned russet and fields lay fallow and brown. The view from the top displayed the surrounding countryside magically. When the weather was clear it looked like an Ordnance Survey map; on other days, clothed in mist or blanketed by heat haze, it looked like an Impressionist painting. It did not matter what the season or the mood, the hill was always welcoming, always comforting. Generations of courting couples, families or lone individuals had made the mile-long journey, yet it was rare to meet anyone else up there. The hill made each person believe it was for them only, like an all-enveloping Earth Mother with many children. At the same time, it seemed to be a benevolent presence, guarding the village without ever appearing menacing the way some hills and mountains can.

They sat on a moss-covered stump, talking. Flora had not met many men, only the lads around the village. She watched Seth as he spoke about his work and his love of horses. She liked the way he talked affectionately about his mother and sisters. He made her heart beat faster when he looked straight into her eyes as he spoke openly and honestly. He was unaware of his own attractiveness or the effect he was having on her.

15

The sun was well down, though it was still light and the clouds gathered in the distance, heralding the coming rain.

"We'd best walk back now," he said, getting up.

He pulled her up and held onto her hand as they started the return journey. Flora stumbled on the rutted and uneven path and he steadied her, smiling down at her.

"Will you come walking with me next Sunday?" he asked earnestly.

"We'll see. It's drawing in so early now," she said.

"I want to see you," he told her solemnly.

"Depends on the weather. If it's not good, you could call on us at the cottage."

He smiled, relieved that she had agreed to meet. They strolled past the cottages of Upper Abbots and straight down to the main road. Turning past the public house, they walked towards Church Lane. It was almost twilight as they approached Orchard Cottage. Seth stamped his feet as they waited for Flora's mother to come out from the scullery so that he could pay his respects. William, Flora's father, came out too.

"Drawing in now, lad. You and your dad got all of your hedges done?"

"Yes. We're almost set for the winter, Mr Henty," replied Seth.

"You two had a good walk?" Flora's father grinned at them.

"Yes, Pa, we have."

Flora turned to Seth and reiterated how much she had enjoyed the afternoon.

"See you next week, then?" Seth looked searchingly into her brown eyes, while still lurking awkwardly in the cottage doorway.

"Yes," said Flora gently. "See you next week."

DECEMBER 1906

Louise Henty was a tall, slender woman approaching her forties. She had large brown, enquiring eyes and a matter-of-fact manner that she had passed on to Flora. Her life was busy and fulfilled; family, the house and livestock kept her busy most of her waking hours. Her parents, Victoria and Joseph, needed her help, and she spared time to meet with other village ladies to keep the church clean and shining. The ladies also organised the Harvest Supper and other celebrations that arose throughout the year.

She looked fondly at her eldest daughter on the opposite side of the table, rolling out pastry.

"You're seeing quite a bit of the Hawkes lad, aren't you?"

"Mmm."

"Is he nice?"

"Yes, Ma. He thinks the way I do about things and he doesn't laugh when I tell him my daydreams."

"Your dad had a drink with his father last week and he says he talks of nothing but you." Her mother smiled.

Flora said nothing.

"Maybe you could tell him he's welcome to come for dinner on Boxing Day," she continued.

Flora carried on rolling pastry silently.

"Your dad and I would appreciate seeing something of him…" Her voice trailed off.

"Oh Mother, you mustn't think that this is anything serious; we just enjoy talking and sharing our thoughts. I don't want any fuss," pleaded Flora.

"Well ask him anyway; I think he'd like to come," her mother insisted.

Bill ran into the scullery.

"Be careful with those eggs," warned his mother. "You're supposed to be helping, not breaking them. And see those hens don't follow you in again!" she shouted as she left the scullery to put some pies in the oven of the range in the living room. She shooed the hens out, and they ran clucking and extending their necks in indignation.

Young Louise came down the stairs and propped open the door at the bottom.

"I'll take up the rest of the linen, Mother, and then I've finished," she called.

"Thank you, dear. That's a great help. Come and have a cup of tea and try a rock bun before we start the supper."

They all sat down for a few minutes, enjoying being together. Bill got up and said he was going to join his father for the milking. As they munched the fresh cakes, their mother commented lightly that Seth would be joining them on Boxing Day.

"Oh, Mother," moaned Flora.

"Mother! Can I bring…?" enthused young Louise.

"No, you can't," stated her mother emphatically. "Most certainly not. Whatever next?"

"Well, why can Flora…?" wailed Louise.

"Enough, Louise. There's time enough."

Flora and her sister looked at one another in mutual sympathy.

There was a knock on the front door and Aunt Elsie appeared. They gossiped a while and then began the preparations for supper, which was the main meal of the day.

"I was talking to Elizabeth Mallish," said Elsie. "They're coming up with their Victor on Boxing Day." She winked at young Louise. "Why don't you all come? Mother and Father will be coming for tea," she added.

"That sounds nice," said her sister.

Louise and her aunt exchanged conspiratorial smiles and, after staying a while longer, Elsie bade them all goodbye. When she had gone, Louise hugged her sister, Flora, and proclaimed that it was going to be a lovely Christmas.

"I'll be your sweetheart," she hummed to herself, dancing around the living room with an imaginary partner.

CHRISTMAS 1906

Christmas is always a lovely time, but especially so in a farming community. People relied on each other a great deal for help and assistance at periods throughout the year, so now, during what was a relatively quiet time for farmers, they enjoyed the festive season together.

It had not yet snowed in Abbots Ford, but it was cold enough for them to expect it. Villagers were making their way towards the church on Christmas Eve as they always did. They carried lanterns in the pitch-blackness, calling out 'season's greetings' as soon as they saw a light dancing towards them. The service was at five o'clock, to allow farmers to attend to the evening milking, wives to make final preparations for the following day and children to go willingly to bed after hanging a stocking or sock on bedpost or mantelshelf.

The church was decorated with garlands of holly, heavy with berries this year, and the altar displayed the celebratory white cloth tonight, after the purple of Advent. People crowded into the surprisingly warm church, their warmth and that of the candles making it seem cosy for once. The voices quietened as Reverend Orrins led his wife and family to the front pew and pottered beside the pulpit before joining the choir at the rear of the church. Mr Williams, the headmaster, wore a surplice, being a member of the choir, and Miss Taylor was there, fussing about the Christingle oranges and candles that some of the children were carrying to represent Jesus as the Light of the World.

Young Mark Bates, the blacksmith's son, began to sing unaccompanied, in a clear, silver soprano, "Once in royal David's city, stood a lowly cattle shed."

The congregation rose as the choir, followed by Reverend Orrins and his chaplain, processed up the aisle. Miss Trent played the organ for the choir to join in the second verse, who gradually reached their places in the choir stalls. The congregation sang the third verse well, relieved at being allowed to join in. Little children, who were carrying the Christingle oranges, sat along the front by the chancel steps for the rest of the carol service, which was traditionally interspersed with the nine lessons of the Christmas story. The service ended with everyone singing *O Come All Ye Faithful* and, uplifted and feeling full of the spirit of Christmas, they went purposefully on their separate ways.

As William and Louise Henty walked home with their family, they chatted and laughed happily. William and Charles carried on up to the farm to milk the herd, while Louise, her daughters and younger son, Bill, went into Orchard Cottage to check up on the hams that they had left cooking slowly on the top of the range. The aroma greeted them as they opened the door.

"Can we have some now, Ma?" pleaded Bill.

"Just wait until tomorrow," replied his mother. "Come and help me to get supper and put more mince pies in. You girls can set the table."

The living room of the cottage was large, with a window at either end. At the front was a bay window, boxed in with a cupboard and seat. On the wall opposite the front door was the black-leaded range with a fire grate on the left and double oven on the right, which was cosy on those cold winter nights. Over the fire rested a grid where the kettle boiled or a pan bubbled. A circular lid towards the back gave access so that fuel could be added and, when it was closed, it was hot enough to simmer saucepans; tonight the hams bubbled quietly.

The mantelpiece was carved oak, draped with a damask cloth and dotted with greetings cards. At the far end of the room on the same side as the range was the door to the solid oak, curved staircase leading to the two bedrooms. In the middle of the living room stood an enormous table that was always covered with a maroon velour cloth with tassels. An oak dresser stood against the long wall, housing all the family china and dishes. In front of the window at the far end of the room was a low cupboard, also covered with damask cloth, and next to it, the grandfather clock ticked reassuringly in the corner near the scullery door. In front of the range sat a horse-hair chaise longue, and to one side, William's capacious battered chair. Two pictures hung on the walls; one was a drawing of a horse, the other was a water colour of the village. Both had been done by Louise's brother, Stephen, before he was killed in the Boer War. The floor was tiled and, in front of the range, was covered by a large red and blue carpet that William and Louise had woven themselves when newly married. On this night, sprigs of holly decorated with red ribbon adorned the mirror over the mantelshelf, and the pictures. The red wool curtains were closed against the night and, when Will and Charles returned, their two sheepdogs would curl up in front of the fire. Just now, Bill was sitting toasting bread on a fork by the fire and leaving a pile of toast to keep warm on top of the range.

The girls carried on with their tasks, Louise humming *O Come All Ye Faithful* once again. There was a knock, and Seth stood framed in the doorway.

"Hello, I thought I'd drop in with this for Flora," he explained.

Flora, daubed with flour, emerged from the scullery and took the wrapped gift from him.

"Open it in the morning, not now." Seth smiled as he instructed Flora.

"Merry Christmas, Mrs Henty."

"Merry Christmas, Seth. How's your mother coping? Everything ready?" asked Louise.

"More or less." Seth laughed.

He nodded to young Louise and ruffled Bill's hair.

"You're coming to Auntie Elsie's on Boxing Day, are you?"

"Yes, Mrs Henty. Looking forward to it."

He turned to smile at Flora.

"See you on Boxing Day then."

Flora saw him to the door and watched as he disappeared into the waiting, expectant night.

BOXING DAY 1906

They were helping to get the meal ready. Flora and her sister prepared vegetables while their mother carved meat and looked at the pudding bubbling on top of the range. Bill had gone to help his father and brother with the morning chores at the farm.

They put on the best white linen tablecloth and set everything neatly upon it. Flora looked at the grandfather clock. Seth would be here soon and she had no time to go upstairs and look in the mirror. William came in, big and glowing from the cold.

"It'll freeze us all out yet," he growled as he moved everyone aside by his very presence. He was a man of medium build, with untidy brown hair and crinkly, twinkling blue eyes that were full of humour. He had a broad, mobile face that only rarely showed displeasure. He loved Louise deeply and they were a good team. They had married young and worked hard on their farm and the

21

cottage, and were now reaping the benefits. He washed his hands and mopped his face, using a bowl at the far end of the narrow scullery. Patting himself dry, he turned and looked at his family.

"You look pleasing in all your finery," he observed.

"Who might be coming? You aren't got up for your old dad, Flora," he teased.

They heard Seth's call simultaneously. Going back to the living room, Will greeted Seth expansively.

"Seasonal greetings to you, lad!"

"Thank you, Mr Henty," replied Seth as he stepped into the warm and bustling room. "And the same to all of you." He looked around for Flora, who suddenly appeared from the scullery.

Her dark hair was escaping from a new red ribbon and her eyes shone as she looked over at Seth. She pushed the errant tendrils back behind her ear and pretended to be busy with something on the already perfect table. She had seen him briefly at church on Christmas morning and they had managed to speak to one another. Flora had thanked him for the cameo brooch he had given her for Christmas and now she fingered it nervously as she looked at him.

"Almost ready," said her mother cheerily. "You men sit down and we'll serve."

They enjoyed a meal of cold roast chicken and ham. They had crackers left over from the day before. Will got out some ale and he, Charles and Seth enjoyed a glass or two. They talked and joked, and read out silly riddles, and everybody laughed. Young Louise was happy too, because she would be seeing Victor Mallish at her Auntie Elsie's at teatime.

When everything was cleared away and Will was having a nap, Louise sent the young ones out. They wrapped up well in hats, mufflers and gloves as, though it had not snowed yet, it was still very cold. Flora and Louise had new red woollen berets to wear and they looked fetching on their hair with their fresh young faces. They took Will's sheepdogs, Bracken and Holly, with them and walked down Church Lane towards the main road. They carried on to the crossroads and aimed for open land. Flora and Seth walked hand in hand while Louise and Bill ran on ahead throwing wood for the dogs to fetch. They turned to look at the couple deep in conversation; Bill observed that soon Louise and Victor would be just like them. Louise, embarrassed, shoved Bill, because he had detected how she felt about Victor Mallish. He rolled down a steep bank, narrowly missing the stream, but he was covered with mud.

"Ma'll kill me!" shouted Bill. "Look what you've done now, you stupid girl!"

"Who are you calling stupid?" retorted Louise. "You're the stupid one!"

"Now, now. Come on Bill. We'll rub the mud off." Seth helped Bill up to the bank and removed most of the offending earth. "Let the rest dry and it'll brush off," he advised.

Flora comforted Louise, who was distraught.

Seth teased them and chased them through the woods on the way back to cheer them up; he could not catch Flora. They arrived back noisily, explaining all at once. Louise organised them and eventually was able to ask if they were ready to go to Aunt Elsie's.

"Are we all here?" queried Will.

"Yes, all ready," said young Louise and Bill in unison.

They walked the short distance to Aunt Elsie's cottage and were met by a gaggle of relatives and friends, wishing them belated season's greetings, but sincere for all that.

"Where shall we put all that food?" asked Louise when she saw the spread on her aunt's table.

"Don't worry, a few games, and songs round the piano, and your appetite will be back again." Elsie laughed.

There was another explosion of greetings as more people arrived.

"He's here, Flora, he's here. Oh look how handsome he is. I can't bear it. Is my hair all right?" bubbled Louise as she spotted Victor.

Seth laughed kindly at her discomfiture and took Flora's hand, guiding her to a seat. Presently, one of their friends sang a carol in a deep bass voice while everyone joined in the refrain. Grandma's eyes were moist as she looked around at the company, but she recovered when Grandad insisted on doing a turn. Flora and her sister sang *Oh for the wings of a dove* to much acclamation. They managed to eat the tea Auntie Elsie had provided and people were sitting in groups, some in comfortable arm chairs and sofas, while others perched on the arms of chairs.

They were reminiscing and gossiping, the way Christmas and New Year makes families do.

Seth caught Flora's eye and nodded at the door. She understood the message and got up to follow him to the scullery.

"You have a nice family," he said quietly.

"So have you." Flora was surprised, for he sounded wistful.

They stood looking through the glass of the door at the stars in the clear sky on the night after Christmas.

"Christmas always makes me sad," admitted Seth.

"Why?" she asked gently. "It's like a new beginning."

"Maybe I'm just thinking... Oh, I don't know." He sounded weary.

"What's the matter, Seth?" Flora was concerned.

"It's nothing really. Our Ruth's little girl has been taken bad and they think it's scarlet fever."

"Seth, I'm so sorry. You shouldn't have come."

He interrupted her, turning her to him and looking down at her with a strange look in his blue eyes.

"Not come? Not come? When I can think of nothing but you? When I can hardly wait until the next time I see you?"

Seth turned away. Flora waited, a shy girl, wondering how she could let him know she felt the same. She touched his shoulder and he turned.

"Seth..." She looked at him questioningly. "How can I...? I... I miss you as well when we're not together."

His eyes softened as the oil lamp flickered. He touched her arms, then traced the shape of her face with his fingers. She looked at him, wonderingly, marvelling again at everything he was. Gently, slowly he kissed her. He put his arms around her and she felt the softness of his lips. He pulled away and they looked at each other as though they had experienced a wondrous revelation. He kissed her again, holding her close, and she stood still, amazed by how she felt. When they pulled away, he held her at arm's length and said softly, tenderly, "Merry Christmas, Merry Christmas, Flora, my love."

NEW YEAR'S EVE 1906/7

Seth had invited Flora to spend New Year's Eve at his parents' house at Drakes Farm.

"You'll still have to be in by half past nine," warned her mother.

"Can Seth come in when he brings me home?"

"Maybe for half an hour." Louise smiled.

Flora wore her best frock, which was made from heavy cotton. It was deep red with little flowers dotted over it and had a high, decorative lace collar. She borrowed her mother's cape to wear on the cold afternoon.

"We'll see you later then," said her mother when Seth called for her. "Have a nice time."

Seth's family were overwhelming to Flora. They were noisy, argumentative and amusing. He had three brothers and two sisters, of whom Flora was much in awe. Ruth was twenty-five and already had three children, and Rebecca was a year younger and had two little ones, with another one due at any minute. His brothers were raucous, indulging in horseplay with their small nieces and nephews as well as among themselves.

James Hawkes was, on the surface, a quiet man who never appeared to do anything or command anyone, yet he ran his farm like clockwork, with the help of his sons. Charlotte, his wife, was not the most organised of housewives, but everything that had to be done was done, eventually. Her family adored her, as she was a warm and generous woman.

"This is Flora, Ma," said Seth proudly when he took her in.

"Come in out of the cold, dear," said Charlotte.

"Who is this, Uncle Seth?" asked a pretty little girl.

"This is my girlfriend," Seth told the child.

His brothers hung about, hands in pockets, smiling at Flora. She was introduced to all of them and she shyly nodded and smiled.

"I'm making a cup of tea," announced Charlotte. "You girls can come and help me."

Flora stayed where she was, next to Seth. He was aware of the effect his family was having on her and put his arm protectively around her. When the novelty of her presence had worn off, she and Seth were able to exchange a few words without an obvious audience.

"Are you all right, love?" he asked her.

She nodded, not really sure.

"We'll be having tea soon. Dad will be in then."

The daughters of the house distributed cups of tea and Rebecca stayed to talk.

"You live in Church Lane, don't you?" she asked.

"Yes, Orchard Cottage," replied Flora.

"Are you related to the Henty's at Marsham?"

"I'm not sure," Flora responded. "We have relatives all over the place."

Rebecca laughed sympathetically. "So have we!"

Tea was a hectic and entertaining meal. The interaction between the brothers and sisters and their parents was friendly and teasing. James, Seth's father, had nodded wordlessly to Flora when he had arrived in. After cleaning up the debris of the meal, there was more frenetic organisation as the children were washed and put to bed, for they were all staying the night. The evening flew past, singing songs, playing games and cards and talking. Flora found herself drawn to the family as they revealed themselves to be friendly and sincere people. It was time for Seth to take Flora home. They called out good wishes for the coming year as Flora and Seth made preparation to leave.

"Thank you for the tea and a lovely evening," Flora told Charlotte.

"You'll have to come again soon," the older woman suggested.

Seth put his arm around her waist as they walked through the cold evening and she did not dissuade him.

"What do you think of them?" he asked.

"They're nice," she said. "Friendly and nice."

"They liked you. I could tell," he told her, obviously pleased.

He explained the family history to her, and some of his siblings' idiosyncrasies. They laughed as they walked, and she compared her brothers and sisters with his.

When they came upon an old barn at the edge of the lane, Seth pulled her over towards it.

"What are you doing?" she asked.

"Come here. I want to kiss you," he informed her cheekily.

"Maybe I don't want to be kissed," she suggested.

"Oh I think you do," he said masterfully.

She put her face up to his and allowed herself to be kissed. Their faces were cold and he hugged her close to him, nuzzling her to warm her.

"I love you," he told her. He kissed her again, revelling in her soft warmth. They were both aware of feelings aroused that had to be controlled, and pulled apart breathlessly.

"We'd best be on our way," she said quietly.

They did not speak for a time as they approached the main road through Abbots Ford, but walked in thoughtful silence. When they reached Orchard Cottage, a noisy gathering greeted them. Louise and Will had Elsie and Ed, Louise's other sisters, Catherine and Ann, and their husbands and children, and Will's sisters, Emily and Mary, and their families.

"This is worse than our house," whispered Seth in her ear.

Flora grinned at him, agreeing.

"You know, Flora, it would be a shame not to join these two families," he told her.

"What do you mean?"

"I love you. I want to be with you all the time," he said seriously.

Flora had been aware of her growing love for Seth for some time, but she was only seventeen.

"I love you too," she said softly.

"Be mine? Be my wife."

"We're too young, Seth. We can't think like that."

"We can if we feel the way we do," he replied.

"Ma and Pa would never allow it. No, it's too soon," she told him emphatically.

When he had gone, Flora joined in her own family celebration with only half her mind. Her thoughts kept returning to how she felt when she was with Seth, whoever else was there. She felt whole, complete and real with him. He gave her a feeling of warmth and security, and her feelings when they kissed were beyond her understanding. Yet she was too young to enter into the lifetime's commitment of marriage. Common sense told her that, for the time being, she would have to see less of him and dampen down the relationship.

JANUARY 1907

"Isn't it all a bit quick, Flora?" reasoned her father.

"It's true, Mr Henty, but we love each other and my parents say we can have the old cottage at Briersham," put in Seth.

Flora's parents looked at each other doubtfully.

"I suppose she has to go sometime," said her father.

"But you're both so young," reiterated her mother.

"Mother, we know how we feel. I'm eighteen in two weeks' time. Please can we become betrothed then?"

"Oh, Flora – if you're both so sure... And Seth, your parents agree?"

"They've known for a while now how I feel about Flora," said Seth seriously.

It was obvious to Will and Louise that the young people were very much in love. Both of them were sensible and they were aware that Flora had always known her own mind. Even so, their heads told them that the couple should wait a while, though instinct told them it would work. Seth explained that, as it was now January, they had thought a wedding at Easter would be convenient – between lambing and harvest.

Will put out his hand to Seth. "Welcome to the family, son," he said.

Bill jumped excitedly around the living room, having come out from his hiding place in the scullery.

Louise asked eagerly, "What about your dress?"

Charles came running downstairs to see what all the commotion was about.

"Well done, Seth, but you'll never quell her temper." He grinned, hugging Flora.

They all laughed and Seth met Flora's eyes with the message that there would be more than her spirit to contend with. They were an attractive couple and were excited about their future marriage and life together. They had grown to know one another well through the late autumn last year. Seth was Flora's first boyfriend, but Seth had walked out with a number of girls. He was considered a catch in the village. One girl had gone on to marry a local boy, but another left to nurse in London, broken-hearted, so they said. Flora loved Seth's quiet strength and his sense of humour; she liked his easy manner with the women in his family and his charm towards her own. They were very much in love.

"We'll meet your parents, Seth," said Will Henty, "and arrange a wedding."

FEBRUARY 1907

Seth and Flora were at his parents' house where they had been talking about the old cottage where they were to begin married life. Seth's family liked Flora and his parents were happy that they were marrying.

"It's as dry as a bone, Flora. Come the weekend; John, David, Arthur and I will sort it out ready for you," reassured James Hawkes.

Flora looked doubtful. They had walked over to see it earlier that afternoon.

"It didn't look as if anyone could live in it," complained Seth.

Flora sat silently and Seth's mother brought in some more tea.

"I've some lovely material for the downstairs curtains and some old made-up curtains for upstairs," she offered encouragingly.

"Sunday. We'll do it Sunday. That's decided," stated James.

They drank their tea dispiritedly and Seth prepared to walk Flora home. When they reached the end of the lane, he challenged her.

"Well where will we live if we can't live there?" he asked hotly. "You tell me! They're only trying to help."

"I don't know, but I'm not living in that horrible, rat-infested old heap of stones," said Flora with finality.

"See what it looks like when my dad and all of us have cleared it," begged Seth.

They walked in silence. It had been so exciting, planning their wedding, and now it looked as though everything would be spoilt if they had nowhere to live.

"My mother will stop the wedding when she sees where you're taking me," sobbed Flora.

Seth tried to take her hand, but she shrugged him off.

"Leave me be. You're a selfish oaf, Seth Hawkes!" she cried.

It began to rain as they approached Orchard Cottage.

"I'm going in," said Flora, and went straight down the steps, through the door and into the house. Seth stood forlornly wondering how he could bring her around. A derelict cottage was nothing compared to their marriage and future life together, surely? He walked home disconsolately in the pouring rain. Where was their love now? His mother welcomed him without fuss and threw him a towel for his hair.

"Wait 'til Flora sees what you can do with Plumtree Cottage, son," she consoled.

"It's no good, Ma. She doesn't love me. It's just an excuse, all a mistake."

The following Sunday Seth, his father and brothers took their tools, brushes, ladders and everything they needed and set to work on Plumtree Cottage out at Briersham. It was a village two miles from Abbots Ford and half a mile from Seth's parents. It had no shops or inns, but could boast two churches. Plumtree Cottage was in a lane off the through road, and was reached by a cart track. It was a pretty little house, built of grey stone, with tiny windows, one of which was missing. The roof was grey tiled and one or two of these were also missing. A porch on the front of the cottage guarded the oak door. The low front wall was covered with ivy and creepers, and one side of the cottage displayed ivy as far as the chimney. Inside, there was one large room at the front and a scullery at the back; stairs ascended from the scullery to the upper floor where there were two bedrooms. It did indeed look almost a ruin, because no one had lived there since Seth's great-aunt had died some years before. James and his sons set to work, regretfully clearing out some nesting birds as well as other muck and mess that had gathered.

"It'll be a while before you'll be able to live in it, Seth," said his brother, John.

"Oh I don't know. I'll keep on it every minute I have before the wedding."

Seth was as good as his word, and his father and brothers helped whenever they could. Will and Charles joined them, building the new window frame and helping James with the roof. They were lucky with the weather, for it was a bright, dry February. They all turned up to distemper the inside walls once the cottage was weatherproof. Will mended the range and got it going to help to dry it all out, as well as keeping the workers warm. Both the mothers had their sewing machines out to make the curtains and chair covers. The happy pair had been given most of what they needed to start married life by family and neighbours. Will had made them a huge dresser – the top of which came off or they would never have got it inside the cottage. Flora's grandparents were giving them a brass bedstead and had made the feather mattress to go with it. Grandfather Bryant, Seth's grandad, had made them a very fine pine table and chairs.

Seth had taken Flora back to see the cottage as soon as it was weatherproof and clean, though not decorated or furnished.

"What do you think, Flora?" he asked anxiously.

"You have worked so hard. You all have," she said. "I'm sorry, Seth. I've been nasty to you."

"No, my little duck, you were right. It looked a sight."

Seth put his arms around her to comfort her. He stroked her hair as she cried a little, because she was ashamed about how she had behaved. He kissed her forehead, then her nose and, finally, her mouth. Flora responded and he held her tighter and picked her up. He was running his hands urgently over her body.

"Seth, no… no." Flora pulled away, afraid of his response. She stood back and pulled her blouse and jumper straight, and patted her hair.

"Not long 'til our wedding now, love," he commented.

"Time enough," responded Flora tartly.

EARLY MARCH 1907

Flora's mother and sister were busy making her wedding frock. Louise was to be her bridesmaid, so they were making a new frock for her too.

"Stand still," complained their mother. "You are a fidget."

Flora was having a fitting. Her gown was fine white cotton gauze underlaid with muslin. It had a high neck and long gauze sleeves, and was decorated with pin-tucks and Tambour-work embroidery made by her grandmother. Her bonnet would be trimmed with fresh spring flowers, gathered and arranged by her mother, and a small veil.

"It's just how I thought it would be," said Flora happily. "It really is beautiful, Ma."

"Let's hope it will be by the time you've finished twisting and turning. Keep still!"

Louise finished the hem and told her daughter she could get down from the chair on which she was standing.

"Mind the pins!" she warned as they helped her out of the garment.

"Shall we do yours while I've got you captive?" Louise asked her other daughter.

"Yes, and I can help you," offered Flora.

Young Louise climbed into her new frock. It was pink muslin with a delicate flower print around the hem.

"Oh you look lovely!" exclaimed Flora, as it was the first time she had seen her sister wearing it.

The two women placed the pins around the hem, with instruction from the wearer. The elder Louise said nothing, but her patience was wearing thin.

"Enough for now," she said when they had finished.

She took the two gowns on hangers and placed them on the back of her bedroom door.

The wedding preparations were going well. The wedding breakfast was going to be at Orchard Cottage and Louise was being helped with the cooking. Her mother, Victoria, and her sisters, Elsie, Catherine and Ann, were assisting her. There was a goodly number of people coming. As well as their own family and friends, there were all Seth's family; the list seemed almost endless.

Louise was spring cleaning the cottage, helped by Flora and young Louise. William became increasingly bewildered by all the frantic activity.

"It would have had to be done anyway," said his wife when he commented, complaining.

"Will there be room for all those people?" he enquired.

"Just pray that it's a nice day," she told him.

The small cottage at Briersham was also taking shape. Flora took her mother and sister to have a look at it.

"It's lovely, Flora," said her mother, who could see the possibilities.

Young Louise did not say much at all, because to her it still looked ramshackle.

The menfolk of both families had worked hard to restore it so that Flora and Seth could start their married life there. Curtains hung at the windows and all the furniture they had been given was in place. Flora had been thrilled by the look of the cottage with the new white distemper on the inside walls. Her bottom drawer collection was taken and installed at her new home. As well as underwear, it included embroidered sheets and linen, towels, blankets and cloths, but most especially, the quilt she had been making and that her mother had begun when she was born. It consisted of pieces of material from all the frocks and garments Louise had made for herself and her daughters through the years. Her grandmother had given her a very special bone china tea set that had in turn belonged to her mother. "Your troubles will fade when you drink a cup of tea from these cups, Flora," her grandma had told her.

Seth had been working in the small garden, digging it over and planting seeds when it was time, so that they would have something growing later in the year.

"Doesn't it remind you of us, Will?" Louise smiled at her husband late one evening.

"Doesn't seem all that while ago, Lou, either," he replied.

"I think they'll be all right. They're so right for each other," mused Louise.

William and Louise had a strong marriage. Will worked hard with the farm with very little time off, but the life was just that – a life, not just a job. He was blessed with strength and good health, as was Louise. She too worked hard looking after her family, her home, her parents and her animals. Her egg money gave her an element of independence, though the income from sheep was put back into buying new livestock and money from the plum harvest was used in the household. The children in the family, as was the custom, were included in the tasks from an early age. Louise had made time to read with her sons and daughters, and also managed to spend time with William.

"I'm proud of you – you're a good woman," said Will matter-of-factly.

Louise smiled across the fireplace at him. "Time for bed, I think."

They went into the small downstairs front room, which was their retreat from the world, prepared for bed and nestled warmly into the soft feather bed.

"You're still a bride to me," whispered Will in her ear as she drifted off to sleep.

EASTER 1907

Easter in Abbots Ford was one of the best times of the year. Winter safely over, the recurring themes of birth and renewal were empirically demonstrated by the activities and events around the countryside. Primroses grew in profusion on the banks at the sides of the lanes, from where children gathered them, competing for who could collect the most bunches for the trellis screen, put up especially in the church for Easter Day.

The weekend after Easter sunbeams shone dustily through the stained glass window in the church and the remnants of the Easter primroses were being replaced and refreshed. The shining trumpets of the daffodils displayed in vases around the church heralded Flora and Seth's wedding day.

Mrs Wilton and Mrs Mallish moved quickly and efficiently between the displays, making sure that they were just so. Two other church helpers dusted and busied themselves between the ancient pews, beating a hassock here and there, and straightening hymnals.

At Orchard Cottage, there was an atmosphere of well-controlled excitement. Louise Henty had worked assiduously to organise everything, from the wedding breakfast to the clothes her family would wear, down to the finest detail.

Flora sat contemplatively, looking into the oval mirror on her bedroom wall. Her sister was dressing in their mother's room to allow her to dress in peace and quiet for her wedding. She knew beyond doubt that she loved Seth, and he her; she had never been more sure of anything. After today, she would no longer be regarded as a young girl, but as a married woman. Her role would change, as would people's perception of her. She would still be her parents' daughter, but no longer a member of their household; still be their baby, yet a woman. Even in the eyes of God, she would be someone different: a man's wife. Instead of her mother's helper, she would be a homemaker; instead of a sweetheart, she would be a lover. One day, instead of a child, she would become a mother. By taking this one immense step, because of her love for Seth, she would alter everything. The love, care and comfort of her family's home would become once removed; she would have her home with Seth. The enormity of the decision she had made filled her with an almost unbearable sadness and longing for all the things that had been and would never be again. Yet there was also hope and delicious anticipation; the thrill and fear of the unknown, the untrodden path. Her father and mother would always be there for her, she knew that. Her love for Seth and his for her would be the foundation upon which they would build this new life, and maybe even, this new family. Unimportant thoughts drifted through her mind; would this be the last time she would dress alone? Would she miss Louise? It had been fun sharing a room with a sister. They had confided various mysteries as each embarked on womanhood; they had giggled and blushed over lads, compared notes on clothes, moaned of each other's untidiness, complained of a candle burning late while one of them read.

Flora was gazing at her wedding gown. It had happened according to their plan and Flora delighted in its full skirt, narrow waist and fresh delicacy. She brushed her hair carefully and called her mother to help her into her frock. They talked of nothing very much, just details of what was happening and what they had to do. It was a conspiracy of not admitting to the pain, while acknowledging the joy of the occasion. Her mother placed her bonnet, decorated with freesias, with Grandma's veil attached to it, on her dark hair.

"No wonder Seth is so bewitched by you," said her mother happily. "You've never looked lovelier."

Her mother and sister held her skirts and helped her down the narrow, curved staircase. William Henty heard their approach and opened the door at the bottom; he stood back with a quick intake of breath.

"About time," he commented gruffly. "But you do look very nice." He glanced at his wife and younger daughter, and his look told of his pride in them all. "You all look nice," he added.

"Where are the boys?" asked their mother.

"They went round to the church to help Seth's brothers show people to their pews," he told her.

"Did you see how they looked, William?"

William, being a farmer, only wore a suit to church on Sundays and always felt stiff and uncomfortable in his high collar and formal clothes. He assured Louise that the boys looked a credit to her.

"You look beautiful too, dear," she told her younger daughter. "Pink suits you well," she added.

After looking around to see that everything was ready for their return, Louise placed a lilac hat on her still-dark hair and stuck in the hat pin she had been holding between her teeth. She smoothed down her jacket and skirt and picked up her bag. Smiling at them, she said, "Well, I'm going now. I'll see you there."

Aunt Elsie and Uncle Ed had been standing out on the path waiting for her and they set off to walk the two hundred yards to the church. Samson was shiningly groomed and handsome in the traces as Will handed his daughters into the carriage he had borrowed for the occasion.

"Ready, my beauty," he said and they drove around to the church, waving to neighbours and children on the way.

One of the Bates boys stood with the horse, while Flora got down and straightened her gown, while her sister tweaked her veil.

"You're a beautiful bride, love," said a neighbour as they walked up the narrow path leading to the church.

Rev Orrins met them at the door. "Beautiful day, Flora. Good turn-out," he said. "Are we ready?"

He gave a sign to Miss Trent and Flora took her father's arm. She took a last look at her sister and began the journey up the aisle. "Praise my soul the King of Heaven," sang the congregation.

People turned to smile at them and Flora found that she was enjoying herself, the beauty of the music sweeping her along. As they neared the chancel steps, Flora looked at Seth, who had been watching her progress all the way. They both turned to look at Rev Orrins as he began with the time-honoured words. "Dearly beloved, we are gathered together here in the sight of God…"

Flora took in the surroundings: the lovely, familiar old church looking its majestic spring best; all their family, friends and neighbours standing behind them witnessing their marriage; her dear father standing beside and a little behind her, waiting to respond when Rev Orrins asked 'Who giveth this woman'. She could smell the spring flowers, lovingly arranged, both in church and for her to wear. Best of all, Seth beside her, looking dashingly handsome in his new suit. His hair was slicked back and she noticed that he had cut himself shaving that morning. She glanced up, following the line of the back of his head and neck as he earnestly made his responses. *Oh God, how I love him. Please let us be happy,* she prayed fervently.

William watched the proceedings and waited for his cue. He had not been prepared for how he had felt when he first saw her coming down the stairs. Was this lovely young woman really the little girl he had known, remembered so well? The girl who had lived with him and Louise until last night? *Who giveth this woman? Not me,* he thought. *Doesn't seem five minutes since she was being christened in that font back there!* Will was jolted out of his thoughts as Louise sidled around, having taken Flora's bouquet from her. He glanced back at his wife. Louise stood, looking beautiful today, holding onto the front of her pew. Charles and Bill had walked with her to her place and joined her in the front row. As the organ music had swept over her and Flora had come into view, all she could think of was the little girl with dark hair at her Confirmation, solemnly making her vow, wanting to do the right thing. Here she was again, the same girl, making another sort of vow. At that moment, Seth looked down at her daughter with such love that Louise was reassured. *My William looks handsome as well,* she thought, *even after all these years.*

They were signing the register and their parents were talking quietly and smiling. Then it was time to emerge as man and wife. Mendelssohn's *Wedding March* rang out as they smiled their way down the aisle and out into the spring sunshine. The guests followed, showering them with petals and rice.

"Beautiful service, wasn't it, Will?" observed Jacob, his father.

"Yes, Dad, beautiful." Will kissed his mother.

"Doesn't seem that long since it was you and Louise," she said.

"No, Mother. Just what we were saying the other day."

Seth's parents hovered near the couple and his brothers and friends shook his hand in congratulation. Flora waited, bemused, while people kissed her cheek and told her she was beautiful. Relatives stood gossiping in the graveyard; there was milling about and spilling out beyond the lych-gate. Eventually, William saw Flora and Seth into the carriage to drive back to Orchard

Cottage and that was the signal for everyone to walk round. Louise, her mother, Victoria, and her sisters were already busy uncovering food and putting a selection of meats out onto plates. The wedding cake stood on the table in front of the window. Flora's grandma had made it and Aunt Elsie had decorated it.

"Oh my dears, come in," Louise welcomed the newly married couple. She kissed them both, as did everyone else who had arrived before them.

It was pleasant enough for people to go out to the garden at the front of the cottage and some of the young ones went out into the orchard. The families mingled, as many of them knew each other. It was quite an occasion when a popular couple was wed. The wedding breakfast was enjoyed and Flora's father said a few words when they drank to the health of the bride and groom. Seth responded and his brothers and friends hooted and teased him when he mentioned his 'wife'.

People gradually said their farewells and, amid a hail of good wishes for their future, it was time for Flora and Seth to leave for their own home. Flora found her mother having a quiet moment in her bedroom.

"Mother, I left my flowers on Seth's grandma's grave. Thank you for everything – it's been a wonderful day."

Louise hugged her daughter to her.

"You're going on a long adventure, you and Seth. We're here if you need us, but you're a wife now – Seth comes first."

"I know, Ma, I know."

Will put his arm around Louise's shoulders as they watched Flora go home with Seth. Seth's parents and some of his family accompanied them, for Briersham was not far from where they lived. Young Louise, Charles and Bill stood with their parents to see their sister off.

"See you tomorrow, Flo," called Charles.

Flora turned for a last look at them as she rounded the corner at the bottom of Church Lane.

I'll see them all tomorrow, she comforted herself.

They were tired when they arrived at Plum Tree Cottage. Seth had been along that morning to lay the fire and his mother had lit it earlier, making it cosy to come home to.

"Shall we have a cup of tea?" asked Seth.

"Yes, that would be nice," said Flora and she filled the kettle and set it on the hob.

"I should take off my frock and get changed."

Flora went out to the scullery and up the pine staircase to their room. Fresh flowers stood on the dressing table. It turned out later that Seth's sisters had put them there. Flora struggled with her buttons, twisting to try to look in the mirror and undo them. She heard Seth's footsteps on the stairs and sat on the chair to take off her shoes and stockings.

"What's going on here?" asked Seth as he came into the room.

"Nothing's 'going on'. Just me trying to take off my wedding finery."

"Let me help," he suggested.

"Just the lower buttons; I can manage the rest."

Seth fiddled with the tiny buttons and loops.

"Oh stop it, I'll manage," complained Flora, turning around.

Seth took her in his arms and kissed her tenderly.

"Hello, my little married duck."

Flora relaxed and returned his kiss.

"You go down and I'll be down in a minute to make the tea," Flora said.

Reluctantly, Seth left the room and Flora managed to change into one of her other new frocks. She looked fetching in it. It was pale apple green with sprigs of leaves over it. As she busied herself in the scullery, Seth came behind her and put his arms around her waist.

"Sit you down, Seth Hawkes."

"Not when I can kiss my wife, Flora Hawkes." He laughed and kissed her neck.

There was a knock at the door and Seth's brother, John, and sister, Rebecca, came straight in.

"What's this?" teased John. "Mother sent us up with something in this dish for you to eat tonight."

"That's thoughtful; thank her, will you?" said Flora.

They were shown around the new home and joined the newlyweds for a cup of tea.

"You're well organised." Rebecca laughed when Flora produced biscuits from a new biscuit barrel.

"Ma made them and we brought them up yesterday with some of my things," explained Flora.

The evening drew in as they sat talking about the wedding.

"We'd best be off home now," said John, and with yet more farewells they left in the dusk.

Flora bustled about, clearing up the cups and saucers and putting the dish of meat and potatoes into the oven. Seth followed her about, getting in her way.

"You could light the oil lamps," she told him hopefully.

She needed one of her new aprons to protect her frock, and lit a candle, putting it in a candlestick to carry upstairs and find the garment. She did not hear Seth come up the stairs and into the room and jumped, startled, when she turned and saw him.

"You are so lovely, my Flora," he said quietly.

She had put the candlestick on her dressing table and the shadows danced and jumped in its yellow light. Seth had shed his tie and stood in his best white shirt with the sleeves rolled to the forearm, where he had been lighting the oil lamps. His eyes burnt into her as he moved towards her purposefully and stroked her hair. She looked up at him and put up her hand to touch his face.

"I can't believe we're married," she said.

She touched his mouth and he turned her hand over and kissed the palm.

Suddenly, he took her in his arms and, with increasing desire, kissed her face, her mouth, her neck, her breast.

"Seth, oh Seth," she said as he undid the buttons on her frock effortlessly.

They consummated their marriage with tenderness and love. Flora had known something of what to expect, as her mother had told her two evenings before, and she was a farmer's daughter. Seth had tried to contain himself and be gentle and kind, for he knew that Flora was innocent, a virgin.

"Do you believe we're married now, my love?" asked Seth passionately at the height of their lovemaking.

"Oh yes, Seth, oh yes," she replied.

They fell asleep exhausted in one another's arms, oblivious to the oil lamps burning downstairs and a stew cooking the night away in their new range; oblivious to everything except their love.

Chapter Two

MAY 1907 – JANUARY 1908

The sun was low on the distant hills at Briersham. Flora loved it when it was clear enough to see as far as the horizon. The spring had been a lasting one and the trees and hedges looked fresh and lush after the early rain. Flora and Seth were sitting in the scullery having tea. They had worked hard to make the cottage welcoming. Blue gingham curtains in the scullery were bright and fresh, framing the windows that looked out on the view of the countryside. The door was open to the back garden where, on good wash days, Flora put her linen out to dry. Unusually, their scullery had a fireplace, as well as the range in the living room. It made it pleasantly cosy in winter and gave a focal point to the small room. Flora was lucky that there was a water pump in her garden and that she did not have to carry all the water she used very far.

"Try the scones," she suggested.

"No, I won't be able to eat at Ma's if I do, love," said Seth.

Flora drew around the knots in the pine table with her finger.

"Seth, Catherine Redford asked me if I'd like to work in the shop twice a week."

"No. You're not doing it," said Seth adamantly.

"But why?"

"Because you're not and that's an end to it."

Flora knew better than to pursue the subject further; if that was how Seth felt about it, then that was that.

"There is something else…" began Flora.

"What?"

"Reverend Orrins has asked me to take Sunday school."

"But it's the only time we have on our own, to ourselves!" shouted Seth.

"It's only for an hour, Seth," pleaded Flora.

"Yes and three quarters of an hour there, the same back and another hour for a 'cup of tea' at your ma's."

"It's only once a week…" she began.

"Week in, week out – what about me?" Seth was really annoyed.

Flora went over to him and put her arms around him.

"Sunday school is good for the children and they reckon I'll be useful 'cos some of them remember me."

"Aren't there other people who can take them?"

"They've split the class in two and Rev Orrins' Rachel is taking the younger ones – I'm having the older ones," explained Flora. "You could come with me, for the walk. I'd need you there in the winter in any case," she went on.

"What, to defend your honour?" joked Seth, capitulating as he picked her up in a tight embrace.

"I'm not staying around at your ma's." He released her suddenly at the thought.

"You could see your Rebecca; she's near enough."

"What, and have her little savages jumping all over me for an hour?" Seth protested.

"Some of the 'little savages' would be in Sunday school with me." Flora laughed.

"Oh, all right then," conceded Seth.

"Are we friends again then?" asked Flora.

"Yes, of course we are – we never stopped."

Flora and Seth were settling down well in their new lives. Flora enjoyed running the little cottage and still managed to go back to Abbots Ford almost every day to help her mother. They had gone around to the whole family on visits to say their 'thank yous' for wedding presents. It was fun being a grown-up married lady.

That evening they were going to visit Seth's parents. He had his arm around her as they walked in the early summer's evening.

"Are you glad we got married?" Flora asked.

"No, I'm not! I hate it."

Flora pummelled him around the back with her hands in mock rage.

"No, I love it. I love you."

They had reached the house where Seth's parents lived. Drakes Farm House was a house rather than a cottage. It sat high above the road, reached by a flight of steep brick steps. Further on up the road was the entrance to the farm and everyone used that way in: through the double gate, which was always left open, across the yard and along the side of the vegetable garden to the back of the house. It was a comfortable, happy house with solid furniture and enough room for James and Charlotte's large family. Grandma Hawkes visited often, spending a few weeks at a time with them.

Charlotte got up to greet them, and nieces and nephews immediately clung onto Seth's legs.

"Swing us, Uncle Seth, swing us!"

Seth took them outside and swung them around in turn until they were dizzy. His sister, Rebecca, whose children they were, was holding four-month-old David. Rebecca was telling them that she was 'expecting' again.

"Not already, Becky!" said her mother in dismay.

Rebecca merely smiled and cuddled David closer.

Seth sat at the piano and played a few notes of a hymn. James Hawkes sang a snatch in a light tenor voice and Seth joined in again on the piano.

"Play *Three Blind Mice*, Uncle Seth," requested young Robbie when they had finished.

They all sang the nursery rhyme, which Seth and his father sang in harmony. Charlotte was making tea.

"Flora, did you let me have that dish back, love?" she asked.

"Which dish, Ma?" queried Seth.

"The stewing dish I sent you a meal in the day you two got married."

Seth stifled a laugh and Flora blushed, remembering the blackened, abandoned vessel.

"I'll bring it when I come tomorrow, Ma," he promised.

James sat in his chair smoking a pipe. His wife was handing out treats to the grandchildren while the grown-ups talked. Seth and his brothers worked hard at Drakes Farm. They had a herd of two hundred Friesian cows, as well as growing cereal crops, and

45

there was always plenty to be done. It was a man's life, and the community revolved around the men and their work. The men always came first and, in theory, their word was law. They gave little credence to the furore that surrounded women's suffrage and had firm views on the news that had filtered through to them.

"I don't reckon on these women voting," said Robert suddenly. "Lot of rubbish if you ask me."

"Yes, that Pankhurst woman should go home and look after her husband," said Seth.

James remained silent. Charlotte was disorganised about some things, but her thoughts on this subject were clear.

"Now you boys listen," she began.

"Oh, Ma, not all that again," moaned Rebecca.

"You listen too, my girl."

Flora's ears pricked up. Seth's family often had volatile debates amongst themselves, but it was not often that Charlotte voiced an opinion. Flora's mother and aunts had dismissed the whole thing as a flash in the pan, but Flora had seen the justice in the ideas being put forward.

"Look at you young women. Look at Flora here," said Charlotte. "They get married and, as soon as they do, they are looking after things as though they've done it forever, and the men expect it."

"That's easy," interrupted Robert.

"It's not easy," insisted Charlotte, "and it is hard physical work, the work we do."

"Let it be, lad," said James.

"We have brains in our heads. Why shouldn't we have a say in what goes on?"

The men were silent and the girls stunned. Flora looked shrewdly at Charlotte. *She's more interesting than I thought,* thought Flora. *No wonder Seth is never boring!*

+ + +

Charles went about his business on the farm while most of family life flowed gently past him. He had thought he would miss Flora when she married, but he saw almost as much of her, she was at Orchard Cottage so often. He was an ideal big brother and eldest son; impartial and understanding, he even managed to be patient with Bill, who was seven years his junior and idolised him. Charles and his father worked well together and got on most of the time; an added advantage for Will was that, because Charles lived at home, he paid him less than the average farmhand.

Charles had been smitten with Emily Hastings, the girl who had won the 'Farmer's Girl' competition at the Harvest Dance: she had also won his heart. The relationship appeared to be serious, although Charles had not mentioned marriage. They made an appealing couple, both being tall and attractive: Charles with his dark hair and intelligent brown eyes, she blonde and beautiful. Nothing had marred their courtship and they were popular among the young folk in the village.

Emily had been behaving strangely in recent days, avoiding Charles and saying little when they were together. He tried to persuade her to confide in him during a pleasant walk on a warm evening when the blossom filled the air with subtle scent.

"I know that something is troubling you. If you don't tell me, we'll never get anywhere," he cajoled.

"That's just it, I think we have got somewhere," she said cryptically.

"What do you mean?" He was baffled.

"I think I'm... you know..."

"You're what?"

"Expecting."

"Expecting what?"

She said nothing, but kept her eyes downcast and blushed.

"Not a baby?" He was aghast. "But you can't be! We haven't... I haven't..."

"Haven't what?" she asked, looking up at him with innocent blue eyes.

"Haven't done anything to make you... expecting," he said firmly.

"We kissed. We've kissed ever such a lot," she asserted. "And anyway, I know."

"Look, Emily, I don't know how you think you know, but I can tell you that you can't be."

"I'm so worried," she whispered, tears beginning to course down her cheeks.

"Talk to your ma about it," advised Charles. He knew that Emily had not been out and about with any other lad, and in any case, young people did not indulge in what they considered to be carnal activity before marriage. "Promise me you'll talk to your ma, or someone?"

She nodded and he wiped her eyes.

"Come on, I'll get you home," he said quietly.

He kissed her cheek and left her at the gate to her house.

"See you tomorrow, love," he told her.

The evening had ended sooner than planned and he decided to walk to the Partridge Inn and enjoy a pint of ale before going home. The jovial atmosphere and welcoming shouts were comforting and helped him to regain a sense of perspective. He knew that it was not possible for Emily to be pregnant, but it had still been a shock for her to think that she was. He joshed and joked with his friends, yet at the back of his mind the thoughts intruded. What if she had been? Did he want to become a father at twenty? Did he want marriage? He would have stood by her if she had been expecting a child, but Emily as a wife? The ale flowed down his throat and his laugh became louder as the evening wore on. Perhaps he would have a word with Flora; she would be able to advise him. By the time he made his way home he was grinning foolishly to himself, imagining himself the father of a fine, strapping son. *Perhaps it wouldn't be that bad,* he thought as he let himself into the slumbering cottage.

JUNE 1907

Flora busied herself in the scullery, preparing the meal in time for Seth's return from Drakes Farm. She had placed a vase of flowers on the windowsill and smiled to herself as she peeled vegetables. They had had an argument the previous evening, because he had gone straight to the Partridge Inn after he had eaten. He had been contrite this morning and, after he had apologised, they had made love and he promised that he would spend more time with her.

"Hello, love," he greeted her, coming in and kissing her ear.

"Nearly ready. Here's water to have a wash," she offered.

"What have we got for tea?" He leant over to peer in the saucepan, which she took through to place on the range.

"Busy this afternoon?"

"Aye, and it's hot work in this weather." He washed and sat down at the table, ready to eat.

"Didn't tire yourself out too much this morning, then?" she teased.

He put an arm around her waist. "Take more than that to tire me." He laughed.

When they were eating, Flora told him that she had promised her parents that they would walk through to see them later in the evening.

"Not tonight, Flo," he said apologetically. "I'm playing darts at the Partridge."

"After all you said in bed this morning, you're still going out?"

"It was arranged. I can't let them down."

Flora said no more. She felt betrayed and angry, and thought that if Seth could not see the injustice of the situation, then now was not the time to enlighten him. He changed into a clean shirt and prepared to leave.

"You'll be all right, love? See you later," he said and, with a flashing smile, turned her heart as he went down the path to the lane.

JULY 1907

Charles had asked Flora to take a turn around the orchard with him. The weather had been oppressively hot and they were glad of the respite in the coolness that the evening brought.

"What is it, Charles?" asked Flora when they had been walking for a while. "I know there's something on your mind."

She looked intently at her elder brother. He had always been the strong one, the sensible one; now she sensed that it was he who needed advice.

He took a few moments before he began to explain the problem to her. "It's silly really, Flo. You know I'm keen on Emily?"

She nodded so that he could continue.

"You know that I would never, you know what I mean, I would never take advantage of her."

"I know that," agreed his sister.

"A couple of months ago, she thought…" He laughed nervously, embarrassed. "We'd kissed, and she thought…"

Flora nodded again.

"I can guess what she thought!" she muttered.

"The problem is, I'm confused," Charles told her. "I was happy enough going about with her, but when I really thought about it, she's not the one I want to marry – spend the rest of my life with."

They walked towards the wall and stood looking across at the church.

"How do you know when you've found the right one?" he asked.

"You'll know, Charles, believe me, you'll know! Even then, it's not roses all the way…"

"You don't think I'm wrong just enjoying walking out with Emily, with no serious intention?"

"No, Charlie, no. You're young. She's young. Enjoy yourselves, behave yourselves and make no rash promises!"

"You're a comfort, Flo. Thanks for listening. I've worried about it a lot recently," he said gratefully.

They returned to Orchard Cottage and, although Louise knew that Charles had confided in his sister, she said nothing.

"You're just in time for a fresh brew," she told them, pleased that they got on well.

When she had enjoyed her tea, Flora prepared to go home to Briersham.

"I'll walk with you," offered Charles. "It's such a nice evening."

Their mother did not get up to see them off, but remained in her chair knitting.

"See you tomorrow, Flora," she called out as they left.

The two strolled down Church Lane, talking animatedly. Charles was relieved to have unburdened himself to his sister, for he valued her opinion. They turned the corner by the piggery wall and walked along the main road towards the Partridge Inn. They were deep in conversation when, simultaneously, they heard a familiar laugh.

"Sounds like Seth!" observed Charles, turning towards the sound.

Flora followed and they approached the inn. The two people were standing close together, the tall form that was Seth leaning towards a girl in the shadows. He murmured softly in her ear and she responded with a low giggle. Without a word, Charles and Flora turned away and continued walking towards Briersham.

"Wonder who she was?" asked Charles eventually.

"Seemed to know her well," grumbled Flora.

"Didn't seem right to butt in, did it?" commented Charles.

"Too embarrassing." Flora laughed mirthlessly.

"I see what you mean about it all not being a bed of roses."

"No. He's been coming to the Partridge a lot lately. In fact, we've had harsh words about it," she told him.

"And there I was, telling you about my silly problem."

"Not silly at all, Charlie. I'm glad you did. At least we can talk to each other. Ma and Pa would look at it all differently. Seems more serious somehow if you tell them about it."

Flora was silent then and Charles said nothing either. He knew that she was upset, but, if she did not want to discuss it further, neither would he. They reached Plum Tree Cottage.

"Come in for a cup of tea," she said.

"No, I'll get back, Flo, thanks. Don't take it too much to heart. I'm sure there's an explanation," he comforted. He turned and went back along the track, waving as he disappeared behind a high hedge.

Flora felt empty, alone. What should she say to Seth? What could she say? She would have to think of something; that was certain. She went into the cottage and pottered about doing unnecessary chores. It was too early to go to bed, and in any case, she wanted to stay and talk to her husband. While she was putting linen away in a drawer, she came across the shrivelled remains of half a dozen conkers that Seth had given to her the previous autumn. She looked at them in the palm of her hand, picking them up and turning them over, remembering how he had smiled down at her when he gave them to her. Was it all over so soon? Her tears dropped one by one onto the dried seeds until she clenched her hand around them and pounded her knees in frustration. "How could he; how could he?" she repeated aloud, asking her mirror for answers.

When Seth returned she was sewing in the scullery.

"Up late tonight, love. Didn't expect to see you," he told her.

"No, and I didn't expect to see you earlier this evening either," she replied, not looking up.

"Oh yes?" he said nonchalantly. "Where was that?"

"I was walking home with Charles and we saw you talking to a girl just outside the Partridge."

"That was our Arthur's girl. She was looking for him."

"You seemed very friendly," said Flora, relieved.

"Well, she was upset. They'd had an argument," explained Seth reasonably.

"You're still going to the Partridge a lot," said Flora.

"Don't keep on," Seth told her, in a tone of voice that meant that he did not want to discuss it further. "Time for bed," he added.

"No, I think I'll stay a while longer," Flora said.

"Come on, come up with me," he cajoled.

"No. You go on. I'll be up in a while."

"So that's the way it's going to be, eh?"

"I only want to finish my sewing."

He took her work from her and put it on her basket.

"You'll not be strange with me, only because I spend a couple of evenings having a pint of ale," he told her quietly.

"I'm lonely here on my own and I can't come with you," she told him plaintively.

"Flora, if a man can't have a sup of ale after a hard day's work, I don't know what the world is coming to."

"Why can't you sup your ale at home with me? It's why we got married, isn't it?"

"It's not the same, love. I drink with my pals."

"Then you can bed with your pals from now on, because if my company's not good enough for you, I'm not sharing my bed with you." She turned and went upstairs, intending to lock the bedroom door against him.

He followed her into the room.

"I know you don't mean that," he told her, trying to embrace her.

She pushed him away and he missed his footing and stumbled against the chest of drawers.

"Want to play, eh?" he taunted. He threw her onto their bed, pulling at her clothes roughly.

"Seth, no!" she screamed.

He was kissing her face and neck and tugging at her bodice.

"I said no, Seth, and I mean it." She became angry and struggled against him.

He seemed to become someone else, with only one thought in mind; she could not believe it was happening and began to sob, terrified. Seth stopped suddenly, coming to his senses.

"Flora, my love. I'm sorry," he said, stroking her hair and wiping her tears. He cradled her, rocking her like a child. "I love you. I didn't mean to hurt or frighten you."

Eventually they fell asleep, a disturbed, intermittent sleep. Flora awoke to find Seth kissing her eyelids and mouth slowly in the half-light of dawn. Expertly, lovingly, he made love to her and she responded to his gentle touch. He whispered his love for her and made them feel whole again. They made love in regenerative apology and later with passion and dedication to one another. Never, they vowed, would they allow anyone or anything to come between them again.

HARVEST – AUGUST 1907

The heat was oppressive and only made bearable by a light breeze that played through the hills around Abbots Ford. The trees, in full leaf, were beginning to look as though they would benefit from some rain. Insects buzzed, but everything else was still in the summer's day. Scything the corn from its shining golden stalks was the job in hand and the clouds of pollen and dust could be seen long before the fields were reached. The sheaves were tied and left to dry out for a few days before the ears were severed and put into a cart ready to be taken to J.W. Biltons Millers. A few cotton wool clouds soared high in the brilliant blue sky and a heat haze settled on the land; even the cows in the fields just above the farm stood dazed by the warmth. The good weather had lasted more than a week now and the farmers were working all the daylight hours, gathering in the harvest before it rained again. Blackie pawed at the ground and swished his tail against the flies that tormented him. His gentle eyes took in every movement and his ears twitched at the sound of their voices. He stood in the traces of the cart, patiently waiting in the heat to take them all home again. Will gave him a bucket of water to drink.

"Soon be time to stop eh, Dad," said Charles.

"I'd think so, boy," said Will.

They struggled up the hill in the heat of the field where the scything was going on. Flora and her sister wore scarves over their hair. Seth and his brothers were gathering up the corn for her father and he would help them in turn; it was literally all hands to the plough at harvest time when the weather held out.

"Food!" cried Flora and the shout went around the field.

The men wore trousers, shirts and waistcoats and had their heads covered with caps. Seth came over, took off his hat and wiped his forehead on his sleeve.

"Hot work, love. Thanks." Gratefully, he took a swig from a pitcher of ale the girls had carried up.

The other men came over and sat around in the shade of the cart.

"Mother and Aunt Elsie are coming with more," said Louise as the pasties disappeared like lightning.

Flora sat next to Seth, tucking her skirt around her legs.

"Did you make these?" Seth grinned at her and his white teeth sparkled in his handsome brown face.

She teased him at night in their room for his brown face and snow-white body.

"Of course. Mother made the filling, but I made the pastry," she admitted.

Louise was talking to one of the virile young helpers. People came from all over to give a hand at harvest and this boy was from a village four miles away. Flora looked worried as the couple started strolling away around the edge of the field.

"Don't worry," said Seth. "Your Louise can look after herself."

The older Louise and Elsie arrived with more food and drink and threw themselves down on a grassy spot at the edge of the field in the shade of the hedge. Taking off her scarf, Louise fanned her face with her hand.

"'Tis a hot one today, Elsie," she puffed.

Will went over to them and stood talking. Everyone rested for a while; it was hard work harvesting in that heat.

"Where's our Louise?" asked her mother suddenly.

Flora did not want to tell tales on Louise nor did she want to lie to her mother, so she remained silent.

"I reckon she's courting," said one of the helpers, laughing.

Louise had turned sixteen that May, so she was no longer a child. Just as her mother was setting off to look for her, Louise and her companion reappeared, walking around the edge of the field towards the group.

"She's for it now. Our mum's mad," murmured Flora to Seth.

"Hello young man," said Will, pointedly taking his daughter by the arm and walking her to her mother and aunt.

"Nice walk, dear?" asked the elder Louise.

"Yes, thanks, Ma." Louise smiled at her mother, unaware that she would be in trouble when she got home.

Seth had lain back and closed his eyes. Flora took a long piece of grass and tickled his features with it.

"What the...!" he spluttered, and laughed when he saw the culprit. He sat up, leant around and kissed Flora full on the mouth while everyone laughed.

It was time to carry on working and, reluctantly, they struggled to get up.

"We'll be getting back," Louise told her husband.

"All right, love. See you at teatime," responded Will.

+ + +

"Do you really think that is ladylike behaviour for a young girl?"

Louise looked her mother straight in the eye, for they were of a height now.

"Well?"

"He was just a nice lad who was having a break from his work, Ma."

"So you went off out of sight, alone, the first time you met him?"

"Well, no. Everyone was there." Young Louise was beginning to understand what had annoyed her mother. Usually, she knew the boys she met and her mother knew their families.

"Well, don't ever do anything like it again," said her mother finally.

It was not that young Louise had been in any danger, but it was unseemly for a young girl to be alone with a lad she had only just met, even in those circumstances.

"They grow up so fast you hardly notice," Louise told her husband later that evening. They were taking a stroll around their orchard in the cooling darkness.

"Mind that there, love." Will guided his wife around some rusting farm machinery; the orchard was used as a repository for equipment that was broken and they were too busy to mend, or items that would come in useful one day.

"Don't worry, dear. Louise has a sensible head on her pretty shoulders. She just didn't think, that's all."

Will had a soft spot for his younger daughter; Louise was blossoming into an attractive young woman. She was tall, like her mother, but her hair was light brown, almost blonde in summer when the sun bleached it. She had limpid blue eyes, heavy lidded, which appeared to be daydreaming, when, in reality, she was fairly astute.

"I hope you're right, Will," said his wife, still unsure.

"Flora and Seth look happy, don't they?" said Will.

"Oh yes. He's a good lad and Flora looks blooming – yes, she's really blooming. I wonder...?"

"Now, then, my love – what are you thinking?"

"Nothing. No nothing," said Louise.

They carried on in practiced companionship, the hill high above watching over them and the village.

"Feels a bit like rain," said Will as they went in.

LATE AUGUST 1907

"Put me down!" Flora laughed and struggled as Seth hung onto her. He had lifted her from the ladder leaning against a plum tree in her parents' orchard.

"Come on you two, stop larking about." Louise smiled. "We've got plums to harvest; no time for that!"

He put her down, picked up a huge basket of plums and carried them into the cottage. In the scullery, Victoria Bartrup was cleaning and stoning the fruit.

"Thank you, Seth. Here, lad, try this," she said, popping a perfect plum into his mouth.

"Thanks, Gran," he mumbled as he ate it.

"Much more?" she asked.

"It's never ending!" he told her. "We're only halfway through!"

Louise had commandeered as many people as she could, because the fruit ripened all at the same time and had to be harvested immediately. Everyone was willing to help, especially as there was enough fruit to give them all a bucketful of plums to take home. Louise's mother and sisters, as well as Flora and young Louise, were coerced into preparing and bottling fruit, making jam and helping to sell it from the cottage garden. Louise had put a notice on the gate leading from the orchard to the main road, saying 'Plums 2d 1lb'. Already, young Louise had stationed herself in the front garden, with the scales on a table, ready to serve customers who knew from past experience how good the plums were. She enjoyed serving; it was her favourite job. She had always felt unsteady going up a ladder and reaching up into the trees to pick the plums. But standing at the table placing the shiny skinned fruits into the brass pan of her mother's scales, weighing them, putting them neatly into paper bags and taking the money appealed to her greatly. When it was six o'clock, Louise decided that it was time to finish for the day. People had homes and families to go to. She asked if they could return the next day and most agreed. They went off with their buckets full of plums, like trophies.

"Are you two staying for supper?" asked Louise.

"No thanks, Ma. I've got a slow stew on the range," Flora told her.

Seth carried the bucket of plums on his arm and held Flora's hand as they walked home.

"That's a good-sized orchard," he observed. "I hadn't realised how big until today!"

"We used to have such games out there!" she recalled. "We all learnt to climb most of the trees!"

"You were a tomboy, then?"

"I suppose so. Ma tried to make ladies out of us, but it was too tempting with all the trees there."

When they arrived home Flora prepared the fruit and boiled it up with sugar to make jam.

"I love that smell," enthused Seth. "Reminds me of Mother making jam."

They had their meal and went for a walk before the sun went down. They stopped and leant against a gate, looking towards the sunset. Seth kissed her cheek and nibbled her ear.

"Are you happy?" he asked.

"Yes, I'm happy," she told him. "What about you?"

"I didn't know anyone could be as happy as I am," he confided. "I knew I wanted to be with you all the time, because I knew I liked you, loved you. It's how I thought it would be, but better."

"Seth, that's a lovely thing to say." She smiled.

They returned home and made a hot drink before going to bed.

"I wonder what the future holds," said Flora thoughtfully.

"Whatever it is, it can't be better than this," he told her.

She smiled quietly at him, secure in his love, and hers for him.

"Time for bed," she told him. "Race you there."

SEPTEMBER 1907

Seth woke up with a start. It was not the sound of the dawn chorus that had woken him. He listened, straining to hear. There it was again, an awful choking sound. He leapt out of bed and down the stairs to the scullery like an athlete.

"God, Flora, what's the matter, love?"

Flora wiped her mouth and sipped the water she had poured.

"I don't know. I must've eaten something and it's made me sick," she said.

"Sit down, love," advised Seth, wrapping her shawl around her shoulders. "Come back to bed for a while; you're shivering." Seth carried her back upstairs and put her tenderly in their bed.

"I don't feel well," said Flora in a small voice.

"No, love, I know. I'll get a bucket in case you feel bad again."

Seth went off and fussed around, coming back a while later with a bucket and a cup of tea.

"Can you drink this, Flora?" Seth asked gently as he woke her up.

She sat up, looking and feeling very shaky. "Seth, I won't be able to..."

"I know, don't you worry about breakfast. I'll be off in a minute and, when I come back later, I'll make us breakfast," he comforted.

The thought was enough to make Flora want to vomit again. She held her abdomen and lay back on the pillows, trying to think what she had eaten.

Flora slept most of that day and gradually felt better, though still very weak. Seth was solicitous and gently took care of her. That evening she was well enough to cook supper for them both and they sat talking about the Harvest Dance and how last year they had met properly for the first time.

"I'm looking forward to it," said Flora enthusiastically.

"Why's that, so you can come home to my bed, you shameless woman?" teased Seth.

"Certainly not; a lout like you?" she responded. "No," she continued, "it's because it's nice going out together now that we're married. I see all my friends and I feel very grown-up."

"I should think you would – as I said, it's all about coming into my…" He got no further, because Flora had launched herself on him bodily, in his chair.

When they had shared a late hot drink, they went up to bed.

"I'm glad you're better, girl. I was worried," said Seth feelingly.

The same thing happened the following morning and Seth suggested that Flora should see Dr Tanner.

"I do believe I shall," said Flora, feeling washed out. "I'll go along and see Mum while I'm there," she added.

When Seth had left for Drakes Farm, she took the pretty jug filled with hot water and washed herself in the matching bowl. *I'm used to living here now,* she thought as she looked in the mirror. *I love this cottage.*

She brushed her hair and tied it up.

I must be happy – I'm getting fat, she thought, peering in the mirror again.

She relished the walk along the lanes towards Abbots Ford. The trees were just tinged with colour and there was that fresh, autumnal chill in the early morning air. A neighbour caught up with her and they walked together sharing gossip and enjoying the day.

Flora waited a while to see Dr Tanner. His surgery was just a room in his house and the waiting area was his hall.

"Come in, come in, my dear. And how are you?"

Dr Tanner had known Flora all her life, though she had been lucky enough not to have to see him often in his professional capacity. He had, however, been very kind to the whole family when little Jacob had died. Flora could remember his explaining as much as he could about it to her and Charles and Louise. The fact that an adult had taken the time to do so had remained in her memory, because, somehow, when a nice man like Dr Tanner had an explanation – to a child – it seemed as if it might be all right after all. All that sadness and crying may not be the end of their world.

"So what brings you to see me?" he enquired.

Flora explained her symptoms and Dr Tanner examined her.

"Well, my dear," he said after a few questions, "I think you may be having a child."

Flora went numb.

"Had you no idea?" he asked kindly.

"Well, no. We've been so busy – I thought... I couldn't believe... so soon!"

"Wait another month to be sure and in the meantime just eat what you can and drink lots of milk. Then get in touch with Ellie Bates – and good luck."

Flora paid her fee to Mrs Tanner and walked out of the surgery in a daze. She decided against calling in on her mother and, stopping to buy some groceries at the village shop, went back to Briersham. The two-mile walk did her good: it cleared her head. A baby? A child? A boy, like Seth? The thoughts rushed crazily about in her head. She did not know why she was so surprised; she knew the facts of life – she had been brought up on a farm after all.

Cows had calves. Hens had chicks – well, eggs, anyway. Sheep had lambs; pigs had piglets. Nothing more natural... When she arrived home she put some soup on the hob for Seth coming in at midday. She sliced some fresh bread and placed it, unbuttered, on a plate. The plates were put to warm on the hob. Flora was distracted; she was having to concentrate on what she was doing. She gave Ding and Dong, their cats, some milk and sat on the scullery chair, hands on her head. When would the baby be due? *For our wedding anniversary in April*, she thought.

Soon Seth came in, calling her name.

"Flora, where were you, love?"

She appeared from where she had been dusting the living room.

"How are you? What did the doctor say?"

"Oh I'm all right – nothing wrong with me. Come and have your meal."

They sat at the pine table, which Flora did not cover with a velour cloth, though there was a pretty chequered cloth on it now. Seth sipped his soup, breaking his bread into it. He told her about his work that morning: there was still some harvesting to do. One of his father's cows was sick...

"Seth, I've something to tell you, love," she said.

He looked anxiously at her with his wonderful blue eyes.

"Seth, I'm having a baby."

He continued to look at her for a few seconds and then leapt up and hugged her, kissing her all over her face. Serious suddenly, he asked, "When? How?"

She laughed. She had thought all those things too.

"Well, I'll know for sure next month, but it's fairly sure now – so Dr Tanner thinks."

"Flora, I love you so much."

Later they spent the evening talking about nothing else. Seth had even offered to make supper, but Flora was having none of that. They had decided not to say anything to anyone for a few days, until they had taken in the news themselves. They knew how pleased, not to say ecstatic, their families and friends would be. They were so happy for themselves and the future looked very bright.

EARLY OCTOBER 1907

Flora was looking forward to a day with her mother and sister. She arrived at Orchard Cottage early.

"How are you, love?" asked her mother.

"Still a bit sick in the mornings, but not as bad as it was, Ma," she replied.

Louise greeted her as she came in from collecting the eggs.

"Hello, Flo, keeping all right now?" she asked.

"Yes. I was just telling Ma I'm not as bad as I was with morning sickness."

"Reckon you're relieved?"

They brewed a pot of tea and Grandma Bartrup joined them as planned. She was pleased to see Flora, who went through the enquiry about how she was yet again.

"Flora," began her grandmother, "I recall when your Auntie Elsie was born, she didn't stop crying for six months."

"Don't tell the girl that, Mother," scolded Louise. "You'll put her off."

"No, I won't. There's nothing like a babe to complete a girl's life."

"I'm not having any children," announced young Louise.

"You'll change your mind," her grandmother told her.

"I won't; I'm going to make clothes. Design and make them."

"Listen to the child," said Victoria Bartrup, smiling.

"Those Pankhurst women have a lot to answer for," opined Louise. "Giving women silly ideas... Mother, do you remember how ugly our Ann was when you had her?"

Victoria laughed loudly. "Never saw such an ugly child in my life."

"Just as well she turned out to be beautiful," said Louise.

"Didn't you almost have her at the Harvest Supper, Mother?"

"Yes, oh don't start me off on that, dear," pleaded Victoria, laughing again.

Flora looked at her sister and smiled. They enjoyed it when their grandmother, mother or aunts retold the family stories, but sometimes they wore thin, especially now that Flora herself was pregnant.

"Are we cooking or not, Ma?" she asked.

"Yes, dear. Now, when we're done, all the puddings will be steamed at Elsie's in the copper, Ma," Louise explained. "And we'll bake two cakes today in my ovens," she continued. "That all right?"

Everyone concurred and they set to work around the living room table, which was covered with an old cloth. The fruit had been soaking these past twenty-four hours and the girls brought all the ingredients together while the older women prepared the bowls. They talked about everything under the sun, the way women of different generations do. They talked about the coming baby and whom it might take after, but mostly they talked about their menfolk and their foibles. They cleared a space at one end, so that Will and Charles could have their meal sitting at the table. Everyone had a turn at stirring the puddings and making a wish. Later they walked up the lane to Elsie's cottage and supervised while she placed the bowls in her copper to allow them to steam for hours.

"I'm really looking forward to Christmas, Ma," said Flora as they walked back to Orchard Cottage.

"There's a lot to look forward to, Flora. I often thank the Lord for all He has given us."

Flora left then, to go home and cook Seth's dinner, saying a cheerful farewell. She felt happy as she returned to Briersham, humming a medley of her favourite songs as she went.

OCTOBER 1907

"You don't want to be coming up here every day now, love," said Charlotte Hawkes.

"If Flora thinks she can manage, she'll come," said Seth.

"You're a good girl, Flora. I am sorry to be a nuisance."

Charlotte was poorly. It sat strangely on her, for she had always been a strong, healthy woman. Her daughters were helping as well, but there was a limit to what they could do with such young families. Both had young babies and Rebecca was pregnant once more. Charlotte was in a great deal of pain and Dr Tanner had not come to any conclusion about its cause.

"I wouldn't mind, only Jim has never done any household work," she said.

"Don't you worry, Ma," said Flora. "I can manage perfectly well."

They arranged for Flora to do Charlotte's laundry every other week, because Flora would have to cope with her own as well. Every day Flora and Seth would eat at his parents' house, so that Flora could cook for them all there. Charlotte's daughters would look after each other's children while one went along to clean their parents' house, perhaps twice a week.

"Well, that's the main things taken care of, Ma," said Seth. "All you have to do now is rest."

During the weeks it took for Charlotte to recover, Flora grew to know her mother-in-law well and to like her more and more. She was not a good patient in that she would never rest enough, but she was an undemanding person and grateful for all they did. Seth was proud of Flora's ability to take on so much so soon after their marriage, especially when she was expecting a baby. His father did not relish Flora's cooking, but ate everything she gave them. It was just as well, because one evening they had an indication of the consequences if they did not.

"What's in this stew?" Seth's brother, David, asked her.

"Why?" questioned Flora shortly.

"Just wondered."

"It's lamb," she informed him.

He made a face suggesting that it was not the tastiest dish he had ever tried. Before anyone could say any more, Flora had walked around the table and tipped the plateful of food over him. They were all so astonished that no one commented; they all carried on in silence and David retreated to clean himself up.

Later James was recounting the incident to Charlotte, who had eaten in her room.

"I always thought Flora was a quiet sort of girl, but she's a match for our Seth, isn't she?" he told his wife.

It was fortunate when Charlotte began to recover sufficiently to take over the running of her household again, with the help of the girls, because Flora's pregnancy was now three and a half months.

"I can't wait for your baby to come next month," she told Rebecca eagerly. "It's going to be good practice for having ours!"

MID-DECEMBER 1907

By the beginning of December, Flora had almost completed the little toys she had knitted for her nieces and nephews-in-law. She had made lavender bags for all her female relations. When she had finished the shawl for Rebecca's baby she had begun to knit a jacket for her own child. William and Louise had been overjoyed when Flora broke the news to them.

"Our first grandchild," Louise had said. The excitement had spread to her sister and brothers, which had surprised Flora, for she had not expected it to affect them.

On the second Sunday in December Flora and Seth were having dinner at Orchard Cottage after church, but before Flora's class at Sunday school.

There was much laughter when they arrived, because, although they were ready for church, Will and Charles were fixing up holly and mistletoe. Both Charles and their sister, Louise, had partners there that day, and no sooner was the mistletoe up than they were kissing beneath it.

"Come in, my dears, in you come," said Louise. "How are you?"

"I'm well, Mother. I feel really well," replied Flora.

Her father kissed her forehead and they were exchanging news and gossip when her mother announced that it was time for church.

"We'd best go and thank the Lord for His goodness," said Will and, marshalling his family, led them all away.

After an entertaining and filling meal Flora bade them goodbye and returned to St Mary's to take a Sunday school class.

"She's looking blooming, Seth," commented her mother.

"Yes, it's all going well," he agreed.

Thanking his mother-in-law for the meal, he took his leave to visit his sister, Rebecca, who was approaching her time.

Louise Henty was quietly sewing later that afternoon and the evening was drawing in when there was the sound of running feet.

"Louise, Louise! Are you there? Come quickly." It was the doctor's neighbour.

"Flora was taken poorly in church and they took her straight across the road to Dr Tanner's."

Louise and her younger daughter grabbed shawls and followed the woman quickly down the lane.

"Stay there, Bill," she called after her. "Tell Father where we are and tell Charles to go and get Seth from Rebecca's."

Mrs Tanner met them at the door.

"She's all right, Louise. She's lying on the bed in the guest room."

Dr Tanner came along the hall and greeted Louise.

"My dear – what can I say? I'm so sorry – I think she's losing the child."

"Oh no." Louise sank onto the chair nearby.

"Is Seth aware…?" Dr Tanner asked.

"Charles will go and tell him at his sister's when he comes in," said Louise flatly.

Young Louise sat next to her mother, quietly taking in the news.

"Can she come home tonight?" asked Louise, meaning 'home' to Orchard Cottage.

"We'll see how she is in a couple of hours. I'm sure she's better off staying here for now," said the doctor.

Mrs Tanner offered them a cup of tea and, shortly afterwards, Seth arrived with Rebecca's husband and Charles.

Dr Tanner allowed Seth to go in and see Flora.

He bent and embraced her and held her tightly to him for a long time. Flora sobbed her heart out and he knew there was nothing to say.

"You've been working too hard – I should have stopped it," he said brokenly.

Flora said nothing and clung to him. When she had quietened he asked if she would like her mother to come in and she agreed. Later it was decided that she should stay where she was until the following day and Seth went sadly back to Abbots Magna to break the news to his parents.

JANUARY 1908

Christmas had been a healing time for Flora. She had recovered quickly, physically, from her miscarriage and her own and Seth's family had blanketed her with love. The villagers knew what had happened; it was impossible to keep these things private in a place like Abbots Ford. But when she was on her own at home Flora had taken out the fragments of baby jacket, putting her fingers inside the tiny sleeves and running her hands over the miniature pieces. She had cried until she had no more tears and she had raged until she was spent. Why? Her grandmother told her of her three miscarriages before Aunt Elsie had arrived. Flora had looked at Gran with new eyes after that and it had given her the courage to put it behind her and look to the future.

They were all at Drakes Farm on the first Sunday of the year. Charlotte was her old self again and her family was relieved. All the grandchildren were there and even little David was toddling about. Rebecca had still not had her baby and she was feeling very fatigued.

"Don't do that to your cousin," said Ruth.

"They're getting fed up," said Rebecca. "Robert, can't you and the boys take these terrors out?"

So the two husbands, Geoffrey and Robert, ably backed by Seth, John, Arthur and David, took every one of the children out onto the home field to play. James had gone off to see the horses, so Charlotte made tea for her two daughters and daughter-in-law. They gossiped amiably.

"Your turn soon, Isabelle." Ruth laughed as they teased Rebecca about the size of her 'bump'.

Isabelle was a very small, quiet and shy girl and she was blushing now as they talked about the coming event. She said nothing when there were oblique remarks about how Rebecca was going to avoid having any more babies for a while.

"Ma, are these cups new?" asked Rebecca.

"No dear, they've been in my china cupboard. I got them out for Christmas – you remember, Grandma gave them to me," said Charlotte.

"Have you everything ready?" Ruth asked her sister.

"I've been ready for weeks," stated Rebecca, but she was caught mid-sentence by a contraction.

"What? What is it?" Charlotte jumped up, automatically going to fill the kettle again.

"Just sit still; breathe deeply," said Flora calmly.

Isabelle was as white as a sheet.

"I... I think I'm going to be sick," she gasped and ran off outside.

"I'll go and get the menfolk in," called Flora as she too left the room.

"Mother, we'd best put on some pans of water; she had David very quickly," advised Ruth.

"Yes, yes – we'll do that," said Charlotte distractedly.

The men came back in, but not before Rebecca had another contraction.

"Tell them to keep the young ones outside," reminded Rebecca.

It was hastily arranged that Ruth and Geoffrey would take their and Rebecca's children home with them. Isabelle and John went home, as she was not feeling at all well.

Charlotte had recovered her composure and was organising linen and newspaper and making up a fire and the bed in David's downstairs bedroom. She whisked off the quilt and heaved at the bedding and sheets. Flora stayed with Rebecca, encouraging her whenever she experienced a contraction.

"There's no time to get Ellie Bates, Flora. You'll have to help me," said Charlotte.

"You won't leave me, Flora, will you?" pleaded Rebecca.

Seth left to go and fetch Ellie anyway, and his father had disappeared again.

Rebecca wanted to walk up and down and that is what they did. Charlotte made tea and the three of them drank it, trying to be as calm as they could.

Another contraction swept over Rebecca, making her want to crouch low. Flora rubbed her back.

"Let's get you into the bedroom," said Flora and, as they helped her across the living room, Rebecca's water broke.

They got her into the little room and Charlotte lit the candle and then the oil lamp, as by now it was almost dark. Flora went off to bring bowls of boiling water and to clean up the wetness in the living room. She heard a cry from Rebecca and rushed back to her.

"There, there love," comforted her mother.

In the brief respite, they spread the clean sheeting over the end of the bed and the paper on the floor. Charlotte had pulled out a drawer of David's chest and piled the contents on the floor; a pillow and clean blanket were neatly arranged inside in readiness.

A laundry basket was lined with a sheet and placed on the floor nearby. Rebecca's contractions were increasingly regular now, with only a minute between them. She knelt up on the bed, supported by Flora, who remained calm and methodical. Instinctively, she suggested that Rebecca should breathe deeply, and rubbed her back or abdomen when needed. She encouraged her to push when the urge came and dissuaded her when she observed that she should not. Flora worked as one with Rebecca, but remained in control of proceedings. She ascertained that the baby would be born very soon and told Rebecca to lie down. Robert, the expectant father, who had been helping Ruth and Geoffrey home with all the children, arrived back.

"Everything all right in there?" he called, knocking loudly on the door. "Anything I can do?"

They assured him that everything was happening as expected and told him to put more water on to boil.

"Yes, yes! I can see the top of the head; it's coming," said Flora excitedly. She waited at the end of the bed for the baby's head to be born, while Charlotte wiped Rebecca's face.

"Go on, one more push next time and I'm sure you'll do it," Flora encouraged.

"Aaaargh!" yelled Rebecca in the exertion of the huge effort to expel her child's head.

"That's it, that's it! Good girl! Now rest for a moment." Flora supported the baby's head gently until the next contraction. First the tiny shoulders and arms, and then the rest of the body, slithered out into the world, followed by the cord. Flora held the child in astonishment for a few seconds and then instinctively cleared debris away from the baby's mouth. Loud yelling and squalling helped to bring Flora round and she carefully placed the noisy being on her mother's belly.

Flora stood back, smiling at the new mother with her baby. She looked across at Charlotte and back again at Rebecca. The feeling of elation was like nothing she had experienced before, although there had always been a feeling of awe when a calf or lamb was born. Where, a few moments ago, there had been three people in the room, there were now four. Flora had worked hard with the labouring woman, identifying with her completely, and the sense of achievement at the outcome was overwhelming.

"I hope you'll allow us to call her Flora!" said Rebecca, and Flora nodded happily.

The new father was invited in to see the latest addition to his family, and sat kissing his wife tenderly and admiring the new baby.

The two women were tidying up when there was a knock at the door and Ellie Bates came in.

"How are you progressing?" She smiled. "I see your baby's been born, Becky. Congratulations!" She turned to Flora. "You've done well, my dear."

"She did it all," admitted Charlotte. "I'm no good at all this." She laughed, relieved that it was safely over.

Ellie began to do the necessary procedures and washed the baby, who was weighed and checked over, wrapped warmly and placed in the prepared drawer. Robert went out to the scullery to have a glass of beer with Seth, who had come back with Ellie, and James, who had mysteriously reappeared at the right moment.

After a while Flora joined them and explained how it had all happened and what she and Charlotte had done.

"Flora did everything; she was a clever girl," said Charlotte with conviction as she arrived to brew yet more tea.

When Ellie had made Rebecca comfortable and taken her a welcome cup of tea, she joined them all in the kitchen and repeated how well Flora coped.

"You could come and help me," said Ellie.

Flora was taken aback.

"Oh, I don't know about that, Mrs Bates." She laughed. "I only did what had to be done and hadn't time to think about it."

"Some people can cope and some can't. But some people are good at it," explained Ellie, "and you're one of those. Think about it, dear."

They enjoyed the impromptu gathering, toasting mother and baby in tea and ale, and then went their separate ways.

"Are you all right, my duck?" asked Seth as they walked the half mile back home in the freezing night.

Seth was remembering that it was less than a month since Flora had lost her own baby.

"Yes Seth, I'm feeling wonderful," she replied.

They were so attuned that she knew what her husband meant and appreciated his concern.

"Only I thought..." he began.

"I know," interrupted Flora. "I know what you are trying to say. I am not sad, Seth; I'm only happy that it all went so well for Becky and I was able to help her."

Seth loved his wife more than ever in that moment. He stopped and put his arm around her shoulders, pulling her face close to his as he bent towards her. Kissing her nose, he told her so.

"You lovely, unselfish, clever little duck," he murmured, and then kissed her passionately in the middle of the deserted, narrow lane on a freezing January night.

Chapter Three

JANUARY 1908 – DECEMBER 1909

Life was good for Flora and Seth. They were busy, happy and loving. Seth's father had bought up land adjoining Drakes Farm, thus expanding the scope of their work. He had invested in a dairy herd of Jersey cows, so Seth and his brothers were fully employed. Charlotte continued in good health and had retaken the helm of family organisation.

Flora was in Redford's Grocers Shop early one morning towards the end of January.

"How is married life treating you?" asked Catherine.

"Busy," said Flora tersely.

"You look well, dear."

"Thank you – I feel all right," she replied more graciously.

Catherine Redford was a kind woman, but Flora never could make up her mind whether she knew everything that went on in the village because she ran the shop, or ran the shop so that she would know everything that went on in the village.

"Hello, Flora," said a voice pleasantly.

Flora turned to see Ellie Bates emerging from the passageway leading from the butcher's shop.

"Nice bit of bacon today, Catherine," said Ellie.

"That's good, dear," Catherine replied.

Ellie stood talking about nothing in particular with Catherine, while Flora carried on with her purchases. When they were all checked, packed and paid for, Ellie said she was going in the same direction as Flora and they walked together towards Church Lane.

"Have you thought any more about helping me?" she asked.

"I enjoyed helping Becky. I don't know about anyone else..." explained Flora.

"You gave Becky confidence, even though you'd never helped at a birth before. That's what matters. I can teach you the rest."

They walked in silence for a while.

"Give it a try," suggested Ellie. "Come with me on a few visits; see what you think."

They had reached Church Lane, where Ellie parted company with Flora.

"Let me know what you decide," she called as she went on up the main road. "But I do need a sensible girl like you."

Flora and Seth had discussed the option just after the birth of Rebecca's baby, when Ellie had first broached the subject. Flora knew she had enjoyed the experience and Seth had been proud of her, but she had rejected the idea. Now, it appeared Ellie genuinely believed that she could be of use.

Louise Henty was pleased to see Flora and, when she told her mother of her conversation with Ellie, Louise was encouraging.

"God made everyone good at something; seems a shame not to do it," was her advice.

Later that morning as Flora walked home to Briersham, she continued to think about the proposition. Perhaps she would do as Ellie suggested and merely go on a few visits to see how she felt. She could easily recall the elation she had experienced that night at Drakes Farm when little Flora was born. Yes, that was a good idea. She would speak to Ellie in church on Sunday and plan a series of visits.

FEBRUARY 1908

"The baby is underweight – he came a fortnight early," explained Ellie on Flora's first day with her. "Evelyn and Martin are sensible enough people and this is their first child," she went on.

They knocked at the door of a cottage in the middle of a row of six. A young woman about the same age as Flora opened the door.

"Hello, Ellie, come in."

"How are you today, Evie?" Ellie placed her bag on the table and introduced Flora as a friend.

"May I wash my hands?" It was a statement rather than a question, for she went straight through to the scullery and did so.

"How is little Adam today?" she asked.

"He's lovely; no trouble."

"Can you bring him down, Evie?" asked Ellie.

The little boy was thriving, though still not up to normal birth weight. He yelled satisfyingly loudly.

Ellie was kind and deft in her handling of the baby. She examined the umbilical cord, which was almost ready to come away.

"Yes, that's good," she observed, wrapping him up again. "And how are you yourself, Evie?" This question was not just a social nicety, for Evie gave details of her own physical progress.

"You're still managing to feed him yourself?" queried Ellie.

"It isn't the milk that's the problem. He takes so long, it's almost time for the next feed when he's finished."

Ellie suggested that Evie should try feeding Adam at three-hour intervals instead of four. He was so small; he was falling asleep during feeds because they tired him out. Assuring the young mother of her return in three days' time, Ellie and Flora bade her goodbye and left the tiny cottage.

"Evie is managing well. Her mother lives three doors away, so she's a help," said Ellie.

"The woman we're going to now is due to have her third baby next week. They're not well organised, so be prepared!" she continued.

Two small children sat on the path outside the cottage even though the day was bitterly cold.

"Where's Mummy?" asked Ellie.

The child indicated the open door. He could not have been more than two years old and he was wearing a shift of indeterminate colour, which almost reached his ankles. On his feet he wore black leather boots, which looked a few sizes too large. The other child was even younger and had not looked up on their approach. Ellie explained that he was deaf, that his mother had contacted measles during the early part of her pregnancy. They went into the cottage and, at first, Flora could not see anything. When her eyes became adjusted to the darkness, she could just discern the shapes of furniture, but there was so much junk strewn around that it was hard to decide exactly what the room contained.

"Hello, Ivy!" called Ellie. "Are you there?"

A woman who must only have been twenty-five at the most, but looked fifty, came through a doorway.

"That you, Ellie? Who's this?"

"This is my friend, Flora. Hope you didn't mind her coming as well?" said Ellie.

"I know you. Your ma's the stuck-up one in the hat in church, isn't she?" said Ivy.

As most women wore hats in church, Flora could not understand why her mother's deserved special attention.

"I'm Flora Hawkes. I was Henty," said Flora politely.

"Oh yes. That wedding last Easter."

"So how are you?" asked Ellie pleasantly.

"Glad when the little bugger's born," came the reply.

"Can I examine you, Ivy?" asked Ellie.

"No. Lot of fuss if you ask me. He'll come when he's good and ready," stated Ivy.

"All right then. I'll pop back in a few days. What about coats for Adam and Dennis?"

"Haven't got none," said Ivy flatly.

"We'll see what we can do," promised Ellie.

"Bye for now."

They did not speak until they were walking back towards the Smithy.

"Are there many in the village like her? I thought I knew everybody," said Flora.

"She's not too bad," replied Ellie. "Certainly not the worst."

They continued on Ellie's round, visiting expectant mothers and checking up on new arrivals.

"I had no idea it was so busy in our village," said Flora.

"Not just Abbots Ford. It's all out by Abbots Magna, Briersham, Upper Abbots, halfway towards Stoke Magna westwards and towards Steeple Burstead the other way."

Flora was filled with admiration for Ellie. She always managed to appear cheerful and looked after Tom and the children diligently. Whenever she was on her travels around the village, she never gave a hint that she was under pressure.

"I'd like to continue visiting with you, Mrs Bates," said Flora.

"Don't call me 'Mrs Bates', Flora. Call me Ellie. You'll enjoy it. You're at your mother's most days aren't you? If I need you, I'll know where to come," she added.

Flora was exhausted when she arrived home that afternoon; Seth had eaten with his parents at midday. While they had their supper Flora regaled him with stories of what had taken place.

"Are you sure this is what you want?" he asked.

"Yes, but I'll feel better when I know more," she replied.

Later they both sat engrossed in reading. Seth yawned.

"All this talk about babies!" He laughed. "Time for bed."

"Time for sleep," said Flora firmly. "I'm tired out."

They went upstairs and by the time Seth was climbing into bed his wife was sound asleep, dark lashes sweeping her cheeks. He looked at her, smiling to himself. *What a girl,* he thought and snuggled behind her.

APRIL 1908

Louise was exultant. Her parents had said she could go on the church outing to Weston-Super-Mare. The reason for the excitement was that a lad called Albert Hines was going too and Louise thought he was the most handsome boy she had ever seen. She was one month away from her seventeenth birthday and very conscious that she was approaching adulthood.

In the bedroom, which she now had to herself, she hung her clothes to display them while she decided what she would wear.

"Wear something sensible," suggested her mother, popping her head around the door. "Something warm, dear. It could be quite chilly, remember."

She tried on her clothes, mixing and matching them, trying to create something to catch Albert's eye.

The day dawned grey and cold, but Louise was not disheartened. She was up early to have time to prepare and look her best. The night before she had tied her hair up in rags after washing it and, once unwound, bouncy curls covered her head.

She crept down to the scullery to borrow her father's boot polish, which she applied delicately to her eyelashes to darken them. The frock she selected was more suited to a summer's day, but she felt that it flattered her best. She went down to breakfast feeling glamorous and sophisticated.

"What have you done to your hair?" asked Will.

"Curled it," she answered shortly.

"I hope you're going to wear a warm coat over that frock," said her mother.

Bill laughed hysterically when he saw his sister.

"You look just like a panda," he chortled, and had to be banished because he could not stop laughing.

"He's such a silly boy," said Louise frostily when he had gone.

"Remember, your Auntie Elsie and Uncle Ed are going so that you have someone with you, dear," said her mother.

Excitement lent novelty to the journey. Louise sat next to her aunt and uncle, and Albert was opposite on the bench seat. He nodded to her and smiled, and her stomach turned and fluttered. The motor bus lurched along towards the coast, noisy and metallic. It was with some relief that they arrived at Weston. They alighted one by one down the steps and stood about, not really knowing what to do next.

"Pick up at four o'clock," shouted the driver. "Same place. Make sure you're back. I'll not wait for latecomers."

Louise looked at Albert expectantly.

"Do you want to walk around with us?" she asked.

He nodded and they set off to explore the beach. He hardly said a word, but Louise did not stop talking. Elsie and Ed followed at a distance. They could not find the sea. At Weston when the tide was out, it disappeared. The cold wind tore at her hair, making her wish she had put it in ribbons. They were feeling frozen to the marrow when her aunt and uncle came to their rescue to buy them a meal and a cup of strong hot tea.

The sun did its best to penetrate the clouds and brightened the afternoon, even though it stayed cold. Not long before they were due to return to the motor bus, Albert spotted a small lake where rowing boats could be hired.

"Give the little lady a treat, son," cried the owner.

So Albert paid for two tickets.

"Tunnel of love," cried the barker. "Tunnel of love!"

The 'tunnel of love' was only an overhang of branches at the edge of the water, but Louise blushed hotly and held onto the side of a small boat. Albert got in and held onto the side while he pushed off. They moved off smoothly, but he lost an oar and stood up to retrieve it. He leant further and further over until, inevitably, the boat capsized, tipping both Albert and Louise into the shallow water. Louise gulped and spluttered, scrabbling about until she stood waist high in the lake. Her hair hung in rat tails over her face and the boot polish from her eyelashes ran down her cheeks.

"You idiot!" she shouted. "Couldn't you see what you were doing?"

Her frock hung wet and clinging and, all around them, people could not help but laugh.

"Here love, let me help you," said a voice. It was Auntie Elsie, stretching a hand to help her out.

Uncle Ed removed his coat and placed it around her shoulders.

"Are you all right, Albert?" he asked, but Albert was silent.

Elsie sat next to Louise on the journey back. At least it was warm on the motor bus, although Louise shivered all the way home. Albert got off at his stop without a word and nothing was said when Elsie walked into Orchard Cottage with Louise. Her mother went about the job of collecting and heating water for a hot bath for her. When she was clean, dry and warm Louise sat wrapped in a blanket.

"Never mention that boy's name to me again, Ma."

Her mother nodded agreement.

"Boys are so silly. I'll never go out with one again as long as I live."

"As you wish, dear," said her mother impassively.

"And you were right about wearing something warm."

Her mother said nothing.

"Oh Ma, I love you," whimpered Louise and, burying her head on her mother's breast, she cried with embarrassment and relief.

"Don't take on so," said her mother. "It's a bad day only when we can't learn something from it, and I do believe you have."

Her daughter looked up with a watery smile.

"Mothers are nearly always right, aren't they, Ma?"

"Only when they're worried about their fledglings, Louise," replied her mother. "Only when their fledglings are learning to fly."

MAY 1908

Flora had been helping Ellie for a few weeks when Nancy Morgan had her child. Nancy was a young girl who was still at school and had managed to keep her pregnancy hidden from everyone. Flora was at her mother's when one of the older girls from Mr William's class at the school came rushing round to Orchard Cottage that Tuesday.

"Something's happening to Nancy! Come quick!" she panted.

"Wait a minute, Barbara," said Flora, who knew her from Sunday school. "Calm down. Tell me what has happened."

"You've got to come quick, Mrs Hawkes. Miss Taylor and Mr Williams say please come quick!"

Flora and her mother dashed around to the school.

"This way," commanded John Williams. He led them swiftly to a cloakroom at the rear of the school.

"Oh my Lord," said Louise Henty. It was obvious that Nancy was far advanced in labour and was confused and extremely anxious.

"Hot water. Cloths. Paper, please," ordered Flora.

"Take these other children away; my mother and I will manage now," she added.

There was no time to send for Ellie, and Flora and Louise concentrated on making the process as calm and relaxed as possible for so young a mother.

"Please don't tell my mother," Nancy cried at intervals.

"Don't worry about anything for now," advised Flora.

"There, there, dear. Nothing to worry about just now," seconded Louise.

After an hour Nancy's son was born. He was lusty and noisy and Nancy was momentarily delighted with him, until the consequences of his birth impinged on her consciousness again. It was impossible to keep the event secret, for the whole school was aware of what had taken place. The girl who had summoned Flora had been sent to bring Nancy's mother, who now burst upon the scene in the cloakroom.

"My God! What's all this?" she shouted.

"Now then, Mrs Morgan..." started Louise.

"Who is he?"

"What, Mum, what?"

"Who's the father? Who did it?"

"Under the circumstances, Mrs Morgan, I think this is not the time or place for this," said Flora sternly.

"Look at the little boy..." said Louise encouragingly.

"Can't bear to – I'll never look at him. The shame..."

"I'll get Dr Tanner to have a look at you and the baby," Flora explained to Nancy. She continued to organise them all, and arranged for mother and baby to be taken across the road to the doctor's house.

Louise took Mrs Morgan to Orchard Cottage with her to calm her down with some tea and understanding.

"These things happen, Mrs Morgan; she's very young," comforted Louise.

"But it's ruined her life; who'll marry her now?" sobbed Mrs Morgan.

"What about the child?"

"What about it?"

"What's going to happen to him?"

"I hadn't thought..."

"Then it's time to start thinking," said Louise gently.

"I've others at home, four others. All younger than Nancy..."

"How old is the youngest?"

"Two."

"What about your husband?"

"He'll kill her, and whoever did it to her."

"Go home, Mrs Morgan, and tell him, as calmly as you can, what has happened to your family today."

"What about Nancy?"

"Dr Tanner wants to keep her until at least tomorrow," reminded Louise.

"You're right. My Nancy has been through a lot."

"She'll need you."

"Thanks, Mrs Henty. Thanks for the tea."

Louise saw her up the steps from the cottage.

"Good luck, dear."

"Thank you again, and your daughter."

A short while later Flora arrived at Orchard Cottage to find her mother sitting on the low wall that ran from the house to the steps.

"What are you doing, Ma?" she asked.

"Just thinking, dear. How are you after all the excitement?"

"All right. Shame, wasn't it? Where did her mother get to?"

"She came home with me."

"How was she?"

"You know. Not very happy."

"It is a shame. Nancy is so young."

"Nancy's youngest brother or sister is only two. Perhaps they'll be able to 'adopt' Nancy's baby."

"It'll be difficult whatever they do."

"You are happy doing this work, dear, aren't you? Even today, with that emergency, you were very good."

"Yes. Every one is different, Ma. Every one is a miracle; even the little one born today out of wedlock to a girl who is still a child herself."

Flora prepared to go home and cook for Seth.

"Dad and I are very proud of you, Flora."

"Thanks, Ma. That's nice. I'll see you later in the week."

"Bye, dear."

Flora's head buzzed with all the thoughts running through her mind. Mentally, she went through the chores and tasks she would do when she arrived home. She thought of the tiny child she had helped to deliver. It suddenly struck her that she had coped alone, with her mother, but without Ellie. She was pleased that it had all gone well.

I'll have to pop in and see Nancy tomorrow, she thought, *and report to Ellie on what happened.* She quickened her step and held up her head as she neared Briersham. *I'm coming, Seth,* she thought. *I'm almost home.*

JULY 1908

The sun was shining on the village in more ways than one. They were holding the vicarage party and the weather was fine on the day and that summer a motor bus began a regular weekly run to Bristol. Louise Henty decided that she would go on one of the first journeys. Will was too busy with the farm to think of joining her, but her daughter, Louise, was keen to go. The day of the vicarage party was the Saturday before their trip. Young Louise had recovered from her early spring trip to Weston-Super-Mare and was excited about her first visit to Bristol. She chattered about it on the way round to the vicarage, which was situated in a wedge at the back of the church, bordered by the school, the churchyard itself and the Henty's orchard. The vicarage was a large house, rendered and pebble-dashed, and ornamented with enormous pebbles. The windows looked silently out onto both school and church, but inside was different. Michael and Virginia Orrins had five children ranging from age two to seventeen. They were a bright and happy family who were an important part of village life, both as people and with regard to Rev Orrins' position.

Flags were hung from the trees around the garden of the vicarage and bees and butterflies darted and settled. Tables had been erected and covered with cloths or coloured paper, and women and children arranged home-made jams, cakes, household goods and toys ready for sale. Hoop-la, tombola and other games were set in place ready for the visitors. Virginia Orrins was busier than most, checking that everyone had whatever they needed, followed by two-year-old Rebecca and Esther, who was six.

Villagers had begun strolling around towards the garden before two o'clock and by half past two the party was alive with laughter and talk. Barley water was being served and mothers sat on the grass with their younger children, enjoying the shade of the trees. Older children ran freely, playing hide-and-seek between the stalls, trees and people.

At four o'clock Michael Orrins called for their attention and thanked them all for coming.

"We are raising money for the upkeep of St Mary's, so you'll agree it's a good cause. Thank you again, Lady Moira, for opening our party, and thank you to our army of ladies who keep the church looking its best throughout the year."

Everyone clapped and looked pleased; it had been an extremely pleasant interlude. People did not want to leave straight away and remained in groups or helping to tidy up until long past teatime. Flora and her mother and sister had run a stall and sold everything, and were now counting up the fruits of their success.

"Looks a goodly sum, Louise," Rev Orrins commented to Flora's mother.

"Yes, Reverend, we're pleased with the response. We all helped to make the toys and clothes."

Mabel Atkinson strolled towards Flora and engaged her in conversation. Mabel was almost forty and had been married twenty years; she and Geraint had no children and she was known in the village for being 'Aunty Mabel' to all and sundry. Eventually, after talking about the party, she asked Flora if she and Ellie could visit her the following week. Flora's interest was at once aroused, as Mabel must be in need of their professional help. She had been sadly unlucky over the years and suffered numerous miscarriages.

"I'll ask Ellie," said Flora. "When is most convenient for you?"

They agreed on a time and Flora hoped it would suit Ellie.

"I'll let you know if not," she assured Mabel.

"See you on Wednesday morning, all being well."

Partly due to Flora's own character and also to the professional code of ethics Ellie had instilled in her, Flora said nothing to her mother on the way back to Orchard Cottage and Louise knew better than to ask, even though Mabel was her contemporary.

"I'll go off home now, Ma, and see what my man's been up to this afternoon," said Flora, and waving them farewell, headed off for Briersham.

+ + +

Ellie and Flora sat in Mabel's neat living room drinking tea.

"I am amazed; I still can't think it's true!" said Mabel happily.

"When was the last miscarriage?" queried Ellie.

"Five years ago. Now, because of my age, I thought it was the 'change'."

"Reasonable enough assumption." Ellie laughed.

"Well, dare I mention it to Geraint?"

"Oh yes. There's no doubt, Mabel. You're about four months gone."

Mabel's face shone with delight and Flora was pleased for her.

A late chance to have a child was a blessing when you had been as unfortunate as Mabel and her husband. Flora knew how she felt; it was only seven months since her own disappointment.

"I'll pop in once a month for the next three months, and then once a week. You're a very special patient!" joked Ellie. "Take care of yourself. Don't overdo things. You know what to do, Mabel," she continued.

They sat gossiping a while longer and then made their excuses to leave.

"Look after yourself," said Flora.

"Thanks, dear, I will," replied Mabel with feeling.

As Ellie and Flora carried on with their rounds, they contemplated the fickleness of fate.

"Such a shame. Mabel should have had a quiverful of children by now," observed Ellie.

"At least she'll have one," said Flora.

"God willing," added Ellie as they walked up the path of a house that was still celebrating the arrival of a twelfth child.

+ + +

Esmerelda Thorndyke was an artist who had lived in the area all her life and ignored most of the villagers. She lived in an elegant Georgian house that had been neglected since her husband's death. The façade of Fourwinds looked intact, but closer inspection belied the initial impression. Inside, she used only certain rooms and no one knew the condition of the others. Esmée, as she called herself, kept dogs; mostly mongrels, but she loved golden retrievers and had four. When anyone approached the house, the sound of barking was enough for most visitors to retreat unless they were intent on seeing Esmée.

Ellie and Flora were going to see her, because she had sent a message asking them to visit her. As they went up the drive, the baying began.

"Are they dangerous?" asked Flora nervously.

"I'm not sure; they sound it, don't they?" replied Ellie.

They knocked on the front door, using the usual brass knocker, shaped like a Gorgon's head. When there was no response, they went gingerly around the side of the house, looking for another entrance. They found the back door and were about to knock when a dog came flying at them from behind.

"Down Bertrand," said a commanding voice.

The mongrel lay down, panting and harmless.

"I was in the garden. Did you knock?"

They nodded and Ellie told her who they were, even though they both wore navy frocks with white collars and cuffs, so that it was obvious that they were nurses of some sort.

"I know you, Mrs Bates. This young woman is something of a stranger, though I recognise her name."

"My father-in-law has Drakes Farm," said Flora helpfully.

"Ah yes, that's it. I purchase milk direct from them."

"You said you wanted to see us."

Esmée had been picking her way through the overgrown garden during the exchange and now stood beside them. She was a very large woman, though not tall. Her hair was titian and flowed around her face in extravagant curls. She was in her forties and still had an attractive face, from which her huge blue eyes now scrutinised Ellie and Flora.

"Come inside; it's hot out here," she said.

They went into a wide passageway, tiled with black and white marble. She led them into a huge kitchen, which was surprisingly clean and neat. She placed the trug she was carrying on the scrubbed wood table and proceeded to pour lemonade for the three of them, from a jug she brought out from the walk-in larder.

Flora looked around admiringly. A vast built-in dresser housed all kinds of china, pottery and crockery. The range, which was not lit, boasted four ovens, and there were two sinks, each with long draining boards. Two comfortable chairs sat beside the range and it was obvious that one was used by the dogs because of the squashed cushions and hairy, soiled covers.

"I wanted to see you because I have a problem," explained Esmée. "A medical problem."

"In that case, you should contact Dr Tanner, Mrs Thorndyke," Ellie told her firmly.

"I don't want to call in Dr Tanner," said Esmée.

"But we are midwives and monthly nurses," said Ellie.

"I know that. I have a problem of a delicate nature and I wanted your view. I don't want to talk to a man about it, not even if he is a doctor."

"Well, that's a bit different," said Ellie, relaxing. "How can we help?"

Esmée told them about her symptoms and they discussed what might be wrong.

"Will you allow me to mention it to Dr Tanner?" asked Ellie.

"Yes, I suppose so," agreed Esmée.

"We could benefit from his advice and I would like to bring him in for the diagnosis," said Ellie.

She showed them out through the front door and they passed a high, elegant room reached through a wide archway off the hall. They could see its faded grandeur and much of the furniture was covered with dustsheets, because it was now Esmée's studio. She waved an arm airily as they passed and said, "The light is best in there; it's an ideal place to paint."

They walked down the drive, unmolested by dogs or their barking.

"What an amazing place!" said Flora.

"Yes, I haven't been there before. It must have been beautiful once."

"When will you see Dr Tanner?"

"We'll see him together. Perhaps in the morning, if that's convenient for him?"

"All right, Ellie," agreed Flora.

They continued on their rounds, grateful that, although their job was a busy one, it was never dull.

AUGUST 1908

"Mother, come along; we'll miss it."

Louise Henty was fiddling with her best hat.

"I am not going to the big town looking like a country bumpkin," she protested. "The motor bus will just have to wait."

"If it waits for everyone all the way to Bristol, it will never get there," reasoned her daughter. "It isn't a horse and cart, Ma!"

"Don't fuss, child," retorted Louise.

Young Louise finally chivvied her mother around to the village square outside the Partridge Inn where the bus was scheduled to stop. A number of people had gathered, all dressed in their Sunday best. They were all excited, but pretending not to be, as though they went on a motor bus every day of their lives.

"Lovely day for it," said Margaret Bartrup, who also happened to be Louise's cousin.

"Yes, Maggy. You looking forward to it?"

"Oh yes. Been meaning to go since it started."

"They say they do a nice tea in Pringle's," interjected Mrs Wilton.

"Shall you be buying anything for the shop?" asked young Louise.

Mrs Wilton explained to her that she was seeing a wholesaler about new fabrics and trimmings, knowing how interested the girl was in such things.

"What about paper patterns?" continued Louise.

"Not this time; that's a different company."

Just then the sound of the motor bus alerted them to its arrival.

They had been standing back from the road beside the wall of the piggery and their view had been obstructed. The motor bus rattled along noisily and stopped in the middle of the road. Archie Summerhill stepped down to allow them on board.

"Good morning, ladies and gentlemen."

The passengers climbed up the steps of a converted Model T Ford van. The bench seats were installed lengthways so that the passengers faced each other. When everyone was seated Archie climbed into the driver's seat and his son, Christopher, collected the fares. The bus rumbled and rattled along the narrow lanes towards Steeple Burstead, where they took on more passengers. It was so noisy that it was impossible to hear any conversation.

Louise was starting to feel a certain queasiness in her stomach when suddenly the bus ground to a halt, the engine puttering out.

"What's the trouble?" asked a gentleman. "Why have we stopped?"

"Everybody out," said Archie with such an air of finality that no one argued.

"Too steep. The bank," explained his son.

"You'll all have to push," stated Archie.

"Push?" asked Mrs Wilton, incredulous. "Push what?"

"The bus, woman, the bus."

"I am not pushing a bus," she said categorically.

"Then you'll have to wait here 'til someone else comes for you."

They all went to the rear of the bus and, while Archie put it into gear, pushed.

"Ready? One, two, three – push!" shouted Christopher.

Nothing happened. They tried again. On the third attempt the engine spluttered to life and the motor bus motored off up the hill.

"Hey wait for us," shouted the man again.

"No good him waiting, sir. You all get on again and same thing'll happen."

So they all trudged up the hill to join the empty bus and continued their journey.

Young Louise could not remember a more exciting day. She had never been to such a large town before and she was fascinated by the diversity of people. There were foreigners about, because the port was busy and thriving, and shipping arrived and departed on a daily basis. They caught sight of the square-rigged ships moored near the vast warehouses at the docks as the bus trundled towards the city centre.

As they found their way through the town, Louise's eyes popped as she saw the fashionable clothing worn by ladies and the way they had primped their hair. Neither woman had been prepared for how sore their feet would become while trudging the hard pavements, trying to see as many shops as possible. They had lunch in Darcy's, another experience new to young Louise, who avidly watched the waitresses who were dressed like 'tweenies'.

They returned to the motor bus stage laden with purchases and climbed up the steps of the bus laughing and elated by their trip. Young Louise took in the scene as the vehicle made its way through the town and the built-up city centre gradually gave way to green countryside, where she began to feel at home again. After Steeple Burstead, she relaxed sufficiently to nod off to sleep.

"We're home, dear," said Louise, shaking her daughter.

Slightly disorientated, she collected her parcels and bags and alighted outside the Partridge Inn once more.

Will had arrived home just ahead of them.

"Did you have a good day?" he asked.

While they made supper, they told him all the details of their trip. Almost as soon as she had eaten young Louise bade them goodnight and took herself up to bed.

"I'll look at my new things for a while, Ma, but I'm so tired I think I'll retire for the night," she said.

Her mother chuckled and admitted to her husband that it had been a tiring, but thoroughly enjoyable day.

"It's an amazing city, isn't it?" she remarked to Will. "So much to see."

"Give me Abbots Ford any day!" he answered.

"Oh, I agree," she said. "I certainly wouldn't want to live there or go by bus every day."

"People don't know anybody up there," complained Will. "They live among a lot of strangers."

Louise kissed her husband fondly and made ready for bed.

"Can't think why I'm so tired," she told him.

"Mixing with all those strangers," he muttered, half to himself. "You wouldn't catch me up there, even for a day."

SEPTEMBER 1908

Charles had been footloose and fancy free for some time. He had vowed to remain that way after the fright Emily had given him, when her lack of knowledge of the facts of life had led her to believe that she could have been pregnant by him. It was nothing of the sort, to their joint relief. He was attractive enough for any number of local girls to agree when he asked them out, and this is what he did.

Will had been to a cattle auction and met an old friend who had heard on the grapevine that a villager in Abbots Ford was thinking of selling land. Armed with this prior warning, Will took Charles and went to see Albert Matthews to discuss the matter, as the land abutted their own. Mrs Matthews served tea and Beatrice, her daughter, helped to carry the trays in. Charles looked up to see a striking blonde girl crossing the room. She was of medium height and her hair was put up at the front, but left hanging in a golden curtain down her back. She wore a fitted frock that was gathered into a small bustle at the back. It was a most beautiful shade of sapphire blue, which seemed to match her eyes as she smiled at him on the way out of the room. She had an air of confident quietude and Charles was instantly attracted to her. He drank the tea and listened to the discussion, but his mind kept wondering if the apparition he had seen was spoken for, or available. Fortunately, she came back again to pour more tea and, when Charles leapt to his feet as she came in, her father introduced her. Will merely stood and nodded, but Charles took her hand and her father had to ask his name and formally introduce them.

Their business over, they took their leave of Mr Matthews and made their way home.

"She took your fancy, boy, didn't she?" observed Will.

"She was very attractive, Dad," responded Charles.

"Yes, lovely girl, but I'd watch that one!" he told his son.

They explained everything to Louise when they returned home and agreed that the terms were good. They would sleep on the decision and contact Mr Matthews in a few days.

+ + +

The business was completed satisfactorily and Charles took the opportunity of asking Beatrice out, as he had never seen her at any of the usual village functions. To his delight, she agreed and they made plans to attend the Harvest Supper together in two weeks hence. His step lightened and he was agog with anticipation. He could hardly wait for the last Saturday in September and planned well in advance to look his most immaculate, for Beatrice was no ordinary girl.

OCTOBER 1908

Flora was so busy helping Ellie Bates and still making time to help her mother three times a week, as well as running her own home, that Seth put it to her that a separate wash house with a copper would be a help.

"Help!" she shrieked delightedly. "Oh Seth, it would be heaven."

"Well, most of our harvest is complete and I reckon I could make time before the bad weather comes to build it. The others'll help if they can."

While the living room was a good size and the scullery of the cottage had room for Grandad's pine table and chairs, Flora had to heat water for everything on the range in the living room, carrying it to the scullery for use. Seth's idea was to build a brick extension at the side of the house to make a wash house and a downstairs bedroom.

"I'll build in the copper, love," he explained. "You can build a fire underneath – it'll have brick all around," he went on.

Flora was elated. She often brought linen home to launder after a birth, to help the new mother. This would make it easier, and on bath night she could heat water all in one go. Seth's father knew a builder who would help with the foundations and some of the building, and Flora's father and brother would do the carpentry for the windows and doors. They began the work the following week, but did not complete it before winter set in.

Seth had gone back out to work on the new building for a couple of hours after his midday meal before he left for Drakes Farm to help with milking. The foundations had been hard work, but now that it was beginning to take shape Seth was keen to get on. His youngest brother, Arthur, was helping him and, at twenty, was a big strong lad.

They were using large pieces of local stone for the building and the two of them were lifting a huge piece into place. Neither of them knew afterwards how it happened, but it slipped out and fell on Seth's foot. Arthur could not lift it on his own, so he ran all the way back to Drakes Farm, half a mile away, to alert his family. James and John could not be found, but David was there and returned with Arthur with all speed. Flora had left earlier to see her mother and to do some shopping in the village, so in the meantime Seth had lain all alone, drifting in and out of consciousness with pain.

Arthur had not waited to make Seth comfortable or cover him for warmth, so by the time his brothers returned he was not at all well. Shock had set in and, along with the loss of blood, Seth was worried and confused.

"Cover him up," said David, "and get him a pillow or something."

David tried to assess the situation and was horrified how pale Seth was. When they had made him more comfortable it was obvious that they had to remove the rock from his leg and foot quickly. By this time Charlotte had bustled along from their farm, having followed the boys more slowly.

"Seth, dear, where are you?" she shouted on arrival.

David hurriedly diverted his mother into the scullery to put on the kettle for some hot, sweet tea for them all. He knew her reaction to the emergency would not be helpful, especially when it involved Seth, her favourite. Going back to the patient, David prayed silently as he and Arthur struggled to lift the weight from their brother's damaged limb.

"All right, my lad," said David. "Keep 'un still."

Seth was writhing in agony and David knew that they had to stem the blood swiftly. He took off his scarf and wrapped it tightly around Seth's thigh. Arthur had gone into the new building to collect some of the wood waiting to be fashioned into window and door frames.

"Will these do to keep his leg straight?" he asked.

"Good lad," said David encouragingly. "Saw them the same size, as long as his leg."

When Flora arrived home they had fixed Seth's splints and helped him into the scullery where his mother was trying to make him drink the sweet tea she had made.

"Oh my Lord!" said Flora, sizing up the situation at once.

"He needs to see the doctor then," she said when the boys had informed her exactly what had happened.

"I'll run up and get the horse and trap," volunteered Arthur.

Seth's colour was marginally better now that he was warm and not losing so much blood, but they could see the pain was intense.

In an amazingly short time, Arthur returned with the transport and they carried Seth to the cart.

"He's best off left lying down in the back," suggested David.

Flora brought another blanket and, making sure that he was comfortable, Flora, Arthur and David drove him to the village to see Dr Tanner.

+ + +

"How are you feeling, love?" asked Flora.

"Lot of pain," said Seth quietly.

"Feel like eating anything now?" she ventured.

"No."

"Not even some of this soup? I've put in some of my dried herbs," she tempted.

"Oh, all right," he said unconvincingly.

To her relief, Seth managed to drink some soup and ate a chunk of bread, which he broke and put into it.

"Poor love."

He was silent. Doctor Tanner had not been very optimistic about Seth's leg and foot when he first saw it. Seth had lost a lot of blood and his limb was badly damaged. Doctor Tanner had set the bones and sewn him up, immobilising the foot, ankle and calf with plaster.

"Rest, rest, rest, young man, is what you'll need," the doctor had commanded. "It won't heal if you are up and about too soon."

"Just as well you did it now – not too much doing at the farm," said Flora.

Seth was still silent.

"Your dad and the boys will manage what there is to do just now, won't they?" she carried on.

"Didn't get the wash house done, did I?" complained Seth.

"Fancy worrying about that!" Flora cradled his head in her breast. "As if that's what I am worried about!" She smiled fondly at the absurdity of it. "Just rest and get well," she said.

"Mmm." He rested in her bosom contentedly. "You know what, Flora?"

"What, love?"

"It was only my leg got damaged."

"What do you...?" she began, and then saw the glint in his eyes.

"Rest is what Dr Tanner said." She laughed.

"Where are my sticks – or better still, come here to me, wench!" he teased. "We won't bother to go upstairs."

Flora made herself comfortable, sitting on the floor, being careful not to touch the damaged leg. He kissed her hungrily and she responded with a passion of her own. They made love there in front of the fire, its light and warmth caressing their bodies.

"Seth, your leg..." said Flora.

"Let's just carry on, love," he replied. "I can't feel a thing."

NOVEMBER 1908

Charles was besotted with her. She held him at arm's length and he did her bidding. His parents were worried.

"He's never been like this before," his mother had observed.

He was neglecting his work if he wanted to see her and it seemed that she was often deliberately awkward about their meetings.

The Harvest Supper had been a success and Beatrice had been at her most alluring. Laughing and happy, she had flirted outrageously with Charles in public and then cooled alarmingly in private. She seemed to have depths he wanted to discover and he could not see her often enough. They had been out walking on Saturday or Sunday afternoons and he had been invited to spend one or two evenings at the Matthews' house, where the time had dragged as they sat with her parents, making excruciatingly boring conversation, for they had nothing in common.

On a cold, bright Saturday in November, his father had allowed him to borrow Samson and the trap to take Beatrice for a run. They were well wrapped up against the cold and snuggled on the seat together as they made their way towards Steeple Burstead.

"Are you all right, Beatrice?" he asked her solicitously.

"Yes, I'm enjoying it," she assured him.

They journeyed on until they arrived at the pretty village, where Charles tied the horse to the post outside the inn and they went for a walk around. The main street was wider than that of Abbots Ford and a memorial stood in the middle of the village square. Cottages and shops lined the square and main thoroughfare, and people went about their business, stopping to chat with neighbours here and there. It was the essence of tranquillity and order, and the couple walked around looking in the shop windows. Beatrice took a particular interest in shops whose wares were for ladies and she entered the draper's shop to buy threads. Charles waited outside, embarrassed in case there were any items of a personal nature on view.

The lady behind the counter wore a severe black frock with a small white collar. Beatrice told her what she required and the woman went to one of numerous small flat drawers to collect the thread. A large glass counter and display case contained discreetly arranged ladies' underwear and the walls of the shop were lined with wooden drawers of differing shapes and sizes. The effect of all the wood, and the cramming of merchandise on every surface, was to muffle sound, and Beatrice felt as though she was in a velvet-lined jewellery case. The woman eyed her beadily as she stood for a moment, thinking of anything else she might require. It was a novelty to see a stranger in her shop and the woman took in every detail of Beatrice's apparel.

"If there's nothing else...?" said the woman.

Beatrice paid for her purchases and took them from the woman, thanking her.

Charles turned as Beatrice went down the steps.

"I thought you were never coming out!" he joked.

They returned to the trap and Charles turned Samson for the journey home. He felt joyously happy; he liked having the horse and trap and Beatrice beside him. It gave him a feeling of completeness, somehow.

They had arrived at the Matthews' house. He tied Samson to the gatepost and handed Beatrice down from her seat.

"You'll come in for a cup of tea?"

"Yes. Thank you," Charles replied.

The house was empty when they went in. Her parents were absent, and the servants gone for their afternoon off.

"I'll go..." Charles offered.

"No, come in; it's quite all right," she told him.

They took the tea into the morning room, which was at the rear of the house and comfortably furnished with sofas and a love seat. They talked and laughed about the sour woman who had served her in the draper's shop and the people who had stared at them in the village. Beatrice put down her cup and saucer and turned to Charles.

"I like being with you," she said, suddenly serious.

He was taken aback. It was rare for her to voice her feelings in this way. She leant towards him and he kissed her, for it was unavoidable, and he was not averse to it. He was apprehensive about behaving like this in her father's house and it made him nervous.

Beatrice had other plans, though, and her kisses became more demanding.

"Come to my room," she whispered urgently.

"We can't..." he said, horrified.

"There's no one here!" She laughed. "Come on!"

She led the way, pulling him by the arm. He did not notice the details of her room, only that it was a bower of floral fabrics and feminine knick-knacks. They did not disrobe entirely, for there was no time, such was the urgency of her desire, and, in consequence, his own. They were lying panting on her bed when they heard the voice.

"Where are you, Bea?"

Her mother's voice grew ever nearer as she called out, while ascending the stairs.

"Quick, out through that door," she instructed Charles. "It'll lead you to the spare room, then you'll have to try to get downstairs unseen."

Charles thought that his heart would burst out through his chest wall, so hard was it beating. He remembered in time to get his jacket and dashed into the next room just as her mother opened the door.

"I need to refresh myself," said Beatrice airily. "Did you see Charles downstairs?"

"No dear. The horse and trap are outside, but there's no sign of Charles."

Charles had managed to make his way to the garden and came in as though he had been for a stroll.

"Good afternoon, sir," he greeted Mr Matthews.

"I see you've been out in the trap, boy. Where did you go?"

The two men were talking when Beatrice, full of decorum and once again the 'Ice Maiden', came into the room.

They sat taking tea with her parents before Charles could escape. He could hardly meet her eye, but she was shameless, for she looked smoulderingly at him whenever she thought that her parents' attention was elsewhere.

"I'll see you tomorrow?" he enquired as he took his leave.

"As much of me as you want," she whispered wickedly.

+ + +

It was the rattling on the door that woke Seth first. Flora had slept through it, but was roused when Seth scrambled out of bed to hobble downstairs. She heard the sound of urgent voices and got up to investigate. Seth met her at the top of the stairs.

"Geraint Atkinson. It's Mabel…"

Flora turned back to her bedroom and, without stopping to wash, got dressed.

"What's the time?"

"Three o'clock. Want a cup of tea?"

"No. No time, thanks," she replied.

She pecked him on the cheeks and told him she would see him when she returned.

The journey with Geraint was quite terrifying. He knew the road and his own horses, but she had never travelled along these lanes so fast.

When they arrived at the house Ellie had everything under control.

"Thank God," she muttered quietly as Flora entered the bedroom.

"Hello, Mabel," said Flora as cheerfully as she could.

Mabel was in the throes of a contraction.

"I think she's been in labour on and off for fifteen hours, but she tried to stay quiet and hoped it would stop, because it's five weeks early," explained Ellie.

"Even so, it seems to be a big baby, doesn't it?" said Flora.

"Trouble is, it's breached. I think we're going to have to call in Dr Tanner. I'll go and tell Gerry."

Half an hour later, Dr Tanner arrived. He examined Mabel and consulted with Ellie and Flora in the scullery.

"She's tiring fast and the babe is distressed," he said.

"It doesn't look hopeful, does it?" asked Ellie.

"I think we'll have to chloroform her," said Dr Tanner.

"We'll prepare her," said Ellie.

The three professionals went about their work efficiently and speedily. Mabel's labour continued throughout the morning and into the afternoon, until at teatime she was delivered of a still-born son.

There is never a time for a professional person to become emotionally involved with clients; certainly not doctors, nurses and patients. It was hard for those three people, who knew Mabel and Geraint as neighbours and friends, not to be sucked into the grief and heartbreak of the broken dreams and sterile life of a pleasant couple. Their hopes had been raised too many times over the years. When Mabel had accepted her childless state, she had been given this last chance. Now, it had been arbitrarily snatched away.

"Pop over and get Rev Orrins," suggested Dr Tanner. "Though God knows how he can help, for I don't."

"Are you all right, Flora?" Ellie noticed that she was looking drained. "Come into the scullery."

Flora wept. "I'm so sorry, Ellie. I'm letting you down."

Ellie was brisk.

"Have some tea. No, you're not letting me down. All the time you've worked with me and you've never been less than professional. This is a very sad day. You'll not cry again, but the sadness, the tragedy of it, you'll never get over that."

Geraint entered the tiny room.

"Have some tea, Gerry?"

"What? Oh – yes, ta."

"So sorry, Gerry. We all are."

"Yes."

"I'll be back later today."

"Yes."

"Rev Orrins will be over to see you both."

"Yes."

"We'll be off then."

Geraint continued sitting as they left.

"Poor man, doesn't know where he is," said Flora.

"Not the time to tell him just now, but he should count his blessings."

"Blessings?" Flora was shocked.

"Yes, blessings. He nearly lost Mabel as well."

Flora was silent as they walked through the village. "That seems hard," she said.

"You've got to be hard, Flora. It helps people, in the end."

Flora Hawkes carried on walking, silently. She had just crossed the line between being an amateur and a midwife, in spirit, at least.

DECEMBER 1908

"Are you going to Seth's family for Christmas dinner?" asked Louise Henty.

"I don't know, Ma, we haven't talked about it," said Flora.

"You know we'd love to have you here," continued her mother.

"I'll talk to Seth about it and let you know, shall I?"

"Yes, dear. How is he now? His foot seems to be healing well, doesn't it?"

"He's being a bit of a baby, but he's getting about on it," said Flora, smiling ruefully.

"So it'll be spring when he carries on with the wash house?" enquired her mother.

"Yes, he's not ready for heavy work and anyway, it isn't the weather for doing it."

"All in good time. Do you know, I saw Nancy in the village the other day," said Louise.

"Really? How is she?" asked Flora, interested.

"She was out with her baby. What a bonny little boy!"

"Did she say where they are living?" asked Flora.

"She's with her grandmother, but they see her parents every day. Her father is gradually coming around to the idea. You couldn't help but love the little chap."

"It's amazing what happens when babies come," said Flora. "However many they have already, once they're here, they love the new one just as much."

"You like working with Ellie, don't you?" observed Louise.

"Yes, Ma. It's wonderful; she's so nice to work with. She's a generous teacher."

"Your time will come, dear. I know it in my bones," said her mother.

"I'm in no hurry," said Flora confidently.

Her mother had completed her ironing and took the flat irons she had been using to cool in the scullery. She folded the blanket and sheets with which she had padded the end of the table and put them to air on the wooden clothes horse. Flora had always enjoyed watching her mother iron; the smell of freshly laundered garments and linen, mingling with the lavender water her mother used to dampen them, would remain with her always.

"That's that for now," said Louise with satisfaction. "And now it's time for a cup of tea before I start the supper."

+ + +

Seth had agreed that they could go to Orchard Cottage for Christmas Day.

"We can go to Drakes Farm on Boxing Day; they'll all still be there," he told Flora.

"There's some kind of meeting at the vicarage on Christmas Eve after the service. Reverend Orrins told Ma on Sunday," she informed him.

He pulled a face.

"You'll come, won't you," she said, laughing and tweaking his ears.

He smiled at her and caught her by the waist, pulling her towards him as he sat on a kitchen chair.

"Only if you'll come upstairs with me now!" he bartered.

"Is that all you think about, Seth Hawkes?" she teased. "I'm making supper."

"Supper can wait," he said authoritatively as he steered her up the stairs.

+ + +

The atmosphere was electric at the Christmas Eve service. The anticipation of the children crackled like a current in the air. They were all well muffled and covered, because snow had fallen heavily and gleamed, twinkling through the darkness from roofs and windowsills. It crunched beneath their feet as they made their way to the church, adding to the excitement. The adults were no better, being almost as awestruck as the children by the beauty of the new snow and its immaculate timing.

They sang the well-loved carols earnestly and with gusto. Local luminaries read the lessons, as well as the headmaster and the head boy and girl of the school; this was considered to be a great honour for them. Paul Bates, the blacksmith's son, was head boy that year and acquitted himself well.

As they emerged from the church out into the snow, the goodwill spilt out with them. Children were impatient to go home in readiness for the special festival.

"Don't forget there's a Yule Cup and mince pies at the vicarage," called Michael Orrins. "Virginia is expecting a good few of you!" he added hopefully.

The Henty family, along with Flora and Seth, made their way down the path towards the vicarage. The lights shone out, guiding them towards the door. One of the vicar's children had been appointed to door duty and opened it as they approached.

"Hello," said the bright-eyed girl.

"Hello. Thank you. You're Mary, aren't you?" said Louise as they went in, wiping their feet thoroughly.

"Yes, I am." She nodded.

"Merry Christmas, Mary," said Will as he passed.

They were guided into a spacious drawing room. A fire crackled in the grate and guests stood near it, warming themselves. The heavy curtains were drawn and on every surface of the sturdy oak furniture stood plates of mince pies, Christmas cake and other goodies.

"Welcome!" said Virginia Orrins. "Would you like some Yule Cup? Well it's a sort of punch, actually." She chuckled.

"Most definitely yes, please," said Will.

The sons of the house, Luke and Paul, were in charge of serving the punch, which, as it was being served to children as well, Will took to be innocuous. Virginia's mother was serving tea and Louise opted for that.

"How lovely, thanks a lot," she said on receiving hers.

It became more crowded as other people arrived, but they spread themselves around the ground floor of the vicarage, talking, laughing and gossiping.

Young Louise watched quietly as her parents conversed with friends, and Flora and Seth stood talking secretively to each other. Bill had gone off with his friends to look around. Her attention had been caught by the vicar's eldest son, Paul, a handsome youth with fair hair and brown eyes. He was the same age as Louise, seventeen, and was confident and friendly. He came around, asking if anyone would like more of his punch, and she held out her glass.

"Hello," he said.

"Hello," she answered, looking at him as though mesmerised.

"You're Louise Henty, aren't you?"

Louise had liked Paul ever since they had been at school, but he had always been remote, unattainable, not interested in girls. She could tell that he had changed and was showing an interest in her.

"What? Oh yes, I'm Louise," she said, as if coming out of a trance.

"You've changed!"

"How do you mean?"

"Well, you've grown up a bit."

"So have you." She smiled, relaxing more.

"That's better. I thought you'd seen a ghost."

"Sorry. I was miles away."

"Do you want to come and sit in the library? It's quieter in there."

She looked around to inform her mother, but the elder Louise was so involved in animated conversation that she went without saying anything. The room was obviously a retreat for the younger element, for Louise recognised some of her friends gathered there. Paul pointed to a large leather chair in the corner and she sat on it while he perched on the arm.

"Looking forward to tomorrow?" he asked.

"Yes, it's going to be busy, though."

"Same here. It's always busy for my father."

"Of course."

"Why busy for you; have you people coming?"

"Yes, well not 'people' – just my sister and her husband, and my grandma and grandad to dinner, then aunts and uncles later on."

"The usual." He laughed.

They found that they had much in common and Louise could not believe what was happening, for Paul seemed to be enjoying himself as much as she was. Her parents came looking for her eventually and she got up to go.

"Hold on," said Paul. Then more quietly, embarrassed, he asked her if she had plans for the following Friday.

"Yes, no, I don't think so," she said, flustered.

"There's a dance, the Christmas dance at the village hall," he told her.

"Oh yes, that. I'm going." She laughed.

"To the dance?"

"To the dance!" she said.

"Then will you come with me?"

"Yes, that would be nice."

"Can I call for you about six-thirty?" he asked.

It was agreed and she said goodbye to everyone and was spirited away by her family.

Louise Henty smiled as they trekked home, and squeezed Will's arm.

"You were getting on well with Paul, weren't you? Did you see that, Flora?" she teased.

"I'm going to the dance with him on Friday," she announced haughtily.

She was teased mercilessly throughout Christmas about it, but hugged the knowledge to her all the same. She, Louise Henty, was going out with the handsomest boy in the village. He had asked her! She could hardly wait for Friday to come and in the meantime was a pleasure to live with.

JANUARY 1909

"Another year!" said Charlotte. "Another year and I'm getting older all the time."

"You're not old on your own, love," said James comfortingly.

It was New Year's Day and they had seen most of their family over Christmas. Charlotte was excited, because John and Isabelle had broken the news that Isabelle was expecting a baby.

"About time too," muttered James, sucking on his pipe. "I thought that girl would never calf."

"Jim!" exclaimed Charlotte.

"Well, you know what I mean, with her pale, wan ways."

They said no more on the subject, as Seth hobbled into the scullery on sticks, followed by Flora.

"Hello, dear."

"Hello, Ma," said Seth, collapsing into a chair near the range. "Everything all right, Dad?"

"Come and see what I'm making," said Charlotte to Flora.

They disappeared into the living room where Charlotte was midway through some embroidery.

"You managing everything?" Seth asked his father. He felt guilty, because he was not pulling his weight; in fact, he could do very little, because of the injury to his foot.

"Yes, lad. Quiet time of year. Leg's not your fault."

"John's wife expecting then?" went on Seth.

"About time. I told your mother. How are you?" James nodded at Seth and stressed the last word.

"What? Oh, we're all right. Flora likes helping Ellie. Seems to have put all that behind her."

"Well you can't leave it too long, boy," said James.

"I know – but it'll happen when it'll happen."

They sat in relaxed silence. Flora and Charlotte returned to make tea.

"David and Peggy are getting wed in the summer," announced Charlotte.

"That's nice," said Seth. He and David had not always seen eye to eye, but, since his accident, Seth had found David changed.

"She's very young, isn't she?" commented Flora.

"She thinks he's the cat's whiskers," said Charlotte. "That's what matters."

They had just sat down and poured tea. There was a knock at the front door.

"Who can that be?" asked Charlotte, for no one came that way.

James lumbered out through the living room and there was a mumble of voices when he opened the door. He came back looking solemn.

"Seems you're needed round home, Flora, love," he said.

Flora paled, sensing bad news.

"What is it, Jim?" asked Charlotte.

"Just Edgar Williams. He's come from Abbots Village. Says they want Flora home. Wouldn't come in," reported James tersely.

"I'd best go now, Ma," said Flora.

"Yes, you get straight off, dear."

It was a two-mile walk to Abbots Ford, so James got out the horse and trap to take them.

"What about you getting back?" he asked as they clopped along the narrow lanes.

"We'll get by, thanks Dad," said Seth.

So he let them down outside Orchard Cottage and took the trap towards Upper Abbots on a round trip home.

"Oh, Flora. I'm so glad you've come," said her mother, starting to weep. She looked as though she had cried a great deal already. "Your grandad has passed away, Grandad Joseph."

Flora put her arm around Louise's shoulders. "Oh Ma, I'm so sorry. When?"

"It was this morning. He got up and had his breakfast." Her voice broke and she blew her nose. "He said he would just go out and look at the garden, and Grandma found him on the path."

"How's Grandma?" Louise began to cry again, so Will told them that she was very upset, but calm.

"I'll make some tea," said Flora and set about organising it.

Young Louise and Bill sat about looking sad; Charles was absent. Flora asked where her brother was and Will explained that Charles and Beatrice were at the cottage with Grandma.

"Shall we pop in and see her, Ma?" asked Flora.

Seth had been sitting silently at the far end of the living room, feeling unequal to the family grief.

"How will you get back?" asked Will.

Flora and Seth looked questioningly at each other.

"I'll get out the cart when you've been to see Grandma," said Will obligingly.

Not much more was said. Flora would return the next day to see her mother again. Seth gathered his sticks and struggled up the two steps to the lane.

"'Bye, Ma. See you tomorrow," said Flora, and they set off slowly up the lane towards Victoria Bartrup's cottage.

+ + +

The bell tolled solemnly, announcing the passing of Joseph Charles Bartrup. The frost still covered the ground, sparkling, despite the greyness of the day. The carriage was pulled by a sturdy black cob for Joseph's last journey. The family had arrived, quiet and dignified, the ladies dressed all in black. They surrounded Victoria Bartrup, physically and emotionally. The man they were saluting had played a different role for each of them and he had been good and kind. They sang the hymns he had chosen himself, with vigour, not wanting to let him down. He was buried in the churchyard, where his parents lay.

The mourners shared sombre sustenance at Orchard Cottage. Not many of their own generation were left, but Victoria took strength from her family around her. Then they went their separate ways, each with their own memories, but Victoria's were the longest and most poignant of all.

SPRING 1909

Flora spent a great deal of time with her grandparents. She had been his favourite grandchild; living close by had helped. He had been part of her everyday life, all her life, so she had many memories. But they were not ready to share them yet – it was too soon; that was tacitly understood. It meshed them together, all of them, like a gossamer web.

Flora talked about the loss with Seth. He was young and strong, and gradually recovering, so they walked up the hill and sat talking.

"Do you believe there's a God?" she asked him.

"You know I do."

"Why is there death, then?"

"You know what the Bible says."

They discussed it endlessly. They both witnessed birth and death regularly, but it was different when it was someone you loved. They came to no conclusion, but made rash promises to each other in the event of either of them dying.

Seth held her at night when she wept for her grandad, and for her sad grandma, who was a shadow of her real self. Gradually, she assimilated the loss, became used to his not being there and gained the strength to be a stoical comfort to Victoria Bartrup.

APRIL 1909

Louise and Paul had been going out together regularly since their date at the Christmas dance. He was a pleasant young man with a crazy sense of humour, which complemented Louise's vague and dreamy moods. They had wonderful days together, going out with friends and spending time with one another's families.

They had gone for a walk on Easter Sunday afternoon and were enjoying the spring sunshine.

"Which is your favourite season?" she asked him.

"I like them all; which is yours?"

"Whichever one we're having. Just now, I like spring best," she told him.

"It'll be sad when autumn comes," he observed.

"Don't you like autumn?"

"I'll be going to Cambridge and I'll miss you," he said.

"Cambridge?"

"University."

"You're going away?"

"I thought you knew."

"No, I didn't."

The mood changed and Louise was quiet.

"I'll be home on holidays."

"But you'll meet all kinds of people there, brilliant people."

"You're the one who is important to me," he told her.

They were walking through Abbots Woods and sat on a fallen tree trunk. He put his arm around her shoulders.

"I won't forget you," he said. "I love you, Louise."

She turned and looked him in the eyes. "Do you, Paul? I love you too."

They kissed gently and looked into one another's eyes again, trying to see into the future. They knew in their hearts that they were probably too young for their feelings to withstand such a parting.

"Let's enjoy now, enjoy the summer," he suggested.

"Mmm," she agreed.

They kissed again and carried on with their walk.

"What will you study?" she asked him.

"I'm reading Classics," he said.

"You're lucky to be going. I wish I was," she confided.

"Don't give up. Do what you want to do."

"It's different if you're a girl. It's harder," she told him.

"Don't let that stop you!" He laughed.

"You don't understand. Everyone expects a girl to just get married and have children. I won't."

He smiled at her then. "I think you will; you're a loving person."

"It's a shame I can't do both, like men," she opined.

He laughed loudly. "I detect a discussion about 'votes for women' coming on."

"You won't forget me, will you?" she asked him.

"No, I won't ever forget you," he promised.

They continued through the greenness of the burgeoning woods in the springtime of the year, in the springtime of their lives.

MAY 1909

Flora could hardly contain her delight. The most exciting event had been when Seth pronounced himself fit to work again, and that Dr Tanner had agreed. James was happy to see him return, for Seth's sake as well as his own. Once the better weather began, Seth carried on with the wash house and bedroom. He was not alone, because, as promised, his father and brothers and Will and Charles helped as much as they could. Now it was complete and ready to use. Seth had just put the finishing touch by painting it with white distemper and, now that it was dry, Flora hung the curtains she had made. He had built the boiler in, utilising the chimney for the fireplace in the scullery. The copper was set off the floor, enclosed at the sides and, when filled with water, a fire was lit in the space beneath and the washing boiled. She could heat water for everything, because there was a tap to syphon off however much she needed. They kept the hip bath in the room, because it was always cosy there, and an ideal place to bathe. A door led from the scullery to the wash house, which also had a door to the back garden, so that Flora could take her washing straight out.

The bedroom was reached by a door at the side of the range in the living room and the window looked towards the front of the cottage. They would gradually collect what they needed to furnish it. Flora could not believe the difference the space made to their home and the convenience of the wash house made her the envy of female family and friends.

"Oh Seth, I can't tell you how pleased I am," she said.

Seth beamed with pleasure at her delight. He was pleased with the result himself.

"Let's light it and try it out," he suggested.

Flora rushed backwards and forwards to the pump in the garden, fetching the water and filling the copper, while Seth collected the kindling and wood to light the fire. Before long, smoke was belching from their chimney and the water in the copper was warming up.

"Let's have a bath," said Seth conspiratorially.

They closed the new back door, drew the curtains and used the hip bath and the tin bath, because they had enough hot water for both, and splashed about like children, soaping each other in turn and then rinsing themselves.

"Oh, Seth, this is wonderful!" exclaimed Flora happily. "Such luxury, and so easy!"

They emerged from their baths and he wrapped her in a warm towel, having wrapped his around his waist.

"You are so beautiful, and funny and daft, and I love you very much," he told her. He picked her up and, leaving a trail of wet footprints across the scullery floor, carried her upstairs and placed her on their bed.

They made love that Sunday afternoon, in the delight of being young, married and happy, and because they could see their lives together taking shape and form.

"Perhaps we made a baby," he said.

"Perhaps we did." She smiled up at him.

"Plenty of time, anyway, for that. I like having you to myself," he told her, "when I can prise you away from everyone else." He began to kiss her again. "Let's just try once more," he said roguishly.

SUMMER 1909

It was an interesting and busy summer. Isabelle had had her baby a month early, in July, and he arrived with no problems at all. Ellie and Flora were both in attendance and teased her about how she had had to go home when Rebecca was having baby Flora, because just the thought of it had made her ill.

"And here you are going through it yourself!" joked Ellie.

John had hung around 'like a lost sheep' as Ellie said, and was bursting with pride when they called him in to see his son. They decided to name him Richard, after his father.

"Another one for Charlotte and James to spoil," commented Ellie, tight-lipped with mock censoriousness.

Isabelle recovered from the birth quickly, and the new parents proudly displayed their son at David and Peggy's wedding. They were married at Abbots Magna church, being closer to Peggy's parental home. The Hawkes family turned out in force and took up most of the tiny church. It was a picturesque place, with a tall, thin spire. It was situated on a slope and the churchyard slanted away, below the church itself. Peggy made a pretty, petite little bride. Her frock was made of cream brocade and cut simply, allowing the beauty of the material to speak for itself. For the same reason, trimmings were kept to a minimum. Her bonnet was trimmed with artificial orange blossom and she carried a white prayer book, rather than a posy.

Her mother never stopped weeping throughout the service and no one knew why, for Peggy and David were going to live in a house close by. They were in Briersham, not far from Flora and Seth. The family was expanding.

AUGUST 1909

Esmée Thorndyke sent another message to Ellie Bates. The previous year she had been everlastingly grateful that Ellie and Flora had quickly settled a medical problem that had been worrying her for many months and that she thought was serious, serious enough to threaten her life.

113

Esmée was just emerging from her bereavement. It had taken almost five years for her to recover from the death of her husband. They had never taken any part in village life, because his work had involved travelling abroad much of the time. Her painting had kept her company and given her solace, as she poured her feelings into executing her works.

Now she was giving a party at Fourwinds and had invited Ellie and Flora and their families. They walked up the drive and were amazed by the difference a year had wrought. Although the house still displayed a sadly passé splendour, it was tidy. The garden had been spruced up and flowers grew where none had been before. The general air of neglect was gone and the place was redolent of happy times in the past.

Esmée came out to greet them. She was wearing a flowing silk robe with fluid sleeves, in vibrant colours.

"Hello, my dears," she effused. "Welcome to my simple gathering. Introduce me."

Ellie introduced her husband, Thomas, and daughters, Bonny and Jenny; her sons had declined to attend.

Esmée greeted them all like old friends, even kissing the girls. Flora introduced Seth, and Esmée immediately began to flirt with him, even though she was almost the same age as his own mother.

"Dear boy, come with me," she instructed, taking Seth's arm familiarly. "There are people I want you to meet."

Following slowly behind, Flora smiled at Ellie and Tom. Ellie's girls giggled and nudged each other; they had never met anyone like Esmée before. Seth was being introduced to some of her artist friends, and he politely said 'hello' and was drawn into the group. He turned to include Flora, and they listened as the Bohemian types discussed politics and art and the Fabian Society. Both Flora and Seth were interested in what they had to say and Seth found himself contributing to the discussion.

Ellie and Tom walked around admiring the garden, and both met people whom they knew, for Tom dealt with all the horses for miles around and Ellie delivered most people's babies. They spent an enjoyable afternoon, gaining insight into another way of life.

After a decent interval, both couples thanked Esmée and departed. As Seth and Flora walked home to Briersham, they mulled over the occasion.

"They are different to us, aren't they?" said Flora.

"Yes, but not in what they really believe," suggested Seth.

"The women had as much to say as the men," continued Flora.

"Yes, and the men let them." Seth laughed.

Flora was silent for a while.

"You and I discuss things at home," she said.

Seth nodded.

"So why can't I say what I want to say in front of people, like your family?"

"You do!" he exclaimed.

"Not really, not about important things."

"Things like what?" he asked.

"Things that they were discussing this afternoon, those women. Things you and I talk about at home."

"Because women don't," said Seth.

"Those women do! I do, at home," she averred.

"I don't know why," said Seth, becoming impatient. "How do I know; it's not my fault."

"Yes, it is. You're a man," she said sulkily.

"And don't you forget it!" he teased, trying to cajole her into a better mood.

"Don't think you can get around me!" she warned.

Seth could not understand it. They had enjoyed a perfectly pleasant afternoon and now he was in her 'bad books' because of the attitudes of men as a whole, when he himself had done nothing to annoy her.

"I'll never understand women," he said.

Flora walked on ahead. Why did she take on these moods? Why had her mother and grandmother been able to settle and accept their lot? What was different now? The thoughts tumbled around in her head. They had arrived home. *Perhaps it's not a good thing to meet new people after all,* she thought as she put the kettle on for tea. *Perhaps I shouldn't think so much.*

SEPTEMBER 1909

After the sadness of losing Grandad Bartrup at the beginning of the year, Flora had decided to enjoy her busy life and accept events as they presented themselves, but she was not prepared for the event that arose that autumn. Charlotte had asked her to call on Rebecca in Abbots Village to collect some material Rebecca had bought from Wiltons for her. Flora chose an afternoon when she had been to see Grandma Bartrup and, after popping in to see her mother, she walked through the village to the row of cottages where Robert and Rebecca lived. Flora could hardly believe that their little Flora was now twenty months old, and she was looking forward to seeing the children and having a gossip with Rebecca. She knocked as usual and went straight in.

"Becky!" There was no response and no sign of anyone in the neat rooms. "Becky" she repeated.

There was a noise from upstairs.

"Becky, are you all right?" she called up.

When no one answered, she went up slowly. The stairs led straight into a bedroom; it was obvious that it was the children's room. She knocked at the door to the second room and slowly opened it. Flora stood frozen with horror as she witnessed a couple on the bed, in the middle of the act of love. It was Robert all right, except that the woman was not Rebecca, but a village girl, Mary Hessop. They both looked at her for what seemed like hours, but then Flora gathered herself and fled back down the stairs, out of the cottage and along the road. She was utterly shocked, and turned down the lane towards Abbots Magna, hoping that no one had noticed her ruffled demeanour. When she arrived home she had retrieved her composure, but her mind was still in a whirl. Should she mention it to Seth? Certainly not to Becky. What about the next time she met Robert? She decided to mull it over and not say anything to anyone for a while.

That evening Flora asked Seth about his old flames. At first he dismissed them as not worthy of discussion, but after persuasion he explained, "Well, Mary was a nice girl, but in the end we didn't think the same way about important things."

"What about Liza?" asked Flora.

"She was all right, but always wanted her own way," said Seth.

"And what about all the others?" asked Flora flirtatiously.

"Never mind about them," he said, encircling her in his arms. "Just come on up to bed."

"Would you ever...?"

"Would I ever what?"

"You know. Another woman?"

"Don't be daft. What's brought this on?" Seth was beginning to be irritated.

Flora explained how she felt and Seth said something that surprised her.

"Our dad had a – well, a 'girlfriend' once."

"Seth! Never! Your dad...?" She was aghast.

"Yes, Our mum turned a blind eye and it all blew over."

He saw the expression on her face and said softly, "Don't worry, girl, I'd never do that to you." He turned off the oil lamps and they went upstairs hand in hand.

+ + +

Louise got ready slowly. It was the last time she would see Paul until he returned at Christmas. His family were sad that he was going, but glad for the opportunity of continuing his education at the historic university. Louise had been invited to lunch with them all and it was a sombre meal. Virginia Orrins tried hard to be bright and cheerful, but she was going to miss her eldest child and she could not muster the will to lift their spirits.

Louise and Paul went for a walk up the hill before he had to catch the bus taking him to Bristol to join the train for London, and thence to Cambridge.

They walked hand in hand, strolling slowly.

"Be good while I'm away," he told her.

She nodded, trying not to cry.

"I'll write; make sure you reply," he instructed.

The September day was beautiful. It was warm, with blue skies and high wispy clouds contrasting with the deep autumn colours below. It was as if nature was mocking them, for their mood did not reflect her beauty.

"I hope you settle in quickly," said Louise.

"Everyone will be in the same boat," he reminded her.

They walked in silence, the unspoken thoughts and vows heavy between them. Neither wanted to tie the other down, yet they wanted promises for themselves.

"I'll be thinking about you all the time," she said.

"I know; I'll be thinking of you, back here at home."

They stopped to kiss, long and lingering. He stood back and touched her face, as if committing it to memory, deliberately.

"Time to go back," he said with finality.

They stood in a little crowd, waving as the bus trundled off up the hill. His sisters wept and his brother blinked back tears. Louise did not go back to the vicarage with them, but went home to throw herself on to her bed and let the heartbroken tears flow.

Her mother knocked on her door half an hour later, with a cup of tea on a tray.

"May I come in?"

Louise nodded and her mother set down the tray and sat on the chair.

"I've been preparing apples for storage; I'm exhausted," she told her daughter. "Flora was here. Auntie Catherine has given them a bed for their new bedroom, and Charlotte Hawkes gave them a chest and wardrobe. She's been longing to use that room, dear, and says do you want to spend the night there tonight? I said 'yes' on your behalf, so she'll have made up the bed."

Louise liked the idea.

"Yes, I'll go. Tonight, you said?"

"Yes. They've got Seth's brother, David, and his wife, Peggy, going for supper. You'll enjoy it."

Louise the elder smiled to herself as her daughter collected the things she would need to spend the night at her sister's home. What she had said was true; Flora did want to use the room, had wanted Louise to go there. Flora had even, only recently, been given the bed by Catherine. *Two birds with one stone,* she thought as she went about her business.

NOVEMBER 1909

Flora sat in her bedroom, which faced the higher fields at the front of the house. She had just watched Seth go back down the track towards Drakes Farm. He had left earlier in the cold darkness of the November morning to do the milking, and returned at half past nine for breakfast. They had sat down in the cosy scullery together and eaten eggs and bacon and talked about mundane, everyday things. Flora looked around the room they shared. The magnificent brass bedstead given to them by Grandma and Grandad took up most of the room. It was covered with the patchwork quilt she and her mother had lovingly made. It was a pretty room, enhanced by Flora's straw hat, colourful ribbons and a bunch of wild flowers Seth had given her, lying dried out on her dressing table.

Maybe this time, she mused. She knew she was carrying a baby even though it was early days yet. She was not as sick as before, but she recognised the feeling. Flora had not told Seth, for she wanted to be sure before raising his hopes. She had seen a number of births now and was well-prepared, but it was different when it was happening to you. Flora went into the other bedroom and opened a drawer in the chest there. The tiny coat was still in pieces, wrapped in cotton. She opened the material and spread out the sleeves, back and two tiny fronts. Her hands ran gently over them, picking them up, placing them together. Tears ran silently down her face, her quiet heart acknowledging, finally, what she had lost. She would wait and rest; she would prepare and look forward. She would take nothing for granted and she would pray.

DECEMBER 1909

The last notes of the song faded and everyone clapped enthusiastically. Louise Henty blushed as she nodded to her small audience in thanks for their appreciation.

"Wonderful," cried Will, proud of his talented wife.

They were enjoying Boxing Day at Orchard Cottage. Charles and Beatrice had announced their betrothal on Christmas Day. Will stood in front of the fireplace and raised his tankard to the company packing the living room.

"Health and happiness to Beatrice and Charles."

The toast was echoed and drunk by everyone. The happy couple blushed and smiled at each other.

"When's the happy day?" called Uncle Ed.

"The spring, but we're not sure exactly when," said Charles.

Will called them to order again and said that Seth had something to say. Seth stood, embarrassed, and told them that he and Flora hoped for a new arrival in the New Year. Her mother and grandmother already knew, but there were more congratulations all round.

"Another toast," said Will. "To the new baby."

They drank the toast and Seth put his arm around Flora and hugged her. Later Flora went and sat with her grandmother.

"How are you, Gran?"

"I'm fine, dear."

"Time for memories, isn't it?" said Flora.

"It's always time for memories, dear," replied Victoria.

"We all still miss him, Gran."

They sat silently for a while, lost in thought.

"Life goes on," said Victoria, as if to herself.

"There's a lot to look forward to," said Flora encouragingly.

"Yes," said Victoria, brightening. "Yes. Your baby, Charles' wedding."

"Grandad would want you to enjoy these things," said Flora.

"Yes. You look after yourself, dear."

Flora went and found Seth; handsome, strong and youthful. Had Victoria and Joseph felt like them, she wondered? Seth sensed her preoccupation and looked quizzically at her, one eyebrow raised.

"Nothing," said Flora. "It's nothing. Just, I love you," she whispered.

It was like a circle, constantly going around, slowly but inexorably. Flora was going to play her part in the pattern; as Gran had said, life goes on. So much to look forward to...

They said their goodbyes and began the walk home.

"I'm scared about the baby, Seth," she admitted.

"I know, love. Everything is going to work out, you'll see," he promised.

They trudged, arm in arm, through the pitch-black night. Flora thought about her grandad. *If it's a boy,* she thought, *maybe we'll call him Joseph.* The velvet blackness guided them home.

Chapter Four

FEBRUARY 1910 – DECEMBER 1911

Flora was happily settled into her pregnancy. She spent more and more time at home, just visiting Abbots Ford to see her family, and avoiding heavy work. Louise, her sister, was nearly nineteen and Bill just sixteen. They were productive helpers for their parents. Flora had decided against helping Ellie for the duration of her pregnancy and she was enjoying some time to herself. She was by no means lonely, especially as Seth's brother, David, and his wife, Peggy, lived nearby, and Peggy was expecting a child in August, a month after Flora.

There was one problem that bothered Flora. She had never said anything to a soul about what she had witnessed the previous autumn at Rebecca's cottage; she had done her best to put it to the back of her mind. If she thought about it at all, it was to deduce that the shock of the situation had made Robert think again about his behaviour. He had never given any acknowledgement that he was aware she knew. It was not until she and her new sister-in-law, Peggy, were talking one day when she visited the cottage that Peggy reminded her.

"That Robert is a handful, isn't he?" she said.

"How do you mean?" asked Flora.

"Well you know… at Christmas," said Peggy, going red.

"I don't understand," said Flora.

"He likes the women, doesn't he? No wonder poor Becky has all those children!"

Flora was surprised, even after what she had seen.

"How would you know?" she asked frostily.

Peggy was aware that Flora was uncomfortable discussing the subject.

"He kissed me at Christmas," explained Peggy.

"Oh is that all," said Flora, relieved.

"No, I was on my own, in the scullery at Drakes Farm. You know, when we all got a bit merry on Christmas Day?" she went on.

"Yes."

"Well, he..." she stopped.

Flora said nothing.

"He kissed me – hard, not just a Christmas kiss. And he pushed himself against me."

Flora could hardly take it in.

"Are you sure?" she asked. "Really sure? Anyway, he was merry; so were you."

"No, Flora. He meant it – I could tell."

Peggy was embarrassed now.

"Oh Peggy, how dreadful. You poor thing," said Flora, the truth dawning on her.

Robert and Rebecca's fourth child had just turned two and Rebecca had said she did not want any more babies, certainly not for a long time. Mary. Peggy. Who else?

"Best not to say anything to anyone. I'm glad you told me, though."

Flora and Peggy had become good friends; they continued to chat, mostly about babies. When Peggy left, Flora mulled it over. Poor Rebecca. Did she know? *Best just to forget all about it,* thought Flora. *Best to put it behind us.*

APRIL 1910

It was Charles' and Beatrice's wedding day. His parents were perturbed about the effect she had had on him. Will confided to Louise that their son had become hard, more cynical, and that he could only put it down to his relationship with Beatrice, as they knew of nothing else that had altered in his life.

The couple had a house on land her father owned at Upper Abbots, and there had been all kinds of trouble and disagreement over its refurbishment. Beatrice and her mother seemed intent on doing everything their way, whether Charles approved or not.

They favoured Victorian grandeur with heavy velvet curtains and long drapes covering furniture, whereas Charles preferred a lighter touch, especially as their new home was a cottage. It was a large cottage, but a cottage all the same. He decided to accept their arrangements and change things once they were married, when he hoped to have more influence over Beatrice.

There was excitement in Abbots Ford over this wedding, because two prominent families were involved. Word had gone round as to the time it was to take place, and villagers began to loiter, waiting to see the bride.

The weather was unsettled and there had been rain in the morning. It had cleared and now the scudding clouds were lighter, with the wind blowing changes in the sky all the while.

Albert Matthews had hired a Brougham to transport himself and his daughter to church. People gasped in admiration when they saw Beatrice, for she was an elegantly beautiful bride. Her gown was fashioned from figured silk, overlaid with delicate cream lace. The neckline scooped modestly and a train trailed behind her. She wore orange blossom in her hair, and a veil covered her face and cascaded down her back. Beatrice had not asked either of Charles's sisters to be matron or maid-of-honour, and neither had she asked anyone else.

Louise and her younger daughter had made clothes for themselves and Flora. Flora's ensemble was voluminous, because her baby was due in only four months. Her frock was red and white cotton with a large chequered weave, all the better to disguise her condition. Her little red hat perched jauntily on her dark hair. Young Louise had chosen lilac patterned muslin and a lilac silk bonnet. Their mother wore a light wool suit dotted with a Paisley pattern. They were pleased with their efforts, because they wanted Charles to be proud of them.

They walked sedately round to the church, accompanied by Will, Seth and Bill in their best Sunday suits, and Charles in his new wedding suit. Charles was nervous and his best friend, Peter, joked quietly with him to ease the tension, which was palpable in the air.

Reverend Orrins greeted the family warmly and had a special word for Flora and Seth. Guests arrived and found their places, and an air of expectancy lit their countenances.

A trumpeter fanfared the music *Trumpet Voluntary* as the bride began to walk up the aisle on her father's arm, and Beatrice's mother wept silently in her pew.

The wedding breakfast was held at the Matthews' home and servants slid unobtrusively around serving the meal. It was a formal occasion executed in a spirit of formality. The speeches were stiff and pompous and the humour of Charles and his best man was not appreciated. The two families did not mix freely, but remained each within their own orbit.

Louise and Will were relieved when, the happy couple having left on their honeymoon, they and their family could return to Orchard Cottage and cogitate on the course their eldest son's life might now take.

Charles and Beatrice had gone to London for their week-long honeymoon. Beatrice was entranced with the city, the sophistication and the people. They were staying at a smart hotel near Hyde Park and she felt as though she was in heaven as she strolled with her handsome new husband through the Royal Park amid the fashionable people of the capital. She wore her 'going away' ensemble, a white wool skirt and jacket, with an elegant little black hat on her upswept hair. Charles thought that she was wonderful; he had been overwhelmed by the sight of her as his bride, and equally her choice of clothes on their honeymoon. It had not yet penetrated his mind that there was a possibility that he would not want to keep her in the manner to which she was accustomed, even if he could afford it.

Their wedding night was a dream come true for both of them. The luxury of their hotel cossetted them and lulled them into the mood for love. The romance of the occasion and a wonderful meal, served efficiently and eaten lingeringly, accompanied by fine wines, had sent them up to their room on a cloud of sexual euphoria. Beatrice was a temptress, using every ploy of seduction to enslave Charles even further. By the end of the week, he was hers.

They returned to Abbots Ford and started life together happily. Beatrice took advantage of her new status as a married woman and was seen out and about more than before. Her father had, until her marriage, the power of control over her. It was commented upon that Charles was a good man and a strong man, but was he the man to subjugate a woman such as Beatrice?

MAY 1910

There was a great sadness in the country. Everyone was speaking of it: King Edward VII had passed away. The last real link with Queen Victoria and, therefore, the Victorian and Edwardian eras, had passed with him. They had all liked 'Bertie' as his mother had called him; he had been a man's man. The heir, George V, was an unknown quantity, and so was Mary, his wife.

The Henty family had gathered at Orchard Cottage after church.

"Are you going to London?" asked Louise.

"No, the charabanc is full now," said Charles regretfully.

"You weren't quick enough reserving the seats," said Beatrice. Charles ignored her.

"There'll be pictures in the papers," said Will. "Anyway, not everyone can go."

"It's a dreadfully long way," put in Louise.

"It would make a change to go somewhere," said Beatrice truculently.

"Come to our house for tea later," suggested Flora.

"We're going to Mother's," answered Beatrice curtly.

"Thanks, Flo, we'll come next week if that's all right?" responded Charles.

They discussed the changes the King's passing would bring, little knowing the full, awful extent of them.

"They say the Kaiser and the King talked it over and sorted it all out when there was trouble a few years ago," said Will.

"There's no telling what the Kaiser will get up to now both his uncle and his old grannie are gone. Drunk with power," said Charles.

Seth nodded in agreement.

"Well, time we were going now, Ma," said Charles, getting up to go.

They said their farewells and he left, taking his sulky wife with him.

"We're off now as well, Ma," said Flora. "See you tomorrow." She looked closely at her mother's face. "Don't worry about him; he's happy," she reassured her.

Seth was thoughtful on the way home.

"Your Charles has got a handful with that Beatrice," he commented.

"They'll be all right," said Flora. "Charles wouldn't have chosen anyone really horrible. Maybe she was in a hurry to get to her mother's."

Seth patted her bump affectionately as they walked.

"How's Seth junior?" he asked.

"I'm feeling fine and so is little Seth," she replied.

"You look beautiful, Flora. It suits you."

"You're not bad yourself." She laughed.

They arrived at Plumtree Cottage and he picked her up, pretending to stagger under the load as he went into the scullery.

"You're a lump!" he said.

"And whose fault is it?" she teased.

Flora put their roast beef into the oven and they sat for a time talking about their families, but still she did not mention Robert.

+ + +

Louise was not a Henty and a Bartrup for nothing. She was sensitive and loving, but she had spirit, and it had come to her aid through the last few months. When Paul returned for the Christmas holidays they had greeted each other ecstatically and spent every minute they could in the other's company. As the seasonal celebrations wore on, though, Louise became aware that he had changed. He was still the same pleasant young man he had been before, but he was more aloof. They continued to write to each other when he returned to Cambridge, but the Easter holiday had proved to them both that they were no longer a couple. Neither had anyone else in mind, but the life had gone from their relationship. They remained friends and carried on their correspondence until eventually it petered out naturally.

Her experience of loving a boy like Paul made her yearn for something other than she saw around her in Abbots Ford. She decided that she would follow her own dream, and arranged to work in a fashion house in Bath. The time had come to tell her parents.

"Mother, I'll be all right! I'm nineteen now, remember," she reasoned.

"But you've no experience and you've never been away from home before," reiterated her mother.

"It's all set, Ma; I'm going. They're very nice people and Lizzie Bartrup works there as well."

"It's no good, Louise. She's determined to go," said Will. "It's what she's always wanted to do."

"The digs are lovely," went on their younger daughter. "The proprietor is very strict. No men at all are allowed." She giggled. "But we can have visitors in the drawing room between ten and four o'clock, with permission."

Her parents looked despairingly at each other. Flora did not contribute to the discussion, but sat silently listening.

"Cousin Lizzie has the room next to mine," Louise added hopefully.

"When are you supposed to go?" asked her mother abruptly.

"Beginning of next month," said Louise flatly.

"Well, you know we'll all miss you," stated Will.

"Pa, it's only fifteen miles away. A bus goes direct from Steeple Burstead. I'll be home at least once a month," she told him.

When Louise had gone to the sanctuary of her room, her mother made her feelings known.

"I'm not one to fuss, but she's too young to go all that way and live away from home."

"Young girls leave home all the time, you know that," he reasoned. "Two years and she can do as she likes anyway."

"Don't worry, Ma," said Flora at last. "She'll be all right; she's a sensible girl."

"I hope you're right, Flora," said her mother vehemently. "I certainly hope you're right."

JUNE 1910

Esmée Thorndyke's daughter had come home. Madeline had been living in London since her father died, for she had fallen out with her mother over her inheritance. She did not enlarge upon exactly what, if anything specific, had brought her back to Abbots Ford, but Esmée was delighted to see her.

Madeline was taller than her mother was, and slender; she had the same titian hair and blue eyes and was pretty rather than beautiful. On her first morning home, they sat in the garden beneath the trees enjoying breakfast. Madeline verged on the Bohemian and did not wear a corset; she had donned a loose, robe-like frock and had wound a scarf fetchingly around her head. She lounged back in her chair, swinging her long legs and smoking a cigarette.

"Maddy, you really are the end!" laughed Esmée.

"Don't be so old-fashioned, Mama," she replied and changed the subject. "You are looking better, you know," she told her mother.

"I'm feeling better, dear. It's such a relief; I thought I'd never recover from your father's passing."

Madeline sat reflecting on life and death.

"I still miss him, you know," she added.

They reminisced about the man they had both loved and laughed over happy memories about his funny ways.

"Anyone about?" called a masculine voice, disturbing their mood.

"Who is it? We're out here!" shouted Esmée.

"Seth Hawkes, about the hunter," he shouted back.

"Oh Seth, dear boy!" said Esmée as she rose to go and meet him.

Seth was looking bronzed and handsome in a white shirt unbuttoned at the chest. He came round to where they had been sitting and Esmée indicated to a chair.

"Sit a while, Seth, while you talk to Maddy about her horse. Have you met Maddy? No, you probably haven't. Madeline, this is Seth Hawkes who helps the blacksmith sometimes. Seth, this is Madeline, my daughter."

"Hello," said Seth, at his most charming. "Pleased to meet you. It's your horse is it?"

"Yes. I've stabled her at Windsor and ridden to hounds nearby, but she's been brought down here and the journey has done her no good at all," she explained. "I wonder, could you look at her?"

Seth agreed and she took him to where the horse was stabled while at Fourwinds.

"There's a girl," said Seth assuredly as he felt the horse's fetlocks. Expertly, he examined them and noticed that she had a wound on her rear leg.

"Crepance. It's possible she's damaged it with her other shoe. You should've had her shoes removed for the journey," he advised her. "I'll bring her something that will help," he promised.

"You're so good with her; you obviously like horses," said Maddy admiringly. "You're used to doing heavy work, aren't you? Look at the muscles on your arms!" She put an elegantly slim finger and thumb on Seth's biceps and tried to squeeze. "Oh." She giggled. "They're like iron!"

Seth smiled, showing perfect white teeth.

"I wonder," she began, "There's a very large trunk still standing in the hall; could you carry it upstairs for me?"

"Yes, certainly I can," Seth told her.

They went through the rear corridor, up some steps, through another passageway, opened a door and were in the main hall.

"There it is, Seth." She pointed. "Are you sure you can manage? It is dreadfully heavy."

Seth pulled on the leather strap at one end of the trunk; it was too large to lift bodily and would have to be manhandled up the stairs. It was easily accomplished and she followed him to show him where to take it.

"Along the corridor and then second on the left," she said.

She opened the door to what was obviously her bedroom and Seth placed the trunk in there.

"Oh, Seth," she simpered. "How can I thank you?"

She stood close to him, close enough that he could smell her perfume, close enough to look down into her beautiful eyes.

"No need, Miss Thorndyke," he told her confidently. Looking her straight in the eyes, he said, "About the horse. I'll sort her out and have her ready for next season before you know it. You'll soon be enjoying a ride on her, no doubt about it." With that, he turned and walked downstairs, paid his respects to Esmée and left, smiling to himself.

+ + +

The village was in uproar. Helen Marshall had been attacked on the bridle path leading up to the forge. A constable had come up from Stoke to find the criminal, and every man in the village between the ages of twenty and thirty-five was suspect.

Ellie Bates was to speak to the girl, who was in shock, and Flora was asked to help, because she was nearer the girl's age. At first, they could not persuade her to say anything at all, so great was her distress.

In the meantime Constable Bunce interviewed every man who was within the age range, which included the young men in the Hawkes and Henty families. Some people were extremely indignant that this shadow had been cast over their menfolk.

"Love, can you tell me what happened?" asked Ellie softly.

"If only to stop him doing it again…" added Flora.

They were sitting in the living room of Helen's parents' little house, which was crowded with furniture so that they all seemed to be sitting close together. There was a smell of cabbage in the air, which made Flora want to be sick.

"Perhaps if your mother went outside?" suggested Ellie.

They had been trying to find out what had happened for a week.

"No, no. I couldn't talk about it to anyone," whispered Helen.

Flora spoke quietly to Ellie and made a suggestion.

"Sometimes it's easier to talk outside, going for a walk, than face-to-face," said Flora. "Will you come for a walk with me?"

When Helen agreed, they decided to take a shortcut through the back of the village and approach the hill from another direction; that way they should meet no one. They set off and it was a long while before either of them spoke.

"Your baby is due soon, isn't it?" ventured Helen.

"Yes, end of July." Flora smiled.

"Are you scared?"

"No. I've seen lots of births. It's hard work, but nothing to be afraid of," she explained.

They reached a fork in the lane and headed towards the hill. Helen was struggling with the dilemma: Flora knew she wanted to purge herself of it all. Then she spoke.

"What he did... hurt."

At once, Flora was alert, but she said nothing and they went on in the warm sunshine.

"It was getting dark. Didn't know who it was..."

Some birds twittered and flew from tree to tree, and a low mooing interrupted the silence as they walked beneath the overhanging branches.

"I was so frightened." Helen stopped and looked at Flora, who could see the terror being relived in the girl's eyes.

"Come and sit here, Helen," suggested Flora, guiding her to a grassy knoll.

Flora struggled to get comfortable and Helen sat almost facing her.

"He pulled me down."

They rested in silence and Flora folded her hands beneath her large belly.

"He... He... touched me," she whispered eventually, disbelievingly. She began to cry, quietly, like a little girl, in short hiccoughing sobs.

Flora could feel her anger rising at the perpetrator of this much pain.

Quietly, Flora asked, "Helen, did he… did he… do anything else to you?"

At this, the girl turned and buried her face in Flora's breast and sobbed until her whole body shook. She cried with great gulping intakes of air and screamed angrily, incoherently, except for the words 'shouldn't have done it' repeated again and again. Flora put her arms around Helen and held her tightly for a very long time, until the sobs began to subside. She knew that it was not the time for explanations or comforting platitudes, so she just rocked Helen backwards and forwards, saying nothing.

"It's as bad as we feared," explained Flora to Ellie.

"It's a manhunt then," said Ellie grimly. "We'll have to tell Constable Bunce."

Helen had agreed that Flora should tell the police the truth and then Helen's mother had taken her away, far away, to stay with her grandmother in Scotland.

When news filtered out about what had taken place, an anonymous printed note was pushed through Ellie's door. It said that the sender had seen Robert Davis, Rebecca's husband, coming through the fence from the bridle path at the relevant time, adjusting himself 'as if he had answered a call of nature'.

+ + +

They had arrested Robert at their cottage, in front of all their children. According to Rebecca, they had been rough and upset the little ones, but the police said it was because Robert would not go with them quietly. Rebecca could not go and visit him at Stoke where they had taken him, nor did she want to. James and Charlotte Hawkes were bewildered, Ruth could not take it in and all the Hawkes sons were both angry and bemused. Flora had grave misgivings about the event; still she had not confided in anyone about Robert's known peccadillos. Yet she was disbelieving; even knowing what she did, she could not believe that Robert had made this heinous attack on a young woman.

The cogs and wheels of the process of law ground into action and the gossip continued.

"Thank goodness Helen's mother took her away," Flora said to Seth one day with a sigh.

Seth would not talk about it and went about his business in a sullen fashion; he would not or could not explain his feelings, even to Flora.

Ellie came out to the cottage to see Flora and examine her.

"All's well with you, my girl. He's not going to be long a-coming."

Flora smiled contentedly. "He's been a good boy – not too much jumping about."

"He hasn't the room, girl – he's a big one! You're all right, what with all the upset?" asked Ellie, scrutinising Flora's face as she answered.

"Yes – it's just been so bad for everyone – in the family, I mean."

"How's Becky?" asked Ellie.

"No one knows. She won't see anyone, not even her mother," said Flora, perplexed. "She's walking about the village like a mad woman."

"I'd best go and see her," said Ellie. "I'll go today."

Ellie knocked at the door and waited. She could hear the children, but no one answered the door.

"Can I come in?" she called, opening the door slowly.

She was horrified at the scene that met her eyes. Rebecca had refused to allow any of the children to stay with grandparents, aunts or anybody at all. They were cowering, even the two older ones, in a corner of the once-neat room. Food was everywhere and so was disorder. The air smelt foul, as Rebecca had locked most of the windows and back door.

"Come here, my little love," cooed Ellie. "Come and see Auntie Ellie."

The two younger children responded to her approach, but the others stayed where they were.

Ellie asked, "Where's Mummy?"

All of the older children nodded towards the upper floor.

"Auntie Ellie will clear this up in a minute. Shall we put the fire on, so we can make some dinner and a cup of tea?"

The children nodded mutely. Ellie gathered up materials to light the fire and left it to kindle. She went up the wooden stairs full of foreboding and entered the furthest room.

"Becky. Are you all right, dear?" asked Ellie softly.

Rebecca stirred, but did not waken. Ellie gently shook her. It was obvious that something was seriously wrong and Ellie ran downstairs and instructed young Robbie to go and tell Dr Tanner to come as quickly as he could. Little Mary was now seven, and Ellie dashed off a note to Catherine Redford at the shop, with a request for Angus or Graham to bring a horse and trap to take the children to their grandparents at Abbots Magna as soon as they could. Mary ran off eagerly with the message.

Rebecca was taken to the hospital in Bristol, as Dr Tanner said she was in a catatonic state. Her family all visited her, but she did not seem to know them. No one told Robert about the plight of his wife and family.

EARLY JULY 1910

"Well, aren't you looking bonny!" Louise kissed her sister on the cheek and stood back, looking at her.

"You look well too." Flora laughed, fingering the elegant frock her sister was wearing.

"Your mother thinks she's grown," quipped Will.

"Of course I haven't grown – you don't grow at nineteen – do you?"

They all laughed, happy to see Louise looking so like herself. Their mother was in her element, bustling about as if she had too much to do to bother with any of them, to hide how pleased she was to see them.

"Not long now, Flora," said Louise, smiling towards Flora's enormous bump.

"No – I'll be glad when it's over; it's dreadful in this heat."

"How are you getting on?" asked Charles.

"It's wonderful. So interesting, and we're very busy," said Louise.

"What about where you're living?" asked her mother.

"You and Pa should come and see for yourselves," said Louise. "There's room to put you up one night – it would make a nice change for you both."

"Yes, we'll come, but is it a nice place?" repeated Louise.

"Yes, it's lovely. It's not like home, of course, but it's comfortable. It's certainly different," she told them.

"Whereabouts is it?" asked Will.

"It's in the town, in the same street where I work," she went on. "There are other girls about my age and we all eat together. Mrs Standing cooks the meals."

"Is the food good?" asked her mother.

"Not as good as home, and I'm looking forward to this."

She eyed the saucepans bubbling on the range.

They sat down to a meal together and gossiped, swapping news avidly. Nothing was said about the attack or its outcome. It seemed too dreadful to mention at this happy gathering. Louise was staying the night and her mother would probably mention it later, on their own.

"Where's Beatrice?" asked Louise, as if she had just noticed her absence.

"She's at her mother's," said Charles casually.

Will and his wife glanced at each other, and the knowing look passed unnoticed by their hungry children.

Afterwards, Will got out the trap and took Flora home.

"Can't have you walking all the way home fully laden." Her father laughed.

As they clopped along, Will enquired about the Hawkes family. "How are they, Flora – I mean, really?"

"Oh, Dad – it's terrible. Rebecca is still very ill and Seth's parents have the two older children, while Ruth and Geoff have the young ones. I go in and look over the cottage when I'm in the village – but there's no word about Robert."

They drove on in silence. Hardly anyone in the village could credit it, but facts were facts.

JULY 1910

It was the end of July when it happened. Another girl from the village was attacked, in almost the same place, at the same time and in the same way. Her name was Adelaide Hirons and she had screamed so blood-curdlingly that Tom and Ellie Bates and their family had heard it. Tom and his sons, now sixteen and fourteen, had run out and caught a man red-handed. It turned out to be Sidney Percival, whose widowed mother lived in Church Lane, not far from Orchard Cottage. Sidney had been on the run from the army and living rough. He also admitted to the attack on Helen and was eventually declared insane.

+ + +

Charles and Beatrice were having trouble settling into the routine of married life. Beatrice wanted her own way in everything and, while Charles gave way over issues that were relatively unimportant, there were some occasions when he had to make his position clear to her; that he would make a certain decision or that something would be done according to his wishes. She spent a great deal of time with her mother and, at times, because they could not afford to employ a cook, there was no meal on the table when Charles came home from Peartree Farm. Indeed, there were times when Beatrice had eaten at her parents' house and there were not even plans for a meal when Charles returned home. Naturally, this led to rows, for Charles had never had to make even the simplest meal for himself and was absolutely incapable, and unwilling, to do so merely because his wife would not come home from her mother's house.

"Where have you been?" he shouted at her one summer's evening.

"At mother's," she replied icily. "Don't shout at me."

"I called in at your parents; you weren't there!" he shouted again.

"I must have left," she said dismissively.

"You'd never been there!" he said emphatically. "You were not there this afternoon," he repeated.

"I meant Margaret's, I was at Margaret's – for tea," she amended hastily, obviously prevaricating.

"You're lying," he stated, certain of himself, certain that she was hiding something. He took her by the shoulders, forcing her to look at him. "Beatrice, where were you this afternoon?" he asked reasonably, more quietly.

"I... I..." She dissolved into tears, crying prettily. "I'm so sorry, Charles." She wept. "It was going to be a surprise..."

"Why did you make me think...? Oh, never mind. I'm sorry; let me wipe your tears. Let's not see these eyes wet with tears."

He held her close to him. He was aware of being manipulated, but he loved her and was glad to have her as his wife. Perhaps a child would be on the way soon and that would draw them together, he thought. Beatrice became more amenable after these quarrels and peace governed their home for a while.

AUGUST 1910

It was a sweltering hot day and Flora was feeling low.

"I'm fed up with this, Seth. I wish he'd come soon."

"He will, love, any day now," said Seth comfortingly. He rubbed her back. "Not long now."

Seth had come home for a while, but had to return because they were busy with the harvest.

Everything was ready for the baby. Will had made a large crib and a baby chair that swung backwards so that a young baby could use it. The layette was complete, as it seemed that everyone in the family had been knitting. Louise had made six tiny flannelette nightgowns for the baby, and two pretty shifts for Flora to wear after her confinement, when it was too hot for nightgowns.

When Seth had gone back to Drakes Farm, Flora went upstairs to look at all the baby things they had collected. She opened drawers filled with tiny clothes and tidied them again; she folded and unfolded the baby linen. Feeling thirsty, she had a drink. *I'll go for a walk,* she thought, and went up the cart track away from the lane. The fields were full of golden corn swaying in unison in a gentle breeze, rippling groups of corn stalks here and there. The sky was clear blue and it felt fresher outside. She stopped and leant against a tree sucking a piece of grass, splitting it to see if she could blow a note the way she had as a little girl. Thoughts ran through her mind, her attention darting to first one thing then another like the butterflies going from flower to flower in the hedgerows. Her parents were going to visit Louise in September, just to stay the night. Seth would help Charles and Bill with milking. She thought of her parents travelling on the bus, together, on their own. Gran was looking well these days; she visited old Mrs Saunders regularly. She had taken to going to see poor Mrs Percival each day, now that they had taken her son off to the asylum. Flora carried on walking, watching the birds wheeling around in the sky. So light, birds. Free. Rebecca's husband, Robert, was free now; poor Robert. Poor Rebecca. The children were still with their grandparents and with Ruth; Robert was too upset to cope yet. He travelled to see his wife each week, but she was still poorly. Could she take in what he had said? Not Robert – it had been someone else. They were sorry. There was something strangely relaxing about being solitary and allowing one's thoughts to run on; surprising where they led. Suddenly Flora doubled up. "Oh my Lord," she said aloud. The pain passed after a while. She knew she should get back and stopped now and then to allow a contraction to pass. She was relieved to arrive home.

"Where have you been?" asked a voice from the scullery as she went up the path to the cottage.

"We were worried about you." It was her mother and Aunt Elsie.

"Well I'm glad to see you – I've been out for a walk; it's so hot…" Flora lent on the back of the scullery chair as another wave swept over her.

"Elsie, you know the way to Drake's Farm?" asked Louise urgently.

Elsie nodded.

"Go up there. Tell Seth to get Ellie Bates for Flora."

Elsie went off, running, on the errand.

"I'm all right, Ma," said Flora, grinning tightly at her mother.

"Different now it's you, isn't it?" responded Louise.

They brewed some tea and shortly Seth came rushing in.

"Are you all right, love?" he panted.

Elsie came puffing in a while later and gratefully they drank the refreshing tea.

"David's gone to fetch Ellie," Seth explained. "Thought I'd see how you are."

"As you can see, I'm fine. Stop shirking and get on with your harvest," said Flora.

Seth stayed to finish his tea and, with reassurances ringing in his ears, he went off to carry on working.

"Thank goodness for that," commented Louise. "He'd have been in the way."

Seth was in the way because Flora was not much further on in labour when he returned late that evening. Ellie had been, and gone home again after examining Flora. Louise went home to make the evening meal, promising to return later, and Elsie went with her. Flora did not feel much like eating, so Seth had chunks of bread with cheese. She was still having contractions regularly, but was happy pottering about.

Ellie came back at ten o'clock and decided she need not stay, so she went home, offering to call in to give the latest news to Louise and Will. They waved her off and went back inside, neither of them feeling able to start anything constructive. Finally Flora said that she was tired and would go to bed early.

"There's a good girl," said Seth, stroking her hair. "You have some sleep."

She only wanted a sheet over her, so he draped it around her and went downstairs. To her surprise, Flora slept, fitfully, for a few hours. By the time the strong contraction woke her, Seth was beside her and it was dark. She got up and crouched. "Seth," she said. "Seth, wake up!"

Seth jumped out of bed, awake instantly.

"I think this is it," she said, wincing with pain.

"I can't leave you to go and get Ellie – what shall I do?"

"She'll be back, don't worry," said Flora.

Seth rubbed her back when the pain came. She needed to go out to the water closet and he helped her downstairs. While she was there, Seth went back and filled pots and kettles with water, which he put on the specially lit range fire. Everything else had been in place for two weeks.

"I think my waters have broken," she said when she came in.

As the sun was beginning to light the horizon in the east, Flora's pains increased in intensity and, just as Seth was regretting being on his own with his wife, Ellie's cheerful voice called at the back door.

"How are you, Flora?"

"Come on up, Ellie," shouted Seth, never more pleased to see anyone.

At eight minutes past nine, Flora's baby was born.

"It's a girl," said Ellie, delighted.

"Oh my darling, my love," said Seth, who had stayed in the room during the birth, because it seemed the most sensible thing to do. Flora wept with relief and joy as Ellie placed her newborn daughter on her chest.

"A girl!" she cried, surprised and elated. "I was sure it was a boy!"

Shortly after, when Ellie had made her comfortable, and at exactly the right moment, Flora's mother arrived.

"You clever, clever girl," she said. "What are you going to call her?"

"Alice Louise," said Flora firmly.

"How lovely," said Ellie.

"They'll call her Elsie," predicted Louise, laughingly.

Flora looked at the tiny face that, even now, displayed the look of her own family, but was topped by surprisingly light hair.

"It doesn't matter what they call you, you're beautiful!" Flora told her baby.

SEPTEMBER 1910

Louise sat in her room in the boarding house in Bath. She was feeling extremely homesick, for she had been to see her family, including the new addition, Flora's baby, Alice, at the weekend. The room was tiny, but bright, because of the large window. It contained a narrow bed, a chest of drawers and a single wardrobe. The floorboards were bare, but her mother had given her a rag-rug from home to brighten the room and to give her something cosier for her feet to wake up to on the cold mornings to come. It was lit by a small oil lamp that stood on the chest, flickering at intervals. She was tired; the day began at six o'clock for work at seven, and they carried on, almost without a break, until six o'clock in the evening. She had only been with the company a few months, but she was impatient to learn more and was depressed that all she did was sew. There was a knock on her door.

"Can I come in? It's Alex," said a voice.

"Yes, come in," said Louise.

"They're wondering where you are – tea's being served," she told her friend.

"Not hungry," said Louise.

"Come on down anyway; you could just have a cup of tea if you don't feel like anything to eat," suggested Alexandra.

"I don't feel like company tonight, if you don't mind," Louise told her.

"You shouldn't sit all alone in your room, though."

Louise began to weep and it was so unlike her that Alexandra was mildly alarmed. She put her arm around her friend's shoulders.

"Come on, don't worry. What's the matter?"

"I've been home for the weekend, and…" This brought on renewed weeping.

"I know. I know how you feel. I've come from London remember, and I'm lucky if I see my family once a year! They wouldn't really notice if they never saw me again, mind." She laughed.

"The baby is so sweet and my sister is so happy. Sometimes I wonder if I'm doing the right thing being here, away from them all. Perhaps I should be meeting someone, getting married…"

"We all feel like that. But being here doesn't mean we won't get married one day. We aren't nuns, are we?" She laughed again. "We might as well be for all the men Mrs Standing lets us see!"

Louise smiled through her tears, and Alex went on, "Did you know that Sophia smuggled a lad into her room on Friday night?"

Louise was suddenly brighter.

"No, tell me all," she insisted.

"Promise you won't say anything to a soul?"

Louise agreed, nodding.

"Well, June and Felicity kept Mrs Standing talking and the others made sure the maid stayed downstairs while Sophia ran down at a prearranged signal and let him in. He ran up those stairs like a cat after a mouse!"

Louise laughed and Alexandra put her finger to puckered lips.

"Ssh," she told her.

"He stayed all evening, 'till bedtime," said Alexandra, making a knowing face.

"What happened when he left?" asked Louise.

"He couldn't shin down outside; it was too high," said the girl. "So Margaret had to pretend to be ill and they called for Mrs Standing, in her night robe…"

The idea of this vision sent Louise into helpless laughter, and Alexandra had to smother her momentarily to stop her. "Ssh, you're meant to be unwell or sad," she reminded her. "Anyway, there she was in her night robe and cap, looking at Margaret by the light of a candle, while Sophia's beau crept downstairs literally behind her back!"

"Oh, Alex, how wonderful," said Louise admiringly.

"Not that wonderful – you wouldn't do it; I wouldn't do it," she said disapprovingly.

"But it's so romantic," avowed Louise.

"Maybe," agreed Alexandra grudgingly. "Are you feeling able to come down and eat at least something?"

"Yes, I suppose so. I should really, shouldn't I?" said Louise. She drew the curtains and plumped up her pillows before peering in the mirror to look at her tear-stained face.

"Just rinse your face with cold water when we go downstairs; no one will suspect anything," Alexandra advised.

"Thanks, Alex," said Louise gratefully. "I don't know what came over me."

"We all feel like that at times, don't worry. And don't keep things to yourself in future!"

They went down to the brightly lit, friendly dining room where all the other girls were gathered.

"Come along, girls, you must be on time for meals," complained Mrs Standing.

They took their places and grinned at the others.

"There's a dance on Saturday. Anyone coming?" asked a raucous cockney named Betty.

"Oh yes," they all agreed. "Wouldn't miss it!"

Louise smiled to herself, thinking how miserable she had been a short time ago. *It's not too bad really,* she thought. *At least I can go home when I want,* she reminded herself. *And that's a comfort.*

OCTOBER 1910

Rebecca was coming home and Robert could hardly contain his delight. He had had help to make the cottage homely and neat again and he walked around looking at everything with new eyes. There were all the treasures they had collected over the years they had been married, and all the things that Rebecca had lovingly made or sewn. He was collecting the children that afternoon and James and Charlotte had gone to bring their daughter home from the hospital in Bristol. Dr Tanner had explained that shock had been the cause of Rebecca's illness and, now that she was rested, she was much improved.

"She'll still need your help," Dr Tanner had told him. "You'll have to help more with the children. Remember, what happened wasn't your fault. Let no feelings about all that interfere with you and Rebecca."

Robert nodded. He knew that to be true, but he still had feelings of guilt over other issues.

The children had been cared for with love while they had been parted from their mother; Robert had seen them often. Charlotte had been sensible and explained to the two older children that their mother loved them, but was not well enough to look after them for a while, and Ruth had spoken about Rebecca often to the two little ones, reassuring them of her return.

It was an affecting scene when Rebecca came into her home after many months' absence to see her family again. The children, shy at first, threw themselves at her and their grandmother wept a few tears. James blew his nose, cleared his throat and said, "We'll see you at the farm tomorrow, then."

They were all going for a family dinner.

"Thanks, Ma, thanks Pa," said Rebecca gratefully.

The children, who were used to meeting all the family often and usually hardly observed greetings at all, clung to their grandparents.

"See you tomorrow," said James gruffly. And with promises of special cakes and treats, Charlotte and James went back in the trap to Abbots Magna.

That evening when the children were tucked into their own beds, Robert and Rebecca sat beside the fire in the cottage living room.

"I've prayed for this, Becky," said Robert.

"It's nice to be home."

"You do know that…" began Robert.

"Don't. Don't start with all that again."

"I was only going to say, you know I love you. Only you. Always will." Robert was not usually a demonstrative man, within his marriage.

"I know. We've a long way to go, Rob," said Rebecca.

Still, deep in her heart, whatever the evidence to the contrary, Rebecca harboured doubts about her husband's involvement in the whole business. Yet she knew he was not capable of that behaviour, hence her ultimate confusion about her feelings for him.

"Whatever the journey is like," said Robert, "I'll always be there with you, you and the babies," he promised.

DECEMBER 1910

"Well you're a lovely girl, then," gurgled Peggy to Flora's baby, Alice.

Alice was four months old and beginning to take notice of her surroundings. Peggy was visiting Plum Tree Cottage with her own little daughter, Charlotte, who had been later than expected and had not arrived until mid-September. The babies were both lying on a blanket before the fire with their mothers watching them.

"How do women with more than one baby do it?" asked Peggy in admiration.

"Do what?" asked Flora matter-of-factly.

"Look after them!"

"What, more than one baby? Don't see why not."

"You're lucky. Alice is a good baby – she sleeps all night, doesn't she?"

"Yes. If she wakes up, Seth gets up."

"What if she wants a feed?" asked Peggy.

"Seth gives her boiled water."

"Boiled water?"

"Yes. That's what she has. So she doesn't bother waking up!"

Peggy decided she would try it with Charlotte.

"I could do with the sleep," she commented dryly.

Flora had decorated the living room and the fireplace in her scullery with holly and red ribbon, reminiscent of the room at Orchard Cottage at Christmas. The babies were focussing on the reflection of the fire on the shining leaves above. Although it was only early afternoon, it was dull enough for the flames to light the scullery; it felt cosy, but exciting.

Flora brought two cups of tea as she sat on the chair at one side of the fireplace.

"How do you think Rebecca is now?" asked Peggy.

"She's much better, thank God," said Flora with feeling. "Everyone is helping."

They sat silently thinking about what had happened.

"Rob's a different man," went on Flora.

"And the children?"

"Seem all right."

"I'm glad Robert's different, for Rebecca's sake," said Peggy. "I sometimes wish that David was a different man."

"Why, what do you mean?" asked Flora.

"He's been bothering me again," said Peggy, going red.

"Bothering you?" Flora was not sure what she meant.

"You know, in bed." She looked down at the baby.

"Oh, that," said Flora, as it dawned on her what Peggy meant.

"Does Seth bother you much now you've got Alice?" she asked.

"Not 'bother', Peggy! Love! It's what husbands and wives do when they love each other. It isn't meant to be a bother." She laughed at the notion.

"So you and Seth still...?"

"Great heavens, yes! Why not?"

"It's just that I don't... I..."

The babies began crying simultaneously and Peggy picked up Charlotte.

"Is it time to go home before it's dark, then?" she cooed.

She wrapped up her baby and placed her into the depths of a huge pram, piling blankets on top.

"Thanks for the tea, Flora," said Peggy as she pushed the pram down the track towards the lane. "See you next week."

Flora picked up Alice and looked at her fondly.

"Did you see your new cousin?" she asked her baby.

Alice squirmed in her arms and protested.

"All right. Time for your bath," said Flora and, putting the child into her padded chair, she began to prepare the water and equipment for her bath.

"Daddy home soon," she crooned as she splashed warm water over the baby's tiny back.

She was sitting feeding Alice when Seth returned home. He looked around the room, with its Christmas decoration, soft oil light and dancing flames. Then he looked at his wife and contented daughter and said, "You're good to come home to, Flo, you really are."

+ + +

The gramophone was emitting unusual music from its speaker, which was in the shape of a horn. There were people everywhere as Flora and Seth made their way through the hall, trying to locate their hostess. A tall Christmas tree stood in the hall of Fourwinds, twinkling with candles. Flora thought that she had never seen anything more beautiful. People bumped into them, laughed and continued on their way.

"I can't see any of them," said Seth.

"Well, I don't know what the daughter looks like anyway," moaned Flora.

They struggled past the throng until they reached the salon. Looking through the archway, they could see Tom and Ellie deep in conversation with another couple. They approached tentatively, but, before they could reach them, Esmée materialised and wished them 'Merry Christmas', kissing them both energetically.

"How lovely it is to see you again! You did wonderful things to Strumpet," she assured him.

Flora raised her eyebrows and looked questioningly at her husband.

"Ah she's a lovely mare. Good as gold," he said enthusiastically.

"Maddy was so pleased! She's ridden her at every meet this season with no problems at all. She'll want to thank you personally. And how is little Flora? How is the new babe? Not so new by now." With that, she departed and circulated among her guests.

Flora and Seth went to Ellie and Tom, who had by now spotted them.

"What a party," said Ellie, shouting to be heard above the din.

Tom nodded to Seth, who smiled back in greeting. Some of the people began to dance and the group moved away to give them room. None of them knew any of the other guests, but they recognised people they had met at Esmée's summer gathering the previous year.

"Do you want to dance?" Seth asked his wife.

She grinned and nodded, and they took to the floor. Ellie and Tom watched them before joining them.

Puffed out and breathless, they went to find somewhere to sit when the dance finished. There were people on the stairs, people on every available seat, even people on the floor. Seth went to the kitchen in search of chairs and was surprised to come across Madeline coming in the opposite direction.

"Seth, how wonderful! Just the man I wanted to see! Mother told me you were here. You are a gem. Strumpet has never performed better. I must find a way to thank you, but for now…" She was standing two steps above Seth, and put her arms around his neck and kissed him.

He was so surprised that he did not resist and it was at that moment that Flora came upon them on her way to look for him.

"Seth!"

Her voice made them break apart.

"Oh hello, you must be little Flora," said Madeline, unperturbed. "I was just thanking Seth for all his help." She carried on upstairs and left the pair there.

Flora glowered at him.

"I thought you said you only helped them out with the horses? Are you sure that's all you helped with?" she asked sarcastically. She too then went upstairs and Seth followed.

Later in the evening Madeline compounded the insult to Flora by grabbing Seth for a dance and becoming overly familiar with him in front of everyone.

On their way home Flora was angry.

"You were enjoying it, admit it," she complained.

"There was nothing I could do," Seth extemporised.

"You didn't have to enjoy it," she accused.

"Come, Flora. You're not being fair."

"We'll see how fair you'll be if it happens the other way round," she predicted harshly.

It was a sad way to end what should have been a wonderful evening, for it was their first evening out since the birth of Alice.

Flora decided there and then that, come what may, she would give Seth a taste of his own medicine.

JANUARY 1911

Flora had taken Alice to Orchard Cottage and her grandma had come down the lane to see her great-granddaughter.

"She's the spit of you when you were a baby, Flora," commented Victoria Bartrup.

"You're getting spoilt, aren't you?" Flora told the baby while Alice lapped up all the attention.

"She's a bright one," said Louise as Alice looked at them in turn. "Been here before, haven't you?"

"Can you stay till Dad and Bill come home?" asked Louise.

"No, Ma. I'd best get back for Seth."

"Come on Sunday, dear," suggested Louise.

"All right. That's a good idea."

"Charles is bringing Beatrice; it'll be nice."

Flora thought *will it*, but remained silent.

"Strange girl, Beatrice," observed Victoria.

Louise said nothing and helped Flora up the steps with the pram. They waved as she went down the lane towards the main road.

"I am worried about Charles and Beatrice," confided Louise to her mother.

"Everything will work out in time," comforted Victoria sagely.

+ + +

They were all back from church and had given Flora birthday presents. The room at Orchard Cottage seemed full with them all there. Bill was now as tall as his father and brother, being almost seventeen. Seth was holding Alice in his arms and looking on fondly as his wife opened her presents.

"Oh how lovely," cried Flora when she saw the brooch her parents had given her for this twenty-second anniversary.

"Pearls are so unlucky," said Beatrice.

"It's very pretty," enthused Charles, glowering at his wife.

"It was my grandma's" explained Louise happily.

"Why, it's a family treasure." Seth laughed.

"I thought that Flora was the family treasure," carried on Beatrice sarcastically.

"Well, let the family treasure help her mother to dish up this dinner we're having," said Will lightly.

They all sat down around the huge table; there were eight adults, as Victoria Bartrup had joined them. Alice was asleep in a cot upstairs, having been fed already. They passed dishes around the table and admired the food.

"So sad about Florence Nightingale, wasn't it?" commented Louise.

"Yes, we'll be fortunate if we see her like again," replied Victoria.

"She made things different for nurses," continued Flora.

"The Lady with the Lamp."

"Never married, did she?" asked Beatrice after a while.

"No, I don't believe she did," said Louise.

"Clever woman," retorted Beatrice.

They had custard with the bottled fruit pie. The jug went around the table and, as Charles passed it to Beatrice, she dropped it.

"You fool." Beatrice said it with such vehemence that they were all embarrassed.

"No harm done," said Louise. "Easily cleared up."

"Easily cleared up! Look at the mess on my new frock." Beatrice was red in the face and furious. "I'll not stay here to be insulted!" she shouted and, grabbing her coat from the little front room, she flounced out, leaving them all aghast.

Charles started to follow her, mumbling apologies to the gathering.

"I'd leave her this time, lad," said his grandmother. "Let her cool off at her mother's – that's where she'll be going."

So Charles, relieved, sat down and they carried on with their meal. The family tried to ignore what had happened and to continue with the small celebration, but they were sad about Charles's obvious discomfiture and worried about the state of his marriage.

"Told you he had a handful there," said Seth to Flora when they were pushing the pram on the journey home.

"Yes, I hadn't realised it was so bad," said Flora thoughtfully. "Maybe I'll try and talk to Charles about it soon," she added.

"I've got a handful as well," said Seth lecherously as he put his arm around her waist.

They were all tired when they got home, what with all the visiting. So they put Alice in her cot to sleep for a while and snuggled into the feathery softness of their bed for a nap.

"Nap, my eye," said Seth happily as he cuddled Flora's scantily clad body. "Come to me, my little duck."

Flora let her worries evaporate as she spent a cold January afternoon in the arms of her husband.

FEBRUARY 1911

Flora had smarted for weeks after the humiliation of Madeline's public flirtation with Seth. She had vowed to get her own back, but time paled the situation into insignificance as they had continued with their lives and Seth had demonstrated that it was she, and only she, with whom he was in love.

Flora had put Alice in her cot for a nap one bright February day when there was a knock on the back door. She pushed her hair back behind her ears and answered it. There stood a young man whom she recognised as one of Charles's friends, who had been at Charles's and Beatrice's wedding the previous spring.

"Hello," she said pleasantly. "What can I do for you?"

"Flora," he said, and was immediately tongue-tied.

"Come in. Do you want a cup of tea?"

"Yes, that would be nice," he said.

She chatted as she went about brewing the tea, and took him into the living room to drink it beside the fire. She thought that perhaps he had come to talk to her about Charles and maybe Beatrice too.

"Flora, I've been meaning to come and see you for a while," he began.

She nodded.

"I know you're married," he continued.

She waited.

"I'm in love with you," he announced.

Flora was taken aback, because it was so unexpected.

"I'm not just married, John, I'm happily married. Not that it would be any different if I was unhappy," she told him.

"I know. I knew that is what you'd say. I expected nothing less of you. But could I see you now and again?" he begged.

Flora felt awkward. He was a personable young man and she was embarrassed by his attention.

"Why don't you find a nice girl of your own?" she enquired.

"I love you," he said simply.

"John, it's really no good. I love Seth. I'm very flattered and everything, but..."

"I only want to see you sometimes," he interrupted.

"What do you suppose Seth would have to say about this?" asked Flora.

"I know it seems a ridiculous request, but I've been so unhappy trying to forget about you."

"I'll have to speak to Seth, but I don't think it's a good idea for you to come and see me."

"I would never hurt you, you know."

"It didn't cross my mind that you would. Think how you would feel if you were Seth."

"I'd be the happiest man alive," he answered.

"I'm very flattered," Flora told him, "but I have to get my baby up from her nap now and you'll have to excuse me, John."

He agreed to leave and Flora breathed a sigh of relief. He had been polite, but she had been afraid. It was not what she had had in mind when she had wanted to make Seth jealous. She would have to tell him, though, and he would be angry, not jealous. She shivered, even though the fire was warm. *Maybe I'll have a word with Charles about it as well,* she thought as she roused Alice from her sleep. *Can't be too careful.*

MARCH 1911

"Well, I will need some help to do it," said Will. "That would be good, Seth, thanks."

"I expect our dad and David would be willing."

"The more the merrier, lad. Douglas Aylmer will oversee it, and he's got two men working for him, but the heavy work on the foundations will need more than that."

Will was building an extension to Orchard Cottage. He had decided to put a two-storey addition on to the end of the existing building; a huge scullery, more of a kitchen, on the ground floor, and a large bedroom for himself and Louise above.

"I'd like a really big window in the kitchen," enthused Louise. "Looking out onto the garden."

"We're having a window in all three walls of our room, you know," he explained.

"Isn't that a window too many, Dad?" queried Flora.

"Not when you see it, girl, not when you see it."

"The new bedroom will be the width of the cottage," said Louise. "There'll be room for two big wardrobes, as well as our bed, and two chairs, my dressing table and wash stand," she went on excitedly.

"And still room to swing a cat." Will laughed.

"Ma, it sounds lovely," said Flora. "We were ever so pleased with our new building," she added.

"About time you young 'uns filled that new bedroom of yours," teased Will.

"All in good time, Will, all in good time," said Louise.

"So when do we start?" asked Seth.

"Next Monday."

"Shall we bring tools?"

"Well, maybe spades. I'm not sure what Douglas has got," said Will.

They sat down to tea and Will played with his little granddaughter.

"You're a bonnie one, little Alice," he assured her.

She gurgled happily on his knee and Louise looked at them.

"You're as bad as you were first time around."

"Too busy first time," he said.

Louise raised her eyes to the ceiling, for Will was as busy now as he ever was. The building work would keep him occupied as well.

"Rooms for little 'uns to stay," he explained to the baby.

Flora and her mother exchanged glances as if to say 'Men! But we wouldn't be without them'.

MAY 1911

The owner of the fashion house where Louise and all the girls worked was giving a show. There was tremendous excitement, because, as well as his collection, he was allowing them to submit sketches from which he would choose a winner, and the design would be made up and included in the show. Louise had not been home for a long time because of bad weather in the winter and the extra work generated by the show. She was writing a long letter to her parents when someone knocked on the door.

"Come in."

It was Mrs Standing.

"There's a Mr Fredericks to see you, Louise," she said.

Louise paled. Mr Lucien Fredericks was the owner of Maison de Lucien, where they all worked.

"I've shown him into my sitting room," Mrs Standing told her. "You can talk to him there."

Louise patted her hair and looked in the mirror. She still wore the cream blouse and brown pinafore frock all the girls wore for work, but had loosened the black taffeta bow around her neck. She re-tied it and went downstairs.

"Mr Fredericks?" said Louise nervously.

"Don't be worried, my dear. I expect you're wondering why I'm here?"

Louise nodded.

"I wanted to divulge the news personally and privately. I have chosen your design as the winner, to be made up for the show."

All the colours of the rainbow flashed in front of her eyes and she thought she would faint, but she was still standing there when he asked, "Are you all right, young woman? I said, are you all right?"

"Yes, Mr Fredericks. Oh yes, I am all right!"

"You're shocked, I can tell. We'll announce it in the morning at the workshop." He gathered his hat and cane, and Mrs Standing, who had been hovering, showed him out.

"Good news, dear?" she asked when she returned to the room.

"The best, Mrs Standing. I've won the competition."

"How marvellous! I'm very pleased for you," said Mrs Standing sincerely.

Louise went back to her room and included the good news in her letter.

"I would rather have come and told you myself, but I am going to be busy helping to make up the garments in time for the show," she wrote. "I'll be home as soon as I can to tell you all about it. Please think of me in the next week or two."

Louise could hardly sleep that night. All the things that might go wrong came into her mind as she tossed and turned. She visualised all the changes she would make to her design, and completely reconstructed it in her head, over and over again. She was wan and tired as she prepared for work in the morning, but, as the news emerged and people congratulated her, she began to feel better.

"Good news can sometimes make you feel as awful as bad!" she laughingly told Alexandra.

The sun shone and the elegant crescents of Bath were the perfect setting for Louise's happiness. As well as winning the competition and supervising the making of her design, it was her birthday! Twenty! Her mother had taken the bus and arrived unexpectedly one day. They only had half an hour together, but, as she said, one could not allow such special occasions to pass by without seeing the happy girl.

Louise was taller than Flora or their mother. She plaited her honey coloured hair when she washed it, and it dried into a frizz of wavy tresses, which she tied back at the top of her head, allowing the rest to flow down her back. Her large blue eyes and wide mouth ensured that she was an attractive girl. She had retained the faintly coltish movements of her early teenage years, her long limbs giving her a tendency towards clumsiness.

She had worked until the small hours, making final adjustments to her ensemble. The girls were all up especially early to be at the Salon of Maison de Lucien in readiness for the lunacy that passed as a fashion show. The apprehension and excitement mounted as the appointed hour approached. All the workroom girls were backstage to help the models dress or to complete last-minute alterations. The 'models' were spoilt society friends of Lucien, some of whom were down from London, and they nearly drove the seamstresses and tailoresses to distraction with their finding fault and fussiness.

It had been a success. Lucien was on a cloud of euphoria and kind to everyone. In the end, the models, the press and the clients had all liked the collection and Louise's design had warranted special mention – and applause. She was literally flushed with success and pleasure at the party after the show. Alexandra, Sophia, Louise and some of their friends were standing talking when a young man approached and stood quietly on the edge of the group. Eventually he tapped her shoulder and asked if she was Louise Henty.

"Yes, that is me." She smiled.

"I thought your design was perfect," he told her.

"Thank you. It was very exciting to win," she replied.

"What made you choose crepe de chine for a style like that?" he asked.

She began to explain and broke off suddenly. "Didn't you think it worked?" she queried.

"Yes, but I wouldn't have thought of it," he said.

"It was the movement of the material, and the colour," she explained, becoming enthusiastic at once.

He smiled. He had an attractive smile. He was not handsome in the generally accepted sense, yet he was pleasing to look at. He had dark brown hair, oiled and dressed close to his head, and mocking green eyes. His nose and mouth were large, giving him the appearance of a friendly dog.

"Are you doing anything this evening, Miss Henty?" he asked.

"Yes, I'm sorry. I'm going out with my friends – more celebrations! I had a birthday recently."

"Would it be impolite to ask which anniversary?" he enquired.

"My twentieth; I'm getting on!"

"Not at all, Miss Henty. I am twenty-five myself and I consider that I am in my prime."

Her friends were giggling and talking behind their hands, so she tried to bring the conversation to a close.

"May I see you tomorrow?" he persisted.

"Yes, all right. When?" she asked.

"May I call for you at two o'clock?"

"Yes, we live at 49 London Road," she told him.

"By the way, my name is Gordon," he said. "Gordon Chapman. See you tomorrow, then, at two." He gave a small bow and left them.

Louise blushed as her friends quietly teased her, but she was pleased all the same. He seemed like a nice man.

JULY 1911

Fourwinds was the centre of village attention and gossip again, because they would all have the chance to go inside and look around. Esmée had completed enough work to warrant an exhibition. It would not be merely her paintings on display, but the sculptures and weaving of some of her friends. Madeline, who had returned to London at the beginning of summer, was coming down especially for the occasion, and bringing a group of friends.

The house looked perfect. Esmée had gradually been having it decorated and it was looking more how it used to when her husband was alive. Her paintings were hung in the salon, hall and dining room. The weaving was exhibited in the study and Thaddaeus's sculptures were displayed in the library.

Madeline was taking her friends around to view her mother's work on the morning of the opening.

"It is an acquired taste, Maddy," said one gentleman.

"Dear boy, no. Mother's very avant-garde," explained Madeline.

"I like it," offered a young woman.

"Too bright for my taste," opined another.

"Exactly, it's a question of taste."

"What do you mean?" Madeline swung round on the gentleman.

"Whether one likes it, dearest, personal taste," he said hurriedly.

Esmée came along behind them.

"Or that it's tasteless, perhaps, Guy?" she asked lightly.

"Not at all, Esmée," he said smoothly.

"What do you think on the whole?" asked Esmée. "Have you seen the other rooms?"

"Not yet, Mama, but the house looks wonderful."

"Almost time for lunch. Do you think we shall have many visitors?" asked Esmée.

"Should do, Mama. They'll all want to see the house," said her daughter cynically.

"We'll see," said Esmée, who was not so sure. "We'll see."

The Johnstone family turned up that afternoon: Sir Matthew, Lady Moira and their daughter, Fiddy. They appreciated the work and Sir Matthew bought a painting.

"Must support our local artist," he said patronisingly.

Esmée served tea for them in the garden and Madeline and her friends joined them, making witty small talk. The event livened up when Esmée's artist friends came, as they all admired each other's work and were fulsome in their praise. The prognostications about the visitors were inaccurate and they failed to materialise.

"They'll get used to it. They'll come next time," Esmée consoled herself.

Her friends remained through the evening, and Madeline's group were staying the night and motoring back to London the next day. All was not lost. Esmée had confidence and faith in her work. The villagers were grudgingly accepting her permanently in their midst; approval of her work could wait.

SEPTEMBER 1911

They had gathered yet again, with good reason. An excellent harvest, Seth's birthday, belated celebrations of Alice's first birthday and the completion of the Orchard Cottage extension. Louise was beside herself with delight at the extra space; the scullery was obsolete, except as a store room and large cupboard. A small passage led from the living room to the new kitchen. It was the full length of the living room and almost as wide. At one end, facing the front garden, was the huge window Louise had wanted. Her sink was placed so that she could look out on her garden and up the lane; if she glanced upwards, she could see the hill. There was a small window in the long side wall and, owing to the lie of the orchard, ground level was not much below it. The chickens could look in at Louise and when she had first seen this, she had been convulsed with laughter. They had seen themselves in the dark reflection of the window and been pecking at the glass; their beady-eyed look of bewilderment had caused the hilarity. Best of all, Will had built a privy, with a door directly from the kitchen. No more going outside in all weathers! Upstairs, a door to the right at the top of the stairs led to the new room. It was light and airy with three large windows as planned; one looked onto the stretch of orchard at the back of the cottage, one at the side and one was directly above the large kitchen window below. Will had made a new table and chairs, and a dresser for the kitchen. It was convenient for providing for a large family. Their family had recently grown again, as Victoria had been invited to live with them. She had the small front room, which had been Louise and

Will's, because she had begun to have difficulty managing the stairs.

"Happy birthday, little mite," said Victoria to Alice, who could stand and take a step or two.

"Happy birthday, Seth."

Louise gave him a small gift; their gift to Alice had been a push-along truck with wheels and filled with bricks – all made by Will. They were all in good spirits and Louise was enjoying showing them the new rooms. Young Louise was home and had brought her young man with her.

"Gordon will be comfortable in with Bill, won't he?" her mother had whispered.

"Yes, Ma." Louise had laughed.

The older Louise had invited Rebecca, Flora's sister-in-law, and her husband and family. Rebecca had been brave, entering into village life again with energy and courage.

"Hello, Rebecca, hello Robert," said Louise. "Can you find your way in?"

"Hello, Becky," said Flora. "Have a sandwich."

Rebecca greeted Flora and Seth, and made a fuss of Alice.

"She's getting so big," she commented. Her own children all looked well and happy. They were growing fast too.

The company had more room to mingle, but it still seemed crowded. Members of the family and neighbours popped in and went off again. Flora was moving about the rooms, seeing if anyone needed more tea or cider; there were enough people to keep an eye on Alice for her. Charles and Beatrice had arrived earlier and, although they were not acting like young lovers, they seemed quite friendly towards each other. Flora went to collect cups and saucers from the corner of the living room and overheard voices coming from behind the closed door of the old scullery, which already contained a store of apples and plums. She opened the door slowly to see who it was and at first could not see anything; her mother had blacked out the window and door glass to stop light getting to the fruit.

"Well, what are you going to do about it?" hissed a female voice.

"There's nothing I can do. It's all over; has been for a long time," came the answer.

"I'll tell your wife... your family."

"Hurt her and I'll, I'll..." the male voice hesitated.

"You'll what?" The female voice was harsh. "You said you loved me," she continued.

"I thought I did, but that was then."

"I took so many risks, especially once I was married."

Flora knew she should close the door and go away, but her instincts kept her there, listening.

"What's all this?" asked Charles jovially.

He had come across Flora at the door, not realising there was anyone in the old scullery. He pushed the door open. Limited light from the living room fell into the small room. Beatrice and Robert stood transfixed, mouths agape.

"Charles, I think we should leave them," said Flora.

"No, I think we should stay," said Charles adamantly.

"Well, go in and close the door. All these people..."

Both Flora and Charles entered the scullery and closed the door behind them.

"Well?" asked Charles.

Beatrice looked down and reddened.

"It's nothing, Charles," she said quietly.

"We had an affair," stated Robert boldly. "It was before you married..."

Before he could continue, Charles raised his fist and hit him. Robert lay on the floor, injured, blood coming from his mouth.

"If you want the truth, it carried on after you were married – but only because she wanted it to!" he shouted.

"Keep your voice down," said Flora. "The visitors..."

"You bastard," said Charles between clenched teeth, pulling Robert up by the collar, ready to punch him again.

"Don't worry, Charles," said Beatrice triumphantly, "I punished him! I wrote the note telling Ellie he attacked Helen Marshall."

Charles let go of Robert and Robert fell back to the floor. All three, Charles, Robert and Flora were frozen, stricken and horrified.

"You did what?" whispered Charles, incredulous.

"Oh God," said Flora in supplication.

Robert continued staring at Beatrice, the consequences of what she had done to him and his family flashing through his mind.

Then, before anyone could stop him, he was up and lunging at her. Charles and Flora moved to stop him before he had done any harm, but Beatrice still had not done. She turned on Flora in a frenzy. "You think your Seth is so perfect. Ask him about that girl his Arthur is courting; I've seen him with her. I've seen them together!" Her voice had gradually risen until she was screaming at Flora.

Without thinking, Flora reacted and slapped her hard across the cheek; the woman was hysterical.

Louise opened the door and asked, "Is everything all right? What's going on?"

"It's all right, Ma, we'll sort it out," said Charles.

When Louise turned away, closing the door, puzzled, Flora turned to Charles.

"Take her home, lad, take her away. Right away."

Robert stood up, straightening his clothes, ruffled in the fracas.

"Are you all right, Rob?" asked Flora, concerned.

"Yes. Don't say anything to Becky about all this, will you?"

"No."

"One day," he said, sadly going to the door, "one day, I'll tell her. Not yet."

Charles took Beatrice out through the scullery door.

Flora took a deep breath, tidied her frock, patted her hair and went out into the living room to join her parents' guests. Seth found her and whispered urgently, "Where have you been? I've been looking for you."

"Don't ask me now, Seth. I'll tell you later," she said.

She moved between the noisy groups of people who were happily celebrating the Henty family's good fortune. Flora looked at them all, laughing and conversing. *Dear Lord,* she thought. *If only they knew; if only they knew.*

+ + +

Charles took Beatrice to live in Salisbury; he found work as a farm manager and they lived in a tied cottage. Louise and Will had to be told why, because the loss of Charles to Will's farm was disastrous. The accusation Beatrice had made against Seth had been purely malicious, because she was consumed with jealousy against Charles's family.

Robert, who had changed, became more morose and introverted. He had already been proved innocent, yet his dilemma was that to produce the final incontrovertible evidence would mean introducing Beatrice as a witness to admit what she had done, thus hurting more people. Almost certainly, in her defence, she would also have made public her affair with Robert, thus exacerbating his wife's pain further. So he had to accept the situation. Flora tried not to be bitter, but she missed Charles. Worst of all, it was a secret she had to keep from Seth. His family, but especially his sister, Rebecca, had been too hurt already to reveal the extent of Beatrice's culpability. Why did people hurt each other? Flora carried on with her busy life and tried to comfort her parents, who for diverse reasons sorely missed their eldest son, Charles.

DECEMBER 1911

"I can't believe it's Christmas again already," said Victoria Bartrup. "It doesn't seem long since we last made the puddings and cakes."

"I know, Mother," said Louise. "It comes around quicker every year."

They were looking after Alice while Flora went to see Ellie.

"Look at that little one toddling about," said Victoria fondly. "Doesn't she look the picture?"

"Charles and Beatrice are coming for Christmas," said Louise casually. "They're only staying one night."

"Where will Louise and Gordon stay?" enquired Victoria.

"Flora says she has room for them; it'll be much nearer than coming all that way from Bath."

"Seems so long since we saw them. It was odd how they moved away suddenly like that. Did you ever find out why, dear?"

"No, Mother. I think Charles thought her mother had too much say in what went on."

Victoria had Alice on her lap beside the fire when Flora came back.

"Hello, my little lovely," she crooned as the toddler ran unsteadily towards her. "Hello, Ma. Hello, Gran."

"Did you sort out your business with Ellie, dear?" asked her mother innocently.

"Yes Ma – and you might as well know, 'cos I know you're bursting. Seth knows already – yes, I am having another baby!"

"Oh how wonderful, Flora," said her grandma.

"What a lovely present to us all for Christmas!"

"Well, not exactly for Christmas, Gran." Flora laughed. "More like early next July."

"That's wonderful, dear," said Louise. "Can we tell everyone when they come?"

"I suppose so – no reason why not."

"You are looking after yourself, aren't you?" queried her mother.

"Of course."

"Well, I know you. Never a thought for yourself," she chided.

"A little brother for you, Alice," said Gran, hugging the small girl.

"That's what Seth said," remarked Flora. "I don't mind as long as it's all right." Flora sat in the other chair, thinking. *Four generations,* she mused. *Four generations of women in our family. Gran, Ma, me and Alice. Makes you feel good. Makes you feel hope for the future.*

Chapter Five

JANUARY 1912 – MAY 1914

Seth came in cold and hungry. He shouted upstairs when he could find no one about.

"Where are you, Flora?"

"Shhh, I've only just got her off to sleep." Flora came down the stairs to the scullery. "What are you doing home?" she asked accusingly.

"Come to tell you that Peggy's had a little boy. This morning at five o'clock!"

"That's wonderful. Who told you?"

"David, of course. He came up to Drakes Farm. Peggy's ma is with her. David will go home early. Thought I'd come and have a cup of tea and tell you."

"Do you know what he weighed?"

"No, Peggy will tell you all that."

"Are you going to see Tom today?" she asked, changing the subject.

"No, he's not too busy at the moment. With all the snow, people haven't been able to get out and the horses don't need to be reshod so often," he explained.

"Alice has been a pest this morning," said her fond mother. "I caught her trying to go up the first few stairs!"

"I hope you haven't been lifting her about; she's a ton weight," he said, concerned.

Flora was almost four months pregnant and was taking care not to carry Alice about more than was necessary. Alice was a dear little girl, always daydreaming and amenable. She had given them no cause for concern and her large blue eyes gazed out contentedly upon the world.

"John was around again," she informed him.

"Damned nuisance. It's a shame your Charles has moved away; he'd be the one to deal with him again. I'll punch his nose for him!"

When Charles's friend had professed his love for Flora, Seth had been so angry they decided that Charles should speak to John. Charles was equally annoyed, but, as Flora was his sister and not his wife, he could deal with it more effectively. John had seemed to realise that he could not maintain any kind of relationship with Flora and had left her alone for some months. Recently he had taken to calling round again, always when Seth was absent, and, as Flora was expecting a baby, nobody wanted her to be unduly upset or worried.

"I feel so sorry for the man," said Flora.

"No need for that! He's off his head," said Seth forcefully.

"Off his head for taking a fancy to me?" she teased.

"You know what I mean. It isn't normal. Can't take no for an answer."

"He says he's concerned about me, being pregnant and all, and wants to keep an eye on me."

"I'll keep an eye on him if he's not careful," said Seth, becoming angry.

"Don't worry, he's harmless enough," Flora assured her husband.

"If it wasn't so mucky out, I'd take Alice in her pram and go and see Peggy and the new baby," continued Flora. "I've knitted a lovely suit for him."

"Best not to go out today, love. I'll go with you on Saturday; only two days' time."

"Only a week and a bit until Arthur's wedding," she observed.

She agreed to wait until Seth could accompany them to David and Peggy's because of the poor weather conditions.

"Don't open the door if that simpleton comes back," he told her. "If he comes in here again, I'll not be responsible for my actions!"

Seth returned to work and Flora made herself busy around the house. She was looking forward to the good weather coming, for she wanted her spring cleaning out of the way early this year. She hummed as she dusted her ornaments in the living room. As she bent towards the windowsill, she suddenly felt a stirring in her womb. It was only like a butterfly wing touching her face, but she was sure. *I wonder who you are,* she thought. *Are you a boy like Seth or another pest like Alice?* She smiled and continued with her work, content to potter and to wait.

SPRING 1912

Esmée was in the village stores. She had a large order and Catherine was collecting the items with her guidance. Always willing to hear snippets of news, she was pumping Esmée.

"You've a big party staying then?" she asked.

"Not exactly," said Esmée, preoccupied with her list.

"Your daughter coming down?" she persisted.

"Perhaps."

"You'll want the same order next week?"

"I'm not sure."

Esmée was giving nothing away. She was not being deliberately secretive; she had much on her mind! Her eldest child was returning home; her son, Giles, who had been in India, was returning for the first time since his father's funeral. She had been young when he was born and he was the apple of her eye. Her depression had, in part, been caused by his departure shortly after her husband died.

He was a major in the army and his tour of duty had run on. He had made his life in India for the duration and chosen to stay rather than take the option of returning to England at intervals. She was glad that she had rejuvenated the house and recovered her spirits, for his return.

Madeline arrived in a flurry of suitcases and trunks. She had been driven down by a young man, who stayed the night. Esmée employed a local man to do the garden and jobs around the house, and he carried the luggage inside. Madeline had always been in competition with Giles, who was two years older. She had been spoilt by their father, but endeavoured to achieve a happy relationship with her mother.

He was arriving on Monday, after spending the weekend in London. Esmée and Madeline were up early, supervising the final preparation of Giles's room. Esmée was nervous and excited. She could not sit still long enough to eat breakfast, far less relax.

He had arrived. He had come by taxi cab from Bristol. She stood at the door and watched as he alighted from the vehicle. He was not wearing uniform, but was in mufti. He turned and smiled.

"Mother."

"Dearest boy! How are you? Welcome home." She kissed him.

Madeline greeted him with sibling banter. "About time! You've escaped the parent long enough!"

She, too, kissed him. His luggage had been deposited on the gravel on the drive and he paid the driver, who scrunched away out of sight.

"You're looking well, dear," said his mother as she slipped her arm through his while they walked inside.

Giles was tall and fair haired. He had a strong square jaw and far-seeing deep-set blue eyes. He moved with the easy grace of an athlete, and while he was professional in his attitude to the army, his approach to life was relaxed.

Esmée rang the bell for tea and they sat in the morning room that looked over the garden.

"The old place is looking very chipper," he observed.

She told him about the work she had commissioned on the house and what had been completed. They asked him about his journey, both from London to Abbots Ford and from India to England. They looked at him as he spoke, unable to believe that he was really there; taking in his features again, and mannerisms, enjoying his persona. He was different. He was five years older, now thirty. But it was more than that. His experiences without them, far away in another country, another way of life, had developed facets of him that they did not know.

He ran his hands over his eyes.

"Good heavens, is that the time?" exclaimed Esmée. "Dear boy, do go to your room. Have a rest and a bath. You must be spent."

"I will if you don't mind. Just get the feel of the place before dinner."

He went upstairs and Madeline left to organise more tea. Esmée sat a while longer, the anticipation and apprehension evaporated. He was home.

She could not quite believe it, it had been so long. It was like seeing him as a stranger, because he was altered, older, a mature man. He was like his father at the same age; naturally she could detect echoes of her own family also, in his face and manner. It was strange how understated we are, she thought. She had wanted to take him in her arms and never release him, to devour him. He was hers and yet he was not, any longer. She no longer had proprietary rights over him or his time. She remembered him as a little boy, clinging, thin and needful of her. It was a relationship unlike any other. One's own child, grown to adulthood, so dear and known and loved, yet stranger to one than someone one did not know at all: stranger because of the familiarity, the assumption that one did know them. All the while, she struggled to allow them freedom, to let them go; while at the same time, they equally struggled to be free and in so doing, tied themselves ever more tightly to her, to the family, from which they yearned release. She thought about her own parents and realised that her love for her husband had given her the key to freedom from them; had allowed her to venture out into life. It would change when her children found partners. Madeline returned with the tea tray herself.

"They're busy preparing a special dinner, Mama," she explained.

Esmée looked at her daughter. Would that she could locate the key to her freedom too.

MAY 1912

It was Gordon's first visit to Orchard Cottage, or even Abbots Ford. He and Louise were staying the night, but Gordon was being put up at Aunt Elsie's. Will made an effort to be in on time to wash and change. He and Bill would have to return for evening milking, but he would be there to meet Louise's boyfriend when he arrived.

Gordon and Louise were good friends. They had many interests in common, but most of all, their jobs. Gordon was a tailor, trained to make men's clothes. When he had had the opportunity of working in a fashion house, he had taken it, and now he had a senior position.

Louise maintained that he was a friend and not a boyfriend. She did not want to tie herself down with complications in her life, because she was enjoying it just the way it was. She and Gordon were inseparable and Gordon told her that he loved her all the time, but she only laughed. So he accepted the status quo and gradually became indispensable to her, as he knew he would.

Although his family lived in Bath, he had never ventured out in this direction before.

"It's lovely countryside," he said as the bus travelled towards Abbots Ford. He had never felt the need to travel far afield in any direction. Bath held everything he required from life. When the bus set them down and rumbled away, he looked around him. "Small, isn't it?" he remarked.

Louise laughed. "What did you expect? I described it to you!"

They walked the short distance towards Church Lane and down to Orchard Cottage.

"Ma! Hello, Ma, we're here!" she called.

Her mother had been at the far end of the old scullery and came out not having heard them.

"Hello, dear," she said delightedly when she saw Louise. "And this must be Gordon. Pleased to meet you."

The kettle was already boiling and Louise made them all tea. Will came in from the orchard and kissed his daughter.

"How are you, my dear?" he asked. He turned to Gordon, "I've heard all about you!"

"Not all bad, I trust, Mr Henty?" responded Gordon.

"Flora and Seth will be along later for tea," Louise explained.

Gordon had obviously become familiar with the names, for he nodded.

"So are you both still busy, at work I mean?" asked Louise.

She always enjoyed hearing her daughter's stories from the workroom and salon. She had been to the workrooms and met some of the girls Louise had spoken about. Bill popped in to meet Gordon and joined them for a cup of tea before going out again.

"Perhaps you'd like to go up the lane to meet Elsie," suggested Louise. "Louise will take you and you can leave your bag there for later on."

While they were gone, Flora, Seth and Alice arrived.

"He seems ever such a nice man," her mother told them, while Will played with Alice.

He had made a monkey between parallel sticks, which somersaulted when the sticks were pressed. He seemed as entertained by the toy as the child was. Flora was becoming large now and the walk had tired her. Her mother had sent her up for a rest on her own bed when Louise and Gordon came back again. Louise went in to say hello. She tiptoed in, in case her sister was asleep.

"Hello." She grinned. "You got twins in there this time?" she teased. She pulled a chair over and sat near the bed. "How are you?"

"I'm fine," said Flora, looking pale. "How are you?"

"Never better. Ma and Pa seem to like Gordon."

"Yes, I'm sorry to be up here. I'll be down in a minute."

"Don't worry. Take your time," advised Louise. "Alice has grown, hasn't she?" she added.

"Yes, more of a pickle than ever!"

Louise went downstairs and, leaving Flora to rest, helped her mother to organise supper. By the time it was prepared, Flora was downstairs.

"This is my elder sister, Flora," Louise introduced her to Gordon.

He smiled into Flora's eyes and she liked him at once. It was important to Louise what her family thought of him, because even though she insisted that he was not her beau, he was more than an ordinary friend, apart from the fact that he was male. Alice was taken with Gordon. She could not take her eyes from him all through supper.

"Man," she kept repeating, pointing a small chubby finger at him.

They all laughed, including Gordon.

"Pest," said Flora, pointing at Alice.

That made them all laugh again and Alice joined in, not knowing why. The laughter eased the mild tension that had been in the air and Gordon was easily assimilated into the family group. Her mother, Louise, warmed towards him more and more.

After they had cleared away the meal and Will got the trap out to take Flora, Seth and Alice home, Louise took Gordon for a walk up the hill. It took longer than they meant to, for she was detained at intervals by neighbours asking how she was and she had to introduce them to Gordon. It was beginning to darken by the time they arrived at the crest, but it was a beautiful evening, so it did not matter. They sat on a bank together and, after an interval, Gordon took her hand. Louise had not allowed their relationship to include any kind of physical contact and she was taken by surprise. She turned to look at him.

"Louise," he said.

"Gordon, you know what I..."

He put a finger to her lips. "You wouldn't have let me come to Abbots Ford with you if you didn't love me," he stated.

She shook her head and started to speak again, but he interrupted.

"You wouldn't have brought me up the hill if you didn't love me," he added. "I've heard you speak of it often enough!"

"But I..." said Louise.

"I love you, very much indeed," Gordon told her, and, delicately at first, kissed her lips. They drew apart and searched each other's eyes. Then he kissed her again, more firmly, exploring her mouth with his own.

"Oh Gordon," she breathed.

"It was right to get to know one another first," he admitted, "but oh how I've waited for this." He kissed her again.

They held hands on the way back and she left him at her Aunt Elsie's cottage.

"See you in the morning," he told her softly.

"In the morning," she repeated, and went down to Orchard Cottage like someone in a dream.

JULY 1912

Flora could not make up her mind. The weather was perfect, which was lucky for the vicarage party. Should she go or not? It was within a fortnight of when her baby was due and, if she went, some people might frown on the idea. They would think she ought to be at home resting instead of gallivanting around the village. That was enough to make her decide. She would go. There was no reason why not, for she felt as fit as a flea. Alice would like the event and they would see her parents and many friends; yes, she would go.

She put Alice into her pram, wearing a new frock she had made; because she had grown so fast, hardly anything fitted her any more. The child looked at the passing scene, taking in every detail. Flora spoke to her as they walked along the lanes, pointing out birds or rabbits which she might like to see. They went straight to Orchard Cottage, where her mother scolded her for walking so far in the heat of the day.

"Put your feet up here for a while," she instructed.

The cottage was cool and dark and Flora gratefully did as she was bid. Louise took charge of the lively toddler, taking her out into the orchard to see the chickens.

"Tickens!" repeated the child earnestly when her grandmother told her what they were.

"Yes, chickens," said Louise. She took great delight in her small granddaughter, who reminded her more of her own Louise than Flora. It was a strange trick of family resemblance, that, she thought.

They strolled slowly around to the vicarage.

"Are you still carrying?" chortled one of Flora's friends. "Thought you'd have had it by now."

Flora grinned ruefully. She had heard that comment over and over again from her family for the last month.

"Everyone knows it takes nine months," she whispered to her mother. "Why do they think I should have my baby quicker than anyone else?"

"Take it in good part, dear," said Louise. "Some of them are just sympathising."

They walked around the tables and stalls, and Alice toddled with them, falling over on the grass and discovering a daisy. Flora made her a daisy chain, which she proudly wore, allowing no one to touch it. While others sat on the grass to rest, Louise went to find a chair for Flora. They drank barley water and gossiped contentedly in the sunshine. A shadow fell over Flora, making her turn to see who stood there.

"Hello," said John.

"Oh hello, John," replied Flora. "Fancy seeing you here! I'd thought you'd be taking some nice girl out to Weston on a day like this."

"I already have a nice girl," he told her.

"That's nice, John, what's her name?" asked Louise.

"Flora," he said, looking at Flora, staring at her.

People shifted uncomfortably and one or two mothers got up and took their children with them.

"Not this Flora!" Louise laughed. "She's already spoken for!"

"But she's mine, really," he insisted.

Louise stood up. "Come on now, John. You can't say these things." Louise knew John because of his long friendship with Charles. She had had a hint of what had been happening, but was unaware how to deal with this situation.

"I think it's time to go home, Alice," said Flora, getting up from her chair.

"You're so beautiful, Flora," he said. "Especially now that you're nearly having our child."

Flora had been willing to humour him until now, but that was too much.

"Go away!" she shouted. "Leave me alone."

People stared and Louise went to fetch Reverend Orrins. She explained briefly and he walked quickly towards John.

"Come along now, John. Come into the vicarage where it is nice and cool," he suggested.

"No, I can't leave Flora; she needs me," he told him.

"Flora's mother is here to look after her; come with me," he repeated. Michael Orrins decided to take John's arm, just in time.

John made a grab for Flora, but did not reach her. Flora turned to move away, stumbled and fell heavily onto the ground. There was a horrified silence before people were suddenly everywhere. They materialised beside John and led him into the vicarage study, to be detained there until Dr Tanner could be called. They gravitated towards Flora, gently helping her to a sitting position. Louise held Alice out of the way, comforting her, for she had seen her mother fall and sensed that all was not well.

"Are you all right, Flora?"

Ellie pushed her way through the crowd. She had only just left the group before John had appeared on the scene and someone had alerted her to what had taken place.

Flora was disorientated. It had all happened so swiftly. The heat, the shock and the crowd made her momentarily confused. She looked for Alice, calling her name, and was reassured when her mother's voice was telling her that Alice was with her. Suddenly, everything clarified into stark relief as the pain gripped her. She bent over, then swung back, writhing on the ground.

"Right. Stand back everyone," Ellie commanded. "It's all right, Flora. Everything will be all right."

She consulted with Louise, who, taking two sensible friends with her, went back to Orchard Cottage with Alice. When the pain had eased, Ellie asked Flora if she could stand up. They helped her to her feet.

"Can you walk, dear?"

Flora tried a few steps and found that she could.

"Never mind about that," said a booming voice.

Ellie's husband, Tom, strode through the crowd and gently picked up Flora and carried her to her mother's home.

"Put her on my bed, Tom, thank you ever so much," said Louise, showing him upstairs to her room.

Flora smiled wanly at him.

"Sorry I'm so much weight," she told him.

"Light as a feather. If you were all the weight I ever had to lift I'd be a happy man," he said.

Another pain gripped Flora and she turned on her side, the better to cope. Ellie, who had followed them round to the cottage, took Louise out of the room.

"I think she's started. Will it be acceptable to use this room?"

When Louise concurred, Ellie gave instructions and Louise went to collect the necessary items. Alice was being entertained by friends downstairs and was unaware of the drama around her. Tom had offered to fetch Seth from Drakes Farm and left at once. Word had travelled of what had taken place and neighbours called at intervals asking if they could be of help. They went on their way reassured that Flora was in capable hands and that everything was under control.

"It won't be long now," said Ellie at teatime. "The second is usually quicker."

Seth arrived, but nobody thought it right to inform him yet of the events that had led to his wife's labour. Time enough for that. He paced up and down like a lion, waiting. He relaxed for a time with Alice, before Louise put her to bed in the small front room where Victoria slept.

Flora's little girl was born late that evening, to the delight and relief of Seth, her family and the village, when they learnt of it. Louise and Will crept in to see her and the baby in the early hours of the following morning.

"Hello dearest girl," whispered Louise. "All over."

"Hello Ma, Pa," said Flora weakly.

They admired the new arrival.

"What do you think you'll call her?" asked Will.

"Dorothy. Her name is Dorothy," said Flora, lying back on the pillows contentedly.

SEPTEMBER 1912

Charles had come to Bristol on business and decided that he could not miss the opportunity to see his family. He had not met the newest member, but had heard about the near disaster leading to her arrival. He had been deeply saddened to know how disturbed his friend had become, to the extent of his having to be hospitalised for his own and others' protection.

When Seth had been acquainted with the facts, his anger had been such that, for a short time, they feared for his reason. He had spent an entire afternoon chopping wood, speaking to no one, until he was exhausted.

Charles was staying the night and having an evening with most of the family. Flora had come along on her own to have supper with them.

"Shame Louise can't be here," said Will. "Then we really would be a family again!"

"It hasn't changed," said Charles. "Somehow I'd expected that it would."

"That's what Louise always says. It's because you change when you go away," said his mother.

"How's your job, son?" asked Will.

"I'm enjoying it. It's a big farm. We've got six regular hands and bring others in when we need them."

"How is Beatrice?" asked Flora.

"She seems better now we're not near her parents," said Charles. "It was like a fresh start for her, going to Salisbury."

"That's good news, son. We want you to be happy."

"I went to see John while I was in Bristol. He didn't know me," Charles told them sadly. "The doctor said he was already ill and became fixated on Flora. It was a gradual process, until he truly thought he was her husband."

"Very sad case," said Will, shaking his head.

"It's his family I feel sorry for," said Louise.

"I'm going to see them tomorrow before I go and see Seth, Alice and Dorothy," said Charles.

They were eating silently and mulling over what might have happened when Bill came in. He had been delayed, finishing a job at the farm.

"Hello, Charles," he said, pleased to see his brother.

Charles stood up to shake his hand.

"How are you?"

"I'm well. Sorry I'm late, Ma. I'll get washed. Back in a minute."

"He's grown!" commented Charles. "He's a man now, not a boy any longer!"

"If you could see the girls he's taking out, you'd know the truth of that!" His father laughed.

Bill had grown into a personable young man. He was agreeable and cheerful. He had grown tall and had a round, open face. His hair was light brown and his gently mocking eyes were blue.

"Is it true about you?" Charles asked him.

"Is what true?"

"About you and the local girls?"

"Whatever they're saying – no." He laughed.

Victoria sat quietly at the end of the table, enjoying the repartee.

"How have you been, Gran?" asked Charles.

"Can't complain. It's been easier since I came here," she told him.

He could see that she was not herself. She had not completely recovered from her husband's death, but she had regained her enjoyment of life. Now, because he had not seen her for a time, Charles could see how frail she had become. While it saddened him, he accepted it as being part of the rotation of life and living. He would say nothing to his mother. She had probably noticed in any case. He felt sentimental, being back with them. They were so familiar and dear to him. His life with Beatrice was not smooth, though it had its compensations. He chewed his food, looking at each of them in turn. Mother had not changed, calm, reliable, sensible as ever. He regretted not working with his father now. Will had not changed, bluff, competitive. Flora, with two babies, yet she was the same. Bill, all grown up.

"It's good to be here," he told them.

Louise looked shrewdly at him. "It's good to have you here. Pity Beatrice isn't with you, but we'll settle for you," she told him.

She worried about him, but as there was nothing she could do; she trusted that his upbringing would always see him through his problems. Beatrice was an intractable problem, but he must love her or he would not put up with her, Louise reasoned.

When they had finished their meal and had sat talking and reminiscing, Charles walked Flora home.

"I'm so sorry about John, and everything," said Charles.

"So am I. Sorry for him, I mean. He seemed a nice lad."

"He was."

They walked in silence for a while.

"He always liked you, you know," Charles told her. "Said you were the ideal woman."

Flora was unaccountably sad.

"Don't dwell on it, Flo. It isn't your fault. Who knows about the workings of the human mind?"

"Seth was just angry. I couldn't make him see that it was sad," she confided.

"He probably envisaged what could have happened. You could have been hurt; you could have lost the baby," said Charles.

"I know," admitted Flora. "He's so headstrong at times, though."

"Perfect foil for you, sis. Always thinking everything through!"

They had reached Plumtree Cottage. Charles went in long enough to say hello to Seth, and began the walk back to Abbots Ford. Did he miss living here, among his family and friends, he mused. Yes, he did. On the other hand, he would not change his life with Beatrice for anything.

NOVEMBER 1912

The day was bitterly cold and snow threatened the sky. The landscape looked stark and bare as the cortège passed along the main street in Abbots Ford. Victoria Bartrup was going on her last journey and her family had gathered to pay tribute. Louise and her sisters, Elsie, Catherine and Ann were the only ones left, as James and Stephen were long gone. They were all dressed in black, walking close together. Their husbands and children followed at a distance. Reverend Orrins was sincerely sad. Victoria and Joseph had been the kind of people whom he regarded as the 'backbone of England' – an England that, he considered, was passing away into history. They all remained dry-eyed and controlled, the way she would have wanted.

The gathering was at Elsie's cottage. They walked up the lane past Orchard Cottage and went into action, organising the food for everyone. When everything was done and people had said what they always say on those occasions, the four sisters could be found in Elsie's bedroom, weeping together for their mother.

"She would tell us to stop crying and get on with it," said Elsie, sniffing.

"She always did," reminded Catherine.

"How will we manage without her?" wept Ann.

"We will," said Louise. "Because we're just like her."

"She hasn't really gone while you're around, Louise," said Elsie.

They smiled at each other through their tears. "Not while any of us is here!" they agreed.

DECEMBER 1912

Louise was home for Christmas. Her parents were looking forward to having her back for a few days. Bill dashed in looking for hot water to have a bath.

"Is there enough, Ma?" he called as he rushed about, getting ready. "Can I clean my shoes in here?"

"No, Bill. Of course not," said Louise impatiently.

"It's cold in the kitchen," he moaned.

"It isn't; it's just nice and warm in here!" she told him.

"The scullery used to be cold, but the kitchen benefits from the range on the other side of the wall."

"Well I'm cold," he repeated.

"No blood, this generation," muttered his mother.

"What time does Louise arrive?" he asked.

"Six o'clock bus," said Louise, preoccupied with her baking.

He went into the kitchen to have his bath, putting the screen around. Louise and her father arrived in shortly afterwards and she greeted her mother delightedly.

"What's that dreadful noise, Ma?" asked Louise.

"Bill's having his bath." Her mother smiled, raising her eyes to the heavens.

Louise went through and shook the screen around him while he bathed.

"Hey, stop it, who's that?" he shouted in alarm, afraid that he was going to be exposed as naked as the day he was born.

"It's me!" Louise shouted.

"Hello, Louise. I'll be there in a minute," he assured her.

Louise and Will were happy with two of their offspring at the table that night. Louise was still emotional about her mother's passing and Will was glad that their younger daughter had managed to come home, because it cheered her so.

The next day was Christmas Eve. They were all looking forward to the ritual of preparation and going to church. Louise hugged herself in pleasure that two of her children were under her roof that night.

+ + +

Flora, Seth, Alice and Dorothy had just arrived. Louise was astounded at the change in the children since she had last seen them only a month before. Little Dorothy was taking in her surroundings and Alice knew even more words than before.

Seth kissed Louise, making a rude remark about her new hairstyle.

"Take no notice of him. He knows nothing about style," teased Flora.

They were having a cup of tea when there came a knock at the door.

"I'll go, Ma," said Louise and, opening the living room door, stood in the minute hall to open the front door. Neither was locked, but merely closed against the cold.

"Gordon!" Louise was shocked to see him standing there.

Everyone laughed and her mother said, "Bring him in, out of the cold!"

Louise was suspicious. "You're not surprised, are you?" she accused. "Did you know he was coming?"

"I'm afraid so," admitted her mother.

"I had to ask if I could come!" he reasoned.

She was thrilled to see him; it was exciting to have him at her home at Christmas.

"You'll be able to come to the carol service," she told him.

Later they sat beside the fire in the living room. Her parents had gone up the lane to Elsie's for an hour. Her aunts would be there also; it was the first Christmas without their mother.

"Your family are so welcoming," Gordon told her.

She smiled happily, the firelight making her face glow.

"I'm not just here for Christmas," said Gordon.

Louise looked at him, surprised. "What do you mean?"

He kissed her tenderly and took a small box from his jacket pocket.

"Louise, I'm here to ask you to marry me."

She was taken aback.

"Say something." He laughed.

"Oh, Gordon," she moaned.

"What's wrong?" he asked, worried.

"You know how I feel about marriage…"

"But you love me. I love you…" he pleaded.

"It'll spoil it."

"No, it won't. Your parents, your sister, people in my family have happy marriages!"

"But my work, I'd have to give that up!"

"No, you wouldn't," he insisted.

"What if there were children? I would then!"

Gordon was devastated. He had been sure that she would agree. They had been friends for close to two years and their relationship had moved on after their kisses on the walk up the hill when Gordon had first visited Abbots Ford.

"I want to marry you, even if it means not having children. We'll open our own shop, or something. Anything, to be with you," he told her.

"Gordon, I'm sorry…"

"At least wear my ring…" he begged.

"A ring is a promise; I can't make that promise," she said sadly.

"Put it on your right hand. Think of it as an early Christmas present – a half promise. Don't reject me completely, please."

"All right. Half a promise. If I get married, it will be to you. But I'm not," she reiterated.

Gordon was sad. He had hoped that it was the right time. He knew that Louise did not want to follow the usual pattern of marriage and children, followed by a lifetime of drudgery. He knew that she was a talented designer who had a future and he was willing to accept all that if he could marry her. He had been patient so far; he would wait. He slipped the ring onto the third finger of her right hand.

"A half promise," he whispered as he kissed her.

"A half promise," she agreed.

JANUARY 1913

Flora and Seth laughed, hardly able to believe it.

"We were going to see Peggy and David's new baby this time last year and here we are again!" said Seth.

"They didn't mean to have another one so soon," Flora reminded him.

"Are you ready, Alice?" her father asked.

"Yes, Daddy. Go to see new baby now."

They arrived at David and Peggy's little house just in time to see the new baby before he was put in his cot after his bath and morning feed. They had called him John and he was the image of his father. Albert was not quite one and Charlotte was almost three and a half, so Peggy had her hands full. Flora teased her often about the chat they had had about David 'bothering' her.

Charlotte and Alice played happily together and even little Dorothy joined in.

Seth and David stood laughing in the scullery, while the girls looked through a bag of baby clothes that Flora had brought.

"Really, Albert's things will be enough for John; you might be able to use these yourself one day!"

"Not too soon, I hope." Flora laughed. "Mind you, when I held John just now, I felt broody."

"What! When Dorothy is only six months old? I won't let you cuddle John again," she teased.

They stayed for a cup of tea and prepared for the walk home.

"Thank you for the lovely gift; it's a beautiful pram coat," said Peggy, kissing Flora.

On the way back, Seth talked about his brother.

"David looks really happy. I never saw him as a family man before they had the children, you know."

"He's good with babies," agreed Flora.

As they approached their cottage, they saw that someone was waiting for them. Seth recognised him at once, but Flora was not sure who it was.

"It's John's brother, Samuel," Seth told her.

"Hello, Sam," said Seth as they reached him. He looked ill and did not look at Flora.

"Can I talk to you on your own?" he whispered to Seth.

"Course! We'll get the little 'uns indoors. Come in, have some tea."

He refused the tea, but waited patiently while they organised the children. Seth took him into the living room and, a few minutes later, came back to the scullery alone. He looked shocked.

"Where's Samuel?" asked Flora.

"He wanted to go out the front doorway," Seth told her.

Flora raised her eyebrows in surprise.

"Sit down, Flo," he said.

"What on earth is wrong?"

"Flo, it's John."

"Yes, what about him?"

"He committed suicide two days ago."

Flora felt her skin creep. For a moment she did not know how she felt, but then a deep sadness permeated her being.

"Oh my God," was all she could say.

"He was extremely ill, Flora."

"I know," she answered in a small voice.

"He would not have come out again. You know that, don't you?"

"Mmmm."

She went about the business of making their meal, talking of the children and thinking about John and his family. She knew that she was not to blame, but still there lingered a feeling of regret.

"Such a waste," she said when Seth told her yet again to put it behind her. Flora would not dwell on the tragedy overlong; it was not in her nature. But she knew that it was one of those events in life that would leave scars on everyone who had known John. The waste of life before its allotted time was always a cause for despair.

As she lay in bed that night, she thought about the day. Seeing Peggy and David's John that morning had been wonderful. The news of the other John had made them deeply unhappy. Tears slid down her nose and onto her pillow. *A life for a life,* she thought sadly.

APRIL 1913

Louise was getting ready to go out with Gordon. Her friend Alexandra and her cousin Lizzie were in her room.

"I like your hair that way," said Alex.

"I don't think I've ever seen Louise with her hair the same two days running." Lizzie laughed.

"Where are you two going?" asked Alex.

"Just for a walk around the town," replied Louise.

Gordon had been unusually patient; Louise had still not agreed to a betrothal, and wore his ring on her right hand. She was not a manipulative girl and did not take advantage of Gordon, and he was happy just spending time with her. At twenty-two, she did not feel that she was ready for marriage, and especially not children, whom she believed would ruin her chances of continuing with her career.

She pulled a hat down from her wardrobe shelf and, placing it on her head, stuck a hat pin through it. Her room looked more lived in after three years as she had gradually collected knick-knacks and ornaments. There were two pictures on the wall, given to her by her mother. One was a view of the hill at Abbots Ford, drawn by her Uncle Stephen long ago; the other was a print of a family of children, not unlike Louise and her siblings when younger. She had draped her shawl over the chest of drawers, upon which stood a mirror. Louise had stuck seashells onto the frame and draped her ribbons over it. Her dried flowers, collected from walks with Gordon, lay around the room and in vases. The bed was covered with a quilt her mother had made especially; all in all it looked homely, which was the effect she had wanted to achieve.

"He's late," complained Louise, looking at the clock.

"Not like Gordon," observed Alex.

"Come downstairs and we'll brew some tea while you're waiting," suggested Lizzie.

The girls made their way down endless flights of stairs to the kitchen in the basement, laughing and talking to others they met on the way.

Louise was unaware of the passage of time as they gathered cups and saucers, milk and sugar, gossiping all the while. By the time she looked at the kitchen clock again, half an hour had passed.

"Something's happened to him," said Louise. "I know it has; I can feel it in my bones."

"Don't be silly; he's just been held up, that's all."

Another half an hour passed and Louise began to feel fidgety.

"I think I'll start to walk round to his house," she told the girls.

"I'll come with you; I could do with some air," offered Lizzie.

Alex volunteered to accompany them.

When the two girls had rushed upstairs to collect their hats, the three set off around the crescent where they lived. It was a sunny day, but still had a chill in the air. The trees were in blossom and the gentle breeze blew flowers along the kerbs where they had fallen, following the girls as they walked. Louise had hoped to meet Gordon coming towards them. But they went all the way to his house without seeing him. They knocked at the door and stood waiting expectantly. His sister answered, standing red-eyed and silent.

"Maud?" Louise stepped forward, into the hall. "What is it?" she asked.

"Gordon's... an accident," she said, and began to weep.

His brother joined them.

"There was an accident. As he left here... don't know what happened, but the wheels went over him. It looks bad, Louise."

The blood drained from Louise's face and her mouth was dry. "Where...?"

"The hospital. Cathedral Street."

"I'll have to go," said Louise, turning to leave at once.

"Have a cup of tea first," said his brother.

"No, I want to see him," insisted Louise.

"We'll go with you, of course," said Alex.

The three girls went along the street.

"Mother's there already," called his brother.

The hospital was, unusually for Bath, made in red brick. Ornate cornicing and scrolls decorated the roof edge. The girls went in at the main door, but were directed outside again to another entrance where accident victims arrived.

"Come along now! Is there any need for all this milling about?" barked a voice. A stern nurse, wearing what appeared to be a starched white linen butterfly upon her head, shepherded them to one side of the tiled corridor.

The tiles were brick shape below the black strip to the floor, and square above it. Lurid green and bright terracotta were the colours favoured by the builders of the early Victorian hospital and Louise felt bilious just looking at them.

"We're looking for a friend," stated Lizzie courageously.

"Why do you think your *friend*..." She accented the word 'friend' heavily. "Is here?" she demanded.

"He's had an accident," said Alex.

"Name?" she ordered.

"Gordon. Gordon Chapman."

"Ah yes, the young gentleman." She sounded more human for a moment. "Sit over there on those benches," she told them.

She marched away and disappeared through a huge partition that did not reach the high ceiling. Louise looked around nervously. The other two did not say anything. People were hobbling about with crutches, feet or legs in plaster. Children bawled, the sound echoing around the cold hardness of the walls. A shriek emanated from behind the partitioned wall and they were unable to tell whether it came from male or female, adult or child. Nurses bustled, shoes squeaking, at speed across the marble tiled floor. Another younger, more sympathetic nurse came over to them after a while.

"Mr Chapman is being seen to. I'm afraid you'll have to wait for quite a while," she said.

The girls nodded.

"We'll all wait," said Alex.

The never-ending parade of people in varying degrees of suffering passed in front of their eyes as they spent the afternoon and early evening waiting.

Louise thought about Gordon. What if anything happened, really happened to him? What if there was no Gordon? It did not bear thinking about. It dawned on her that she must love him if she felt like that. Was love knowing that you could not live without somebody? What about that other part, the part she was not very particular about? Did it matter?

"You can see him now." The voice penetrated her thoughts like a knife.

She jumped up involuntarily.

"We'll wait for you, Louise," said Lizzie.

The nurse led her down the corridor and into a huge ward lined with beds, all neatly tucked in. She walked over to him.

"Gordon. It's me, Louise."

He opened his eyes and smiled slowly. His face was bruised and she could see the beginnings of a black eye. His head was bandaged and his arm in a sling. She tried hard not to cry.

"You only had to say if you didn't want to come out with me," she joked weakly.

They could only look at each other. It was too painful for either of them to speak. She would not, could not stay long. She leant over to kiss him gently.

"Gordon, I love you," she whispered in his ear.

He smiled again and mouthed the words back to her. He had closed his eyes again.

"Gordon?" she whispered.

When he opened his eyes, she held up her right hand. Slowly, she removed his ring from her finger, transferred it to the other hand and placed it on the third finger of her left hand.

"I love you," she repeated.

He tried to lean towards her, but the discomfort was too great. He groaned.

"What are you doing to my patient, young lady?" asked the stern nurse.

"She's just agreed to marry me," he mumbled.

"In that case I'll turn a blind eye. But only two more minutes," she ordered, turning with just a hint of a smile on her face.

JULY 1913

Esmée pottered in the garden. She needed a rest from painting. There was another exhibition in a fortnight and she wanted to finish two more pictures before then. It never worked when she was under pressure, when she put a time limit on herself. She had invited a friend to stay for a while. Anna was a long-standing intimate who had also known Esmée's husband. She was the same age as Esmée, but had never married. Giles wandered out to see his mother. He strolled up the garden, hands in pockets.

"What time do you expect her, Mama?" he enquired.

"About teatime, dear."

"Shall I make myself scarce?"

"No, not at all. Have tea with us. She'll be interested to see you," his mother told him.

He wandered back inside. He was at a loose end. It was time to go up to London and find something constructive to do.

The garden of Fourwinds was at its best. Esmée had applied her creative talents and, with the help of Mr Timms, it had become a talking point in the village. The roses had been there for a long time, but, now that the undergrowth had been tamed, they were revealed in all their beauty. There was a water garden, which was Esmée's favourite, because she said it calmed her. Lavender bushes edged the path towards the small lake and a stream that fed the lake chattered busily. The house was covered with wisteria, its blooms draping lazily over the tall windows.

Giles sat on the seat watching his mother. She was glad that he had decided to take up a career once again. People who remembered his father were willing to give him directorships to start him off. He smiled to himself as she swatted insects with her secateurs in her hand. The dogs ran about sniffing here and there, going to Esmée for reassurance and then lying in the shade to cool down. Giles's sister, Madeline, had kept him in touch with how their mother had fared in the years after their father died. He had almost returned to England once or twice he had been so worried about her.

+ + +

Esmée had changed into another flowing gown. Unlike her usual vibrant primary colours, this one was palest green with fronds of darker green creating the design. It suited her. Giles had not changed, but wore the white shirt and slacks he had worn earlier. He was so angular and tall that he looked smart in almost anything.

The sun had turned his fair skin a healthy looking pale brown, mildly sprinkled with attractive freckles.

"She's here, dear. I heard the gravel on the drive!" Esmée warned him of her friend's arrival.

"I'll show her in, Mama," he called.

He opened the front door and there was one of the most attractive women he had ever seen.

"I'm sorry," he said. "I thought you were a friend of my mother's."

"I am." She smiled. "Surely you're not Giles?"

"The same," he admitted, nonplussed. He remained standing there looking at her when he suddenly remembered his role. "I'm so sorry, come in!"

"Thank you, I thought you were going to leave me out here." She spoke lightly in a voice that purred.

"Mother, it's Mrs... I'm sorry, I don't know your name?"

"Call me Anna," she told him.

"My dear, dear girl. Anna, how wonderful to see you!" Esmée greeted her ebulliently.

"How are you, Esmée? You look well, fit and well," responded Anna.

They had tea, which was served in the garden. Giles saw to her luggage, leaving it just outside the door of her bedroom. The maid would unpack it later. He rejoined them for tea and sat listening, amused, while they caught up with each other's lives. Anna was unusual in that her hair was cut quite short. It was dark and shining, like her eyes, which were elongated almonds. He could not believe that she was one of his mother's contemporaries, for she looked to be in her thirties. Her clothes were not cut in the fashion of the time either; she favoured a long, dark tunic unlike anything he had seen before. After a suitable time, he excused himself, saying he would see them at dinner.

He could hear them chattering on endlessly as he climbed the stairs. It made him realise how isolated he had become, staying at home for so long. Mentally, he shook himself. His memories and regrets about the beautiful Indian girl he had left behind were fading, though he knew he would never find a relationship like that in England.

AUGUST 1913

Bill hung about the kitchen, getting under his mother's feet.

"Are you waiting for anything in particular?" she asked crossly. "I'm busy."

"I wanted my best shirt," he confessed.

"Your best shirt? Why?" she demanded.

He reddened.

"Oh, I see," she said more tolerantly. "Yes, it's where it should be, in your cupboard."

"I didn't see it, Ma."

"You didn't look properly," she told him.

He turned and went out of the kitchen.

"What's her name?" she called after him.

He pretended not to hear and carried on upstairs. When he came down later he looked smart in his suit and best shirt.

"Who is she?" his mother repeated, grinning at him.

"Nobody you know, Ma," he said evasively.

"I know everyone in the village," she said.

"It's Martha Jackson," he told her.

"I know, Helen Jackson's girl," said his mother delightedly. "Nice family. When did you meet her?"

"Uh, Ma..." he groaned.

"All right, off you go. I'm only showing an interest. Behave like a gentleman!"

Trying to ignore her, he made his way out and off up the lane. He was meeting Martha at her house in Upper Abbots. The sun was still high in the sky, though it was early evening. He felt his spirits rise as he got closer to her house. He did not like his mother prying and teasing him when he took a girl out; it embarrassed him. Martha opened the door to him herself.

"Hello," she said shyly.

"Hello."

"Will you come in?"

He wanted to go straight away, but he knew that her parents had probably suggested that he go in to see them. There was a stilted exchange between him and Mr Jackson, with much false laughter, before he and Martha could make their way slowly up the hill. He breathed a sigh of relief as they left the house, and the village, behind.

"I'm sorry about my father," she remarked.

"Don't worry. All parents seem to be the same."

"You've got two sisters, haven't you?"

"Yes. It was the same with them. My sister, Louise, is living in Bath where she works, and she has a nice young man. Flora's married," he told her.

"I know your Flora. She taught me in Sunday school."

They told each other about their families. Martha was only just seventeen and still helped at home; she had six younger sisters and brothers.

They reached the top of the hill and stopped, looking around as if they owned all the land they could see.

"Makes you feel good, doesn't it?" he commented.

"I love it up here," she agreed.

They could see spots and specks moving down in the village that were people going about their business and enjoying the pleasant evening.

He held her hand on the way back and she looked at him coyly, smiling beneath her lashes.

"You're pretty," he told her.

She blushed.

"Can I see you again?"

"I'll have to ask my father," she told him.

"Ask him if Saturday is all right, then," he said.

They had arrived back.

"Maybe see you Saturday?"

She nodded and went inside.

+ + +

Giles knew that he was susceptible. It had been so long since he had loved a woman. Anna had been at Fourwinds for three weeks and seeing her every day had started to affect him. She was always pleasant, fun to be with and entertaining. He had begun to flirt with her and she responded willingly. One evening, Esmée had to visit one of her Bohemian friends who was sick and she charged Giles with 'looking after' Anna.

"You'll be all right, dears, won't you? Maddy needs me," she explained.

They assured her that, although they would miss her, they would enjoy an evening together. Giles was not the sort of man to plan seduction, but he was never sure afterwards how it happened between him and Anna. He had been aware that he was roused by her, but had not consciously entertained the idea of making love to her; it had not seemed to be a possibility. They certainly drank a good deal; they were alone in the house. She was accomplished in the arts of love and he enjoyed the experience.

They lay together in her bed afterwards.

"What will Esmée say, Giles?"

"She won't need to know."

"I think she'll guess," remarked Anna.

"Will it happen again, do you think?" he asked.

"That is up to you," she told him.

"How much longer had you planned on staying?"

"Another week."

"Then where shall you go?" he asked, getting up.

"London."

"I'm planning to go to London very soon," he told her. "I've been buried here for too long."

"Perhaps we'll bump into each other there?"

"I think that's almost certain," he said, smiling at her.

She gave him her address and, tucking it safely into his dressing gown, he left her and returned to his room. As he reached his door, he heard that his mother had returned. She climbed the stairs slowly.

"Hello, Giles."

"Hello, Mama. How was Maddy?"

"Not good, dear. Not good," she said sadly.

"I'm sorry."

"Did you have a lovely evening with Anna?"

"Yes, Mama, thank you. She seemed to enjoy herself."

"Well, goodnight, dear."

"Goodnight, Mama." He kissed her on the cheek. He did not usually, but she seemed uncharacteristically deflated. It would be best not to let her see how his relationship with Anna had changed. Perhaps he should bring forward his departure. He would sleep on it; at least he was certain now what he wanted to do.

NOVEMBER 1913

Flora and Seth's children were growing fast. Alice was quite unlike her sensible mother. She was developing into a vague little person with flights of fancy even beyond that of the average three-year-old. Dorothy was a serious, independent toddler, the image of Flora. Seth revelled in being the father of these two little girls and he was kept increasingly busy helping Tom Bates at the forge, his love of horses always calling him away from his work on his father's farm. James and Charlotte Hawkes enjoyed their large family and still had David and Arthur, and their son-in-law, Geoffrey, working with them. Arthur had married pleasant, hard-working Doris from Bristol the year previously and they had made their home in Abbots Magna. John and Isabelle now had James and Isabelle as well as Richard, thus James and Charlotte could boast sixteen grandchildren.

Louise and Will Henty were happy with their two grand-daughters, Alice and Dorothy. Louise had become more and more involved in village life since her mother's death. After having her living with them, the void caused by her passing was hard to fill. Louise and Gordon visited Orchard Cottage often and had an 'understanding'. Louise kept putting off her wedding, because she was loath to give up her independence by getting married.

The pattern of the years lent comfort in changing times and the work on the farms demanded attention as it went inexorably on. Whatever happened within families or the world, cows had to be milked and seed had to be sown and harvested. It gave the community a stability and timelessness they all thought could not change, but there had already been rumblings of unrest in Europe over the last two or three years. The death of the king, who had been Queen Victoria's son, had led to instability between England and Germany. Kaiser Wilhelm harboured an uncontrollable jealousy of England and, although closely related to the royal family, could not wait to unleash his power on her.

All that was in the future as Abbots Ford prepared itself for winter and the festive season. Flora, while having her hands full with her own family, left her daughters with her mother when the need arose, in order to help Ellie Bates. She functioned now purely as a monthly nurse, helping mothers with their babies for only the first few weeks. The time Louise spent with her little grand-daughters healed her spirit and gave her plenty to do. Will and their Uncle Bill spoilt them, but there was little harm in that. Flora was going to collect her daughters from Orchard Cottage to take them around to Rebecca's home, delivering presents for the children at Christmas.

"Thanks, Ma," she said. "I'll see you again tomorrow. Say goodbye to Grannie," she instructed the girls.

"Bye, bye, Grannie," said Alice.

Waving, they disappeared around the corner at the bottom of Church Lane.

They hurried along the narrow path edge of the road, around by the piggery and past the Partridge Inn. Flora stopped briefly to gossip to someone outside the grocer's shop and then carried on up the steep path towards Rebecca's cottage.

"It's Auntie Flora!" Flora heard Robbie call to his mother. He was now a tall ten-year-old and seemed to have put behind him any memories of his mother's illness. He helped Flora in with his small cousins.

"Hello, Flora," said Rebecca fondly. "What on earth have you got there?"

"Something for us; something for us!" shouted Rebecca's two younger children.

"No, it isn't." Their mother laughed. She brewed tea for everyone and provided a special cup for little Dorothy to have a drink.

"You're a big girl now, Alice, aren't you?" said Rebecca.

Pleased to see their cousins, and having been cooped up in the house due to cold weather, the six children made enough noise for twenty.

"Thank goodness they're usually all at school." Their mother sighed. "Tomorrow I'll get some peace!"

"How are you?" probed Flora. "Have you seen Ellie?"

"No, I thought I'd leave it 'til after Christmas; I'm not really sure yet."

"Are you pleased?"

"Yes. I can't help but be anything else. It's been a long while."

"You and Robert seem happy."

"Yes, we are. He changed so much after all that… business."

"He's a good man, Becky. As long as you love one another. A baby always brings love with it."

They dealt with an argument among the children that threatened to develop into a skirmish.

"I'll do your tea soon. Play nicely for now; I'm talking to Auntie Flora," said their mother.

"Seth is spending plenty of time at the forge, isn't he?" continued Rebecca. "Our dad says he might as well work for Tom Bates for all the time he's at Drakes Farm."

"He's happy doing it. He loves working with the horses and people are asking for him," explained Flora.

"Well, he'll have to make up his mind," said Rebecca.

"Anyway," said Flora, getting up to go, "look after yourself. Don't worry about Seth – he'll sort it out with your dad. Becky, how does Robert feel about another baby?"

"He doesn't know yet."

"Will you tell him soon?"

"I don't know. I'll wait 'till I'm sure. He'll be all right."

Flora wrapped a blanket around little Dorothy and snuggled her into the big pram.

"Mummy, can I go in the pram as well?" pleaded Alice.

"Oh all right", said Flora, lifting her in with the baby. "I suppose it's a long way for you to walk and it is getting very cold – it's almost dark."

Flora pushed her precious cargo along the lanes towards home. She had stoked up the range before she had left earlier. It should be cosy to go in to.

There was a pot of stew simmering on the top and the delicious smell pervaded her nostrils as she pushed open the door. To her surprise, Seth was sitting in his chair, considerably earlier than expected.

"Hello, dear. You're early," said Flora.

"Man can come home early if he likes," growled Seth.

His dark brows were knitted and he scowled at her, his handsome face contorted. Flora lifted the girls down and, taking off her coat, put Dorothy into her chair. She darted about the scullery taking things out of cupboards, stirring, peeling and talking. Eventually they had their supper and Seth played with his daughters while Flora cleared away and prepared the water and bowls for their wash. When they were ready and brushed she took the clean children to say goodnight to their father in the living room.

"Night, night, Daddy."

"Night, love; sleep tight. Mind the bugs don't bite."

Alice laughed. "What's bugs, Mummy?" she enquired as she went up the stairs. "Daddy always says bugs."

Flora settled them both down in the room next to hers and Seth's and went downstairs.

"Feeling better now, Old Grumpy?" she teased. She sat on the arm of his chair.

"Yes, love. Sorry. Had a row with our dad."

"About you working too much at the forge?"

"How do you know?" asked Seth, surprised.

"Your Becky had a word with me when we went round this afternoon."

"She did, did she! Always on our dad's side, Becky."

"No, Seth. They just want to know. If that's what you want to do, let your dad know and speak to Tom. Won't be long 'til Becky's Robbie will be big enough to help out at Drakes Farm."

Seth pulled her down onto his lap. "You always see things so clearly, Flo."

"Just common sense," retorted Flora.

He outlined her face and features with his fingers and allowed them to wander down her neck to her breast.

"My clever duck," he murmured as he kissed her, with gradually increasing urgency.

"Seth..." she complained. "I'm busy."

"Yes, busy as you'll ever be – for now," he whispered. He pulled her down onto the rug in front of the range and, without even waiting to get fully disrobed, he pleasured his wife.

MARCH 1914

Louise was home for the weekend to discuss the preparations for her wedding and Gordon had not been able to come with her.

"We don't want a big 'do', Ma," she explained to her mother.

"That's all right, dear," said Louise. "Whatever you think best."

"Gordon's family will have to stay in the village," continued her daughter. "Where shall we put everyone?"

They decided that if they sent Bill off to Flora's there would be two rooms at Orchard Cottage. Auntie Elsie had two rooms to spare and Auntie Ann had one, and anyone else could stay at the Partridge.

"Who will make my cake, Ma?" asked Louise gently.

Victoria Bartrup had made all the wedding cakes in the family for as far back as anyone could remember.

"I'll make it, of course," replied her mother curtly. "Elsie might ice it, but I shall make it."

"Thanks, Ma," said Louise, getting up and kissing her cheek. "My dress is going to be simple and I'm wearing a hat," she informed her mother.

"As you see fit, dear," agreed her mother. "Though I do think Grandma's veil…"

"I've made up my mind, Ma," repeated Louise.

They decided that June would be a good time.

"And, Ma," began Louise quietly. "Ma, we're moving back here, to Abbots Ford."

Her mother stopped sewing and looked at her, incredulous.

"What…? How…? Dear, where shall you live?"

"Pa mentioned that the Saunders old cottage is free."

"You mean, your father – he knew about this?"

"Only since this morning." Louise laughed.

"What will Gordon do, dear; doesn't he work in a shop?"

"Yes, Ma. We're thinking about that. We may have plans; there's someone we need to see."

They talked about the wedding breakfast and whom to invite from the village; Louise still had many friends there.

"What about Flora's Alice being my bridesmaid; do you think she would like to?"

"Yes, dear. I think that would be lovely – she's big enough now."

"Gordon has no little relatives, but his two girl cousins are the right age – late teens, I believe. Anyway, I've met one and I'm meeting the other one soon – I'll make their frocks too."

"You'll be busy," remarked her mother.

"Luckily, the Saunders' cottage is habitable and we'll make it how we want once we've moved in," explained Louise.

"Well, dear, there's some of Grandma's furniture out in the barn and I've got some things I can give you. Auntie Elsie has Grandma's old bed, which she said you can have."

"Thanks, Ma, thanks for everything."

Will and Bill came bursting in, hungry.

"What's all this then? No food on the table. Women chattering!" boomed Will.

"I'm starving." Bill smiled at his mother and sister.

They both rose to prepare the dinner, which was cold meat and bread and butter; they would have a roast tonight.

"You didn't tell me Louise was moving back," accused her mother.

"Well, you know now," replied Will fondly as he washed his face. "Can do without that kind of trouble – her moving back," he commented jovially.

"I know you don't mean that," said his daughter.

"Every word, love, every word," he answered as he put his arm around each of his womenfolk.

MAY 1914

Seth and Tom Bates stood at the bar of the Partridge Inn.

"What'll you have, lad?"

"Pint, Tom, thanks."

They exchanged banter with Malcolm and Joshua and some of the regulars, and went to sit down at one of the battered tables.

"So, lad, what's the problem?"

"It's difficult, Tom. My dad…"

"I'm not daft, boy. Your dad needs you on Drakes Farm?"

"Well, yes."

"It's a full-time job, really, isn't it?" said Tom. "Can't even come weekends or that."

Seth nodded.

"You know Mark and Paul do a lot for me, especially Mark. Paul's not so keen – would rather farm. Life, isn't it?" He smiled ruefully.

Seth held his tankard with both hands and looked down at his ale.

"Tell you what. Come one definite day a week. Sort out your work for your dad on the other days."

Seth looked up. "That all right for you, Tom?"

"Wouldn't say it if it wasn't."

"That sounds like a good idea. We'll try it," said Seth enthusiastically.

"Done," responded Tom. "Let me buy you another."

"No, Tom. This one's on me."

They stayed and played a game of darts and then, at closing time, left and went their separate ways. Seth whistled as he strode along. His first love had always been his and his father's horses; farming was enjoyable because of the contact with these fine, dignified animals. At least he would have some time at the forge and still do his stint for his father.

Life was good: a lovely wife, two beautiful little girls and peace of mind. *Yes,* he thought, *I can manage that.*

Chapter Six

JUNE 1914 – DECEMBER 1914

Louise had had enough of the preparations. *I must get out,* she thought. She needed groceries, so she put on her hat and took her shopping bag off the hook.

"See you later," she called to her daughter, who was beavering away on the sewing machine in the small front room of the cottage, where she was completing her bridesmaid's frocks.

"Bye, Ma," called Louise, mouth full of pins. "Ma!" she shouted.

"Yes?" said her mother sharply, peering through the open front window. "What is it?"

"Can you get more thread at Wiltons while you're out?"

"The eau-de-Nil?"

"Please," said her daughter gratefully.

Louise went up the steps and took in the bright, sunny day. *I feel better already,* she thought.

The wedding was in two days' time. They were well organised and Louise had been home for three weeks to help and to finish the frocks.

Gordon was already ensconced in the old cottage at the top of Church Lane. The Saunders had gone to live with one of their sons, as Mrs Saunders was infirm and could no longer look after things. Louise and Gordon were in the process of buying a little shop to sell clothes, 'designs' as Louise called them, in the next village along the main road towards Bristol, Cherwood Wick. They were very excited about the prospect, even if it meant a great deal of work and travelling back and forth to Bath, where they were having most of the clothes made up.

Louise went up the steps of Redford's shop and pushed the door. There was a clang as the bell jangled to warn Catherine of a customer. The sound was redundant, as Catherine and Phoebe were already serving customers. Louise scuffed her feet along the dry boards as she stood waiting. Hams sat on marble covered with muslin, and bottles and jars lined the shelves. Vast crates containing tea, sugar and flour stood to one side of the counter; the enormous brass cash register sat in majestic splendour at one end. A pile of thick blue bags perched neatly at the side of the till, ready for use. Brown paper bags hung on a large hook: three sizes, each size strung together and available at the click of a finger. Farm implements, buckets, bowls and oddments dangled from the ceiling. A young girl assistant stood at a table at the back of the shop, patting butter into bricks ready for sale. Louise became mesmerised by her rhythmical movements and unerring precision. Each piece looked identical and was wrapped neatly, at great speed.

"Morning, Louise! How are you? Everything going smoothly?" called Catherine cheerfully.

Louise jerked out of her reverie. "Yes, Catherine – it's all fine. I need sugar, dear – four pounds, please."

Catherine used a metal scoop with a short handle and dug it into the sugar. She put her hand into the stiff blue bag to open it and sat it upright on the scales. With practiced aim, she put the sugar in without spilling a grain, then the process was repeated, and each time her hands darted and folded and tucked the top of the bags in on themselves to secure them.

"What next?" She smiled as she sat the packages before Louise.

Louise carried on with her list and finally said, "That's everything, Catherine."

Catherine pulled off one of the brown paper bags and, muttering 'tuppence', 'fourpence' and 'a shilling', she wrote the prices on the back. Like lightning, she totalled up the amounts, her pencil flying up and down the list.

"That's nine shillings and fourpence, please, Louise." She beamed.

All the packets and packages were neatly placed inside Louise's bag and she turned to leave.

"Good luck, Saturday!" said Catherine.

She went across the road to the Wiltons' Drapery shop to buy the thread her daughter had asked for, and was stopped for a gossip by a friend. On her way home, she ran through her mental list of things to be done. *I'll be glad when this is all over,* she thought, *but as long as it all goes well, that's what counts.*

+ + +

The day before Louise was married Rebecca had her fifth child, another girl. They called her Amy, after Robert's mother who had died at the start of the year. Flora was unable to be present, but Ellie was and so was Robert. It was an easy birth; she delivered the baby in just two hours.

Flora dashed in to see her early, on her way to help her mother with Louise's wedding breakfast, and to assist in dressing the bride and her attendants.

"Hello, Becky," she said softly, creeping into the room to avoid waking the sleeping infant.

"Hello, Flo – isn't she lovely?" said Rebecca happily.

"Where is everyone?" Flora had only seen Robert downstairs.

"Charlotte and James have the children for a few days, to let me get used to it again."

The baby stirred and Flora peeped in at her.

"She's just like Robert!"

"He's smitten with her already," said Rebecca.

"Once the wedding is over I'll come next week and help out," promised Flora.

She gave Rebecca some small gifts she had made for the new arrival and left them to rest. She paused at the bottom of the stairs before going into the scullery where Robert sat, working on a small piece of farm machinery.

"She's lovely, Robert – and Becky seems well."

He smiled at Flora. "Yes, she's a little gem."

Flora repeated her plans to help out next week.

"That'd be good," he said gratefully.

Flora hesitated. "Rob. You know Louise gets wed tomorrow."

"Yes."

"Charles is here. So is Beatrice."

Robert said nothing. He had not seen either of them since that awful day at Orchard Cottage, with its cathartic results on his life.

"Just thought you ought to know," she said as she went out.

+ + +

The sky was overcast and it was not as warm as they could have hoped. Orchard Cottage was overflowing with people. They had Gordon's cousins staying, who were Louise's older bridesmaids, as well as Gordon's parents. Everyone wanted to help, which made it worse. Will and Bill disappeared early to do the milking and urgent jobs on the farm, Bill having come from Flora's. Seth was arriving nearer the time with his daughters, when Flora would dress Alice in her posh frock at the last possible moment.

As the morning flew by, Flora helped Felicity and Mimi into their frocks in their bedroom. They were giggly girls of seventeen and nineteen, and Felicity, the older one, was using rouge and something on her lips. Flora was amazed by the amount of time they were spending on their hair, especially when they were wearing hats.

"You never know..." Mimi giggled. Her name was short for Jemima.

Flora rushed about, also helping Louise to dress.

"Are you sure you chose the right 'maids'?" asked Flora as she buttoned her sister's frock.

"They're all right," said Louise tolerantly.

Louise's gown was pale magnolia with some beading, but elegantly straight and plain. It suited her and, when she added her aquamarine hat, she looked stunning.

"Oh! Look at my little sis," said Flora. "Wait 'til they see you!"

Alice had a magnolia frock with beading and lace, and eau-de-Nil trimming; the other bridesmaids were wearing eau-de-Nil. Alice behaved like an angel; she was so delighted to be playing a major part in the ceremony and she was impressed by herself in her frock.

"Look at me, Daddy. Look, Grandpa," she said, standing ready for their admiration.

"Why, who is this?" asked Will in mock confusion.

"I don't know, Will. Looks like our Alice, but it can't be..." answered Seth, joining in.

"It's me." The little girl laughed, pleased with her effect on them.

The ceremony was very moving. Louise had put off this day for some years, but now she was sure, and Gordon felt the same about her. Flora sniffed, affected by their obvious sincerity and love. Seth looked down sideways at her, beneath his lashes. He looked incredibly handsome today in his new suit. He was twenty-eight now and had filled out to develop into a muscular man for all his height. His hair was neatly cut, but even so, parts of it came out over his stiff collar at the back of his neck. Flora returned his look. *I'd marry you again,* she thought. He winked at her and she smiled. She looked down at the dark-haired child, so like herself, standing between them, cuddling a floppy doll. *I'm content. Yes. I can say I'm content,* she thought happily.

Charles was looking well; so was Beatrice. At first it seemed strange after not seeing them for so long, but Charles was his old self. There were so many people that they could not really converse for long. Louise and Will, and the bride and groom were pleased they had decided to come; they were staying with Beatrice's mother in the village. Eventually Charles sought out Flora and took her to one side.

"Flo, love. I've something to say. It's different. She's different."

"Put it behind you, Charlie; don't worry," said Flora.

"There's something I need to tell you, and you'll tell Ma and Pa for me. Beatrice is with child – she'll have it by Christmas." His face was alight with joy.

"Oh, Charlie – I'm so pleased for you, for you both." Flora hugged him. "Keep in touch more. We all miss you, especially Ma and Pa."

This really is a special day, thought Flora as she circled, catching up with relatives she had not seen for a while and meeting Gordon's family. *And Charles to be a father too!* She went out to her mother's big kitchen, which, surprisingly, was empty. The weather had brightened up and people had moved to the garden and orchard. She took a tray laden with food and started her journey between the guests. Stopping to laugh and joke with them here and there, she made her way outside. The orchard looked wonderful today; the sun had become warm now that it had appeared, and nicely dressed people were gathered at random beneath the trees. Flora stood talking to some of Gordon's friends, who were impressed by the joint undertaking of the newly married couple.

"A shop!" said one.

"They're both hard grafters, though, aren't they?" commented another.

Flora agreed, but her concentration was suddenly broken by the sound of a low, rumbling laugh and a deep voice speaking intimately to someone. A silvery, flirty voice replied and joined in with an attractive bell-like laugh. Flora put down her empty tray against a tree, excused herself from the group and went to find out who was behind the barn. She went quietly over the grass and peeped around the corner of the wooden structure. She was stunned as she took in the sight of her husband bending elegantly, slowly, to kiss, Louise's flighty bridesmaid, Felicity, full on the mouth. She retreated, not sure what to do, but opted to carry on as if nothing had happened.

They saw the happy couple off to who-knows-where at teatime. Flora's mother cried as she waved her daughter off.

"She'll only be up the lane." Will laughed as he guided his wife back to the cottage. People said their thank yous and drifted off; it had gone well.

"We'd best take these tired little ones home, Ma," said Flora.

"All right, dear. Thank you for all your help. Alice looked so lovely and Dotty was sweet. You looked nice yourself, Flora."

"Thanks, Ma."

They walked home in silence and Seth did not know why. He had thought she was happy, in church, at the wedding. She had smiled lovingly at him. She had looked nice today in her new cotton frock. Good old Flora. Reliable Flora. They dealt with the children, of course, and spoke to them, but until they were safely tucked up in bed that night Flora uttered not a single word to her husband.

+ + +

They sat on the wooden seat just outside the scullery door, in the last rays of the sun setting on Louise's wedding day. Seth put his arm around Flora's shoulders and she shrugged him off angrily. She still had not been able to say anything to him by way of explanation for her silence.

"Tell me what's wrong, love," Seth pleaded. "I need to know what's wrong!"

Her anger rising, Flora's hand moved as if by itself and, with a stinging slap, smacked Seth's face. She had never done anything like it before and for a moment he was shocked.

He took her by the wrist and quietly said, "Enough, woman, enough. If you won't tell me what all this is about, I'm off to the Partridge." He looked at her questioningly.

Flora dissolved into sobs, but Seth was not prepared for any more 'hysterics' as he thought of it and, grabbing his jacket, walked off into the dusk.

+ + +

They had arrived at the station at Minehead in the early evening. The journey had gone smoothly, but they were both weary after the excitement of the day. Gordon called a taxi to take them to their hotel and they sat back gratefully.

"Nearly there, my love," comforted Gordon.

"The trains are so smutty, I think I'll have a bath before dinner," said Louise.

"Me too, I mean, after you." He blushed.

They looked out at the people enjoying the early evening sunshine in the small seaside town.

"Is it far?" Gordon asked the driver.

"No, sir, a few more minutes."

They pulled up outside an elegant building that had a flight of stone steps leading up to a wooden door, which now stood wide open.

Louise looked up at the windows as Gordon paid the driver, who then retrieved their luggage for them and took it into the hotel.

"Good evening, sir, madam," said the clerk.

"Mr and Mrs Chapman," said Gordon nervously.

"Ah yes. Room number fifteen, sir."

A young man helped Gordon with the cases and they were shown to their room.

"Gordon, it's lovely!" breathed Louise.

The room contained a magnificent double bed covered with a red silk counterpane. Red velvet curtains draped at the windows through which Louise could view the sea. A chaise longue sat near the fireplace, which boasted an attractive embroidered screen, and a carpet patterned with red and dark green covered most of the floor.

"Well, here we are," said Gordon, taking a deep breath.

They went around the room investigating its contents before Louise started unpacking her things.

"I shall have a bath now," she told Gordon and, gathering up everything she needed, she went along the corridor to the bathroom.

Later they were shown to their table. The waiter led the way and pulled out the chair for Louise. Smiling, she sat down. He gave them the menu and left them to choose. Louise leant over to Gordon.

"Did you know it was a posh place?"

"Yes, I thought that, as we're only away for two nights, it should be somewhere special."

"I'm enjoying being spoilt." She grinned.

During the meal they talked of their wedding and who had attended, how everyone had looked, what they had said.

"You are beautiful," Gordon told her. "You looked wonderful today. I had no notion that you were going to be such an elegant bride!"

"Thank you." She nodded. "Mother wasn't sure at first."

"Everyone said how elegant you were," he continued.

"Wasn't Alice sweet?" she asked.

"All the bridesmaids were lovely," he answered her. "You worked very hard and everyone knew they were your own designs."

They sat until quite late, talking animatedly, until they realised that the dining room was almost empty.

"Time to go up," Gordon told her.

When they were ready for bed, Louise stood at the window in the dark, looking out over the sea, which sparkled mysteriously in the moonlight. Gordon stood behind her with his hands on her shoulders.

"Lovely, isn't it?" he said.

"Yes." She leant back against him.

"Gordon, I..."

"Yes, dearest?"

"Do you mind very much if...?"

"I understand. Don't worry. There's no hurry." He turned her to face him; she could just see his features in the shadows. He kissed her gently on her forehead, then her eyes and cheeks. "No hurry," he repeated.

They climbed into the vast bed. Gordon leant over to kiss her goodnight and then turned away to face the edge of the bed.

Louise did the same and lay trying to breathe quietly so as not to disturb Gordon. It seemed strange indeed, being in bed with a man, listening to him sleeping with heavy, even breaths. If she moved her leg, no, she almost touched him then. What if she came into contact with him in the night? Eventually, exhausted, she fell asleep. As she drifted off, she could remember thinking, *Married, I'm married. This is for the rest of my life...*

+ + +

Flora had been to see Rebecca early that morning. Both mother and baby were doing well, and Flora was pleased. Her children were with her mother and she was going to Louise and Gordon's cottage to air the beds and prepare for their return; they had only gone away for a long weekend. Flora tried to dampen the anger she still felt about Seth's behaviour at the wedding; she had still not been able to explain and he was equally stubborn.

Flora let herself in and was surprised to find someone already there; a few people, in fact. Felicity and Mimi had been joined by two friends of Gordon's and had continued their visit at the cottage.

"Gordon said so." Felicity laughed, explaining.

"Lou won't mind," agreed Mimi.

Flora was cool and began her preparations.

"We're going this afternoon anyway," simpered Mimi.

Flora carried on with her jobs; she could hear them all talking.

"He was divine," squealed Felicity.

"I thought he liked me," sulked Mimi.

"I like you," said one of the other visitors.

Mimi simpered again.

"When he kissed me, I knew, I just knew!"

"How did he know we were here?" asked Mimi.

"I told him we were staying."

"Were you surprised when he came back?" asked a voice.

"No. I knew he couldn't wait to... you know," said Felicity coyly.

"Did he stay the night?"

"Most of it," came the laughing reply.

Flora carried on working, determined to leave her sister's cottage welcoming for the newlyweds' return.

"What was his name?" asked Mimi.

"Sefton. Sef. No, Seth. That's it, Seth."

"Well, I just hope you were careful," said Mimi. "You know what you're like when you take a fancy..."

"He was worth it." Felicity sighed knowingly.

Flora had heard enough. She had completed all she wanted to do.

"Close the doors when you go," she ordered and, without further ado, she stalked out.

"What's the matter with her?" asked Mimi.

"No idea," said Felicity airily, implying that neither did she care.

+ + +

Flora did not collect the children, nor did she return to Orchard Cottage to see her mother. She turned left outside Louise's cottage and walked to Upper Abbots, turning straight down towards the main road. She marched along, barely acknowledging greetings from neighbours or friends. She carried on walking, neither tiring nor noticing the heat, until, at last, she reached Drakes' Farm.

"Where's Seth?" she demanded of David.

"Don't know, Flora. I..."

She marched on, through the yard.

"Hello, Flora, what a nice surprise," began James Hawkes.

"I want Seth."

"He's out by home field, mending fences," James told her.

She carried on, leaving Seth's father wondering. When she saw him, she felt relieved that he was working alone. What she had to say, she would have said whoever was there. He looked up as she approached.

"What the...? What are you doing here?"

Flora stood staring at him for a few moments, hatred in her eyes. All she could think about was his betrayal.

"What's up, Flora?"

Flora was a well-brought-up young woman, but her temper got the better of her in this situation.

"You complete, you utter, complete and utter bastard!" she screamed incoherently.

Seth stumbled down the bank towards her. He tried to take her by the shoulders.

"Flora!"

"Get away from me, you lying bastard!" she shrieked.

"Flora, I don't under..."

"Don't understand! Don't understand? You conniving, swinish..."

She began to pummel his chest with her fists, and Seth had to struggle to contain her, so great was her fury. By this time David and Arthur had come to find out what was wrong, sent by their father. Flora screamed further oaths at Seth, who, on seeing his brothers, released her. She ran, sobbing and hysterical, down the hill and, taking a shortcut across the home fields, made for home.

+ + +

Seth was perplexed as he strode quickly towards home. What on earth could have made Flora…? He slowed down, his thoughts in turmoil. Maybe? No, she couldn't have… She wouldn't…?

His pace quickened again as he neared their cottage. He went in, carefully, peering in at the open scullery door. He could hear her sobbing.

"Flora, love."

"Don't you 'love' me!" she wailed.

"What is it?"

"If you don't know…" At this, she broke into renewed sobbing.

He tried to stroke her hair, but she pushed him away.

"If you could tell me? I don't know what's wrong."

Flora pictured him and Felicity in the orchard. That was bad enough! But the pictures she had drawn in conversation at the cottage – her and Seth!

With refreshed vigour, Flora tried to batter her husband wherever she could reach him.

"Enough!" he shouted, annoyed. "How can I help when you won't explain? You've been strange all weekend!" he continued.

Flora screamed back and there ensued an almighty row between them, the like of which they had never had before. All the irritations of their lives together came spewing out in a terrible tirade against the other. Accusation upon accusation, bitter and choleric. Finally Flora shouted, "You said you'd never make love to another woman."

Seth was taken aback.

"What do you mean by that?" he demanded.

"You know what I mean," she said sarcastically. "You and that – that trollop, Felicity!"

They had been standing on either side of the living room, but now Seth advanced menacingly towards her.

"Is *that* what this whole pantomime is about?"

Flora ran round the table away from him; she was scared by the expression in his eyes.

"Come here," he ordered.

They stood still for a second, then Seth made a grab for her. She dashed up the stairs, hoping to lock herself in their room – and Seth out.

If Flora was agile, Seth was the fitter. He reached the door before she could close it.

"You bitch!" he shouted as she tried to shut his hand in the door. "You little bitch!"

"How dare you? How could you? I saw you in the orchard with her. I *saw* you."

"So what?" asked Seth challengingly.

"You should have heard her, this morning, talking about when you went back to them, the other night – at my sister's cottage." Her voice had risen to a scream.

"Nothing happened then!" shouted Seth. "Nothing happened."

"You liar," she accused.

"What did she say I did?" he yelled.

He grabbed Flora and held her hard, her arms behind her back.

"Did she say I kissed her, like this?" He kissed Flora roughly, urgently. "Did she say I caressed her, like this?" he taunted. "Did she say I touched her – like this?"

Flora struggled valiantly against her husband's coarse seduction. He was angrier than he had ever been; she had made his life hell for forty-eight hours; she had accused him of God knows what. But he loved her, desired her, and in the turmoil of his mind he thought he could prove it to her. Prove her accusations false. Flora believed him. It did not make sense, but she did. Her kind, sensitive, understanding, loving Seth had been reduced to this. She felt him, wanted him, needed him, but not like this. Finally, their anger and frustrations spent, they lay, sated, on their marriage bed.

Flora felt bruised and bloodied. Seth touched her body, where it was marked, gently. He kissed her tenderly.

"So sorry, love. So sorry." He wept quietly as he held her, and she too was weeping. They held each other for a long time.

Something to think about, thought Flora as she lay there with him, sleeping.

They had caused each other pain, both mental and physical. She did trust him, but when the evidence had seemed to incriminate him, her trust had crumbled. Those silly girls were attractive and she was the mother of two children now, and perhaps she was losing the bloom of girlhood. Her lack of confidence had contributed to the situation. She turned in bed to look at his sleeping face. He looked so young and still devastatingly handsome. She should not blame the girls, she thought, but he still had not explained adequately where he was that night. *Lord,* she thought, *why is marriage sometimes so hard? Why does it have to be like a battlefield?*

JULY 1914

Flora could hardly wait to visit Louise at her new home. It was so wonderful to have her back in the village, let alone in a cottage of her own. She and Gordon seemed to be exceedingly happy and perfect for each other. They had been home for three weeks.

They were excited about their shop and Gordon was at the premises, painting, while Louise spent some time on the cottage. She was distempering the scullery when Flora got there, so it was lucky that she had left Dorothy and Alice with their mother. Louise climbed down from the ladder wiping her hands.

"You look wonderful," said Flora.

She did too. She had caught the sun while on honeymoon and her hair was more fair than usual for the same reason. Even in her oldest clothes she looked elegant, and happiness was the best ingredient of all to her blooming looks.

"Thank you, you're looking well yourself."

They had a cold drink as Louise squeezed some oranges. They were sitting drinking it in the garden when they heard a great deal of noise, giggling and chattering.

"Are you in?" asked a light voice. "Louise, Gordon, are you there?" It was Felicity and Mimi.

Flora groaned inwardly, remembering with regret the trouble they had inadvertently caused between herself and Seth. Louise greeted them warmly, pouring drinks for them.

"Didn't know you'd be busy," twittered Mimi.

They talked about the wedding again and how much they had enjoyed it.

"It was so exciting; everyone in the family was looking forward to it for months."

"It was after the wedding I enjoyed myself," confided Felicity, her blonde curls quivering with the thought.

"Why was that? It sounds interesting!" Louise grinned.

Flora had not wanted to mention her horrible row with Seth to Louise, and in any case, she had not had the opportunity. Nor did she wish to put Gordon's cousins in a bad light just as the happy couple had arrived home from their honeymoon.

Felicity and Mimi were so self-engrossed that they had not realised that Flora was the person who had been in Louise's cottage the Monday after the wedding, tidying up. It made no difference, because they had not really linked Flora with Louise, other than that she was there once again. More importantly, they had not linked Flora with Seth.

"Tell me what happened after my wedding," encouraged Louise.

"Oh my dear, it was wonderful. I met an amazingly divine man, who really fell for me. I'm hoping to see him again while we're here," she explained.

"Yes, we told him we'd be staying here the night and he came to see us," put in Mimi.

"Really?" said Louise, not sure she was happy with what she was hearing; they had met in her new home, after all.

"He didn't take to me, but Felicity had to fight him off, didn't you, dear?" commented Mimi.

Flora's heart was beating so fast, she thought that they would notice it through her cotton frock. She felt as if she might even faint.

"What did you do?" asked Louise. "Was he horrible to you?"

"Oh no, we kissed and cuddled and… you know." Felicity giggled. "But then he wanted to, you know, do it," she told them. "He was so big and strong, he almost did!" She seemed unperturbed by the whole experience and it was obvious that she was not innocent.

"Who is this Casanova?" asked Louise, intrigued.

"It was a funny name…" began Mimi.

"I remember it," said Felicity. "It was Seth."

+ + +

Flora could not believe it. It was happening all over again, just the same as before. Going about her business, she had had her life taken hostage. Those idiotic, cotton wool-brained young women had no notion of the upset they were causing and probably would not care much if they did. Louise knew now. Flora's mind flitted over the thought that her sister might tell them the truth. It did not matter. What mattered was to deal with the almost malicious duplicity of her errant husband. He had sworn to her, more than once, that nothing had occurred between him and either of those girls. He had as good as raped her when she had accused him of it!

Again, she did not collect her children from her mother's house, and again, she went straight to Drakes Farm. This time she deliberately did not attract attention by her demeanour. This time she would speak to Seth quietly, reasonably. Unbelievably, he had gone home. They had finished a field and decided to have a break, an early dinner.

He was fiddling with the boiler when she went in.

"Seth, I want to talk to you," she told him.

"Hello, Flo love, where are the girls?" he asked and carried on prodding the coals.

"Seth, did you hear what I said? I've something important to say to you."

He continued with the boiler for some minutes and then came through to the scullery to wash his hands.

"What is it, love?"

"I've been to see Louise."

"Yes?" He was growing impatient, because there was no sign of his meal.

"Gordon's cousins were there, Felicity and Mimi. You do remember them?"

A strange look darkened his face as he realised that this subject was rearing up again.

"What do you want to say?" he demanded. "Get on with it."

"What I wanted to say..." she began quietly, "was..."

With that she began to sob; great, shuddering, terrible sobs, which wracked her slight body.

"Oh no, not all this again!" he shouted.

"I'm leaving you," she told him, stumbling over the words as they emerged on a sea of emotion.

"Don't be silly!" He dismissed what she was saying as hysteria.

"I mean it, Seth. I'm leaving. I can't live with you when you behave like that. It's no good denying it again."

He had started to repeat what he had said before. He sat on a chair.

"I saw you kissing her, in the orchard. Goodness knows what you did that night at Louise's cottage! My sister's cottage... I can't get over that!" she said with heavy irony.

He had nothing to say.

She continued, "She still doesn't know who I am! She told us, Louise and me, about the 'divine' man she hoped to meet again. Well, here's her chance. You're free to meet who ever you want. The girls are at Ma's and I'm going back there. And I'm not coming home until you're gone. Understand?"

"I love you! It was all so silly... She's nothing to me... Flo?" He was concerned now.

Flora got up and began to put belongings that she needed immediately into a bag. She collected toys for the children and then went upstairs to gather clothes for the three of them.

"You can't do this!" he shouted.

She ignored him. He stood in her way, arms akimbo.

"Please let me do this," she said.

"No, you love me!" He put his arms around her, trying to embrace her.

She shrugged him off.

"Talk about it, please. You can't do this. You can't leave me!" he shouted.

"There's nothing more to say. I've made my decision. I can't trust you and I can't live like that."

When she went downstairs he was sitting on a scullery chair with his head in his hands. She almost felt sorry for him. He had always had his own way in everything. The favourite son, he had always done what he wanted, had what he wanted. It had been so easy. Now Flora was taking it all away. He stood up and went to her. She understood why the girl had responded to him. Facing her, he held her arms and looked deep into her tear-stained eyes. He spoke softly.

"Flora, forgive me. You'd been so strange... for a while... what with the baby and all... always busy. She led me on..."

She looked at him for a long moment and then turned away. She gathered her bags and went to the door.

"Let me know when you're leaving and the girls and I will come home," she said, and she went down the path towards Abbots Ford and her parents' home.

+ + +

Charles and Beatrice were finding happiness together at last. She was still as spirited as ever, but her pregnancy seemed to calm her; she appeared more content with life. They began to visit Abbots Ford more often, always staying with her parents. When they visited Louise and Will, they were relieved to see the change in her.

"You're looking well, dear," Louise told her.

Charles looked on, quiet pleasure suffusing his face. Beatrice did look beautiful; always unusually attractive, her condition gave her an added bloom. She was pleasant to everyone, though the family still did not feel able to include her in the incessant teasing that went on between them. Alice caused much mirth when she insisted on calling her aunt 'Auntie Bee' and young Bill took all kinds of meaning from it. Full of the anticipation of parenthood and enjoying life to the full, Charles became himself again and not the preoccupied, distracted man he had become while coping with his wife's spoilt tantrums. He was surprised to see that Flora and the girls were living at Orchard Cottage.

"What's happened, Flo?" he asked her privately.

"I don't really want to talk about it," she told her brother, her eyes filling.

"Don't then, but listen," he said gently. "You and Seth are right for each other. Always have been. He's a man, Flo; give him some slack. Look to yourself. No excuse if he's misbehaved, but he works hard for you and the girls; don't ever forget how much he loves you." He held her gently, stroking the back of her head.

They had always confided in each other and understood. She wiped her eyes.

"I'm ever so glad it's better now for you and Bea," she told him, and he nodded in assent.

Louise and Gordon were visiting, popping in on their way back from the shop. Charles was full of interest in how they were progressing, and even Beatrice was impressed.

"I must come over and have a look." She smiled. "When I've had this baby I shall want a whole new wardrobe!"

Louise, the mother, looked around at them all. Three of them married, even if Flora and Seth were having a few problems just now. She was content. Will could see that on her face when he came in. He enjoyed it too.

"My Lord, what a crowd!" he complained good-naturedly. "Who can all these people be?"

"It's me, Grandpa!" Alice told him. "Me and Dorry."

He kissed the small girls and went to wash. Louise followed him out to the kitchen.

"All looking well, my love, aren't they?" he said.

She nodded, too full from the well of happiness to speak.

EARLY AUGUST 1914

"My God, no," said Louise as Will told her the news.

"That's what they're saying at the inn," stated Will.

"We're at war with Germany?"

"And Austria and Hungary."

"What's going to happen, Will? I'm afraid."

"Nobody knows, love. It's all up to them politicians." He embraced his wife comfortingly.

"What about the call-up?"

"They need farmers, hon; local lads'll be all right. Enough to do here."

"Are you sure?"

"As sure as anyone can be. They say it'll begin soon, whatever is going to happen."

"My God," she said earnestly.

"We knew something would develop – there's been warning," continued Will.

"Yes, but I never believed it would really..." Louise's voice petered out. She was weeping.

"All our lads..."

They stood together, entwined, praying.

+ + +

The news had gone around the village like wildfire. There was talk of nothing else.

"Who will go, Ma?" asked Louise. "People like Gordon?"

"We don't know. I don't think anyone does. Soon will," said her mother.

Their fears were to be realised. All the young men aged from eighteen onwards were called up and some volunteered. Charles volunteered; Louise and Will could never understand it, but he did. His was a reserved occupation; he was a farm manager. He said that a retired man was taking over and he wanted to fight for his country. He was in the infantry and came to see them, wearing his uniform, before he went. Beatrice moved back to stay with her mother, because she was expecting a baby; she had never really liked Salisbury.

The Wilton's son went into the navy; apparently her father had been a navy man. Victor Mallish was called up; his father had Gabriel to help him. Joshua and Jasper Smythe went into the army – their father had an older brother who could help at the Partridge Inn.

Giles Thorndyke came home on embarkation leave and Esmée could not believe that he was going abroad again, in anger, so to speak.

Julian and Oberon Johnstone, sons of Sir Matthew, went into officer training, and Graham Redford joined up.

Gordon Bartrup, the baker's son, was called up, as were both Tom Bates's lads, Mark and Paul.

Louise's husband, Gordon, volunteered. The list was endless; or almost. Farmers were able to stay to produce food and those over twenty-six were not called up at first. An atmosphere of doom and despair hung over the village as all of its young manhood and blood seeped silently away.

SEPTEMBER 1914

Seth came regularly to Orchard Cottage, ostensibly to see the children. Louise, Will and Bill tried to behave as though everything was normal, for the sake of everybody concerned. Flora had stayed on at the cottage, because she had made no move to return home. Her parents did not chivvy her to leave. Seth was still at Plumtree Cottage, refusing to go. It had been the talk of the village until greater events had overtaken them. Seth was unused to having the children on his own, so Flora was always there when he came.

"Hello, Flo," he said, nodding to her.

She nodded curtly in return. They played with the children in the orchard and chased them around the trees. Seth grabbed Flora around the waist in a skirmish and stood back, almost shyly.

"Sorry, Flo."

She went into the cottage. She could almost believe that he was sorry for what he had done and her heart still turned over at the sight of him.

He had followed her inside, bringing the girls. Louise took them to the kitchen for their tea.

"Flo…"

"Leave me be, Seth," she said irritably.

"We must talk. It can't go on like this," he declared.

"I know. You leave Plumtree Cottage and I'll bring the girls home. Ma and Pa will be fed up with us soon."

"All right," he agreed.

She looked at him in surprise.

"Why the sudden change?" she asked.

"It's not fair to your ma and pa, you being here all this time. I'll go to Drakes Farm tonight, with my things," he offered.

They decided that they would take everything there and then, and that Flora would go home that night.

"Whatever you think best, dear," Louise told her.

"We can collect the rest tomorrow, Ma," said Flora when they had packed up most of their luggage.

They talked of the war as they walked home. Seth had come round as soon as he had heard about first Charles, and then Gordon, to say goodbye.

"So many have gone away," Seth remarked. "I often wish it was me."

It was strange for Flora to be home after so many weeks away. The cottage looked neglected, even though Seth had done his best to keep it tidy. It had an air of loneliness and desolation about it.

"I'd have lit the range if I'd known you were coming," he said. "I'll do it now," he offered.

She let him get on with it, because there was so much to do. She heated water to wash the children as soon as he had the fire going and put them down in hastily made-up beds.

"You might as well eat here," she said grudgingly.

He agreed with alacrity, though it was only a cheese dish she was making. Seth liked his meat.

"This is nice, Flo," he said as they sat at the scullery table together. "It feels good."

"Well, don't get any ideas!" she warned him.

After they had eaten she reminded him that he had to gather his things together to leave for Drakes Farm. Time was getting on and his mother did not know that he was about to descend upon them. He went upstairs and filled a bag with basic necessities. When he went downstairs Flora was sitting on the sofa in front of the fire, enjoying being back in her own home.

"You look comfortable." He smiled, sitting next to her.

They both watched the flames leaping and cavorting.

"Please..." he started.

"No, Seth. Don't say anything. Just go," she said harshly.

"I love you," he told her.

She said nothing. He began to stroke her hair.

"Leave me be."

He leant over to kiss her.

"Seth, don't," she said.

He kissed her again.

"Please, Seth," she said breathlessly. "It's not fair."

He kissed her neck and his hand went to the neck of her frock, undoing it. She could not help herself; he was her love; he was Seth. He leant her backwards until she was lying on the sofa and continued to make love to her. She was almost carried away on the strength of her desire, and his.

"No, Seth." She sat up suddenly. What was she thinking of? He was seducing her as he probably had Felicity, and heaven knew who else! "Go away. You agreed! Leave me alone."

"Oh, Flora," he groaned. "Stop all this! I've said I'm sorry. I'll never do anything like it again. Come on. You love me and I love you. What do I have to do to prove it to you?"

"Go away to Drakes Farm, this minute; that's what you do!" she cried.

He left soon after, dejected and sad. He kissed her at the door, searching her face for even a hint of forgiveness.

"I'll be back. You can be sure of that. I'll be along tomorrow, and the next day, and the day after that, until you give in. And you will, Flo. You won't be able to resist." He grinned at her.

She went in and closed the door, locking it.

The cheek of him, she mused. *Who does he think he is? We'll see who gives up first!* And she went to bed alone, glad to be home again.

+ + +

Flora had been feeling strange for some time. A suspicion nagged at her mind, but she rejected the notion. She could not be. The evidence suggested that she might be, but she put it down to all the upset she had experienced in recent weeks. Seth had been calling in every day, making himself useful, helping with the children, joining her for meals. He began to stay longer each time and everything appeared to be normal, except that he went to Drakes Farm to sleep.

Then one morning, Flora woke feeling nauseous. *Oh my Lord,* she thought. *It's definite. That's just what I don't need now!* She had been denying it to herself for two weeks. She was desperately sick when she got up, and Alice and Dorothy wondered what was happening.

"Mummy isn't very well," she explained to Alice. "Mummy must have eaten something that made her sick."

"Poor Mummy," sympathised Alice.

Flora eventually managed to get breakfast for the children and do the morning chores. She felt weak and washed out. She decided to have a quiet day and remained at home, except for taking the girls for a short walk in the afternoon.

At teatime, Seth arrived.

"Hello, Alice," he said exuberantly, picking up the little girl and holding her high above his head.

"Look what Dorry can do!" She demonstrated Dorothy's latest feat to their father.

They sat down for tea together.

"You're quiet, Flo," remarked Seth. "Everything all right?"

"Mummy's been sick," stated Alice.

Seth smiled. "Sick, eh?" he asked. "Why's that?"

"Must have eaten something that disagreed with me," said Flora miserably.

He said no more until later when the girls were in bed. He went up behind her in the scullery as she was washing up and put his arms around her. She did not push him away.

"Are you all right?" he asked.

She nodded, not speaking.

"You're expecting, aren't you?" he challenged. He turned her around to face him. "I'm moving back home. You need me here, at least for now. If you like, I'll sleep in the spare bedroom," he told her.

He embraced her and she allowed her face to rest on his chest. It felt so comforting, so strong.

"Funny little duck," he said contentedly.

He made up the bed in the spare room and later when Flora went upstairs he kissed her goodnight and sat beside the fire in the living room.

Flora was only just in bed when he came into the room. He lay on top of the quilt stroking her hair, cuddling her, until she drifted off to sleep.

NOVEMBER 1914

The news was bad and getting worse. News of trench warfare filtered through and they knew that U-boats had sunk H.M.S. Cressy. The First Battle of Ypres had taken place at the beginning of October and the loss of life was inestimable.

Although life carried on at Abbots Ford and the seasons rotated unremittingly, there remained a pall of hopelessness and grief over the village. As news arrived of yet another death, the people gathered in the church and, led by Rev. Orrins, they prayed. They prayed that it might end; they prayed for all those lost and they prayed most of all for their own.

Nothing could comfort the bereaved village. Those families that had already lost someone, almost always a son, could not be comforted. The families who knew their lad, or even lads, had gone away to fight, but had no news of them, lived in constant dread. And still the war went on unrelentingly. Reports that were coming back from the frontlines told of terrible, savage slaughter. At sea, H.M.S. Monmouth and H.M.S. Good Hope were sunk by German cruisers. Yet still it worsened: Turkey became involved. People began to think it would never end.

Louise and Will had just returned from the Sunday morning service when a neighbour of Beatrice's mother knocked at the door of Orchard Cottage. The younger Louise and Flora were there, along with Alice and Dorothy; Seth was working at the forge with Tom and Bill had carried on back to the farm to see to a sick cow.

"Sit down, Louise. Sit down, Will," said the woman.

They obeyed and Flora instinctively pulled her children to her. Louise sat on the arm of her mother's chair and placed her arm around the back.

"There's bad news, my dears. Beatrice has had a message."

Louise put her hand to her mouth in terror. The woman's demeanour suggested it was something serious.

"Go on, Janet," said Will calmly when the woman hesitated.

"Charles has been killed."

The horror sank in only slowly, as if it were not real. Janet began to cry quietly.

"I'm so sorry, so sorry," she said.

"Thank you for telling us," said Will. "It must have been hard."

"I'll go now," she said, blowing her nose strongly.

They stood silently for a little longer while Janet Baines left them, and then went to their mother.

Flora put the kettle on to boil.

"What's wrong with Grannie?" asked Alice.

Dorothy began to cry, sensing the sadness.

Flora and Louise were holding their mother tight and Will put his arms around all his womenfolk. They stood in mute grief while they took it in.

Bill arrived home and was informed of the news by his father, starkly, almost formally.

"Your brother, Charles, has lost his life serving his country, son. You are now our only son."

Bill, seeing the effect on his mother and sisters, went at once to his room, stricken.

"We had best see Beatrice," said Louise to her husband.

"I'll get my hat on again and we'll go along now."

"We'll stay here, Ma," suggested Flora, so she and her sister remained behind and prepared sandwiches, rather than a meal, just in case anyone was hungry.

Bill emerged from his room and, on seeing his young face so shadowed by grief, Flora and Louise went to him and they clung together, convulsed by sorrow for the loving big brother they would never see again.

+ + +

Charles William Henty, among others, was mentioned in church the following Sunday. His parents went about their business knowing life would never be the same again. Flora, Louise and Bill did their best to support them – while coming to terms with their own grief. Beatrice had been determined to attend the service, despite the fact that her baby's birth was only a month away; she was supported by her mother and two brothers. Villagers approached her and the Hentys with individual condolences and it was in honour of Charles's memory that they accepted these with great dignity. He had given his all; they would give their best. It was the only comfort they had.

DECEMBER 1914

Just before Christmas Tom and Ellie Bates heard that their eldest son, Paul, had been killed. Under the circumstances, it was agreed that Seth would work permanently at the forge. James Hawkes had been lucky enough to retain all his sons, because they were too old or had a chronic illness. It was deemed that they were more useful farming; so James could spare Seth.

While Ellie was still taking in this catastrophe, Beatrice went into labour. Ellie's daughter, Jenny, a pretty sixteen-year-old, was dispatched on her bike to fetch Flora to assist. Beatrice had asked for her, so Flora came that very evening, calling in to tell her parents and to ask her mother if she could have the children if need be the following day.

Beatrice's mother hovered around getting in the way. Louise Henty called round during the late evening to see how it was progressing. When there was still no news, they sat together, quietly talking over the past. Both women knew what had transpired between Beatrice and Robert Davis, its consequences, and Charles and Beatrice's own problems. None of this was mentioned; only the happier memories. Louise returned home after midnight as the clock welcomed Christmas Eve.

Beatrice's travail lasted right through the next day. Ellie said it was always worse when the woman's husband was not there, waiting. In the early hours of Christmas Day a perfect little boy was born: a gift for the sorrowing village at Christmas. Beatrice had his names already: Charles Paul Noel Henty.

When Rev. Orrins made the announcement during the Christmas Day service, no one minded about the women's tears: Beatrice's mother, Louise Henty, Ellie, Flora and her sister, Louise. There were tears for all of them, from all of them. Yet in the very depths of their darkness, in the shadowed valley in which they found themselves, there was a chink of light. On the anniversary of the birth of Jesus, another little boy had come to bring them hope.

Chapter Seven

MARCH 1915 – JULY 1916

The New Year brought another light on the horizon. In March, Flora's baby was born. Seth had already returned home to Plumtree Cottage when the news of Charles's death had come and Flora was so grief-stricken that he had taken over the running of the house and care of the children for a week. He had been afraid that she might lose the baby and add to her grief. His love and care of her had cemented their relationship, and gradually, as the weeks and months passed, they returned to normality. That normality applied only to their personal lives, as dreadful news still came through of the war.

Flora was baking, with the assistance of Alice, who would be five in the summer, and Dorothy, almost three. They were all rolling out pastry when Flora felt the first contraction. She had thought she was suffering from indigestion earlier, but the speed with which her labour now progressed made her wonder later. Seth took the girls to stay with Peggy while Flora gathered things she would need into the downstairs bedroom. The bed was already prepared and the crib stood ready nearby.

Seth arrived back swiftly, David having offered to fetch Ellie. Although Flora knew that the labour was progressing normally, she was pleased when Ellie's smiling face appeared around the door. The baby, their first son, was born only half an hour after Ellie's arrival.

"Seth, it's a boy!" Flora told him joyfully.

Seth went to his wife, covering her face with kisses. Then he looked down at the child she held close to her.

"Hello," said Seth, smiling broadly.

Flora could see that he was delighted to have a son. He agreed that the boy would be named Charles, after her brother.

"Charles Edward William Hawkes," said Seth proudly.

Somehow, though, the baby was always known as Eddy.

Flora's mother, Louise, was grateful for the extra little one to fuss over. She saw Beatrice and Charles's tiny son almost every day.

It was to be quite a year for new arrivals. Seth's brother, John, and his wife, Isabelle, had produced their fourth child, a daughter called Jennifer, in February. Seth's youngest brother, Arthur, and his wife, Doris, produced a little son, James Arthur, in January, after nearly three years of marriage.

The village of Abbots Ford had settled down after the initial shocks of the war. The bad news continued, with reports of the ever-widening escalation in atrocities and ever more countries' involvement. The latest casualty was Sir Matthew and Lady Moira Johnstone's son, Julian.

Will knew Sir Matthew quite well, but Seth knew him better, because Sir Matthew always liked Seth to deal with his horses. He approached Seth on one of his visits to the forge, asking him to send his father-in-law along to Salisbury House to see him. Will could not think what the gentleman wanted and was apprehensive when he prepared for the meeting.

"I'll wear my best suit," he informed Louise. "Give my shoes a brush, love, will you," he instructed.

When he was ready, Louise inspected him.

"You look every inch a gentleman yourself, dear," she reassured him.

Will stopped off at the Partridge for half a pint of ale on his way through the village to Sir Matthew's house.

"Can't think what he'll want," he told Malcolm.

"Does he own your land – you're a tenant farmer, aren't you, lad?" asked the publican.

"Yes, but Lord Strickland owns my farm," Will assured him.

"Can't think then," said Malcolm.

The Partridge Inn was a much quieter place nowadays. People did not want to be out and about when there was a war on, not when men were losing their lives in some far-distant place.

Will approached Salisbury House by the servants' entrance, only to be shown into the drawing room by Sir Matthew's elderly butler.

"Wait here, sir. Sir Matthew will join you in a moment."

Will held his hat in his hands and stood nervously looking around. It was a room of magnificent proportions. After entering double glass doors, one was on a raised area with a polished wood-block floor. Three shallow steps went down to the main body of the room towards a massive stone Tudor-style fireplace, where today a fire danced and crackled. The whole room was panelled three quarters of the way up with what Will took to be walnut. Chinese and Indian carpets were scattered about the floor and a golden retriever dog lay on one in front of the fire, ignoring Will's presence completely. Solid, highly polished furniture graced the elegant room, and enormous leather chairs and sofas enhanced the look of comfort.

"Good day, my man," barked Sir Matthew, appearing suddenly, without warning. "Nice of you to come." He gestured at one of the chairs. "Sit down, man. No point standing about."

Will sat, but remained silent.

"You must be wondering why you're here?" He smiled kindly at Will. "You're aware," he continued, "that Master Julian, now Captain Julian, has been wounded?"

"Yes, Sir Matthew."

"Shortage of servants. The war, you know."

Will nodded.

"Could you spare that lad of yours – another William, I gather, for three or four days a week to act as manservant-*cum*-companion to Captain Julian?"

Will continued to sit mutely.

"There'd be remuneration, of course, not expecting charity, what?"

"Well, there's the farm..." began Will.

"Two or three days would be a help. Ask your lad, Will."

With that, Sir Matthew disappeared and, two seconds later, the butler came to show Will out again.

+ + +

"Well, I never did!" Louise laughed.

"Quite an opportunity for your Bill," said Flora.

"I've all the opportunity I want with our dad and the farm," said Bill.

"It'd be extra money; that's always useful," commented young Louise.

"Up to you, son. Whatever you want to do. Do you really think you'd manage three days there and four at the farm?" asked Will.

"Come to think of it, Seth's sister, Ruth's boy, Geoffrey, he's fifteen now and he's been helping James. He's a useful size," commented Flora. "He could help you, Dad."

"I'll go and see the man before I decide," said Bill.

"That seems the most sensible idea," said his mother, "because what if you didn't get on?"

"I'll not work for him then," said Bill reasonably.

"You do feel sorry for the poor boy," commented his mother.

"How badly wounded is he?" asked Flora.

"He's in a wheelchair; I know that much," said Will.

Louise put her arm around her younger daughter's shoulders. Gordon had gone off to war last autumn and there had been no word of him recently.

"It'll be a change for you, Bill, and it isn't forever," comforted their mother. "Go and see him soon."

"I'd better get these two ready to go home," said Flora, gathering her daughters' coats. "You too, my little man," she said tenderly, muzzling her baby son.

"I'll walk home with you if you like," offered Louise.

Flora smiled at her sister. "That'd be nice."

Louise pushed the big pram, while Alice and Dorothy skipped along beside it.

"How do you think they are?" she asked.

"Doing well. Everyone's affected."

"Ma looks older."

"She'd look older anyway."

"I look older. Can't believe I've been married only nine months – it seems forever since Gordon went."

They walked in silence, speaking only to the children. Louise was still working at home and travelling to Bath once a month to collect or deliver fabrics or clothes she had made. Their plans for opening a shop had been shelved on the outbreak of war.

"Flora," said Louise thoughtfully, "I wish I'd fallen for a baby before he went."

"Maybe it's for the best," said her sister. "You'll have babies."

"I hope so. You're so lucky, Flo – look at your family now."

Flora laughed. "Sometimes you can have them all, happily."

They both knew she did not mean it. The war was having its effect on many lives in myriad ways; no one could tell Louise what the future held, for her or anyone else.

APRIL 1915

Bill was as nervous as his father had been on his visit to Salisbury House. He stood waiting in the library. He had not seen Sir Matthew, because the butler had let him in and was fetching Julian. He looked around.

"Hello, there!" The voice was cheerful.

Bill turned to see a nice-looking young man wearing a safari shirt. He had sandy hair, cut very short, and shrewd hazel eyes that were too old for his face. He propelled his chair forward with one hand, while holding out the other to greet Bill.

"Hello."

"Nice of you to come, Bill. Come over and sit down."

A maid brought in a tray with silver pots and jugs on it, setting it down on a circular table near the fire.

"Coffee?"

Bill nodded.

"Cream and sugar?"

As they sat drinking, Julian began to explain what Bill's duties would involve.

"I need to be lifted everywhere. Out of bed. Into bed. Out of bath. Into bath. Nuisance, really."

Bill sat listening, taking everything in.

"Need help dressing and, of course, the ablutions."

Bill liked him; he was down to earth and friendly.

"What sort of times did you have in mind, sir?"

"No 'sir' here, Bill. Call me Julian. I spoke with Mother and we thought, if you actually stayed here, slept here, three days a week, you'd be there whenever I needed help."

"Sounds all right to me."

"You could have afternoons or mornings off, once I was sorted out."

Bill nodded.

"Shall we give it a try? Starting on Sunday?"

They agreed and shook hands again.

"Sunday morning, then," repeated Julian and wheeled his chair over to ring for the butler to see Bill out.

MAY 1915

Louise Henty was pushing her grandson, Charles, in his pram in the early summer sunshine. There was nothing unusual in that, as she was always seen around the village with some of her grandchildren. Young Charles was a healthy, bright four months old, propped up and taking in his surroundings.

"We shall pop in and collect the wool for your jacket," she told him. She negotiated the narrow verge along the roadside towards the Wilton's shop.

"Hello, Mrs Henty."

Louise looked round. "Oh, hello, Becky, how are you, dear?" she asked.

"I'm fine. How's little Charlie?" She looked into the pram. "He's lovely. He's like his dad, isn't he?" she ventured.

"Yes, he is," agreed Louise proudly.

"How's Beatrice?" went on Rebecca. "I don't see her in the village much."

"Oh she's bearing up, you know."

Louise admired little Amy, who was as pretty as a picture.

"Well, I'd best be on my way," said Rebecca.

"Bye, dear," said Louise and pushed the pram up the steep platform that fronted the Draper's shop.

She left Charles outside in his pram and went in.

"Hello, Mrs Henty. What can we do for you today?"

"I've come in for the wool I ordered, Mrs Wilton."

"That was the blue, wasn't it?"

Louise agreed and Mrs Wilton went out to the room behind the shop to collect the order.

"I'll buy the buttons now as well. There are none in my button box that would be suitable," explained Louise.

"How are you, Mrs Henty?" asked Maisie Wilton as she wrapped the purchases.

"I'm well, thank you."

They talked about the new rota for the church helpers, then Louise paid for the wool and bade her goodbye.

As she pushed Charles home, she passed the Partridge Inn. Malcolm and his wife came rushing out through the door.

"No, no, not again!" Winifred was crying in despair.

"Dear God, Malcolm, what is the matter?" asked Louise.

"The news just came through. News of Gallipoli." Malcolm swallowed hard, unable to stem the tears. "Tom's other lad, Mark..." He could not contain himself.

Louise stood shivering in the warm sunshine in a small village in England. A good man, of strong yeoman stock, was yet unaware that, on a peninsular in far-off Turkey, he had been robbed of a second son.

JUNE 1915

Louise was excited. She had come to Orchard Cottage full of the idea. One of her clients, a lady of social standing for whom she made clothes, had heard about the project she and Gordon had planned and that had had to be shelved when he went away to war. Mrs Sarah Steatham had offered to help financially, so that Louise could find premises to sell her clothes. All Mrs Steatham would require in return would be a discount on all the clothes she bought. Will had read the agreement and, when Louise said that she thought it was acceptable, he had to concur. She and Alex had been to Steeple Burstead to look at premises and had liked what they saw.

"It needs a good scrub out." Louise laughed. "But all the girls at the workshop said they'll help."

Louise and Will were pleased to see their daughter so animated after all the heartbreak she had known since her marriage a year ago.

"Whatever you think, dear," said her mother.

Louise Henty knew that there were risks involved in any business venture, but she and Will knew that their daughter had a talent when fashioning fabric into elegant clothes. The young needed an outlet for their energies and this was something Louise enjoyed doing.

"Anything we can do to help, Louise, you know we're here," said her father.

"Thanks, Dad." She was grateful. She could always count on her parents.

Her mother had helped during the year she had been married; sometimes just listening to her fears for Gordon, at other times dispensing sensible advice. Her mother had also helped with her work; as an efficient seamstress in her own right, she had co-opted her into assisting with all the work she brought home. During the year, the two women had worked on soft furnishings for Louise's cottage as well as clothes. They had renewed some of Flora's curtains and provided her with frocks for her little girls.

So Louise was relieved that her daughter felt confident enough to plan for the future, regardless of what the present dealt.

"So, I'll go ahead then."

"Yes, and if you ask me very nicely, I'll come along and cut the ribbon to open your shop!" Her mother laughed.

"That's a good idea – and we'll invite all our friends! Get your big scissors ready, Ma," retorted Louise, excitement giving her a thrill of anticipation.

JULY 1915

Bill was finding it interesting working at Salisbury House. He and Julian got on extremely well, for Bill was an intelligent and well-read young man. His attitude to life was refreshing for Sir Matthew's son, who, before the war, had been spending time with the mostly spoilt and vacuous friends of his parents. His experience at the front had matured him, but what he needed now was down to earth, pleasant company, and that is what Bill represented. There was no embarrassment on either side about the services that had to be provided; Bill took everything in his stride. They shared a sense of humour and there was only a matter of two years between them, for Bill was now twenty-one. He had the same straight hair as Flora and blue eyes that sparkled with good humour. They had already developed a reputation within the household for practical jokes, on each other and everyone else. Julian had already had to be rescued from the shrubbery in the garden where he had landed during a race with Bill. On the other days of the week, another lad from the village shared the duties in caring for Julian, and all three of them were sometimes together indulging in horseplay, within the constraints of Julian's disability. Occasionally he became morose and withdrawn over his lack of progress as he saw it, and the pain made him depressed. It was a bad day, though, when Bill could not cajole him into a better mood. Sir Matthew and Lady Moira were grateful to the two young men for the effect they had on their son, even though their more outlandish pranks had an element of the foolhardy.

"The parents are having drinks on Saturday for a few notables," said Julian to Bill. "Want to come?"

"Sounds pleasant," replied Bill casually.

"Anthony is coming, obviously." Anthony was Julian's other helper, whose turn it was to take care of him at that time.

"About six?"

"All right."

+ + +

Seth and Tom Bates had had a busy day. They had delivered a horse to a farm in a village close by and, while Seth had ridden, Tom had hitched up the cart to Ebony and driven along to bring Seth back. They left the newly-shod horse and bartered with the farmer and his young son before making their way through the lanes and home. They could see dots that were men working in the fields at the beginning of the harvesting. Ebony clopped along, swishing his tail and giving his head a shake, which rattled the harness.

Tom gave a low throaty sound that served to steady the horse and held the reigns loosely in his hands. They continued in companionable silence. Tom's hair was very grey now, almost white around his face. The loss of his sons had etched his face with pain and grief and he went about his work surrounded by an aura of infinite sadness. Seth was relaxed and enjoying the slow, rhythmical beat of the hooves on the lane when Tom spoke.

"You're a good man, Seth," he said.

Seth looked at him, surprised.

"You like your work; you're a hard worker. You love the horses."

There was silence.

"You know our Bonnie had her little girl last month?"

Seth knew about the baby, because Flora had delivered her; her mother, Ellie, had felt unable to assist.

"Little Ellie, little Eleanor," said Tom, almost to himself.

Still, Seth remained silent.

"Sometimes, when I'm dealing with these beasts, these horses, I think... So beautiful. Real beauty. Dignity. Elegance, almost."

Seth had never heard Tom say so much at once.

"I work with them – God's creatures. I live in this countryside." He waved an arm to indicate the landscape. "I never thought..." His voice broke and the tears were trickling down his weather-beaten face. "I never thought to question the Lord... my sons, my sons."

"Tom..." Seth spoke with compassion.

"No. Let me be, lad." He seemed to gather himself together. "Seth, I'm giving it up. I want you to..."

"Tom, no!" Seth was horrified, for Tom was by no means an old man.

"I've made up my mind. My Ellie agrees. I've not the heart, Seth, nor the spirit any longer."

"Leave it a while, Tom – think again."

"I've thought and thought, and I know now. Nothing will bring them back. Nothing."

"But why...?"

"I'll help you out, lad. You take over and I'll help you. You're young and strong with a future ahead of you..."

Seth could not persuade Tom to change his mind, but he determined to speak with him another time. He could not believe that Tom was giving up the forge; it was too soon to make a decision. He made his way home to Flora and his family thoroughly bewildered.

+ + +

Bill was wearing his best suit, his only suit. He had filled out so much it was the only one that fitted him.

"Just be yourself, lad," advised Will.

"He's not thinking of being anything else!" said Louise tartly.

Will smiled over his pipe at his son.

"Don't drink more than..." began Louise.

"Stop fussing, woman!" said her husband, exasperated. "You're like an old hen!"

"Are you ready?" asked his mother.

"Ready as I'll ever be!" Bill smiled.

He strolled through the village in the still-warm sunshine of the early evening, stopping to speak to a trio of young ladies, who giggled and flirted in response. When he arrived at Salisbury House, the butler let him in. There were a few people there already, standing with glasses in their hands. The French doors were open onto the carefully manicured gardens and Bill could see people spilling out onto the terrace.

"Oh, there you are, at last," called Julian, wheeling his chair in at some speed. "We thought you'd changed your mind!"

Anthony greeted Bill with a mock salute.

"Not late, am I?" queried Bill.

"He's not late, don't tease," said Lady Moira. "Help yourself, Bill. Tell Hetty over there what you'd like." She motioned to a smartly uniformed maid.

Some of Julian's army friends were present and, as they made a good deal of fuss of him, Bill and Anthony began to feel superfluous. Bill decided to walk around the garden and, taking his drink with him, he went out through the French doors. He followed the path he knew well, which brought him to a box-hedged garden. He passed the elegant statuary and went down towards a miniature lake. He was walking around an enormous shrub when he noticed a girl. She was the most beautiful girl he had ever seen and she was sitting on a boulder at the edge of the water, with her knees tucked up under her chin and her arms wrapped around them. Her elfin face was resting on her knees and it looked sad. She was unaware of his approach. He felt he had to speak.

"What are you doing there?" he asked.

She was so surprised that she jumped involuntarily and almost toppled into the lake. She laughed nervously.

"I'm sorry – I didn't mean to scare you," he apologised.

She stood up and joined him on the grass. Her frock was made of diaphanous, flowing, pale green shift, which added to her air of fragility.

He took in her russet hair and marvellous green eyes, which she had turned upon him.

"Who are you?" she asked candidly.

"I'm Bill, Bill Henty. From the village. I assist Captain Johnstone."

"Oh," said the faery girl.

"Who are you?"

"I'm Fiddy. Short for Fidelia."

"Are you a friend of the family?" he asked.

She laughed. "No, I'm Fiddy. You know." When there was no recognition, she clarified. "Fiddy Johnstone. Julian's sister."

Bill was incredulous. He had worked up at Salisbury House for almost three months, living there three days a week, and he had not even known there was a Fiddy.

"Where have you been?" he asked.

"Oh, away. With friends," she replied.

"I can see it now. You're like your brother." He smiled at her.

"Shall we walk back?" she invited.

Bill enjoyed the party and was sorry to leave. It was going to add to his enjoyment of his job, knowing that the gorgeous creature who called herself Fiddy had come home.

AUGUST 1915

Esmée had not had any exhibitions or parties since the beginning of the war. It did not seem appropriate, even if it might have cheered people up.

Giles had been wounded and was living in London; he and Anna had managed to keep their affair from Esmée thus far. Esmée was drawn into the mood of the village and her sadness included mourning for her good friend and former lover, the sculptor Thaddeus, who had died after a long illness.

In the middle of all the sadness came a little sunshine when her daughter, Madeline, had announced that she was marrying a captain in the navy. Esmée suggested that she should return home to Abbots Ford for the wedding and the couple had agreed. Many of their friends were unable to be there. Some were away in the war or at sea. Others could not travel easily; in any case, people wanted to keep these occasions low-key, out of respect for people's loss.

The church was half-full. Madeline's Uncle Conrad was giving her away. Esmée was pleased; she had not thought that Madeline would ever settle down enough to marry, certainly not to wed in church. Yet here she was. Her husband-to-be stood waiting for her, looking handsome in his uniform, hat tucked under his arm until the service began.

Madeline was stunning. She wore a dress of oyster satin, with delicate peach lace and beading on the long bodice. Her hat had a veil that enhanced her titian hair. She walked modestly up the aisle on her uncle's arm, eyes down, only glancing up now and then. She had no bridesmaids or maids of honour.

When they returned to Fourwinds for the wedding breakfast, it was pleasant enough to gather in the garden before the meal. The ubiquitous dogs leapt around with excitement at seeing so many new people. Suddenly he was there. He had not been home to Abbots Ford since returning from France. He had written.

"You look well," said Esmée. "I had not expected you to look so well."

He kissed his mother.

"Hello, Anna," said Esmée. She had not invited her friend to the wedding, but it was obvious why she was there and Esmée chose to appear to accept it. They had come as a couple.

"Couldn't miss Maddy's nuptials," said Giles, embarrassed.

"How wonderful!" squealed Madeline when she spotted her brother, and introduced him to her new husband.

The two men shook hands. "I've heard a lot about you," they said simultaneously and laughed.

Giles introduced Anna without saying who she was. Madeline said nothing, although she knew what Anna's position was.

The meal was served with the dining room windows opening onto the water garden. It was idyllic and hard to believe that a war raged in Europe. Conrad Thorndyke made a moving, witty speech and Esmée tried not to cry. Algernon, Madeline's husband, replied, embarrassing Madeline with his extravagant praise of her qualities.

Esmée was feeling emotional. She missed her husband, today particularly; her daughter had married at last and her son was attending the wedding with one of her oldest friends as a partner. Finally, she was aware of the missing faces; people who were no longer here.

The couple had gone in a hail of good wishes and farewells. Madeline had hugged her mother for a long moment.

"This is it, Mama. You've got rid of me at last!"

"My dearest girl. Papa would have been so proud of you today." Turning to Algernon, she asked him to take good care of Madeline.

"I shall." He smiled, kissing her on the cheek.

The house became more and more deserted until there were only a few guests remaining.

"We're off now, Mama," said Giles.

"You're going, my dear?" she asked, surprised.

"Yes, Esmée, we thought it best. Not to stay, I mean," said Anna.

"As you wish," she replied calmly, belying her growing anger. She waved them off and turned to find one of her artist friends waiting for her.

"Didn't Anna stay with you for a few weeks some time ago?"

"Yes, Barny. She did. She was my friend."

They walked in silence around the garden, followed by the dogs, sniffing and snuffling. Esmée absent-mindedly threw a ball for them to fetch.

"Isn't life funny, Barny?" she asked.

"Yes, dear," agreed her friend as they walked back to the empty house through the deepening twilight.

OCTOBER 1915

It had taken a long time and a great deal of heavy work, but at last they were ready. Louise had worked herself almost to a standstill getting the little shop and all the stock prepared. The friends from the workshop and her old 'digs' in Bath had taken it in turns to go down to Abbots Ford to stay the weekend or for a few days at the cottage, travelling the two miles to Steeple Burstead each day by bicycle. They had cleared debris, cleaned, painted and decorated the shop inside and out. They had enlisted help from anyone in their families who could sew, to finish the garments on time. Louise's friends thought it all incredibly exciting and took great interest in her designs.

The shop was stained dark oak around the exterior window frames and the name 'Chapman' was picked out in gilt across the top. Mirrors backed the window display, which served to reflect light as well as rear views of the models in the window. The wooden floor inside was stripped and polished, and mahogany cupboards with glass fronts stored the merchandise, which was brought out under the guidance of Louise or her assistants. Two or three mannequins stood around the shop with the most popular ensembles draped on them. Shawls, hats and gloves were displayed here and there on stands and cupboards, lending flashes of colour.

On opening day, everyone had made an effort to be there, except for Bill, who had to stay behind.

As promised, Louise's mother was performing the ceremony. The shop was decorated with autumn flowers and the golden autumn sun brightened the day. A small crowd had gathered, attracted by signs advertising the event. Family, friends, neighbours and locals stood about while Louise Henty, in her best brown coat and hat, fox fur around her shoulders, declared her daughter's shop well and truly open. They all clapped and cheered as she cut the ribbon across the doorway, and followed her inside to have a look around; there were even a few sales.

Flora was enjoying herself until she noticed Gordon's cousins. She tried to ignore them completely, but Alice had other ideas.

"There's Aunt Louise's other bridesmaids," she cried out in a loud voice.

Flora nodded curtly to them and dragged her children away to find her mother. They were serving tea and biscuits to the amiable crowd. Some folk had gone on their way, but there were still a number of people about and an air of celebration prevailed. Suddenly, Louise froze. At first, she thought that she had seen a ghost, for framed in the shop doorway, in uniform, was Gordon. She was aware of her brother grinning somewhere behind him. People seemed to melt away and she went slowly towards him. She put her hand up to touch his face, making sure he was real. He embraced her with his good arm and she threw her arms around his neck.

"It is you! You're really here! How? We didn't know!"

He stood looking at her, drinking her in. "Bill brought me. I went home."

"This is the shop," she said awkwardly.

They became aware of applause and looked around. Everyone was clapping and smiling, knowing what had taken place.

"You did it. You clever girl," he said.

"Not on my own. Everyone helped."

They embraced again, clumsily.

"A cup of tea, do you want some tea?" she asked earnestly.

He laughed, relieved, happy.

"So English. Yes, I'd like some tea."

People crowded around them, kissing and congratulating them both, slapping Gordon on the back, shaking his hand. Welcoming him home to England.

NOVEMBER 1915

Seth had been unable to change Tom's mind about the forge. He was happy to work with Seth, but he no longer wanted the responsibility of running the Smithy and he felt that he had no one to whom he could leave it. Flora had even beseeched Ellie, for Seth felt it was the wrong decision. Nothing much changed; Seth still went along to work every day and Tom and Ellie lived in the Forge House. Tom had more time off, especially if they were quiet, and Seth kept the books. Ellie continued to work hard in and around the village, but both she and Tom spent an increasing amount of time with their daughters and granddaughter.

Seth was gradually becoming happier with the situation; after all, a man of almost thirty ought to be getting somewhere in life. He and Flora had become established members of the community; indeed, in earlier days, Tom and Ellie had often predicted that they would become like themselves: the smith and the lying-in woman. And so it had transpired.

Seth arrived home after a particularly busy day.

"Hello love, only me," he called.

The fire was on in the scullery and the oil lamps were lit, but there was no sign of Flora or the children. He called out again.

"Up here," came the reply. Flora had all three children upstairs in their bed.

"Who's been sleeping in my bed?" teased Seth, but there was no response.

The two girls lay looking at him and the baby was asleep.

When he approached, Flora warned him, "Stay away if you haven't had chickenpox!"

"Oh Lord!" he said. "Not all three!"

"Yes, all three." Flora grinned. "I took them down to see Dr Tanner and he says that's what it is. Apparently everyone has it at school and our big schoolgirl brought it home with her."

"Didn't bring nothing home," moaned Alice.

"We got pocks," informed Dorothy.

"Pocks?" queried Seth, smiling down at them.

"We aren't sure if she means 'spots' or 'pox'." Flora laughed.

"So you're at home for a while?" He raised his eyebrows at his eldest daughter.

"She's upset. She wants to go to school. She thinks she'll miss Christmas," explained her mother.

Alice had begun school that autumn and was an able pupil, if a little vague on occasion.

"Can we stay in your bed all night?" asked Alice, aware that they were discussing her.

"Eddy will have to go into his cot now, but you two can stay where you are," said Flora.

Seth looked across the bed at her, grimacing. The children were all tucked in, fed and clean, despite feeling poorly.

"Night, night."

"Night, night, Mummy, night, night, Daddy."

"Sleep tight, sleep tight," said their father.

"Mind the bugs don't bite," said Alice, laughing.

"Go to sleep now, children," said Flora.

They ate their evening meal talking about their day, by the light of the oil lamp and the fire. Seth looked across the table at his wife.

"That was good food."

Flora smiled in response.

"You're looking beautiful tonight, Flo; you're not getting 'pocks' as well are you? You're flushed," he commented.

"No."

"You look so young," he said fondly.

"I am young," she retorted.

"Why have you let those urchins sleep in our bed?"

"Because they're ill."

"Come to bed."

"You do love me, and the 'urchins', don't you, Seth?" she asked.

"Of course, my duck. Why?"

"Because we're having another one, that's why." She grinned.

"Lord, not again!" he joked. "When?"

"Next summer, about June."

"As I said, come to bed; throw the urchins out!" he demanded.

They went up, quietly laughing, to look at their son and to squeeze into their already occupied bed.

"Serves you right, Seth Hawkes," she murmured in the darkness. "Jolly well serves you right!"

MARCH 1916

Bill could not get her out of his mind. For months since they had met, he had thought about Fiddy constantly. To him, she was like a goddess: beautiful, fragile and completely unattainable. She was Sir Matthew's daughter, Captain Julian's sister, and he could never declare his love. He had to be content with just seeing her whenever he worked at Salisbury House. Fidelia often joined them when he and Julian were having fun, or reading or playing board games. Gradually, they had become a trio, enjoying one another's company, sharing their humour.

Fiddy grew to like Bill enormously, partly because he was good company and nice looking, but mainly because he cheered up her brother, prevented him from falling into the trough of deep depression that hovered, threateningly.

There was to be a party for the young people; more of a celebration really. It was Julian's birthday and he would be twenty-three. Fiddy's friends were invited, to make up numbers tragically depleted by the war. Bill took it as part of his job, but his mother was excited.

"Fancy, you're mixing with the nobs of the county," she observed.

"It means nothing, Ma; it's only because I work up there."

"They've no need to invite you; others could see to Captain Julian."

"Well, I suppose I'm a friend of sorts," he conceded.

"Of course you are. They recognise someone genuine when they see him," she said proudly.

The house was en fête; balloons festooned corners and focal points, and bunting was strung around the rooms. Gatherings had been severely curtailed since the outbreak of war and the whole household was held in happy anticipation. Sir Matthew and Lady Moira had been grateful that their son had been spared when he had arrived home badly wounded a year previously, but celebration had seemed sadly inappropriate; they now felt able to mark his birthday with a clear conscience.

The fresh energy of youth brightened Salisbury House as the guests began to arrive. Some were staying the weekend, and cars and carriages delivered them and their luggage in laughing, noisy, frenetic groups. Efficient servants glided among them, organising the transport of heavy cases into the house. Friends, parted for months, army people, glimpsing a character they had not thought to see again, past lovers, new amours, all gathered at the country house in the unreal and counterfeit world generated by the war.

The party was going well; as the evening wore on the room took on a roseate character as the firelight reflected on the panelled wood and cosy furnishings. Groups conversed intimately in corners and alcoves, elegantly coiffed and dressed. Julian was enjoying himself. One of his brother officers had brought a group of young ladies and Julian was obviously drawn to an elegant brunette in a red frock.

Bill had attached himself to a group and stood, glass in hand, listening. He felt someone close beside him and, looking down, saw that it was Fiddy.

"Hello. Enjoying yourself?" she asked.

He nodded.

"Come and help me fetch Julian's presents," she suggested.

She led the way as they went across the lofty hall to the library, where the gifts had been hidden. It was lit only by three oil lamps, placed in corners, lending sombre shadows to the dark book-lined shelves.

Fiddy bent and picked up three large packages. Turning around, she tripped on her frock and fell, scattering the parcels on the floor.

"Silly me!" she tinkled.

Bill bent to help retrieve them and to assist Fiddy to her feet. As she stood up, he kept hold of her arm and she looked up at him expectantly. He put the gifts on a nearby table and took her into his arms.

"Oh, Fiddy," he breathed. He inclined his head and gently kissed her. "Fiddy, I love you," he whispered.

They kissed again, with growing passion.

"I've loved you since I first saw you," he told her. He was astonished when she responded to his kisses; he had not intended this to happen.

"I love you too, Bill," she said quietly.

There seemed nothing more to do at that moment but gather up Julian's gifts and take them through for the presentation. They both seemed stunned by the turn of events, the unexpectedness of it all. Bill went through the rest of the evening in a daze. His pent-up ardour, from months of what he had thought to be unrequited love, was ready to be unleashed. They danced and he told her he needed her. She smiled that elfin, almost capricious smile, and said nothing.

Later on, when everyone had settled down for the night, which was, in actuality, the early hours of the morning, Bill crept to Fiddy's room. He was unsure what his reception would be, but he was obsessed with the idea of her. When he tapped gently on her door, he heard her say softly, "Come in."

He met with no resistance at all.

JUNE 1916

The war raged on. The Battle of Jutland had taken place. Life in Abbots Ford took on a new demeanour; for a while at the beginning every piece of bad news was a shock, but now they were prepared. They were impervious to the rumours and stories; they even thought they were ready when the true reports came through.

Louise and Will worked hard and helped their children. Louise and Gordon were successfully running the shop at Steeple Burstead and, on what would have been her brother Charles's twenty-ninth birthday in June, told her parents that she was expecting her first baby in the New Year.

Beatrice was included in the Henty family's lives, because they were inextricably linked by the intelligent eighteen-month-old Charles, the apple of both grandmothers' eye. Friendship had grown slowly between Beatrice and her sisters-in-law, but they knew that Charles would have expected them to sustain her through their joint loss.

Bill continued to lead the double life of farming with his father and working at Salisbury House. His relationship with the family remained the same, except for Fidelia. She had been happy to carry on their affair for a time, but she suddenly refused to see him. There seemed to be some kind of trauma going on within the family itself, but Julian never spoke of it. Then, in June, she disappeared to stay 'with friends' and Sir Matthew and Lady Moira seem distracted for some days after her departure. Bill was confused, though he never mentioned it to anyone; for, shortly before she left, she sought him out and said cryptically, "Don't worry; I did not tell them who it was!"

JULY 1916

Ellie and Tom were dear friends of Seth and Flora. They had come to terms with their loss. The loss to the village, of all the young men who would not return, could not be quantified. So they counted their blessings. Their eldest daughter, Bonnie, had given birth to a little boy, whom they called Paul Mark. Eighteen-year-old Jenny was marrying her childhood sweetheart in September. Tom helped out as much as he was needed at the forge, which was good for Seth, with his young family.

They were paying a visit to the forge on a hot, sunny Saturday in July. Ellie had suggested a picnic and invited Flora, Seth and their family, and her daughter, Bonnie, with husband and babies. Seth wanted his children to see the forge, because they wanted to, and it was too dangerous to have them there while the Smithy was in operation. They walked around the equipment asking endless unanswerable questions of 'Daddy' and 'Uncle Tom'. Seth carried his son about, pointing out tools to the toddler. Ellie called them all for the picnic and, when they did not appear, she and Flora went out to find them.

"You don't want to leave this place, do you?" chided Ellie. "I think we'll get them beds out here, Flora!"

Flora laughed and looked fondly at her husband. A moment later she was doubled in pain as a contraction swept through her body.

"Oh Flora!" said Ellie, almost in exasperation. "Not on picnic day, love; can't you hang on?"

"No, I jolly well can't," gasped Flora. "I need to lie down."

"Seth, Tom, take the children back to the house," ordered Ellie.

"I want to stay with Mummy," cried Dorothy.

"Mummy will be in soon," comforted Seth.

"Sooner than you think," commented Flora with heavy irony.

Ellie moved swiftly, efficiently, organising the items necessary in childbirth.

"Make her comfortable," Ellie told her own daughters. "It looks as if she's having the baby out here."

Flora was in labour for only an hour.

"I feel as if I should be in the Holyland," quipped Flora when they moved bales of hay around her for privacy. "I'm in a Smithy instead of a stable."

As if to punish her for the blasphemy, a final, strong contraction wracked her body.

"Push, girl, that's the girl, push," encouraged Ellie.

Just as Flora thought she could bear no more, her baby was born. Seth came near as Ellie said happily, "It's a boy!"

Flora looked down at the crying child and was astounded to see that he had a shock of dark hair. Seth put his arm around her as they both looked at their newest son.

"It's like looking at a miniature version of you." Flora laughed.

"I love you," muttered Seth. He looked again at the baby. "I love you too, whatever-your-name-is."

"What should we call him?" asked Flora, euphoric with a sense of achievement.

"Only one thing you can call a lad who looks like him," said Seth proudly. "Seth".

Chapter Eight

JANUARY 1917 - JULY 1918

After young Seth's birth, when they thought that the news could get no worse, the Battle of the Somme took place throughout the summer and autumn. It was not until sometime afterwards that the true magnitude of the loss became clear: four hundred and twenty thousand British lives alone. David Lloyd George had formed a war cabinet at the end of the year and still the destruction hurtled on.

Life went on much as before in Abbots Ford. Flora and Seth were busy with four children, although both the girls were now at school.

One winter's morning, after Flora had left the girls at the village school and walked round to Orchard Cottage to see her mother, Ellie dashed in on her way up Church Lane.

"Louise is having her baby!" she announced excitedly. "Can't stop!" She disappeared up Church Lane on her bicycle, struggling to peddle against the gradient.

"Poor Louise," said Flora with feeling.

"You know it isn't 'poor' Louise, dear," said her mother. "Let's put on the kettle while we wait."

Flora had intended to return to Briersham; she had more than enough to do. Now that she knew her sister was in labour, she decided to wait.

"You don't mind, Ma, do you?" she asked.

"Mind? Why should I mind? It's lovely to have you here. In a while, when we've had a cup of tea, I'll look after the boys so that you can go and see how Louise is progressing."

It was a dull, cold day and Flora wrapped up well, glad of her new woolly hat and scarf.

"I'll see you later, Ma. I'll be back to collect the girls from school for their dinner," she called as she went up the steps to the lane.

She stopped briefly to speak to Mrs Percival and to tell her that Louise would probably have her baby that day. Mrs Percival had never recovered from the shock of what her son had done, and suffered a variety of ailments. Flora chatted with her and then excused herself, promising to give her news of the new baby. When Flora knocked at the door, Gordon answered, looking so anxious that Flora laughed.

"Have you got the kettle on?" she asked.

"No, no, I forgot," he dithered.

"Well I expect that Ellie could do with a cup of tea," she suggested.

"Hello!" called Ellie, hearing the familiar voice.

"How's she doing?" called Flora.

"Fine. Slow in coming. I'll see how she goes and I may do my rounds and come back."

Flora took three cups of tea up on a tray, smiling as she went into the pretty room.

"How are you?" she asked her sister.

"So far, so good. Nobody told me it would be this painful," she began, and winced as another contraction sent waves of pain through her body.

"I'll be going now. See you later," said Ellie cheerily when she had finished her drink.

"Don't worry, I'll stay with her until you come back," Flora assured her.

Gordon wandered in looking fraught.

"I didn't realise it took so long," he told them.

The two women laughed.

"Sorry to keep you waiting!" said his wife ironically.

Flora stayed until it was time to collect her daughters from school, and went off, secure in the knowledge that Louise's child would not come for a few hours yet and that either she or Ellie would return in good time.

Gordon went downstairs to heat soup to sustain, if not his wife, then himself. He was stirring it absently when Louise emitted a shriek that sent him hurling upstairs two at a time.

"What's the matter?" he panted, dashing into the room.

"Gordon! Something's happening."

Gordon stood for a second, unsure what to do. He knew there was nobody at home in the adjoining cottages from whom he could seek assistance. Incredibly, he had no notion of the actual processes involved in childbirth, nor, until that moment, had he wanted to know.

"Don't worry," he told Louise, picking up things and putting them down again, displacing his extreme anxiety in useless actions.

"Gordon!" said Louise sternly.

"Yes?"

"Gordon, I'm having the baby," she said slowly. "Come over here. Everything is ready. Aaargh."

She allowed herself to be carried along on a crest of the contraction, and Gordon responded instinctively.

"That's my girl!"

She felt the urge to push, push, and relief came with the effort. The pain ebbed away, momentarily. She lay panting and perspiring. Gordon wiped her face and brow tenderly.

"My love…"

"Aaargh! Gordon… again… already!"

She held his arm, using it to push against, as if drawing in his energy to use for her own. The contraction left her breathless, but exultant. Gordon left her side to ascertain the situation. He looked up at her in disbelief.

"I can see…"

"Aaargh! Gordon…"

He rushed to her side as, strenuously, she endeavoured to give birth. He was taken up in the moment; he could not believe the toil or exertion necessary for this natural function. Tears streamed down his face.

"Please God, stop this pain," he called out.

A sound vent the air, taking them both by surprise. Louise leant back on her pillows, in readiness for the last effort. Gordon looked, awestruck, as the tiny, perfect baby slid from her, squalling, announcing his arrival. Gordon held him, showing him to his exhausted wife, who smiled through tired eyes, wet with tears.

"He's a boy, a baby boy!" he told her in amazement.

Louise held the baby on her chest, looking at his limbs, feet, hands. Gordon encircled them both in his arms and his love.

"Good Lord above!" The voice broke the spell over them.

"What's been happening here?" asked Ellie. "Fathers delivering babies? That's not good practice! And who are you to be in such a hurry to come into this world?" She smiled at the new parents and cast an expert eye over the child. Giving Louise a piece of linen in which to wrap her baby, she chivvied Gordon out of the room with instructions to boil hot water again. "Enough for tea and washing babies!" she called after him. She busied herself around Louise and then, taking him gently from her, placed the baby in the crib close by. "You can watch me wash him in a moment when I've dealt with you!"

Gordon soon returned with the welcome nectar. He sat beside the pillows with his arm around his wife while Ellie chatted as she prepared the baby. Gently, she smoothed away the detritus and debris of gestation and birth, speaking softly all the while. Gordon and Louise looked on at the miracle that was their newborn son, taking in the length of his limbs, the sturdiness of the small body and the protests emanating from his lungs.

"Not long now, little man," Ellie assured him.

When he was clean, powdered and dressed in the nightgown so lovingly made by his mother, Ellie returned him to Louise's arms. Gordon thought his heart would burst with pride and love as he looked at his wife and son.

"I'm glad I was here," he said gratefully.

"What are you going to call him?" asked Ellie, enjoying the moment, pleased that it had turned out well.

"He looks like a Charles, and he was so eager to get here. I think we'll have to call him Charles," said Louise.

Gordon nodded in agreement, his perception of the world changed for always by the experience.

The village, and especially the family, was bustling with the news that Gordon had helped to deliver his own son. The men would regard him for weeks as though he had discovered the Holy Grail, and the women with a mixture of amusement and acceptance, as though he had been initiated into a secret society.

There was an element of sour grapes when Flora discussed it with her mother.

"And to think that Louise didn't want children, once," said Flora.

"That was a long time ago," said her mother.

"Not that long ago, Ma," contradicted Flora.

"A long time in experience, dear," said her mother wisely. "Louise always needs a nudge. It took Gordon's accident to make her see how much she loved him, and Gordon's going away to war to show her what was most important in life."

Flora could see that her mother was right. It did sometimes take disparate events to show people how they felt.

Flora was full of the new baby when she went home that night. Seth had stoked the fires up and it was cosy for her and the children to go in to.

"I wondered where you were," he told her.

"It's a lovely baby, so sweet," tattled Flora.

"Mummy, have we got enough babies?" asked Alice. "Because I would like one."

Seth looked at Flora and laughed.

"Just like her mother! I expect you're broody again, even with little Seth here."

"Yes, we have enough babies," Flora told her daughter. "In any case, you have your dollies."

They sat round having supper together before Flora washed them all and put them to bed.

Seth sat with her on the sofa, his arm around her.

"Happy, love?" he asked.

"Yes. It's nice to have good news for a change," she said.

"Want some more good news then?" he asked.

"Yes?" she said.

"Esmée Thorndyke is getting married again!"

Flora turned to look at him, because she thought he was teasing her.

"How do you know?"

"She came into the forge. Wants some help soldering for that sculptor chap she knows. What's his name?"

"Barnabus Mortimer."

"That's him," said Seth.

"Yes?" said Flora impatiently.

"She said she's marrying him in the summer."

"Well I never!" exclaimed Flora. "Who'd have thought it?"

"She's still an attractive woman," said Seth.

"But quite old…" opined Flora.

"Never too old, my love." Seth laughed. "Reminds me, it's time for bed."

They looked in on their sleeping brood before they turned in.

"Don't they look like little angels?" said Flora fondly.

"Just like their father." Seth laughed quietly. "Just like me."

MARCH 1917

Bill was lonely once Fiddy had left. The affair had not lasted long, but he had loved her deeply and the attraction between them had been strong. He still worked for the Johnstone's, helping Julian. It made life busy, for he maintained his three days assisting Julian and four days on the farm. Gradually, he managed to have a day off now and then as Seth's nephew grew to manhood and helped Will for the day.

New homes were being erected on the outskirts of Abbots Ford, which meant new families moving into the area. It was strange for those to whom the village had always been home. They were unused to seeing people they did not know. On a chilly morning in early March, Bill had called into a shop in the village to collect their order for cattle cake. A girl was there with her father and Bill watched her. She was of medium height and build, and had fair hair. He could not see her face at first, but he watched as she listened to the transaction and laughed when Ted Benson joked with her father. They turned to leave and her eyes rested on Bill on the way out.

"Who's that?" asked Bill casually.

"I've got my eye on her; you take your turn." Ted laughed.

"They new?" continued Bill.

"Yes. Live down by Abbots Woods. Those new houses."

"He got a farm then?"

"No. A smallholding. Keeping chickens mainly. Growing vegetables…" Ted told him.

"What's his name?" asked Bill.

"That's for me to know and you to find out," Ted teased.

"Buy you a pint at the Partridge?" offered Bill.

Bill found out later that the family's name was Powers. Archibald Powers, and Jessica was the daughter he had had with him. It was not long before Bill found an excuse to visit the Powers home. The first time he did not see Jessica and went away feeling defeated. He was a determined young man and returned the following week, going straight to the house. A maid opened the door and Bill asked for the 'lady of the house'. He had expected an older woman, perhaps Jessica's mother, but Jessica herself came down the stairs to see him.

"What can I do for you?" she asked politely.

"I thought to see the lady of the house," he said, flustered.

"It is I," she told him.

"Your mother…?"

"My mother passed away last year. What can we do for you?"

He was unprepared for that and turned away, embarrassed. He had been going to put a business proposition, involving collection and delivery of their goods, to the older woman had she materialised. Now he did not know what to say.

"Do you want to see my father?" she suggested.

"No. It's all right. I've made a mistake." He thanked her and went away, red-faced for having made a fool of himself. She had given no indication that she was interested in him at all. He could have kicked himself for his stupidity and clumsy approach. He should have been more patient. Too late now. He turned to look at the house before making off down the road, back to the village. To his surprise, she still stood at the open door. He raised his hand in salute and she waved, an elegant, friendly little wave. He whistled as he walked back to Peartree Farm.

+ + +

Louise had completed all her chores. She was to look after Flora's little boys, which was quite a responsibility, as Eddy was now two and could get into everything. Seth was eight months old and, though he was happy to stay with his grannie, was extremely demanding. Flora would drop them off before she went about her duties with Ellie. Louise arrived with baby Charles.

"Hello, my little love," cooed his fond grandmother.

"He's been restless, Ma. Woke up at four o'clock this morning!" Louise told her mother.

"Teething. Look at the little face!"

"I wondered why he was a bit red," commented Louise.

"And he's dribbling," pointed out her mother.

"Poor little thing."

"I have something I'll rub on his gums," offered the elder Louise. She went out to a cupboard in the kitchen and searched out the clove oil.

"Auntie Louise is here." It was Flora, coming in with her boys. "Hello, Lou," she said. "Where's Ma?"

"She's hunting out something for Charles's sore gums."

"Teething," stated Flora.

There was a crash and both girls rushed through to the kitchen. Their mother lay on the floor awkwardly.

"Ma, are you all right?" Flora knelt down beside her.

Louise groaned.

"Don't move, Ma. Just stay where you are for a moment. What happened?"

"I had a pain…"

"Where?" asked the younger Louise.

"In my chest."

Flora suggested that her sister should organise the children, while she, Flora, stayed with their mother until she could make her more comfortable with cushions and a blanket.

"Will you be all right, Ma, while I go for the doctor?" asked Flora anxiously. "Louise is here as well."

Her mother moaned and tried to get up.

"Stay there, Ma. Don't move."

Flora dashed away to find Dr Tanner. Louise went into the kitchen to be with her mother, taking Eddy with her. She looked at her mother's grey face and her mouth went dry with fear.

I mustn't panic, she thought. *That won't help.* She knelt down and stroked her mother's hair. Flora's son, Eddy, bent to do the same.

"Grannie!" he called.

"Grannie isn't well; she's resting," Louise explained.

"Poor Grannie," repeated Eddy, bending again and mimicking Louise.

It was not long before Flora came back.

"He's on his way," she told her sister breathlessly. "I'll get the kettle on. Let's put the two little ones down for a rest."

They dissipated their fears by making themselves busy, then returning to their mother.

The doctor arrived.

"Where is she?" he asked.

Louise showed him through to the kitchen. "We thought it best not to move her," she told him.

"Good. Hello, Louise! What have you been doing to yourself?" he asked rhetorically and with mock heartiness. He examined her and looked serious, even though his voice remained cheerful. "Have you got a bed in the front room?" he asked Flora.

She nodded.

"Let's get her there. Can you make it up?"

She went to collect linen for the bed in the small front room, while Dr Tanner continued to examine Louise, who was fully awake now and no longer confused.

"You've had a heart attack, Louise," he told her gently. "You'll have to take things slowly for a while. They're making up the bed for you."

She protested about 'fuss and bother', but the doctor persuaded her to remain where she was. When Louise was settled in bed, Dr Tanner went out to the living room to speak to her daughters.

"You'll contact your father and let him know as soon as possible?"

The two young women nodded.

"Can you arrange things so that your mother gets as much rest as she can?"

"Mmmm," they agreed.

Now that she was comfortable, the shock of what had happened was affecting them.

"It's serious, isn't it?" asked Flora.

"Well, she'll have to take life easily for a few weeks. Once she's through that, she's out of the woods." He looked at the two girls. "She's a fighter," he reassured them. "She's not one to give in easily!"

Dr Tanner left after saying goodbye to Louise and giving her stern instructions. Not long after he had gone, Will and Bill came in for their midday meal. Will's family had never seen him respond the way he did to the news of his wife's illness. The blood drained from his ruddy face and he seemed incapable of speaking. He stumbled into the little room to see her. He was extremely relieved to see her sitting up and that her colour was normal. They all squeezed into the tiny space around the bed and furniture and stood looking at her.

She laughed loudly at the sight of them, with their concerned faces, then laughed again at their looks of bewilderment at what seemed inappropriate mirth.

"It'll take more than that to finish me off," she told them firmly. "Get on about your business, Will Henty, and you girls can bring my dinner when you've all had yours."

They remained, unmoving, looking at her, as though making sure that she was really there.

"Off you go," she repeated.

Will stayed behind.

"Are you really all right, love?" he asked. "You gave me a fright."

"Nothing to the fright it gave the girls." She smiled ruefully.

More gently, she told him once more to go and get his dinner. Then she lay back on the pillows, exhausted, trying to gather what strength she had left. Her thoughts were a perplexing muddle. She had been feeling healthy earlier that morning and now it appeared that she was almost an invalid. Her family was obviously desperately worried. *Poor Will,* she thought. She was aware of a terrible weakness, quite unlike her usual state. *I've too much to do to lie here,* she thought. She tried to get out of bed and lay back, too tired to move. Tears slid down her face and she dashed them away impatiently. 'Rest and get well' the doctor had said. Then that is what she would do, as cheerfully as she could. No point in wasting energy railing against fate.

Give me the strength, Lord, she said silently, *and I'll do everything I can to recover.*

When Flora looked in on her mother a little later, she was sleeping. The watery sun crept in, slanting through the window and falling on the end of the bed and the fireplace. There was a certain pleasant, clean smell always in the room, where no Wellington boots ever trod. The white lace and damask cloths on mantelshelf and cupboard shone out in the light of the sun, in contrast to the darker shadows of the rest of the room. Her mother's best ornaments stood about in respectful silence and family treasures guarded the stillness. Flora looked at her mother's face. Her skin was becoming lined, but looked luminous as she lay there. Wisps of grey peppered the hair at her ears and brow. She had remained slender, as angular, tall women often do. A sudden surge of emotion caught the daughter's throat and she wanted to throw herself onto her mother and cry out 'don't leave me, Ma'. But she did not. It was not Flora's way. They would see to it that she did as the doctor had said. "We'll manage somehow, Ma," she whispered. "Don't worry about a thing."

JUNE 1917

In April the United States of America had declared war on Germany and the first American troops arrived in France in the summer. The news of battles continued to come through and the tide of the war was turning. It did the people in the village good to see the new generation thriving and growing, for the standard of care conferred by Ellie and Flora on the young women and their babies ensured that survival rates were high.

Louise Henty had made an excellent recovery from her heart attack. The family had been moved at the response when news of her illness had become known. They had had to limit her visitors to afternoons only, because so many people wanted to see her. All kinds of help was offered; naturally from her own sisters, but near neighbours would go in and make breakfast for Will and Bill after they had done the early milking and morning chores. Flora and Louise were able to keep the household laundry and cleaning up to date so that their mother could relax, knowing that everything was under control.

On a Saturday in early summer, when Louise was almost fully recovered, her daughters and daughter-in-law, Beatrice, gathered at Orchard Cottage with all their children. Louise looked around at her six grandchildren, two girls and four boys. Charles was a good-looking, sturdy little lad of two and a half. Flora's girls were almost seven and five, her boys one and two. Baby Charles was six months. The young women were talking about baby care, teething and behaviour. The older Louise smiled to herself, remembering when her own family was young. Suddenly the peace was shattered by the sound of footsteps, someone running. Bill arrived in the cool cottage living room, hot and breathless.

"Ma, I've come to warn all of you. Frost's farm has an outbreak of foot and mouth."

He bent over, hands on knees to ease the spasm he felt after running all the way from Peartree Farm.

"You'll have to warn Seth," said Flora urgently.

"The whole village will have to be warned!" said Bill.

"I'll walk along with the boys, Bill. Save you the run," offered Flora.

"Everyone will have to get their animals tested. Frost's farm are having to destroy all their herd," he told them sadly.

The women said nothing. In a farming area, nothing struck terror in the hearts of the people more than foot and mouth disease, for it could mean the decimation or destruction of herds over a whole county.

"I'll be getting back. See what Pa wants me to do next," said Bill.

Flora gathered her sons to her and, explaining to her girls what she was doing, they went through the village to the smithy. Beatrice took her leave at the same time and accompanied Flora part of the way. She was still distant at times, as though she thought she was better than Flora and Louise. Having Charles had made her seem warmer and she had needed the support of her husband's family after he died so tragically.

"Charles is growing tall, isn't he?" commented Flora.

"Yes – well Charles was tall and so am I," she replied.

"You'll be telling your father about the foot and mouth?" queried Flora.

"Yes, of course. It'll be the talk of the village for weeks."

Beatrice turned off towards her parents' house. Little Charles waved goodbye to his aunt and cousins, and Flora went on towards the smithy.

"Have you heard?" she asked Seth.

"Heard what?"

"Foot and mouth in the village," she told him.

"Oh my God, no!" exclaimed Seth, stopping what he was doing. "Where?"

"Frost's Farm."

He looked worried. "Had their horses only two weeks ago," he said despondently.

"Seth, no!" she cried.

"Afraid so. Doesn't affect horses, but they might carry it."

"What will it mean? Will you have to stop the smithy working?"

"I'll talk to the ministry. The man will be here before the week's out, I'm sure," he said.

It was utterly disastrous when an area became infected with the disease. The spores were carried so easily between farms, even between counties, on human or animal feet, wheels, and could even be airborne. In many cases it meant the end of a farmer's livelihood, because there was no way to recompense him for the loss of his herd. If he was a tenant farmer and had few or no cash crops, it could mean the loss of his home. Hence, the panic when people became aware of the enemy in their midst.

Flora hung about while Seth walked down to the Forge House to inform Tom. She took the boys to see the horses and baby Seth squealed with delight.

"You're going to take after your pa, aren't you?" she told him.

Eddy showed no sign of fear even though he was tiny, standing next to the massive cob. Ellie walked up the path towards them, drying her hands on a towel.

"Bad news eh, Flora?"

"Yes. Couldn't be worse, could it?"

"Hello you little lads," said Ellie fondly. "How are you?"

Eddy ran to her to be picked up and cuddled. Ellie loved all children, but her grandchildren and Flora's were special to her.

"They might have to close the smithy, put it in quarantine?" she queried.

"Don't really know," said Flora. "All we can do is wait and see," she said bleakly.

"It will seem like a long week," said Ellie. "Won't it little man?"

JULY 1917

"So it's really happening?" asked Ellie.

"Yes", said Esmée, blushing like a young girl. "I'm getting married tomorrow."

They had met in the village and stopped for a chat.

"Is Madeline coming?"

"Oh yes, but not Algy; he's at sea," Esmée told her.

"Will Giles come down?"

I'm not sure," replied Esmée evasively. "But Barry's family are all attending."

"Well the weather looks set to stay nice," Ellie assured her. "Good luck tomorrow, Mrs Thorndyke."

"Thank you, Ellie," said Esmée as she went home, smiling inwardly at the gossip her nuptials were generating.

+ + +

Bill arrived home even more filthy than normal. He had been turning out the cowsheds and, although he had taken off the clothes he had been wearing and changed into some that were marginally better, he could still be detected some distance away.

"Ma!" he shouted. "Ma, I'm filthy. Can you bring water out to the orchard?"

"Use the water straight from the pump and I'll bring you some hot water when you're rinsed off!" she called.

"Ma," he moaned. "I wanted hot water to rinse off…"

"On a warm day like this? Use the cold!" she admonished.

Bill went and did as he was bid, and Louise took hot water for him to wash out in the orchard. He was so dirty that he came inside to have a bath. He heaved off his Wellington boots, revealing thick woollen socks. He had leant on the doorposts and, once the boots were removed, he went in. To his chagrin, the first person he saw was Jessica, the lovely girl he had been trying to meet since the spring when he had first noticed her.

"Oh!" he said, nonplussed.

Jessica smiled. "Hello," she said.

"Do you know Jessica Powers?" asked Louise.

"We've met," he said shortly and went through to the kitchen to have his bath behind the screen.

Jessica was still there when he emerged, which he thought was indelicate. He had needed his bath urgently and she had remained in the cottage while he completed his ablutions.

"You still here?" he asked rudely.

"Bill! Miss Powers is my guest!" said his mother.

"That's all right, Mrs Henty. I must be going now," she said pleasantly.

"Miss Powers is here to discuss her stall at the Vicarage Fete. She is making considerable contributions, all made by her own clever hands," explained Louise.

"I thought my tea might be ready by now," he carried on pointedly.

Jessica rose to leave. "It has been nice to meet you, Mr Henty," she said.

Bill was not sure whether or not he detected sarcasm in her tone.

269

"Thank you for your help, Mrs Henty."

"That's all right, dear. We'll all be there to help you on the day," Louise told her.

"That was unnecessary," Louise told Bill when Jessica had gone.

"It was unnecessary for her to be here when I was having a bath," he responded.

"You were rude," countered his mother.

He said no more. He knew it was true. He had been unduly rude. He had felt awkward and embarrassed in front of an attractive girl. He had felt at a disadvantage because she had been in his own home.

"I'm going out," he told Louise. "Don't bother about tea for me."

She smiled to herself. Her son was so transparent, even Jessica had realised why he had behaved the way he had. No doubt they would meet again soon.

+ + +

Esmée went to church to marry Barry in a car. She wore an elegant silk coffee-coloured chiffon frock with a dropped waistline and a floppy silk hat, covered in pale pink silk tea roses. Esmée had had one happy marriage with Augustus Thorndyke. Barnabus Mortimer was a different proposition, but then Esmée was a different woman now. Their many friends surrounded them as they made their vows, as movingly and as seriously as any young bride and groom. Madeline acted as her mother's matron of honour. Giles and Anna had arrived early that morning. Esmée was pleased to see them both; she and Barry talked and laughed quietly with them after the short ceremony. A few villagers stood about waiting to see the latest bride from Fourwinds.

"You look radiant," said Anna.

"Thank you; I feel well," replied Esmée.

"Are you going away, Mother?" asked Giles.

"No, dear. Not at once. We may go to France in the winter."

Barnabus had a picturesque cottage on the outskirts of Abbots Ford, but was moving into Fourwinds on his marriage to Esmée.

270

"Mama, shall we return home now," suggested Madeline.

The party made its way down the main street from the church towards the house. People smiled and bade them good day and good luck. Esmée did indeed look younger than her years; happiness was a tonic.

Barnabus was a tall, thin gentleman in his early sixties with white hair and a goatee beard. He was dressed in an elegant, pale grey suit and a panama hat. He was a perfect foil for Esmée, being quiet and calm, with inner strengths and resources. She would not always have her own way. He was a charming host, while remaining slightly apart, as if not wanting to appear proprietorial. The group spent a pleasant and relaxed afternoon celebrating the marriage.

"Surely you're going away tonight?" asked Anna.

"No, my dear. We begin married life here. We shall spend tomorrow using Baxter's cart to bring Barry's things over and we both have work to do for the autumn exhibition."

"In October again?" asked Michael Orrins.

"Yes, bigger and better than ever," enthused Esmée.

"We have exhibitors coming from all over the country," said Barry.

"Even London!" bubbled his wife.

"Don't forget the local artists and sculptors," put in Ursula Austin, one of Esmée's artist friends.

"We're not likely to forget you, Ursula." Esmée laughed.

"Perhaps we could advertise the event more?" suggested the vicar.

"It would be an idea to let people in surrounding villages know, even Bristol," agreed Barry.

"We'll put it in the local press," said Esmée.

"Enough of this on our wedding day," teased Barry. "I've heard of nothing else but the exhibition recently; even the wedding took second place!"

Giles made a speech, making clear his and his sister's happiness about the marriage, and Barry replied in his urbane and sophisticated way, causing ripples of laughter around the garden. Gradually, their guests departed, including their children.

When everyone had gone the couple walked around, the dogs trailing behind them. Barnabus knew Fourwinds well, for he had long been part of the coterie of artists and artisans who gathered there.

"My dear, you have made a paradise here," he told her.

"For you to share now, Barry."

"There is so much to look forward to."

"For we two. No ghosts?"

"No ghosts. From now on your Augustus and my Tansy must stay where they belong: in our hearts and in our past. The future is ours."

AUGUST 1917

The village had been let off lightly. Frosts' Farm was in quarantine and all their cattle and sheep destroyed, but after almost two months there were no new cases. Still, they metaphorically held their breath, but as the weeks passed it became less likely. Everyone felt sorry for the Frosts. They had farmed in the area for as far back as anyone could remember. They still maintained that they did not know how it had reached them, but word went about that one of the brothers was a bad lot and had done a deal on new animals he had acquired.

Seth and Tom gravitated towards the Partridge Inn one Saturday evening. They ordered their drinks and stood talking to Malcolm at the bar. Seth listened as Tom argued pleasantly with their host and his eyes wandered idly round, taking in their surroundings. It dawned on him that the old place was looking shabby. The bare wooden floor was uneven and worn and the walls and ceiling could have been mustard, but untold years of tobacco stains had discoloured the plaster. There was a fine wooden surround to the expansive fireplace, but it looked redundant and empty at this time of year. The leather was worn on the seats of the battered chairs and vandals had carved initials on the oak tables that were spread around the room. Gas lights cast a diffuse glow, making the atmosphere more cheerful than broad daylight. The oak bar was polished by Winifred Smythe and by her clientele leaning ever more heavily on it as the evenings wore on. A few generations of elbows had contributed to its antique patina.

Will joined them and brought up the subject of foot and mouth disease.

"Vet says we're out of the woods now," he told them.

"It'll be another month before we know for sure," said Tom.

"They say it came in from Wiltshire..."

"Could be, could be, Seth, lad," agreed Tom. "I'd like to get my hands on whoever brought it here."

"What'll you have?" asked Bill, who had arrived late.

"Another pint of beer, lad, ta," said Will.

"All right, boy. Same here," opted Tom.

"Thanks, Will," agreed Seth.

They took their fresh drinks and sat down at a large table near the curtainless window. Bill paid Malcolm and joined them, slopping his beer as he sat down, pocketing his change.

"Did you hear?" He lowered his voice conspiratorially.

"Hear what?" asked Seth.

"They're pressing charges against Walter Frost."

"No, lad? Never!"

"Tis true. The constabulary have been looking into it. Walter knew what he was doing and he still went ahead. They say it'll kill his father after all he's been through lately," said Will.

"Who pointed the finger at him?" asked Tom.

"Don't know."

"Good thing, whoever did," said Will. "Could have meant the end of all of us."

They sat drinking thoughtfully. Other farms in Abbots Ford and around could have been finished, as well as smallholding livestock. They could not understand why anyone would take such a risk merely to buy stock more cheaply.

"I reckon he should be taught a lesson," said Bill.

"Reckon it's punishment enough, what's happened," said Will mildly.

"He don't care," said Bill. "He's going around just as cocky as he always was."

"Not like you the day Miss Powers was around our house."
Will laughed.

"What was that, then?" asked Tom.

Will explained, "He came down from the farm stinking to
high heaven and covered with dung!"

"Yes, go on. Where does Miss Powers come in?" asked Seth.

"Well, as you might say, it was Bill what came in, not Miss
Powers." Will roared with laughter at his own pun. "She were
sitting there when he came in shouting at his ma for hot water!
There she sat all the while he was having his bath."

The others laughed at the image Will had conjured up. Bill
was annoyed.

"Yes. Would you believe it? Anyone else would have made
their excuses and left. No privacy anywhere, not even in your own
home." He was so indignant that it set the others off laughing
again.

"I needed a good laugh, Bill," said Tom.

"I've got to be off home now," said Seth.

"Or our Flora will have your gizzard for garters," said Bill,
pleased to get his own back on one of them.

"It'll take more than her!" called Seth from the door as the
older men smiled benignly.

Seth walked towards Abbots Magna and Briersham. The
evenings were drawing in surprisingly quickly now. He whistled as
he strode along, looking forward to a longer lie in bed the next
day. The smithy was closed and, unless there was an emergency, he
would go and give an extra hand at Drakes Farm for the
harvesting. He was not sure what had happened at first. He could
not believe it. All he knew was that he was lying face down on the
tarmac of the road and it slowly came to him that he had been hit
on the head. He was so stunned that he lay there for a moment to
gather his thoughts. He put his hand up to his head and rolled
over. He could not see anyone; the twilight was neither light nor
dark as he tried to focus.

He heard scrabbling in a hedge, but it could have been an
animal. Either way, he was too stunned to try to follow. Even in
the fading light, he could see the dark blood on his hand. He knew

that he should try to head for home. He stood up slowly and felt dizzy, so he staggered towards a tree and leant against it. *Who would do something like that,* he wondered. Eventually he was able to continue, slowly, resting now and again as he felt himself fading away. He had no idea of the time, but it was pitch-dark by the time he tottered around to the scullery door of Plumtree Cottage. Flora was there, alone, cooking.

"Where have you b...?" she started. "My Lord, Seth! What's happened to you, love?" She sat him on a chair.

"Someone hit me, Flo," he said, still unable to take it in.

Flora got clean clothes, disinfectant and a bandage.

"Where were you?" she asked gently.

"Coming home along the lane... from the Partridge," he told her.

"You didn't just fall in the hedge then?"

"Someone hit me over the head with something hard, Flo. You can see." Seth swayed, almost toppling from the chair.

"I know, love. Only teasing you. They've almost bally killed you." A terrible thought came into her mind as she said it. What had they been trying to do? "Were you robbed, Seth?" she asked.

He had not considered this. He did not think so. He looked in his pockets.

"No, my money is still there," he said.

Flora did not speak for a while. She concentrated on bathing Seth's head and discovered that a nasty wound was underneath the matted, bloody hair.

"I think Dr Tanner should see this," she told him, trying not to panic. "It may need to be stitched."

"Oh Flora. No," he groaned. "I feel bad enough as it is."

"I'll pop along to Drakes Farm. One of them will go. I can't leave you or the children for long." She settled him in the living room.

"Try not to go to sleep," she instructed. "I won't be long."

She ran the half-mile to Seth's parents' house. All the boys were married now and living away, but someone may be left after working late, or Seth's father would fetch Dr Tanner. Breathlessly, she explained. At once, James harnessed up and rode to fetch the doctor.

When Flora returned home, Seth had fallen asleep and she did her best to wake him. But she could not. His breathing was shallow and he looked pale and clammy. By the time Dr Tanner arrived, she was hysterical.

"He won't wake up, Doctor. Is he dying?" she pleaded.

Dr Tanner went into the room and set about examining Seth.

"He's unconscious, Flora, as I expect you'd realised by now. He's probably suffering a severe concussion. Tell me again what happened."

By this time both James and Charlotte had joined them, Charlotte bringing with her medicinal brandy, which she gave Flora. James listened closely while she told them all what Seth had managed to impart to her before he lost consciousness. When she had finished Dr Tanner turned to James.

"I think the police should be informed."

They all looked shocked.

"Why?" asked Flora.

"Someone has attacked Seth with great severity. He's badly hurt, Flora. The police will want to know about it."

She began to sob loudly.

"There, there, dear," comforted Charlotte. "Don't take on so."

"Will you be able to stay here with her, Mrs Hawkes?" asked the doctor. "If not, maybe her mother...?"

"We'll stay 'til morning, then we'll see," Charlotte told him. "Don't worry, Doctor, we won't leave them alone."

"Seth will need to be watched throughout the night, and if there's any deterioration, I want to know," he told them.

None of them had much sleep that night. Flora was too upset to sleep. Indeed, the same applied to Seth's parents. They all dozed fitfully, examining Seth at intervals. As the dawn broke, Flora was wakened by his voice.

"I'm thirsty, God, I'm thirsty. What the hell...?"

"Oh love, you're all right. Ma, he's all right!" she shouted.

"What are they doing here?" he asked, irritated.

"Hello, Seth. Feeling better then?" James smiled.

"Someone hit you over the head, son," explained Charlotte.

Flora came back with a drink for him. "Kettle's on," she told them.

When they had finished the tea, James and Charlotte returned home, promising to return when they had washed and eaten.

"Doctor says the police will want to know. I think he's right," James told his son.

"They can't be allowed to get away with this," agreed Charlotte.

"Why? I don't understand why anyone would do it," said Seth, still confused.

"Leave it to Constable Bunce," suggested Flora. "He'll find whoever almost killed you." Her mouth was set in a grim, determined line. *I'll even sort them out, whoever they are,* she thought.

SEPTEMBER 1917

It was time for the Harvest Supper Dance once more. Will and Louise and Flora and Seth, among others, had gone along to the village hall to hang the bunting and put up the lights. Seth had had to rest for almost a fortnight in order to recover from the attack. It was the first time many people had seen him out and about, and they were interested to hear from his own lips what had happened. Typically, Seth played it down. The village was in no doubt about how serious the attack was and had been shocked that such a thing could have happened to one of their community. The police had warned Seth not to say too much while they were still investigating the incident, which they, too, regarded as serious.

They went along that evening as a family group, with much laughter and teasing. It was a long time since they had been out together: Louise and Will, Flora and Seth, Louise and Gordon and Bill. Beatrice was there with her parents, sitting aloof and guarded. She did not approach the Hentys, nor venture to offer Seth sympathy for his injury. The fiddles encouraged them onto the floor. Bill danced with as many attractive young women as he could before he noticed Jessica Powers with her father. Taking his courage in his hands, he approached them.

"Will you dance with me, Miss Powers?"

"I see you're decently dressed this evening, Mr Henty," she said, equally formally. She grinned at her father. "Indeed, it's nice to see that you have on any clothes at all!"

There were smirks and stifled laughter all around them. Bill reddened as she accepted his hand to lead her onto the floor.

"Why did you have to say that?" he muttered.

"Because it's true. What you have on tonight is a great improvement on that day."

She could not help but laugh at the expression on his face. She laughed so much that he had to laugh too. They enjoyed the next few dances together and began to talk. He discovered that she was an attractive character as well as an attractive girl. He was enjoying himself.

"You're a very nice person," he told her warmly.

"That's kind of you," she said ingratiatingly.

"I'm sorry," he said. "I didn't mean it to sound condescending."

Jessica was whisked away then, as they were included in a dance set. He watched her as she whirled around with various partners, charming and animated. He wondered if her father would allow him to see her home. It would involve a long walk through the village and out to her home; it would mean half an hour alone with her...

Bill's attention was suddenly caught by an intense conversation between Seth and one of the Frost brothers. There was nothing overtly wrong, more of an instinctive feeling on Bill's part. He excused himself and walked casually over to them. Another of the Frost brothers had joined them. Seth's brother, David, reached the group at the same time as Bill.

"Everything all right, Seth?" asked Bill.

"Time to get some pints, Seth," said David.

The two men escorted Seth to the bar.

"What was that all about?" asked David.

"I'm not sure. Nasty piece of work that Walter Frost," Seth told them.

"What did they say?" asked Bill.

"Told me to mind my own business or they would mind it for me."

The two men grimaced. This was not the time or the place for unpleasantness of that kind, but it could not be ignored indefinitely.

"We'll see to it later," said David. "Enjoy yourself now."

Bill went in search of Jessica and asked her to dance.

"Can I see you home?" he whispered.

"Yes, I've already told my father you'll see me home."

"You have, have you? Fast wench!" He squeezed her around the waist, laughing.

They talked all the way back to her house. She was quick-witted and amusing. She shivered and he put an arm around her shoulders, which she did not shrug off.

"Can I see you again?" he asked as they stood at her front gates.

She nodded.

"When? Tomorrow?"

She nodded again.

"What time?"

"Come for me at three o'clock," she told him. "Goodnight."

"Goodnight," he replied, and watched her go in and close the door.

He smiled as he began to walk back home. He put his hands in his pockets to keep warm and quickened his pace as he noticed, for the first time, that it was chilly. He walked down past the rows of cottages and was approaching the centre of the village when he felt himself pulled in towards a thick hedge. An arm was round his neck, constricting his throat.

"Don't try to struggle. There's two of us here," said a muffled, disguised voice. "Just mind your own business or you'll be sorry." He was propelled violently forward and fell heavily on the road.

He looked around, but there was nothing and nobody to be seen.

He got up, brushing himself down, straightening his hat. *Good God! What is the place coming to,* he thought. He felt it was obvious who had attacked him. But why? This was a problem they would have to deal with; this was not how people in a village like Abbots Ford behaved. He would contact Seth the next day and discuss the situation with him.

OCTOBER 1917

Bill and Seth had decided that it was time to settle a few scores. It was obvious who had attacked them, but Seth had mentioned nothing of his suspicions to the police, who were still looking for his assailant. They decided to meet Walter. They arranged to waylay him one evening as he returned home. It was dark as he walked up the lane, and Seth and Bill stepped out of the shadows. "Hello, Walter," said Seth. "We want a word with you."

Walter took a few steps backwards, startled. "I don't want any trouble," he said.

"That's not what we've heard," Bill told him. "Seems to us you've been looking for trouble."

"Don't know what you mean," said Walter.

"I've been attacked," said Seth. "Bill, here, has been attacked. We want to know why." Seth took hold of Walter's coat lapels. "Well?"

Walter said nothing, but Seth could detect his fear in the darkness.

He shook him and repeated, "Well?"

"You put word out about me," said Walter.

"What word?" asked Seth, surprised.

"Foot 'n' mouth. Saying I started it," went on Walter.

"Go on," said Bill.

"You were heard in the Partridge... saying I did a deal against my own father, and all."

"And you did!" said Bill.

"Didn't know it'd bring disease to the village, though, did I?" He was condemned from his own mouth.

"Leave us alone. And our families and friends. Any more trouble from you, ever, and I tell the police," said Seth. "The only reason we're not going straight to them is because of your father and brothers," Seth continued. "You nearly killed me!"

"Go on, you're not worth the trouble," said Bill, giving Walter a push.

"I wasn't alone!" said Walter as a parting shot.

"Leave him," said Seth. "He's a coward."

The two men walked back through the village.

"Best not to say anything to anyone about this," suggested Seth.

Bill agreed. They went their separate ways, bidding each other farewell.

As he walked towards Briersham, it occurred to Seth to wonder who it really was who had put word around about Walter. *Interesting to find out,* he thought.

NOVEMBER 1917

"I can't do everything, Gordon!" protested Louise.

Gordon was distressed. "You insisted on coming. It's too much and it isn't fair to Charles. He needs to be crawling around, not cooped up in that little room!" reasoned Gordon.

"Don't you think I know that?" she shouted. "He's your child as well; you stay at home with him if that's what you want!" she went on.

The bell warning them of a customer jingled shrilly.

Gordon turned and went out to the shop. "Good morning, madam." He smiled. "What can I do for you?"

He could hear Louise snuffling and weeping in the tiny back room, beyond the fitting rooms. He spent half an hour assisting the customer and she bought nothing.

"I don't know how you can be so two-faced! All calm and smiling out there and so unpleasant to me!" accused Louise.

"Because it's our living." He tried to soothe her and embraced her, pulling her gently towards him.

"Dada." Charles beamed.

"There! Look at him; he's worth everything," he said, looking into Louise's face. "Isn't he?"

"I want to come back to work. Ma can't have the baby, because she's not well enough. I'm not leaving him all that time with anyone else in Abbots Ford, so what on earth can I do?"

"You're doing enough by making and finishing garments at home," he pointed out.

"But I need the stimulation of being out and working to design anything new!" she protested. "When I'm at home in the village, with only the baby for company, my brain addles!"

A voice diverted their attention.

"A-hem," it said.

Louise emerged from the back room to find a young woman with a small child waiting in the shop.

"I'm sorry. I didn't mean to interrupt…" she said, embarrassed.

"It's I who should apologise to you. You must excuse us," apologised Louise.

"I could not help overhearing," she started. "I live along the road, a few doors away. I've two children at school and Angela, who is only two. I'd like to look after your baby for you. I've seen you coming in with him; he's lovely!"

"Well, that's very kind, but…"

"Come to tea one afternoon. Meet my family before you make up your mind."

"How would I reimburse you?" asked Louise.

"A discount perhaps…?"

They arranged a time for tea the next day and the young woman introduced herself as Catherine Baxter.

"Can I show you anything, Mrs Baxter?" asked Louise.

"Please, call me Catherine. Yes, I am looking for something to wear to a wedding," she explained.

"Then I have a number of suitable examples," said Louise.

They spent an enjoyable hour looking through the clothes and Catherine Baxter chose a suit of fine merino wool. Gordon remained in the background, doing the books while Charles slept. When Catherine had gone Louise went to him. "Sometimes it helps to have a woman here," she stated.

"You spend longer than I," countered Gordon.

"Some women may not want to even discuss what they wear with a man."

"Rubbish! What about the great couturiers?"

"You're hardly that, Gordon!" said Louise with an ironic laugh.

There was a certain coolness between them for the remainder of the day. Gordon had not yet come to accept the woman he had married. He did not understand the inner drive, the ambition within her. The women in his family were not like her; they settled down, having many babies and doing what Gordon considered to be more usual women's work. Louise kept a nice home and took pride in it; she made all her own and the child's clothes, and Charles was loved and cared for. Yet still Louise needed something more. Even he, Gordon, was not enough, and at times he felt hurt. He realised now that she was serious about continuing to work; she would even leave her baby with a stranger if necessary. He would check up on this woman; at least she was close by and they would both be able to go along and see Charles at intervals throughout the day. Gordon knew that it was the joy in her work that fired Louise; it was not even an urge to generate a great deal of wealth. They were living comfortably and Gordon enjoyed designing garments. He had thought about it endlessly, trying to accept his wife's restlessness. Perhaps, if Charles was well cared for and he and Louise could pull in the same direction, life would be easier.

DECEMBER 1917

He walked quickly, muffled against the cold. The ground was covered with a thick shiny frost and the roofs of the buildings looked as if they were blanketed with snow. Seth made his way through the village on his way home to Briersham. He had called in at Orchard Cottage, both collecting and delivering food and gifts in preparation for Christmas. They had all decided to have Christmas dinner in their own homes, because Louise, although recovered from her heart attack, was not well enough to do all she used to. They would gather at Orchard Cottage in the afternoon of Christmas Day. He passed the Partridge Inn and glanced towards it. His pace slowed as he realised that there was some sort of celebration taking place and, retracing his steps, he knocked at the locked doors. An ebullient Malcolm Smythe answered.

"Seth! Come in out of the cold. Look who's here!"

"Jasper!" said Seth, not believing his eyes. "You're home! When? How did you get here?"

Jasper Smythe, arm around his mother, laughed. "I was wounded... not badly, but enough to keep me in hospital for a number of weeks. Then they sent me home!" he explained.

"Any news of Jacob?" asked Seth.

The two men shook their heads sadly. Malcolm poured a celebratory drink for Seth, who drank to Jasper's health. He could see that Jasper had changed. He was no longer the young lad who had been called upon to fight for his country. He laughed and joked, but Seth could see his experiences mirrored in his eyes and etched in lines of tiredness and despair on his young face.

"It's truly marvellous to see you safely home," said Seth with feeling, remembering all those who would not return.

They gossiped about the village, but did not speak of the war.

"You'll be helping your pa again, then?" queried Seth. "You well enough?"

"Oh yes. It was my back that got hurt, but they were surprised how good a recovery I made," assured Jasper.

"He can take it slowly for a while," said Malcolm proudly. "He's earned that much, but then I'll be a hard taskmaster." He grinned.

They all laughed, then, at the idea. Malcolm Smythe was one of the friendliest, funniest men in the village.

"I'll be off now. Thanks for the drink and the happy surprise," said Seth, shaking Jasper's hand once again.

"I dreamed of being here for Christmas," said Jasper as Seth walked away.

He pulled his coat up round his neck and tugged his cap further down his brow. The night felt colder than ever after the warmth of the room and the celebration at the inn. Seth had often thought about the war and the men who had to fight in it. At his age, he had been beyond the remit of the call-up, even at the start of the war. He was the only working blacksmith in the area and, as such, was deemed to be required at home. He had always regretted not being able to go to war and to fight for his country, yet another side of him was forever grateful not to have had the experience. His life had carried on its course, while those whose lives had hardly begun had been cut down in the greenness of their years, or altered and tarnished forever. He was almost home. He walked up the path and round to the scullery door. He opened it onto a thrillingly domestic scene. His little sons were sitting in their chairs eating, while his daughters still played in their bath before the scullery fire. Flora was flushed and busy.

"Come in, love. Sit down and have a cup of tea." She kissed him absently.

"Hello, Papa," said the girls in unison.

His boys uttered greeting, baby Seth waving a crust towards him. The warmth, the domesticity, the Christmas decorations and his wife moved him beyond words. He pulled her over and, putting his arms tightly around her waist, buried his face deep in her breast, silently, with only his shoulders shaking.

JANUARY 1918

Jessica and Bill had fallen in love. He loved everything about her; the way she looked, her sense of humour; even her sense of responsibility towards her family commended her to him. He could not spend enough time with her, because, when they were together, it passed so quickly, as to leave him regretting having to part from her. One frosty, bitterly cold day not long after Christmas he put it to her. "I need to be with you all the time."

"I know." She smiled.

"What about marrying me?" he asked.

"That's not very romantic," she observed.

"Nothing to do with romance. This is serious; marriage is serious," he told her.

She laughed uproariously. "You're saying that marriage has nothing to do with romance?"

"Well, it has, if you know what I mean, but it's much more than that," he blustered.

"You make it sound boring! Do I want to marry a boring, unromantic person?" she asked rhetorically.

"No need to be flippant," he scolded. "You know full well what my meaning is. I mean it's not just, well, romance; it's love. I'm saying I love you – enough to marry you."

"I must say that is good of you, Mr Henty!"

"You're teasing me now!" He laughed. He stopped walking and stood to bar her way. "Will you?"

"Will I what?" Her blue eyes glinted with laughter.

"Marry me?" He kissed her longingly.

"Bill!" She was scandalised at being kissed in public, in the broad light of day.

"Say you'll marry me," he begged.

"It's something I shall have to give a great deal of thought to..." she began.

"Fiddlesticks!" he shouted. "Shall you marry me or not?"

Jessica never ceased to be surprised by Bill. He was usually controlled and sensible, but occasionally he could be transferred into an emotional, spontaneous person.

"You'll have to ask my father..."

"Do you say 'yes', though?"

She nodded, laughing again.

"You will?" He could hardly believe it. He kissed her ecstatically. "When shall I speak to your father?"

"Come tomorrow night," she suggested. "Come to supper."

"Are you sure? Won't he know?"

"Probably!" She giggled.

He kissed her again.

"I can hardly believe it," he breathed.

"Where will we live?" she asked suddenly.

"Peartree Farm House," he told her.

"I've often wondered why your parents didn't live there," she told him.

"They don't like it. It wasn't available when my father bought the cottage. Then he extended the cottage and, when the farmhouse became available, they didn't want to move. I'll speak to Pa," he continued, "and arrange for you to look around the farmhouse."

They talked excitedly about wedding arrangements, both enthusiastic and interested. Bill realised that he was looking forward to having a home of his own, as well as making Jessica his wife.

"When shall we get married?" he asked.

"You haven't spoken to my father yet!" she protested.

"He won't say 'no', will he?" said Bill, shocked.

She laughed.

"I've always thought a summer wedding would be nice," she told him.

"We'll need a while to get the house cleared out and ready…" he added.

"There's my trousseau, my wedding frock…"

"Speak to my sister, Louise, about that. She'd enjoy doing it," offered Bill.

They talked all the way up the hill and all the way back down, noticing the freezing weather not a bit. They found themselves back at Jessica's home before they knew it.

"Come in for a nice hot cup of tea," she invited.

Her father sat beside a roaring fire, smoking a pipe. He looked up as they entered the room.

"Hello, my dear."

"Hello, Papa. You know Bill Henty, don't you?"

"Hello, young man."

"Good afternoon, sir," said Bill respectfully.

Jessica went away to make the tea.

Bill decided not to wait until the next day. "Sir, I've something to ask you…" he began.

"I thought you might," said Mr Powers.

Bill looked taken aback.

"You have been walking out with my daughter since the Harvest Supper and all I ever hear about is you."

"I'd like to marry Jessica," said Bill bravely.

"Congratulations!" said her father, rising to shake Bill's hand.

"I can?" shouted Bill delightedly.

"You can!" agreed her father.

Jessica came back into the room with a tray.

"I hear there's going to be a wedding!" said her father.

"You were going to ask him tomorrow!" she accused.

"I couldn't wait!" he said.

Archibald Powers kissed his daughter, with tears in his eyes.

"Your mother would have been pleased," he said, turning away.

Jessica put her arm around him for a moment, comforting him. She poured the tea.

"We'll make tomorrow's supper a celebration," she told them.

He could not believe it as he walked home. He would have to tell his parents and family. She had agreed! She would marry him! There was so much to look forward to. He would have to let Julian and Sir Matthew know that he could no longer work there; he would need time to prepare the house and, once he was married, he would not be able to spare any time. *I'll be a married man, after all,* he told himself as he approached Orchard Cottage in the freezing night.

SPRING 1918

Gradually, the wounded in mind and spirit returned to the peace and tranquillity of Abbots Ford, from the battlefields of Europe. The village drew them in, assimilating them into their world and lives as though they had never been away. Everyone knew they were changed, of course; in some cases, changed beyond recognition. Those young men had witnessed that which no man should have to see, or hear or experience. It sometimes made what was good and right and normal appear banal, trivial and unimportant. This led to frustration on the part of those who had stayed behind, as well as those whose perceptions had been brutally altered.

Seth met a group of the heroes one evening in the spring. He had arranged it with Jasper Smythe, who had fitted in again, helping his father at the Partridge Inn, so smoothly that it was as if he had never been away. Bill and Gordon, Seth's brothers, and old friends were all gathered at the inn. The Wiltons' son had been lost at sea and Victor Mallish had not returned. Jacob Smythe had not come home, but they knew he was wounded and in hospital somewhere. Graham Redford was safely home and Gordon Bartrup, the baker's son, had recently arrived. No one talked of Mark and Paul Bates, or Charles Henty or any of those who had died, but they were among them that evening as the young men of the village gathered in tacit remembrance.

Towards the end of the evening, the Frost brothers joined the group. They tried to fit in, but there was that about them that could not be liked however hard anyone tried. They always managed to say the inappropriate thing or strike a discordant note in proceedings. It was sad, because their father was well liked in the village and the family had farmed the area for generations. Seth could not recall afterwards who introduced the subject, but the outbreak of foot and mouth disease and its origin was mentioned. All the young men had imbibed a quantity of ale and tempers flared.

"Always comes up, doesn't it? It has to be talked of when we're around!" shouted Walter Frost.

"Now then, Walter. No harm meant, no harm done," said Jasper soothingly.

Walter was prepared to take on any of them, fists ready. Graham Redford, son of the butcher, wanted to know more of the details. Bill discreetly told him the outline of what had occurred.

"I can see you talking about me! What are you saying? You opened your big mouth before, didn't you, Henty?" Walter lunged towards Bill, who stepped briskly aside, and Walter accidentally punched Graham.

Graham, who was now a trained soldier, defended himself and sent Walter crashing to the floor. His brother, Christopher, joined in the fray and a fight broke out. The others moved in to part the men, who had to be held back to stop them.

"You bastards!" shouted Walter. "I'll never forgive you for pointing the finger at me."

"It wasn't them," said his brother, Christopher. "None of them."

Walter looked blank. "What do you mean?" he challenged.

"It was me."

Walter could not take it in. He straightened up, arms hung at his sides.

"I pointed the finger! I told them it was you and your dirty deeds brought in foot 'n' mouth."

Walter could take no more. His own brother! Telling him, in front of all those people. His own brother, telling the police. Walter turned without a word and walked out of the inn. The men returned quietly, shaken, to their drinks; muttering, shaking heads. Christopher Frost brushed himself down, put on his cap and followed him.

"Maybe they're not all bad after all," said Bill quietly.

"Depends what you call bad, Bill," said Seth ambiguously.

JULY 1918

Peace was being won at great expense to life. The Peace Conference would take place in Paris at the start of 1919 and a terrible influenza epidemic would steal as many lives as the Great War itself. All that was yet to come as Bill and Jessica prepared for their wedding

Louise Henty was feeling so well that she had taken delight in helping the couple to prepare Peartree Farm House. She had felt duty-bound to do so in the absence of Jessica's own mother. In the event, she had enjoyed herself enormously. They had built a bathroom at the side of the kitchen, and the living room, dining room and three bedrooms comprised a sizeable home in which to start married life. Jessica's father contributed by giving them most of the furniture they needed, some of it new and some from her old home.

"Your mother would want you to have it," he had told her.

Seth and Flora did what they could to help, sharing babysitting with Louise and Gordon to free them to help to distemper each room. Louise's most important task was to remodel Jessica's mother's wedding gown for the bride. It was an unusual frock, being based on medieval lines. Oyster beaded lace was overlaid on shell-pink satin, which suited Jessica's fair colouring. Louise had to raise the waist and alter the neckline and sleeves to fit properly and they were thrilled with the result.

The wedding day was hot and sunny from early on. Jessica's relatives had descended upon Abbots Ford from Devon only the day before. They set to willingly helping to transport food for the wedding breakfast to the village hall. Louise Henty was there early, setting up tables and laying them attractively. She got on well with Jessica's family, which reassured her. They had liked Mr Powers, though they realised that he was not yet himself, because he was still recovering from the death of his wife. Fortunately, his daughter was not moving far away, for Peartree Farm House was only half an hour's walk from his home.

The bridesmaids were three of Jessica's pretty cousins and Flora's two girls, who were becoming practiced experts at the job. It was a late morning wedding and Jessica was travelling to church with her father in a carriage. Seth drove to collect them, joking and endeavouring to relax a surprisingly nervous bride. Local children and villagers waved and called out good wishes as they went along at a good pace.

Flora endeavoured to keep her little boys quiet as they waited inside the church for the arrival of the bride. She smiled at her brother as he waited nervously, too tense even to tease his small nephews. Her mind wandered as she gazed around at the familiar place, absently dandling baby Seth on her knee. The weddings, christenings and funerals that had taken place here... It was the one place that punctuated their lives and it gave them the opportunity to reappraise how they were using those lives. People looked about them expectantly, and then, there she was; not nervous or shy, but wearing a beatific smile. This was not to be a sad day without her recently departed mother, for Jessica was sure that she was with them in spirit for this special occasion. The music bound them in praise to God and the celebration of the marriage of loved ones. The happiness on Jessica's face as she walked slowly towards her husband-to-be reflected the feelings of them all, as they saw that an end to the war was in sight. That afternoon, William Henty would marry his sweetheart, and at least one wartime love story would have a happy ending.

Louise Henty felt that she had slipped unobtrusively into her mother's role as she watched her youngest son make his vows. She glanced at her daughters with their families and it did not seem long since she had stood with them in these very pews, when they were young, on family occasions. She felt fluid in time: able to look both backwards and forwards, remembering and recalling all the generations of women; it was as if she could see the past, present and future.

It was time for the couple to sign the register and she followed Will, smiling at her family as she went past them. She sent up silent prayers for them all, for the newly married couple.

Whatever lies in store, God give us all the strength to deal with it, she thought.

Alice slipped her hand into that of her grandmother and smiled up at her.

"Come on, Grannie. Come and sign God's book. He'll want to know that you've been here," she said.

Louise squeezed the small hand gently, thankfully.

"I think He'll know, Alice. I think He'll know," she said gratefully.

THE END